DEATH WARMED OVER

A Thea Kozak Mystery

Book Eight

Kate Flora

Book and cover design by eBook Prep
www.ebookprep.com

July, 2017
ISBN: 978-1-61417-969-6

ePublishing Works!
www.epublishingworks.com

CHAPTER 1

Home ownership is supposed to be the American dream. I've heard it, read it, even seen it in my realtor's promotional materials. Andre and I needed a house. Someplace with an office for me, a workshop for him. A place where we could finally unpack all our boxes, get my stuff out of storage, and stop feeling like we were camping out. We needed a place where there was no nosy landlady who felt free to comment on our comings and goings and undoubtedly—the floors and walls being flimsy—kept track of our sex life as well.

So why, I wondered, as my phone rang for the seventh time on a thirty-minute drive from my office to the house I was going to look at, did the quest for this dream feel so much like a nightmare? I knew part of the answer: my work life had spilled over so completely into my personal life that I had no time for chasing dreams. In theory, I could concentrate on my driving and on following our realtor Ginger's directions to the place she had described as "absolutely perfect" for me and the man of my dreams, and still conduct business if I needed to. I had Bluetooth. I was hands-free. But the incessant calls that were dogging my journey required undivided attention to my clients' problems. They called for concentration, quick thinking, and useful answers.

I had planned to use this drive to put myself in the right zone. Get my head into kitchens and closets, yards and living rooms. I wanted to be open to the possibilities of this house that had looked so lovely in Ginger's pictures. I wanted to imagine white wicker furniture on the deep, shady porch and our king-sized bed in the roomy master bedroom. Ginger's "absolutely perfect" had to be better than what we'd looked at so far. Awkward layouts, hideous paint jobs. Boxy little rooms with no space for furniture. Kitchens and baths that reminded me of the worst decorating sins of my childhood. It was hard to believe there were still places where people spent their days with copper, avocado, or gold appliances or pink tiled baths and pink-flocked wallpaper.

It wasn't just a matter of needing paint or a little updating. House after house cried out for a serious makeover, if not for being scrapped and starting over. My quest was turning me into an amateur architect, imagining what things would look like with walls knocked down. With dormers. With whole new walls of windows. Some houses were oriented so poorly to the potential of their lots I'd even imagined picking them up and turning them sideways. It could have been fun with the right house but I kept seeing the wrong house. Over the months of looking, I'd become discouraged with house-hunting and a life that needed a makeover, which was why I needed my half hour of attitude improvement.

Instead, I was spending that half hour trying to convince a demanding client to send us the data we needed to complete the report they needed in a few days for their annual trustees' meeting. Data only they had and that was essential for the report. This was not the first such half hour I'd spent with these people, nor the first time they'd promised to get it to me right away. I was out of patience. But clients pay the bills, and this was a big-bill project. Ordinarily, my partner Suzanne, the queen of sweet-talk, would have been handling this. But my day had begun with a six a.m. call from her, saying something didn't feel right and she was seeing her obstetrician this morning.

When I say 'consultant' people's eyes glaze over, but the truth is that our work can be very challenging and we're good at it. EDGE Consulting is a small business that provides important services to independent—read private—schools. We consult on using traditional media and new social media to attract the applicant pool they want. On giving the right, unified 'look' to their website and promotional materials. On branding and their image. A few years ago, the word branding wasn't in my vocabulary, except to refer to something cruel that is done to cattle. Now I'm becoming a branding queen. We also, as was the case with this report, can analyze their application and acceptance trends and compare those with national trends to determine whether their approach needs tweaking.

Then there is my own subspecialty—damage control. I'm the person they call when something bad happens on campus and they need help managing the resulting publicity. Sometimes they also need my help figuring out where their own systems went wrong, so bad things won't happen again. I'm the knight in shining armor. The girl in the white hat. I'm Jane Wayne.

The downside is that the operative word is 'bad.' Lately it seemed like few weeks passed without an emergency call from a school. Most I could handle over the phone, but sometimes I had to show up, hold hands, and occasionally run the whole damage control show.

I already had way too much on my plate. My calendar was stacked with projects like airplanes on a busy runway, which, like a good air traffic controller, I could handle until the call from Ginger's office moved the showing from nine a.m., when it had almost worked, to 10:30, when it threw everything into chaos. The incessant phone calls were bringing on a headache of epic proportions. There is no ring tone soothing enough for a too-busy day. The umpteenth iteration of the opening bars of Pachelbel's Canon quickly loses its magic.

It was the end of March in Maine, affectionately known as "mud season." A time of year when we're all utterly sick of looking out at brown ground and brown grass and brown trees, or a dirty white world of snow banks and icy ruts and yellow pee circles and melting brown dog turds. Where bloated cigarette butts litter the sidewalks outside of restaurants, bars, and every form of public building like an infestation of giant maggots.

Okay. If this was becoming my worldview, I either needed therapy, a vacation, or to have something—like this search for a home—off my plate. I was barely into my thirties and I grimaced so often I was getting permanent frown lines. Soon children would run from me and people would start leaving flyers for Botox and Restylane on my desk. I knew I could improve my mood by going to the gym and getting all charged up with yummy endorphins, but I didn't have time for the gym. Or to buy the new shoes I needed for the gym, because mine were now held together with duct tape. My wardrobe was looking shabby. I needed some spring clothes. I was looking shabby. I needed a haircut. A massage. A chocolate cake picnic with my sweetie.

I wanted a home because home represented normal. I wanted to unpack my books and put them on welcoming white shelves. Unpack my CDs and remember when I used to listen to music. It would be fun to dance around my living room with the sound turned up too loud without worrying about my landlady knocking on the door. Share a bottle of wine on the rug before the fire with my husband without one of us getting a call that would send us out the door.

The Canon began again and the number that flashed on my screen was my mother. Not enough that Suzanne was on my case. My mother, the chronic complainer, was undoubtedly calling to ask for something and while she was at it, give me an update on my many flaws. That wasn't on my agenda, so I let her go to voice mail. The notes had barely died away when they began again. A client, so I answered.

"It's Reeve Barrows, from Stafford Academy. Is this Thea?"

I longed to say, "Wrong number," but said, "Yes."

"We've got a situation brewing and we may need your help."

The line of planes waiting for takeoff got longer. I gathered some facts regarding students selling drugs and a student who'd used the drugs and been rushed to the hospital. "Get out in front of it, Reeve. Limit access to the campus. Remind your faculty not to comment. Ask your students to wait for the facts."

"I don't know if I can do that." He sounded dubious.

"Seriously, Reeve. You have to control the message or your students and parents will panic."

"It's really not my problem," he said.

Then why was *he* calling me? The answer, it seemed, was because the headmaster was nowhere to be found. Gack. I had heard this one before. I asked him to keep in touch as the situation developed and disconnected, knowing he was likely to call back with a full-blown emergency and want me on his campus ASAP. I felt like a pressure cooker about to blow its gasket. I was living too much of my life on alert, waiting for situations to become crises.

The overwhelming demand of work was something I'd vowed to limit when we settled into a home and lived a more normal life. I also wanted normal because it would help me to step away from the last years of my life, which felt like the plot from a fem jep novel or a women's adventure flick. Things kept happening to me that never happened to regular people. I'd been left at the altar when Andre was taken hostage by some crazy religious fundamentalists. I'd tried to help a school with a campus stalking crisis and ended up fleeing from an ax-wielding monster. I didn't sleep well because my mind was filled with horrific images. I didn't want to be one of Angelina Jolie's fictional avatars. I wanted to live in a nice house in an ordinary neighborhood and start claiming my life back.

Something else I wanted that also seemed to be beyond my reach—a family. After my miscarriage, the doctors had said that everything was fine and I should relax and not worry about getting pregnant again. But months kept passing and nothing was happening, making it harder and harder to relax. My clock was beginning to tick. And, as everyone knows who has ever had difficulties conceiving, suddenly it seemed like the whole world was pregnant, including my partner, Suzanne. Expecting her second, Suzanne was sick as a dog, perpetually tired, and noticeably crabbier after a year of being crabby.

As Miz GPS announced that I was approaching the turn onto Joy Lane, where I would have reached my destination, my phone rang for the eighth time. A truck barreling toward me was so far over the line it missed me by an inch. My desperately needed Dunkin' Donuts coffee, carelessly seated in the cup holder, was unseated by my swerve and turned the sleeve and belly of my last decent white blouse a rich café au lait.

I pulled over to do some damage control, rolling down the window to let the coffee fumes and the heat of my temper out as I scrubbed at myself with a handful of napkins, then mopped up the seat and the console. I was five minutes late. Not bad, considering the morning I'd had. Joy Lane sounded like a chatty hostess on one of those unbearable morning talk shows—someone who would coo over Easter cupcakes or baby ducks or a dog that played the piano—not someplace I was supposed to live. But I needed a house, even if it meant living on a street with a ridiculous name. It was a pleasant street. Wide, clean, quiet, and lined with a few big old trees. The houses were large and well-maintained and they were set back from the street behind spacious front yards. It looked like the kind of street I'd grown up on. A street that felt like home.

I took another moment to breathe, and turned off my phone so the next round of calls would go to voice mail. Muttering the word 'home' like a mantra, I pushed Stafford Academy and its student drug problem from my mind and tried to get centered, to be fully present in this search instead of scattered in so many directions.

Then I put the car in drive and poked down the street until I found the house I was looking for. Ginger's little silver RAV4 was parked in the driveway. The 'for sale' sign with her picture swung in a slight breeze. There was an honest-to-goodness white picket fence around the front yard. After a minute, I turned off the engine, grabbed my purse, and got out of the car. Even though it was only mid-morning, it smelled like someone was barbecuing, the kind of smell that makes me hungry for steak or ribs because at heart I'm a carnivore. I've embraced whole grains. Bulgur. Quinoa. Faro. I eat my veggies. I even like my veggies. But sometimes, just like Andre, my hard-bodied detective husband, I really NEED steak.

I let myself in through the gate, closed it behind me, and looked at the broad steps leading up to the front porch. A row of round pillars held up the roof. Along the edge of the porch were shrubs that gave partial privacy and looked like they would flower, if the dirty snow ever left us and spring arrived. What I knew about plants and shrubs wouldn't fill a thimble, but it was something I looked forward to learning.

A wide strip of indoor-outdoor carpeting led to a shiny wooden door. I rang the bell and waited, and then, since the door was slightly open, I let myself in, calling for Ginger and hearing my voice echo in the high-ceilinged foyer. The floors were freshly done, and gleamed underfoot. I wiped my shoes on the doormat and looked around. A formal dining room to my right. Closed pocket doors that would open to what I knew was the living room on my left.

Because the pictures had made it look so special, I saved the living room for last, and wandered into the dining room. Big enough to seat all of Andre's family. All those sisters and their husbands and their children. I pictured the happy chaos of a family dinner. His family, not mine. All their love and noisy squabbles were right out in the open. My family dinners were like White House state dinners with the Chinese. Fraught with underlying tensions and things that needed to be discussed but the time wasn't right and never would be. Andre's family might be big on reproduction and too eager to gobble up our meager free time, but they were otherwise pretty easy to live with.

Creamy white bead board ran up the wall to a chair rail, with lovely blue and white toile wallpaper above. The house was unfurnished, but they'd sensibly left large, white-framed mirrors at either end of the room. My taste ran to paint, not wallpaper, but I could live with this, and I thought Andre, who was sometimes surprisingly traditional, would really like it. My spirits rose. This might finally be our house.

As I went through the doorway into the large kitchen that opened onto a family room addition beyond, the grilling smell got stronger. Whatever they were cooking, the scent had gotten unpleasant with overtones of something burning. Privacy, and a sense of distance from my neighbors, was important. So far, Ginger's gushing hadn't been so hyperbolic as I'd feared. What I'd seen of the house was great, but I wasn't sure I wanted to live in a place where I was so much in my neighbor's pocket I had intimate knowledge of what they were cooking.

I'd barely taken in the warm terracotta floors and rust-flecked granite countertops, glass-fronted cabinets, and trendy stainless steel appliances when I heard a sound from the living room. Not a hello or someone calling my name. It sounded like someone in pain. Maybe Ginger had slipped on the shiny floor and fallen, and that's why she hadn't come to greet me or answered when I called. She was far too polite—and had too much of the realtor's necessary charm—to have deliberately left me on my own for so long.

I retraced my steps through the dining room and the entry hall and shoved back the heavy pocket doors. The huge, bright, front-to-back living room was painted a soothing, soft gray-green. Light streamed in through a wall of windows at the end. In the center sat a single chair. The chair was surrounded by a circle of space heaters, each of them glowing fiery red, connected to outlets by long orange tails of extension cords. Our realtor, Ginger Stevens, was tied to the chair, a thick strip of shiny silver duct tape wrapped around her head and her mouth. Her skin was blackening red and blistered. Her clothes were charred and smoking.

As fresh air whooshed through the door with me, her clothes burst into little tongues of flame and her long russet-brown braid caught fire. Above the smoke and flames, her eyes, wide with pain and terror, fixed on me. She mumbled behind the tape as I stood and stared, frozen in place, trying to process what I was seeing. The horror. The incongruity. The utterly incomprehensible nature of what was happening. Ginger was being cooked. I stood in the doorway, paralyzed.

Then I dove into action.

I sprinted toward the circle. Heat and hot metal seared my ankles as I kicked the nearest heaters out of the way. I grabbed the back of the chair, the paint blistering hot under my fingers. As tongues of flame licked at me, I dragged her into a cooler part of the room. I tore off my jacket, balled it up to protect my hands, and used it to smother the flames from her still-burning clothing and her hair. Then I tore at the tape that covered her mouth and nearly covered her nose, gagging from the smell of burned flesh and singed hair and the horror of realizing that I hadn't smelled barbecue at all. I'd smelled this woman, Ginger Stevens, my kind, sweet, sometimes too chatty realtor, being burned alive.

As I pulled out my phone and dialed 9-1-1, Ginger tried to speak.

"Hush," I said. "Hold on. Hold on. I'm calling for help. I'm going to get someone here to help you. We're going to get you to a hospital, Ginger. It's going to be okay."

I wished I believed what I was saying.

Her mouth moved. Dry split lips. Her swollen tongue trying to form words. I bent down so my mouth was close. There was a faint mumble I could barely make out, a few sounds that seemed like words.

"Don't try to talk," I said, because the effort was so clearly painful. But her effort was extreme. There was something she had to tell me.

"…airy," she gasped. "Bobby." Her blackened hands clawed at the air. "So long. Safe." A grasp for the strength to go on, and then, "Sorry."

As the operator answered and went through her spiel, this call is being recorded, blah, blah, I tried to give her the details. My name. The address of this house. The awful scene, a woman being burned alive. Our need for an ambulance and EMTS. Our need for cops, for a crime scene team because this was no accident.

Now that the tape was off her mouth and she'd delivered her incomprehensible message, Ginger's muffled sounds had become a ceaseless high-pitched scream, a primitive, animal cry of agony. Most people know what a burn feels like. Multiply that times a thousand and you wouldn't even come close. Her eyes had a dulled glaze that made me fear she was dying. That she'd die here before help could arrive.

I could barely hear the operator over the screaming. She kept asking me questions I couldn't answer. Finally, I gave up.

"Just send help," I said. I repeated my number and the address. "Send help. And please, for God's sake, have someone call me and tell what I should be doing for her. If there's any way to help her."

"Please stay on the line," she began.

"Don't be stupid," I said. "I can't stay on the line. I've got to go unplug those damned heaters before the whole place burns down."

The ones I'd kicked over were already scorching the floor, heating up the shiny new finish and adding a hot chemical reek to the already fouled air. It was only a matter of moments before the whole place caught fire.

She was starting to say something about staying out of a burning building when I disconnected. Emergency operators can be amazing. They can talk people in crisis through a lot, they can help people deliver babies and save someone who's choking, but in this case she wasn't helpful. She didn't understand the situation I was in and it was way too bizarre to explain.

I dropped the phone in my pocket and ran around the room, jerking on the cords and unplugging all of the heaters. It was so hot I felt like I was in an oven. Where they'd been burned, my ankles and hands felt raw and sore. I raced back to Ginger's chair and dragged her out into the hall where it was cooler, the chair legs leaving ugly scrapes on the shiny floor.

I tore at the knots, trying to get them undone, wanting to set her free, but they were too tight. Not that she would notice. They were all that was holding her up now. Her body had collapsed and she slumped against them, only semi-conscious. I figured that I couldn't get her out of the chair, anyway. There was no place I could touch her that wouldn't be agonizing. And those knots, those rather strange knots, might be evidence. There might be DNA on them.

Dammit. I was hopeless. Thea Kozak. The woman who couldn't stop being a detective, even when she'd sworn she'd left all that behind her.

The screaming didn't stop. Ginger screamed like I had never heard screaming before, screams of such awful intensity I wanted to cover my ears. I wanted to scream myself. I wanted to beg her to please stop, even though I knew she couldn't, because I knew I would never get those screams out of my head.

I couldn't leave her. I couldn't do anything for her. I couldn't even take her hand or touch her to lend some comfort. The only thing I could do was talk to her. Keep my voice calm and reassuring and remind her to hold on. To stay with me because help was coming.

It felt like I knelt there in the foyer and tried to say comforting things for about four lifetimes, using my charred jacket as padding because the hardwood floor was torturing my knees, while the smell of burned flesh imbedded itself in my hair, my clothes, my lungs, and my brain.

My phone rang several times, but each time, as I answered it, hoping for someone who could tell me what to do or give me a clue about how to ease her suffering, it was another call from work, including one from my partner, Suzanne. Before I could finish saying hello or explain my situation, she was off and running, beginning with, "What the heck are you thinking, Thea, going off to look at real estate on a day like this. We've got a real emergency on our hands."

"I've spoken with Reeve. We're working on it. But I can't talk right now," I told her, "I've got an emergency of my own. Someone has tried to murder my realtor."

I disconnected while she was still speaking. I could probably guess what she was saying, though. She was starting a lecture on staying out of trouble and my need to live a more normal life. Like this was something I'd engineered because things were getting too dull. Or because I couldn't resist helping people. Little did she know how hard I was trying for normal. It wasn't my fault that bad things kept finding me.

I couldn't say how much time passed—minutes? hours? weeks?—before Ginger's screams blended with the scream of approaching sirens. The gate slammed, the front door burst open, and a moving, shouting blend of emergency personnel exploded into the small space, observing, assessing and talking all at once as I pushed up off my knees and backed toward the wall to give them room.

The EMTs went to work on Ginger while a uniformed cop, looking like he was finding it as hard to hold himself together as I was, fixed me with beady eyes, demanded my name, and said, “What happened here?”

“I have no idea,” I said, knowing, from all my experience with cops, that the answer wouldn’t satisfy him, and that soon he’d start pecking at me like a hungry bird, demanding information.

I watched his gaze shift from my face to the EMTs, who were cutting the knots that bound poor Ginger to the chair. As they shifted her, her screams rose to a pitch so shrill they should have shattered glass. They absolutely shattered my nerves.

“Save those knots,” I said. “They may be important.”

He would think me absurd and I didn’t care. Then my stomach gave a violent lurch and I dove for the powder room under the stairs behind me.

CHAPTER 2

The silence after the ambulance had taken Ginger away was so profound it felt tangible, like someone had suddenly stopped hitting me, or like a heavy weight had been lifted off the room. It didn't last long. I'd barely had time to take a breath before the cops started in with their questions.

There were two of them, the cop who'd been first on the scene and another, older one who'd arrived soon after. The older man wore the weary, dutiful sport coat of a detective. His face was fissured with cynicism and disappointment. Maybe the screaming had damaged my hearing, though, because I could see their mouths move, but I couldn't hear their questions.

It was as if we had a bad cell phone connection. Or like listening to one of those distant radio stations you get in the car late at night with a song you really want to hear that keeps fading in and out. I got bits and pieces of what they said, interrupted by static and dropped calls. I couldn't hear anything clearly, or get my focus back, never mind process their questions and give them useful answers.

I tried. Honestly, I tried, because although I have a natural resentment of cops, except the ones I loved, I knew they needed answers from me. Sooner rather than later and in as much detail as possible. Yet somehow I couldn't seem to move beyond the charred, empty chair that sat like Ginger's ghost in the center of the room, surrounded by blackened bits of rope and the detritus of a medical emergency—torn packages, blackened gauze, discarded blue gloves. Thea the great and terrible, natural adversary of bad guys and compulsive rescuer of the downtrodden and the helpless, had become an incoherent, trembling bundle of nerves.

I was ashamed of myself and powerless to do anything about it.

As I watched their faces morph from blank to frustrated, I made a timeout sign. "Look. I'm sorry. I don't know if this is shock or what. Usually I'm coherent. But I can't understand a word you're saying."

Instead of producing the desired results—understanding, a comforting arm, or the suggestion that we move to a different venue where there might be a glass of water or some place to sit down away from such vivid reminders of the horrors I'd just seen—they raised their voices. It's such an oddly universal human instinct. If someone doesn't understand you, talk louder, as though loud static is more comprehensible.

Since my attempt at an explanation hadn't worked, I decided to join their club. I didn't do it gracefully. "Shut up!" I yelled. "Just shut up. Shut up. Shut up. I can't hear you. I can't process your questions. I can't hear anything but Ginger screaming. Yelling at me will not make it better."

I marched through the door and out onto the porch, greedily inhaling the chilly March air as though if I could just take in enough of it I could purge my lungs of the stench of burned flesh and maybe some oxygen would restore my fumbling brain. It was like going from a noisy bar to the circus. The street swarmed with police cars with flashing blue lights, with news vans, and crowds of curious people. I'd forgotten about the blood maggots, as Andre and his cohort called them.

A made-up blonde carrying a large mike pushed past the cop guarding the gate and rushed toward me, her incomprehensible questions streaming from shiny, blood-red lips. I fled back inside.

Motioning for my inquisitors to follow me, I headed for the kitchen, farther from the horrors of that living room. They waited while I bathed my face in cold water and mopped it dry with some paper towels. As soon as I turned back toward them, they started in again, like a pair of mismatched twins.

"Only one of you," I said, pointing at the senior guy.

"What were you…"

In my pocket, my phone vibrated like a trapped bee. I pulled it out and checked the number. Andre. This was the one call I wanted to take.

"I just heard," he said.

"I can't hear," I said. "I can't think. They want me to answer questions and all I hear is screaming. What do I do?"

"Not now." The older cop snatched my phone out of my hand, shaking his head like he was chiding a naughty child.

"Give that back!" I dove for it.

He backed up, holding it out of my reach like a taunting older sibling. "Not until you answer my questions."

My hearing was getting better. Getting angry makes some people less coherent but for some reason it helps me to focus. Yes, definitely getting better, because from the little device that idiot was holding in his hand, I could hear Andre's anxious voice. "Thea? Thea? What the hell is going on?"

"You might want to stop acting like a boob and tell that guy on the phone what's happening," I said, folding my arms over my chest and giving him my best "let's settle down and act like grownups" glare. "He's Maine State Police homicide, and if Ginger dies, you're going to be dealing with him anyway. No reason to piss him off now. Really. Is there?"

Sporty—I had no other name for him, as he hadn't had the courtesy to introduce himself or given me a card, he'd just hollered questions—stared at me like I'd betrayed some trust, even though no trust had been built between us. Or as if I'd taken leave of my senses. Which, in fairness, I temporarily had. But I was coming back now.

"What the fuck?" he said. "You already called the staties?"

"No." I shook my head. "Detective Andre Lemieux," I said, pointing at the phone. "My husband. If you won't let me speak to him, please tell him I'm in shock. That I really need him. Right here. Right now."

In the spirit of people yelling to be sure they were heard, I was yelling now so that Andre would hear me. I wanted to help these guys out. I absolutely did. But I've never understood how bullying people, never mind refusing to listen to people you want information from, is supposed to advance any investigation. It seemed to me that the details of this one were critical. Someone had done something utterly horrific here, and that someone needed to be found and roasted over a slow fire, or at least brought to justice. I was the person who'd found the victim and tried to save her, which kind of made me a victim, too, even if not in the same league. A victim, and someone who could reasonably be expected to be in shock. And they weren't treating me like a victim, or like someone who might be affected by such a terrible experience. They were acting like I was being deliberately difficult.

Meanwhile, Sporty had temporarily stopped acting like someone's mean big brother. He'd lowered the phone to his ear and was talking. As someone who reads people for a living, which consultants have to do almost as often as cops, especially when their clients aren't telling them the truth, I was getting a wealth of information from his face. It appeared that Sporty was getting an earful of Andre's displeasure. My husband, it seemed, was not happy about being unable to speak with his traumatized wife, and he was explaining that now. No way to know if he and Sporty knew each other. It was likely, since the Maine law enforcement community isn't that big. If he did, he'd know that Detective Andre Lemieux was not someone to be messed with.

Eventually, Sporty withdrew the phone from his ear, shook it like it was coated with something that should require a Hazmat suit, and held it out to me.

"Can you hold it together until I get there?" Andre said. "I'm about twenty minutes out."

"I can try." Even as I said it, I felt like I wasn't going to be able to hold it together for two minutes, let alone twenty. "But hurry. The street out there. It's like a circus. And oh my God! Poor Ginger. I've never seen…"

"Tell Lieutenant Scafaro what you saw. Everything you saw. He's not an idiot, even if he's acting like one. It's important, okay? Just keep breathing. Stay calm. And tell him what you know. I'm on my way."

Sporty Scafaro was watching me warily, like he wasn't sure what to do with me now. I wasn't just an uncooperative witness anymore. Not that I ever had been. I was a cop's wife. It complicated the hell out of what he wanted to do, which was yell, bully, and generally be a cop asshole.

I disconnected and put my phone away, ready to make a genuine effort at cooperation. When my honey tells me to do something, I try to comply. Especially when it's cop-related. He's a good cop. And anyway, he was right. Scafaro did need to know things if he was going to find out who had done this to Ginger.

"There's no place to sit," I said. "And we don't want to go out there." I waved vaguely toward the street. "We'll just have to make the best of it. So, what do you want to know?"

Scafaro flipped over his notebook. "Everything. From the beginning. Who are you and why are you here?"

"My name is Thea Kozak," I said. "Ginger Stevens, that's the woman who was…in the…tied to the chair, is my realtor. Our realtor. Andre and I are looking for a house." I gave him the name of the company. "I was supposed to meet her here this morning at nine to look at the house—"

"At nine?" he interrupted. "You didn't call us until 10:45."

"I know when I called you."

I could feel myself unraveling. Oh. God. I had to hang on to my temper. This was going to be hard enough without another shouting match. "Is this how it's going to be?" I said. "You're going to keep interrupting me? Can't you just listen until I've finished and then ask your questions? And stop being so damned accusatory. I'm just a realtor's customer who's trying to buy a house."

Okay. I was not being all sweetness and light. "Please," I said. "I'm just trying to get this out the way I remember it. It doesn't help if you keep interrupting."

"Go on," he said.

"Just as I was about to leave, right around 8:30, Ginger's office called and said she'd been delayed and the showing needed to be pushed back to 10:30. That was a bad time for me, I've got a lot on my…"

I stopped. He didn't need to hear about my day. Just the facts, ma'am, as they say. Among those facts was who had made the call. I tried to remember. It had not been Ginger. Had it been a man or a woman? Either a man, or a woman with a deep voice. I told him that.

"I got here about five minutes late. Ginger's car was in the driveway. I knocked. She didn't answer, but the door was open, so I went in. I called her name a few times. No response. I thought she might be out in the back…in the yard. I knew the house has a big back yard from the listing photos she'd sent. So I started to look around."

Scafaro was scribbling. The other cop was watching me like he was some kind of human polygraph assigned to tell when my body's responses said I'd veered from the straight and narrow.

"Backing up," I said. "When I came through the door into the foyer, the pocket doors into the living room were closed, so I went the other way, into the dining room. I thought I was going to love the living room. I wanted to save it for last."

I rubbed a hand over my face, and when I looked down, I saw my hand was black. My face was probably streaked with black now, too. I probably looked primitive and savage. They could have told me. It wasn't nice to let someone think they looked normal when they were covered in soot. No. Not soot. Charred flesh, burned hair and clothes.

I went to the sink, used the bottle of detergent that still sat there to clean my hands. The soap stung where they'd been burned. I wet a paper towel and scrubbed at my face as I continued my story. "It was only a few minutes. I looked at the dining room and then went into the kitchen. That's when I heard sounds, like someone in pain. I went into the living room to investigate. And I found her."

I started to rub my face again. And stopped myself again, wondering if he might think all this face rubbing was odd. My hands hurt. They were red and tender and had little rows of blisters. I wanted to plunge them into a bucket of ice. But there probably was no ice, and anyway, he was looking very impatient. I dropped my hands and went on. So far, I was all they had.

"Do you think it would have made any difference if I'd found her sooner? If I'd opened those doors first? Will it make any difference?" Would. Will. Was Ginger going to live? Would she even want to? I'd heard the recovery from burns was terrible.

I had no idea how long it would have taken those heaters to do so much damage. Was it minutes or hours? Had that call to delay me really come from Ginger's office? What if it had come from the killer, to give him—her?—time to waylay Ginger and set this up? Had her attacker meant for her to die or just to suffer horribly? But it had come from Ginger's office, because the realtor's name was what had showed up on my caller ID. But now I couldn't remember whether that also came up when she used her cell phone.

I shivered. What had the killer's plan been? This wasn't some random act. No one drives around with six or eight space heaters in their car, never mind all those extension cords. Would they even fit in a car? Maybe the bad guy needed a truck. And why heaters? It was peculiar way to kill somebody. Was I supposed to arrive and save her or arrive and find her? Either one was horrible.

Scafaro cleared his throat and tapped his pen against his pad. He hadn't answered my question. Probably he had no idea, but cops didn't answer witnesses' questions anyway. That was not how they worked. It was all a one-way street.

"As I stepped into the room, I saw Ginger there, in the chair, surrounded by those portable heaters. They were all on full blast. The room was incredibly hot. She was trying to speak—probably she was screaming—but her mouth was wrapped in duct tape. You might be able to get some prints off…"

I stopped myself again. They knew about getting prints from tape. "I ran over there. I kicked some of the heaters out of the way so I could get to her. Then I grabbed her chair and dragged her away from the circle."

I tried to remember what I'd done next. Scafaro tapped impatiently. I wanted to tell him to stop. I was doing my best and his impatience wasn't helping. "I'm not sure what order I did things in," I told him. "I got the duct tape off her mouth. I tried to undo those knots but they were too tight. Then, because it was so hot, I dragged her into the foyer and called 9-1-1."

"At any point, did she say anything to you?"

"She tried. She seemed desperate to tell me something but I couldn't make it out."

"Did she say anything at all?"

I tried to remember.

"Nothing?" The pen tapped twice. Three times. "Not a single word?"

I held up a finger to silence him. Then I closed my eyes and thought back. I felt the hot paint under my hands. I felt the stickiness of hot duct tape as I tried to tear it off her face. The incredible heat of her skin, oozing and crusty against my hands. The tape slippery. Incredibly strong, resisting my efforts to tear it, when duct tape usually tore so easily. The sucking sound when it came away, taking skin with it. The way her eyes had flared open from the pain. Then the way her hands had curled into tight fists and she'd tried so hard to speak to me.

"Backing up," I said. "When I opened those doors the rush of air fanned the fire. Her clothes burst into flame and her hair started to smolder. The first thing I did after I pulled her away from those heaters was to use my jacket to beat out the flames."

Two taps with the pen. "Did she say anything to you?" Scafaro repeated.

"I could only make out a few words. Three words. No. Four. Five? Airy. Bobby. At least I think it was Bobby, 'so long,' 'safe,' and 'sorry.' 'Airy' might have been part of a longer word. Or a name. I don't know. Then she started to scream and she never stopped. I turned on my phone and called 9-1-1."

"I'm going to need that phone," he said.

My phone, which was still buzzing in my pocket, was my lifeline. Everything I needed to do my job resided in that little rectangle of black plastic. Contacts. Notes. My calendar. Everything. No way was I giving it up.

"No," I said. "You can look at it. You can take pictures or screen shots or whatever you need to do. Obviously you can have access to my phone records. But my whole work life is in this thing. My clients need to stay in close contact, as do my co-workers. It would take hours to program a new one and transfer all the data and contacts and my calendar and my notes and my…"

I shook my head. I'd been about to say 'my pictures of Andre,' but I'd found that cops got all cynical and mean when I went sentimental about my husband and our newlywed status. They had no idea what we'd been through to stay together.

"I don't have hours to spare," I said. "I will cooperate in any way that I can, but I can't give up my phone."

"Right," Scafaro said. "Poor you. You don't really care much about what happened to that woman. Ginger Stevens. You just want to be done here so you can get back to work."

He scribbled another note on his pad. "If I want your phone, I am going to have your phone."

Those lines in his face that I'd taken for weariness? They were just deeply embedded meanness. Not the marks of a hard-worn man but the signs of a judgmental man. And a bully. What about that fundamental cop rule: don't let your assumptions get ahead of the facts? This guy was all about assumptions. It depressed me that justice for Ginger might rest in his hands.

If I were the selfish bitch he thought I was, right now I'd be bemoaning the fact that I could never buy this, my dream house, the first decent place I'd seen, a house Andre and I could have lived in. If I were a selfish bitch, I would have run out of the house before calling for help, leaving Ginger and the house to burn.

What about the reality? My ankles were bruised, maybe burned, and my hands were definitely burned—they really hurt. Even a man as blind as Scafaro could see the little rows of blisters from my desperate attempt to save a crime victim's life. I was supposed to go from here to dealing calmly and professionally with a client whose idiotic refusal to cooperate pushed all my buttons, and then a client with what was potentially a genuine emergency who might need me on campus later today, all while my lungs and hair were saturated with the terrible smell of burning flesh.

Selfish bitch? My clothes were ruined. I'd just seen one of the most horrific things a person could ever see and it was going to stir up a lot of bad stuff I tried to keep locked away. I was looking at a lot of sleepless nights, months of nightmares—possibly years of them triggered every time I smelled someone barbecuing.

If I were truly a selfish bitch, I'd be bemoaning the fact that I was probably going to have to become a vegetarian, instead of hearing Ginger's screams echoing in my head. I'd be thinking about scars and my own discomfort instead of trying to recall what I knew about Ginger, and whether any of it might explain the things she'd said.

I looked over at Scafaro, that smug and certain bully. Was this payback because Andre had yelled at him or a personality defect? Either way, if he stayed on the case, I would have to see him again. I could already see that this was not the beginning of a beautiful friendship.

Then our cautious détente fell apart. He decided he wanted my phone, right then and there, and instead of asking, he lunged for my pocket.

My body went into post-shock defense mode. I dove for the corner, cowering in a protective crouch. I folded my hands over my head and started screaming.

And my husband burst through the door like the wrath of God.

CHAPTER 3

The truth is that I'm not big on being rescued. I like to rescue myself. Some people have characterized this as pigheaded or stubborn. Others, including my kindly pediatrician when I was a difficult child, as determined and resolute. Whatever the terms used, the fact is that I'm much more likely to be the one doing the rescuing. But I've learned a lot from Andre about what people do for each other, about sharing the responsibility and letting myself be taken care of.

While this whole business should have been straightforward—I'd tell the cops what I knew and get back to helping my clients with their own crises while these cops went on to do their job—it had been anything but. So right now, the advent of a knight in shining armor with a badge, a gun, and a gleaming gold wedding ring was just fine with me.

After he'd coaxed me out of my corner, I grabbed his shirtfront in two oozing paws and planted my face against his sturdy chest. I listened to his heartbeat while the alpha males exchanged data in crisp sound bites. I wanted to close my eyes, the better to shut them out, but whenever I closed my eyes, I saw Ginger's face and the whole ghastly scene in the living room. Inhaling the comfort of Andre's familiar scent while staring at the edge of his jacket and the blue of his shirt was better.

Eventually, some kind of truce was brokered and Andre nudged me back into telling my story. We'd gotten as far as I'd gotten with Scafaro when Andre's phone rang, and then Scafaro's. Mine, which was set on vibrate, had never stopped ringing. If I'd had it in a different pocket, I could have had a hell of a good time. But that would have counted as being heartless.

The observing cop and I watched them take the calls. Saw them process what was obviously sad news. The worst news. I saw regret pass over Andre's face—we'd both followed Ginger through a bunch of houses. Andre had liked her. Her directness had gotten past his instinctive distrust of realtors. She'd tried hard to find us something that was right and truly understood what that was. The house we were standing in now.

All I saw on Scafaro's face was disappointment that he was losing control of the case. That he was about to become the beta dog in a state where the Maine State Police investigated most of the homicides. But the younger cop, the one who'd been first through the door, looked sad enough for both of them. I thought I remembered that Ginger lived somewhere near here, so maybe he'd known her. Maybe even dated her? He wasn't wearing a wedding ring. I knew Ginger was single, or at least about to be single—she'd mentioned that she and her live-in boyfriend had found themselves increasingly incompatible, and the boyfriend had moved out. She was a little older than the young cop, but these days, the rules seemed to be pretty flexible.

There was something else she'd said about her boyfriend, but I couldn't recall it right now. I'd have to try. In a case like this, who knew what might be important? This was either the act of a psychopath or a deeply angry person.

Ginger was—had been—really cute. While her pearly pale skin and sprinkle of freckles suggested she should have been a redhead, she had glossy russet brown hair that she'd worn in a thick braid down her back, with little curly tendrils that escaped around her face. Thinking about her braid led, inevitably, to seeing it burst into flame, and to the awful smell of singed hair.

That led to all the rest of it.

I turned to Andre, who was between calls in the series he would have to make to summon the necessary personnel to the scene. The MSP crime scene van. Their crime scene technicians. Someone would have to arrange for Ginger to be taken to Augusta, to the ME's office. Stuff I knew more about than I wanted to.

"What kind of a monster does something like this?" I said.

He just shook his head. "The world is full of monsters, Thea. You know that. It's way too soon to speculate about this. We don't know anything yet. Roland's on his way. He'll take your statement, okay?"

He looked across the room to Scafaro. "You'll probably want to sit in, get the whole story, so we can coordinate?"

Scafaro nodded, trying not to look at me.

I had a million questions I wanted to ask Andre, but he had clicked into detective mode and was beginning to run a million questions of his own. For now, my job was to tell Andre's fellow detective Roland Proffit what I knew, then get out of the way so the cops could do their job.

"What do I do 'til Roland gets here?"

Roland Proffit was one of Andre's good friends. I liked Roland a lot. He had a way of making really bad scenes better just by being there, and he had a whole collection of moose stories to leaven the bad times, always a new one to share. It wasn't that he didn't take what they did seriously. They all did. But humor, much of it pretty black and profane, was part of staying sane in the face of so much awfulness. At least the moose stories were light-hearted.

"Ten minutes," Andre said. He looked around at the room we were standing in. The lovely, bright room and beyond it to the family room with its big stone fireplace and sliders out to the yard. "Dammit. Goddammit! Why the hell—"

There were so many why the hells. Why our realtor? Why this house, this house we otherwise could have loved? Why us? Why now? Why? Why? Why? Why could we never get to enjoy normal, some peace and quiet, instead of what seemed like an endless amount of death and violence? Of course it came with the territory of his job. But too often it seemed to come with mine, as well. And now it seemed to be seeping into our private lives, as though together we had our own personal dark cloud that followed us about.

My phone was dancing. I might as well use the ten minutes. "Lt. Scafaro has the number that that call came from, changing the showing time. So you can see if it really came from Ginger's office or her cell. But while I'm waiting for Roland, is it okay if I make some calls? Suzanne had to see the doctor this morning. She's worried about the baby. I'd like to see what's going on."

"Go ahead." He waved toward the family room. "Maybe you want to go out there? We're going to be pretty busy in here."

He paused then, looking at my hands, seeing for the first time that I'd been burned. "They hurt?"

I nodded.

"You want to go to the hospital?"

I shook my head. "Just tell Roland to bring his first aid kit." I hate hospitals and I wasn't going to be a weak sister, taking attention away from the more serious matters here.

I stood at the far end of the lovely, high-ceilinged room, away from the official commotion in the living room and hall, staring into the yard, and at a children's swing set, holding the phone gingerly as I listened to my messages. Checking everyone's schedules in case the school down in Connecticut with the student drug problem needed us to parachute in. Bobby and Lisa were both tied up. Neither of them was free to work with our data-retentive client, though Bobby had some time tomorrow. If they needed someone on campus, Suzanne couldn't go. Lisa was tied up at another school, and Bobby would be better suited to taking over the report. He was a gem, but could be far too nice to stand up to a difficult administration or trustees reluctant to take our advice.

That left me holding the bag, or whatever the proper term was. I wasn't even sure the cops were going to let me go—not when I was their primary witness in an ugly homicide. I almost wished they wouldn't. I didn't want to drive anywhere on crumbling, slushy roads to get someplace where I'd have to put on my white hat and convince recalcitrant adults to act in their own best interests.

I was tired. Tired of winter. Tired of all the crises and emergencies that kept my adrenaline spiking and my suitcase packed. That made house hunting something I had to sandwich in between appointments. That made marriage, reading, movies, leisure and dinners with friends something I hoped to get around to sometime. Andre and I had chosen these lives—or they had chosen us—but we were both tired of feeling like gypsies. Our personal lives felt like they were stolen from our respective callings. It wasn't healthy and it wasn't likely to would get better unless we made an affirmative effort to change. And there would still be the question: change to what?

Today, I had to focus on the here and now. Or heres and nows. What was the term Andre used? Box it up. We had to box up our work lives and pack them away when we wanted to be together. Otherwise, they would sprawl into every available minute. Right now, I had to box up the horrors I'd just seen so I could be available for the Caldwell School, which wanted to know whether they were doing the right things to attract a strong student body but didn't want to share their applications and acceptance data; and, if things boiled over, for Stafford Academy. A consultant who looks and acts like she's just been flattened by a steamroller and smells singed isn't likely to inspire confidence.

We could tell the school to find themselves someone else to nurse them through their crisis. We weren't the only game in town, only, we liked to think, the best one. Or I could wait for Stafford to decide they needed me. Suzanne had called on the way to the doctor while I was dealing with Ginger, and I'd said I'd call her later. Now I called to discuss our options.

Her gloomy secretary, Magda, said she wasn't back from the doctor. Magda's emotional range is narrow. She goes from grouchy to not so grouchy. But she mothers us. Protects us from demanding clients and me from my mother. And makes our lives go smoothly. I was about to hang up when she said, "I'm worried about Suzanne. You've got to make her not work so much."

Like any of us could do that. But I agreed that I would try, even though we both knew Suzanne working less meant me working more.

As I sorted through my messages, triaged my calls, answered a question for a client I dearly loved, and conferred with Bobby about another report we were working on, the horrific business here fell away. The other side of the dilemma Andre and I both faced in our lives was this: while our work lives were stealing away the personal lives we longed to have, we allowed that theft because we both loved what we did. He was a fantastic instinctive detective. A superb reader of people and analyzer of facts. I loved bringing order out of chaos, of helping well-intentioned institutions realize those intentions. We both, in our own ways, dropped into out-of-control situations and brought them back under control. We righted the worlds that turned to us for help.

Right now, with burned hands and a mind filled with horrible images reminding me what I'd just witnessed, I didn't see any way that the world could be righted.

CHAPTER 4

"Thea."

Roland Proffit was coming toward me, his big hand outstretched. Roland's face was a study in contradictions. Lean and severe, thin lipped, with a powerful nose topped by the kindest eyes. His manner was similar. He was quick to assess and act. At 6' 4" he had a strong, imposing presence, yet his manner, especially with victims, with traumatized people, was surprisingly gentle. That outstretched hand wasn't for a conventional handshake, but preceded an arm that wrapped around me and gave me a hug. Followed by eyes that assessed me for damage, and analyzed what I might need from the first aid kit he was carrying.

"I know it was awful," he said. "How are you holding up?"

I waved my phone. "Keeping busy. Losing myself in work."

He nodded. "Things don't change much, do they?"

He looked around. "So where do you want to do this? Nice house. Too bad there isn't a big comfortable sofa." He jerked his chin toward the front of the house. "I'd suggest my car, but it's a zoo out there."

The fireplace had a wide raised fieldstone hearth, like a long bench plenty big enough to sit on. "How about right here?" I said, lowering myself to it. We probably looked pretty funny. I'm tall. He's very tall, so we were folded up like storks. But it was a place to sit, and relatively quiet.

Before he started in on his questions, Roland bandaged my hands, giving me a cute matching set of little gauzy fingerless mitts, shaking his head and clucking as he wrapped me up. I felt him holding back a lecture—something about not going back to work or taking it easy. But he knows I'm one of the tough guys. Anyway, I didn't see how I *could* take time off. People needed me.

Then Roland started to take me through the same questions Scafaro had asked, yet from him, they were very different. Partly, it was his pace. He talked like we had all the time in the world, even though we both knew we didn't.

"Wait," I said, as we settled into our conversation, "what about Scafaro? Andre wanted him to hear this."

Roland shook his head. "I think he's found something else for the lieutenant to do."

Trust Andre to get that right, I thought.

"When you got to the gate," Roland said, "was it latched?"

I considered. "No. The latch hadn't caught."

"What about the front door. You said it was open. How open? Could you see into the room?"

"No. It was almost closed. But when I knocked, after Ginger didn't answer the doorbell, it swung open. So I went in."

"The floors look like they've all been recently redone," he said. "Did you see any signs where someone had tracked in dirt? Did you notice any footprints?"

Anything that had been there would be gone now, or all mucked up, after the flurry of emergency activity. "That's funny," I said.

"What?"

"I did see footprints. Sock prints, actually. Because I could almost, but not quite, see the imprint of toes, like feet in wet or sweaty socks."

"Where?" he asked.

"From right by the front door toward those closed pocket doors. Lots of footprints, actually, like someone had gone back and forth several times. I thought Ginger must have slipped off her shoes, to avoid messing up the floor and wondered if I should take mine off, but there weren't any shoes."

I tried to remember whether she'd been wearing shoes. I couldn't. "And they weren't Ginger's feet. Her feet were tiny." We'd joked about that one day, when she was wearing these darling little embroidered boots and she said they were actually kid's boots. She'd said she also had a pair of those kid's sneakers that lit up when you walked. I was jealous. I've always wanted a pair of those.

"Only leading toward the living room?"

I nodded. "Back and forth."

I tried to recall whether I'd seen any tracks when I went into the living room, but I'd been in such a hurry. And once the door was open, my focus had been on Ginger and that dreadful circle of heaters. "I'm sorry, Roland. I didn't notice. Once the door opened and I saw her…that's all I saw."

"That's okay," he said. "You're doing fine. You said the doors were closed, so you didn't go into the living room when you first entered the house. Why not?"

"Because I expected it to knock my socks off. You know how long we've been house hunting. I wanted to save the best for last." I looked away, biting my lip to stop a bit of 'poor me.'

He patted my arm reassuringly. "So you went into the dining room?" I nodded. "See any footprints there?"

I considered, then shook my head. Those shiny floors had been unmarked. "No. Then I went into the kitchen, but I never really got a chance to look around, because that's when I heard the sound."

"Sound?"

"Someone moaning? Or crying? A muffled sound like someone needed help. So I ran back into the foyer, pushed those doors open, and I saw her."

I stopped. This was the hard part. I decided to let Roland lead me through it.

"Tell me what you saw."

"In front of the fireplace. There was the chair in the middle, with Ginger tied to it, and around her that ring of space heaters."

It was important, I knew, and I was the only person who had seen it the way the killer had set it up. I'd disturbed things trying to rescue Ginger.

"Did you notice anything particular about the heaters? About their spacing or arrangement?"

It seemed like an odd question. My focus had been on Ginger, on processing what was happening, getting her out of there, trying to save her life. I hadn't paid much attention to them. Now I considered. My first thought was that they had all been alike. Evenly spaced around her, like squat, crouching, red-faced beasts with long orange tails. But that wasn't quite right. The two in front of her had been smaller heaters, closer together and closer to her, like her tormenter had run out of big ones.

Or like her tormenter had wanted a particularly fierce blast of heat right in front of her.

I told Roland that.

He walked me through everything I'd done. Whether I'd noticed anything unusual about the room. I hadn't. Had I seen anyone in the back yard? I'd never even looked out there. There had been sheer curtains but not heavy drapes. Light but no view.

Had Ginger said anything to me? I repeated the words, or pieces of words, that I had heard. Airy. Bobby. So long. Safe. Sorry.

He wrote them down. "Nothing else?"

"I don't think so. Roland, I was so shocked…So wrapped up in trying to save her. In calling for help. There might have been something else and I just don't remember. She forced out those few words…it was a struggle for her to say that much but it seemed terribly important…and then she started screaming. I told her not to try and speak, but it was like something she had to tell me. I only wish…"

But there were so many things I wished.

"That's okay," he said. "Sometimes things come back later on. Or things that seemed random suddenly make sense. Connect up with something else you knew. You know how it works. If you remember anything else, tell Andre."

He backed me up, then, to when I first arrived. "What about cars on the street? You said you saw Ginger's car in the driveway. Did you notice any other cars?"

I told him about the truck that had veered into my lane. Largish. Dark green. Pickup. I thought it had a double cab, but wasn't sure. Between the ringing phone and spilling coffee, I hadn't noticed the driver. Or the make. I wasn't much of a witness, if there had been anything to witness, but who goes out to look at a house and conscientiously records everything they see along the way?

Sure, Andre and I have this remembering game that we play. But it's a game. It's play. Describing someone we've passed on the street or seen briefly in a car. It's different under stress conditions when a life is at stake. At least, it's different for me. Maybe he can do it all the time. I'm not usually around him under stress conditions.

That last was almost a lie, given our history.

He wanted to know how the street looked when I turned onto it. I'd noticed the trees. The way the houses were set back from the street. Had I noticed any cars? I shook my head. "I was thinking about living on this street. I wasn't looking at the cars. Wait. I did notice one or two. There was one of those pseudo-Hummer things. You know—the one Toyota makes. A bright, shiny blue. It looked brand new, like the owner just brought it home or he took it to the carwash every day."

I think of certain types of cars as men's cars or women's cars. This was a guy car. Like those open Jeeps. Like muscle cars. Jaguar sedans, on the other hand, I think of as women's cars.

During mud season, cars get pretty dirty. Between dirt, sand, and road salt, they become a universal tannish gray color, no matter what color they were to start with, often with arcs of clean where the wipers have been working. That's why this one stood out. What was the other one? Oh. Right. "And an older car. Smallish. I don't know the make. But it was that kind of odd mallard green?"

"Teal?" he said.

I nodded.

"What about people on the street? Did you see any people? We'll do a canvass, of course, but just in case?" His smile was a bit cynical. "You know how eager people can be to talk to us."

I did know. I replayed turning onto the street and driving down it. Had I seen any of the people who might have been my new neighbors? Maybe the game Andre and I played was working, because I had.

"A grouchy-looking woman out walking a black lab. Hair a slightly too bright blonde, pulled back in a ponytail. She was wearing a Red Sox hat and a pink coat. A woman carrying a toddler in a red snowsuit. An older woman in a black down coat scraping her windshield." The suburbs in the daytime. The population overwhelmingly female. I hadn't even noticed that I was seeing them.

"Sorry I can't be more helpful," I said.

This time Roland's smile was genuine. "You're doing fine. We never know what will be helpful 'til we get into it."

I looked at my watch. It was getting later and later, and my work was waiting. Roland read it right. "Places to be?" he said.

"Always."

"I'll walk you out to your car. Make sure you can get out. Keep those reporters off your back."

"My hero," I said. But in fact, he was. Roland had been there for me during some pretty tough times. Picked me up and put me back together a few times.

"Find the monster who did this, Roland."

"We will. Meanwhile, you keep thinking. What you saw. What you might know. I haven't even gotten to asking you about Ginger Stevens. We can get most of that from her co-workers and friends, but keep your thinking cap on. You're a good observer."

Roland cleared the way, and soon I was back in my Jeep and heading for the highway. But instead of planning what I would do if the Stafford Academy headmaster called, I was pondering Roland's last question. What DID I know about Ginger Stevens?

CHAPTER 5

I pulled over at a donut shop a few miles away. I really needed something to eat, and a donut place was the only kind of fast food I could think of where I might not have to smell cooking meat. Once I was inside, I found I couldn't face the thought of eating, so I just got coffee. I loaded it with cream and sugar and went outside, leaning against the car, trying to air out my hair and clothes a little, and sipped cautiously. I wanted to speed back to the office and bury myself in work, filling my head with charts and graphs that would push images of Ginger aside, use some of my bad energy to bully our recalcitrant client into giving up their data. But first I badly needed airing.

Actually, what I badly needed was a scrub brush to clean out the inside of my head. A shower. Therapy to help me get past the moment when I'd accidentally put my hand on Ginger's arm and her skin had started to slip. Otherwise, that feeling would live with me forever. Andre kept saying 'box it up.' But I had no idea how I was supposed to get these ugly things into a box.

Fingers of wind made sneak attacks on my body like the sudden gropings of middle school boys. While the wind tried to turn me into a popsicle, I closed my eyes and said a prayer for Ginger. I hoped she was in a better place. I hoped there was a better place. But my nature is to fix things, so it wasn't long before I moved on to the question of justice for Ginger and whether there was anything I could do to help.

It was freezing out. One of those days that looks appealing through a car window and is actually miserable. The people going in to get their coffee were red-nosed and grimacing. The weatherman predicted snow for later. When I couldn't stand it anymore, I got in the car, cranked up the heat, and drove to the office. Even with the heat blasting, I couldn't seem to get warm.

On the way, I called Suzanne for an update on her condition and our clients'. Magda said she wasn't back in the office yet. Magda sounded worried, and Suzanne had been gone so long that I was worried, too. Suzanne is a slave of duty, and there was plenty of duty calling today.

I rummaged in the back for some clean clothes, then ran, bunched-up clothes in one hand and my overstuffed briefcase in the other, the bandages cushioning my hands as I crossed the sandy lot to the building. We had a suite of offices on the second floor of a bland beige office building. My feet thudded heavily on the stairs and I was out of breath by the time I reached the door. Something else I was behind on—I was badly overdue at the gym.

My desk had experienced a pink slip storm while I was out. I gathered them up and sorted them into 'needs attention' and 'can wait.' The 'can wait' pile was smaller. On top was one with URGENT in Magda's loopy penmanship, with the word underlined three times. I guess that that meant it was urgent. The message was to call Suzanne at home.

The fact that Suzanne was at home suggested bad news, but when I reached her, she sounded like her usual chipper self. She wanted to plan how we would deal with the situation at Stafford Academy if it escalated, and whether I would need Bobby there as well, when we were so busy.

I said if they decided they needed help, I could handle it. Then Suzanne changed the subject. "I almost hesitate to ask, Thea, but what did you mean about a body of your own?"

I filled her in on getting to the house, finding Ginger, and Ginger's death and she asked me what in hell was my problem? Okay. Suzanne didn't say hell. She said heck. She's a proper, ladylike sort who hasn't spent as much time around cops as I have.

"You're not going to get involved in that, I hope."

"Doing my best to avoid it. But I'm the one who found her, so avoiding involvement is difficult. I'm kind of a major witness."

"You don't need this, Thea. We don't need this. Let the police handle it."

I didn't argue that the police couldn't handle it without civilian cooperation or that the choice wasn't mine because I knew she wouldn't listen. Like my mother, Suzanne is always urging me to live a more careful life, while overlooking the realities of the situations I get involved in. Not that I could see how being careful would have helped me this morning. House hunting was supposed to be a pretty benign activity and it wasn't one easily undertaken without a realtor. I hadn't read anywhere about a rash of attacks on realtors. Maybe I should do an internet search?

But the things I'd observed in that living room suggested elaborate planning and a deep, twisted need to do harm. They suggested that this was personal. Not a random attack on a cute realtor, but a deliberate attack on Ginger.

I couldn't think about that right now. Before I disconnected, I followed up on another of my intuitions—that Suzanne didn't sound quite like herself. She wasn't acting like herself, either, at home in the middle of the day. And she hadn't mentioned the doctor or seeing me in the office later in the day. Something was up.

"So what did the doctor say?"

There was an uncharacteristically long silence. "Bed rest," she said gloomily.

"Serious bed rest or just take it easy bed rest?"

"Serious. Confined to quarters. No being an independent school goddess. No being a domestic goddess. If I want to carry this kid to term, I am confined to my bed. To be waited on hand and foot. Not," she continued darkly, "that there is anyone around here to wait on me." Silence. Then, "I'm already restless and it's only been two hours. Promise you'll bring me work. Send Magda to keep me organized. Not let me lose my mind."

I promised.

Suzanne's form of domestic goddesshood was complicated, because she was the goddess not only of her own home, but, as headmaster's wife at a private school, she was the goddess of the whole community. Half the time, she went home not to her family or her house, but to a tea, or a fancy dinner, or to attend a campus event. Often, as well, she went home to entertain VIP houseguests. Sometimes she was flying off to distant cities to attend fundraisers with alums. Bed rest meant having to find coverage in every aspect of her life. Never mind that she had a small child to care for. If I was stressed, she was on an emotional rack.

We both loved helping schools. It had been a very special moment when she'd asked me to move from employee to partner, and between us, we had built a fine business. But our business depended on quick and responsive personal service. On our individual reputations as much as on our good staff and excellent work. That meant delegation was hard, and because boarding schools were a 24/7 world, we could no more put off attending to things than Andre could when he was deeply enmeshed in a case. Sometimes, though no one would believe it when we said we were consultants, our work also felt like life or death. Or life *and* death, given some of the situations we'd been called on to deal with.

"So. Stafford Academy? Have they called again?" she asked.

"Not yet. But my intuition says they will."

"Mine, too. Look, I'm feeling a little flattened by all this. Let me think about what's on my plate right now that can't wait, and I'll call you."

There was never much that could wait. We both knew that. We agreed that I would handle things at Stafford without Bobby, that I would keep twisting our client's arm to get the data for the report that was coming up on deadline, and that I would hand writing that off to Bobby. Suzanne would call when she got herself sorted out. I didn't mention that I'd probably have to spend more time with the police. Suzanne had enough things to worry about.

"Call me when you can," I said. "And please, no heroics. Don't worry about our clients. Lisa and Bobby and I can handle things if you need us to."

I disconnected and filled in Magda, who had been hovering by my elbow. Her gloomy expression got gloomier until I said, "And she wants you to go to her house to work with her, as soon as we figure out who's going to take on which projects and which ones she'll keep."

"She wants me to go there?"

"That's what she said. She needs you"

Though she would vehemently deny it, I was sure I saw the trace of a smile. Most of all, Magda needed us to need her, and Suzanne was her special pet. There was an added benefit. If Magda had to go to Suzanne's house, she might also get to see Paul, Jr. She considered Suzanne's little boy her grandchild, never mind that she had several of her own, and Suzanne and Paul both had living parents. It could be worse. She might droop about like an oversized Eeyore, but Magda also made our work lives work.

Magda mollified, or at least informed, I dove into the rest of the pink slips and spent most of the next two hours on the phone. It was only then that I realized I'd dumped my clean clothes on my visitor's chair and was still wearing smelly soot-and-coffee-stained clothes.

I dashed to the ladies' room, did a quick swipe at my face and arms, and changed into clean clothes. Clean clothes helped, but the worn-looking woman in the mirror needed a facial, a vacation, and an infusion of daily multiples. I told her I was working on it—not a total lie—and went back to traffic control.

In the five or six minutes I'd been gone, the pink slips had managed to have sex and produce offspring. At least, that's how it looked. There was a message from my husband wanting to know how I was doing and saying not to expect him for dinner. One from Roland Proffit, asking me to call. And one from the data-retentive client, saying they were putting it together and would have it for me by the end of the day. So far, nothing from Stafford, but when a client puts you on standby alert, you stay on alert until you're sure the crisis has passed.

I called the client who was sending me data. I wasn't sure what their definition of "end of the day" was, but my clock said it was nearing 4:30, and sometime in the next hour, I hoped to get enough done so I could go home, take the world's longest shower, and then crawl under my bed and moan for a while, doing the decompressing from this morning that I hadn't had time for yet.

The client, in the way that clients will, put me off, saying they'd call back in "the next hour." I wasn't planning to hold my breath.

The clock ticked on. Bobby had a question. Lisa called from the school where she was working and she had a question that required me to find and send her some information. Bobby needed the name of an expert we sometimes used. Suzanne needed her Daytimer and some materials from her desk. A board that was in the process of hiring a new head of school called with some questions and wanted to know if I could sit on in their final set of interviews.

I checked my calendar and said yes.

The clock ticked on. The data didn't arrive. The client didn't call back.

My stomach rumbled like an angry beast but I didn't know what to feed it. I tried to return Roland's call, but he didn't pick up. I hated phone tag. Real tag was fun. Exciting and infused with a sense of danger. Phone tag was boring and infused with a sense of time wasted and clocks ticking, as well as the frustration of being unable to complete a necessary task.

I'd been concentrating on my office phone, but a buzzing from my purse reminded me that my cell phone also wanted attention. Some days, I amuse myself by dreaming up appropriate tortures for the people who thought all these electronic devices would enhance our lives. Too often, the way they demand our obedience is more in the nature of those electric shock collars that people use to train dogs. Only now we're all busy training each other. Or ourselves. My phone was constantly startling me with the tones to announce arriving text messages and reminders about what was on my calendar. Sometimes even in the middle of the night. Youngsters may have a handle on how to manage these devices. I find them rather willful little beasts.

Andre, dear man that he was, had called to ask if I was doing all right. Then he had called to ask when I was coming home. Then *if* I was coming home. And finally, to let me know that he probably *wasn't* going to be home anytime soon, so if was I coming home, I'd better just go ahead and eat something. I tried calling him back and went to voicemail. Marriage by phone tag. Described like that, it didn't sound appealing, though the truth was that when we were together, we usually had a pretty great time.

Roland had called the office but he'd also called my cell to set up a follow-up interview, hopefully one that could take place soon. There was heavy emphasis on the soon. In his message, he expressed surprise at how little information anyone who knew her seemed to have about Ginger, and hoped I might know more. She was a mysterious person, he said. Her co-workers knew little about her, other than some vague details about her stormy relationship with someone named Randy. No one knew about any parents or other relatives or could recall her ever having mentioned them.

No one could direct him to her best friends, or even to any casual ones.

Her neighbors described cordial, but distant, relationships. They'd observed no one coming or going from her apartment other than Ginger herself or the boyfriend, Randy. Roland couldn't even locate that ubiquitous Maine feature, the nosy elderly neighbor who sat in her window and kept tabs on everyone. He hoped I might know *something*.

Normally, cops shared almost nothing, so I was surprised at how much he'd told me. Maybe it was to secure my cooperation. There was a note of desperation in that "something."

Why me? I was just one of her clients. Someone who'd spent some time with her looking at real estate. Tromping through attics and basements discussing furnaces and plumbing, wiring and sump pumps was not ordinarily considered the foundation of a close relationship. In the time we'd spent together, Ginger had been outgoing and confided things about her life quite easily. She was bubbly and cute and seemed like a fun person to spend time with. It was odd that she wouldn't have had a raft of friends and be on great terms with her neighbors. Even odder that the people in her office couldn't fill him in a whole lot better than I.

Of course I would do whatever I could to help. It was just that my goal right now was to put this morning's awful events behind me as best I could and immerse myself in my clients' troubles. It looked like Roland wasn't going to let me.

The divinely charming Lt. Sporty Scafaro had called to tell me that I'd left my jacket behind and they were going to keep it as evidence. As evidence of what, I couldn't guess. Proof that I really had used it to beat out the flames? Or did he expect that on further inspection he'd find receipts for eight space heaters hidden in the lining? Or maybe tiny flecks of orange plastic from unreeling all those extension cords?

Oh man. I needed to stop this. I needed to still my cranky mind and keep a louse like Scafaro on a back burner where he could simmer without causing me any grief. Right now, my back burners were getting pretty crowded.

On the front burner was our unresponsive client. We couldn't just say to heck with the report. We had way too many hours in and needed their check for our bottom line. I tried once more and didn't get an answer. I looked at my e-mail and the fax, but nothing had come in. If it came in the morning, we were going to be hard pressed to get the report done on time. One more thing that would make tomorrow another miserable day.

I sighed and reached for my coat.

The phone rang. Every instinct said to let it go to voicemail, but I am a slave of duty, and the caller ID said it was Stafford Academy.

"This is Reeve Barrows," the voice said. "Is this EDGE Consulting?"

"Reeve, it's Thea."

"Thank god," he said, "we really need your help."

My heart sank.

CHAPTER 6

By the time I got off the phone, it was after six, and I'd agreed to be at Stafford by nine the next morning. That meant leaving at the crack of dawn. Reeve had a genuine dilemma. Two students—one a venture capitalist's daughter from Manhattan, the other a minority scholarship kid from the Bronx—had been selling Molly to their classmates. Molly. MDMA. A club drug. Bad enough by itself, but one of their customers had gotten happily high and dehydrated, then hyperthermic. She'd gone outside to cool off, passed out, and nearly died of hypothermia.

She was recovering at a local hospital and her parents were threatening to sue. The VC parents were helicoptering in with lawyers and entourage in tow. VC daughter and minority boyfriend were trying to get each other off the hook. Cops were circling. As soon as the word got out, reporters would be everywhere. And the headmaster was AWOL—at some off-site meeting and not responding to his phone.

I asked a bunch of questions, made some notes about steps to take, repeated the basic instructions I'd given him earlier about controlling information flow and securing the campus. I made sure he had the school's lawyer and head of trustees in the loop. I cut him off when he tried to tell me it wasn't his problem. Until the Head of School resurfaced, it was. I said I'd call him in the morning from the road with some further instructions. Then I grabbed my stuff and headed for the door before the phone rang again.

I needed to try Andre again. Schedule some time with Roland—the first twenty-four hours being critical and all that. I was so tired even the drive home felt daunting. Finding a body and getting grilled by cops—even friendly cops like Roland—takes it out of you. I still hadn't eaten, but there are very few places that serve food that don't smell like grilled or fried meat. I'd have to drive to Portland if I wanted vegetarian or vegan cuisine, so I wasn't sure what I was going to do. I'm way too young to feel tired. That's what I tell myself. Other times, I wonder if I have some fatal disease that just hasn't been diagnosed. On my rational days, I think I suffer from a middle-years version of old timer's disease—no timer's disease. Most of my friends have it, too.

I threw my stuff in the back seat and told Siri to call Roland.

When he answered, Roland sounded tired and cranky. "I've called you a dozen times," he said, "and you don't call me back. You know this is a critical time for us. You want the monster who did this to walk because we can't get good information?"

"But I did call you back."

Roland didn't respond.

His anger wasn't directed at me. But despite what he'd said in his messages about people not having much information about Ginger, I was still puzzled that he considered my information significant. I'd barely known Ginger. Our conversation had been girl talk in the car driving to see a house, or casual stuff as we walked through one. This was when he should be spending time talking to her co-workers and friends, to her family. He should have tracked down that sketchy boyfriend she'd been complaining about. Pressing them, not me, even if they claimed not to have known her well. He should be searching her place, going through her things, reading her mail. What I knew ought to be way down the list.

I didn't help matters by pointing all that out, though. He already knew it. He must be drawing blanks if he thought I was important. Besides, it's not easy to blow off a guy who's intimidatingly large, a very talented interrogator, and a friend.

"Sorry, Roland. I've got my own crisis here. Suzanne's on bed rest and I've got a school that's in deep trouble with students selling drugs on campus."

"What do they expect you to do?" He sounded puzzled. Another one of the people who think because I'm a consultant I must do something utterly boring and there is no urgency about my work.

"Handle the press. Handle the parents. Help them deal with their upset students. Get someone in who can scare them—the students—silly about drugs. Protect the school's reputation and keep this from causing major attrition in next year's entering class. All the usual. So what's the emergency?"

"When are you going to be home?" he said. "I really need to talk to you. And I don't mean phone chat. I mean a lengthy face-to-face interview about Ginger Stevens."

"I've just started home. It's going to take me about twenty minutes, depending on traffic. But I don't know much I can help. I barely knew her, Roland."

"That's my problem, Thea. Everyone barely knew her. Neighbors. Co-workers. Except maybe for her boyfriend, and he's vanished. Co-workers and neighbors say he was living there as recently as last week, but there's no sign of him at her apartment. And I mean no sign. No clothes, no stuff, no hairs or fibers. I've never seen anyone move out and leave no traces behind, especially a guy. It's almost as though he doesn't want to be found."

That was strange, even if it was an unpleasant breakup. "Maybe Ginger was so glad to see him go she literally wiped him out of her life," I suggested. "I know she was feeling pretty negative about him. What about her car? Her clothes? The laundry bin? The mattress pad? There must be some traces of him. Some fingerprints. What about the underside of the toilet seat?"

I couldn't believe I'd just said that. I blame Andre. Living with him has made me far more cop-like than most people. I've even occasionally been accused of being a cop myself. Usually by people who don't like cops.

He sighed. "We're checking the car. We struck out everywhere else. Look, let's meet up somewhere."

"Roland, I honestly don't know. I'm tired. I've got a lot of work to do tonight, and it's time sensitive, just like yours. And I have to leave for Connecticut at five a.m. Maybe tomorrow night?"

"Tonight," he said, in a tone that brooked no argument. "I'll buy you dinner."

"Only if there are no roasting, frying, or grilling smells, Roland. You know of any place like that?"

"Your place, then," he said. "I'll bring something."

This was the moment when being more "cop-like" became a negative instead of a positive. Except that I did want to help. He wasn't going to hear me if I said no anyway.

"I'll call you when I'm home."

"Will you call me?" There was a pause, and I thought he regretted being so negative. Confirmed when he added, in a softer tone, "How about when you're ten minutes away?" Unable, at the end, to avoid pressing the time thing.

Now he wasn't the only one who was getting cranky. "Don't treat me like a difficult witness, Roland. Okay? I've been up to my ears in stuff, too. I've been working every second since I left you. I haven't eaten all day and I'm out here on the highway surrounded by people who seem scared by a few snowflakes."

Living in Maine was spoiling me. Except for the occasional burst of fight or flight, which caused timid drivers to pull out right in front of me and then drive a tentative, aggravating twenty miles an hour, the drivers here tended to be pretty competent. Mostly, if I found someone riding my bumper, they were what Mainers called "from away." But tonight, maybe just because they were exhausted from so many winter storms, everyone seemed to be being unnecessarily cautious.

"Sorry, Thea. It's just that there are so many odd things about this case."

I was going to ask "like what?" but I needed to concentrate on driving. I could get the details when we were face-to-face, which was soon enough for me. I wasn't eager to revisit the horrors of this morning, and when I sat down with him and he started asking questions, I would be right back there.

Before I disconnected to check in with Suzanne and Bobby about the Stafford situation, I had one more suggestion for him about the missing boyfriend.

"About that boyfriend. You should check her purse and her wallet for his fingerprints, because one of the things she mentioned to me when she said they were breaking up was that he'd been helping himself to her money, going right into her wallet and taking it while she was sleeping or in the shower. Her purse and her wallet probably have his fingerprints all over them. She said she'd started locking her money in the glove compartment of her car to protect herself."

"Great tip," he said. "And a small mystery solved."

I figured he meant a stash of cash in Ginger's car. I was well on my way to earning my junior achievement badge. We agreed I'd call when I was close and he'd find us something we could safely eat. I went back to navigating traffic. The swirl of snowflakes was getting thicker and there was the promise of a "wintery mix" overnight. By the end of March, after a long and miserable winter, the words "wintery mix" are like nails on a blackboard. Everyone cringes and wants it to stop.

I was on the phone the rest of the way home. I updated Suzanne and left her to her rest, though she'd get little of that as she figured out how to parcel out her work to our staff. Then I called Bobby to bring him into the loop on the status of the report for the data-retentive client.

Bobby's husband answered, his voice wary and querulous as soon as he knew it was me. He believed it was his job to protect Bobby from us, even though our small staff had a great relationship and no one took advantage of anyone. Quinn was a chef, and worked in a world where taking advantage seemed to be the norm. He never believed in any reality that was different from his. I'd long ago give up trying to change his mind and settled for knowing that we both loved Bobby and wanted the best for him.

"We've got an emergency and I need to speak with Bobby," I said.

I chose the word 'emergency' to cut through his usual layers of protest and it worked. A moment later, I was filling Bobby in on Suzanne's situation and briefing him about the problem at Stafford Academy. "I'm off to Connecticut in the morning. You'll have to pick up the slack on that report," I said. "I have no idea whether they'll actually come through with that data in the morning. If you don't have it by ten, call me."

"No problem," he said.

Is it any wonder I love Bobby? He's what my mother would call a 'sweet-natured boy'. Having him around makes the whole world better.

"If we don't get the data, we're going to finish that report anyway," I said. "We'll just do what we can and write, 'estimates pending correct data' wherever we need to."

"How about a nifty set of initials," he said, "like ACDSD?"

It sounded good. Very official. Almost military. "What is ACDSD?"

"Asshole client didn't supply data."

"I love you, Bobby."

"Take it easy, Thea," he said. "Things are going to be fine."

Every office needs an optimist like Bobby. I said I'd talk to him in the morning and disconnected.

* * *

My briefcase was bulging with work I hadn't gotten to. After a few more calls, I'd turned my phone to vibrate and it had been dancing the rest of the way home. I knew what some of it was about. Conference planning where the organizer wanted to lay off everything onto me and Suzanne—a place we'd been before with a conference organizer who'd then had the temerity to get herself killed at the conference. Some small, but serious, issues at two client schools where they wanted to discuss the details of on-campus suspensions—calls I had to return. Everyone wanted a piece of me. Ignoring the rest of my messages, I called Roland and told him I was ten minutes out.

By the time I pulled onto our street, I'd been pecked by so many beaks I was a lace doily remnant of the woman who'd set out in the morning to buy herself a house.

However grueling Roland's questions, right now I welcomed the respite. He would deal straight with no game playing, wasn't going to nickel and dime me about a bill, and he wasn't likely to have had a sudden bout of amnesia.

As I pulled into my driveway, though, I wished I'd found a way to put him off. I used the word 'home' because this was where we slept and hung our clothes. But this place felt so little like home it could plunge me into instant depression. A curtain twitched as our landlady, Mrs. Ames, did her routine check on my arrival. The apartment was nice enough, but from the outside, the house looked as tired and worn as I felt. I'd always hated the fact that it was painted a color that only belonged in black raspberry ice cream. The walls of dirty snow didn't help.

Dammit. Dammit. Dammit. I pounded the steering wheel. I lived in a freakin' purple house with a man who was never home. I was never home. I couldn't find a house to buy no matter how hard I tried. How was I ever going to achieve a simpler life when just getting up in the morning immersed me in messes like this?

True to his word, Roland had brought us both safe, meat-free dinners—two huge, messy eggplant parmesan subs and a plastic tub of salad. Very wise choices. He got out plates while I found him a beer and poured myself a glass of delicious Bogle Phantom, a wine I chose because I loved the name. Besides, if I drank too much Phantom, I'd never get drunk because the wine really wasn't there. I could tell myself I just had a phantom drinking habit. My father, much as I love the man, also has this phantom habit. I believe he needs it in order to live with my mother.

Roland looked as tired as I felt. We weren't either of us as resilient as we used to be—as Indy says, it's not the years, it's the mileage—and investigating murder and child abuse was a hard business. Harder, even though cops are tough, when the murder is gruesome. Though few would believe me, consulting was tough, too. I'd been on the phone almost constantly all day, interviewing, reassuring and cajoling. The only easy conversation had been with my husband. In the brief minute or two that he'd allotted me, Andre had been kind, caring, and concerned for my state of mind. Also, as was too often the case, unavailable. He didn't know when he'd be home. At least he expected to be home. Tonight I definitely didn't want to sleep alone.

Roland and I settled in the living room, spread our food out on the coffee table, and went to work.

"Sorry I was a grouch earlier," he said. "I haven't eaten all day."

As we ate, he filled me in a little on why he thought anything I could tell him might be helpful. "Here's the thing," he said. "Not only do we have little to go on in finding her killer, we don't even know who our victim is."

Of course we did. I was there. I saw her. I burned my hands trying to save her.

I set down my sandwich and stared at him. "What are you talking about, Roland? It's not like she was burned beyond recognition or anything. It was Ginger."

"Not so simple, Thea. That's the name she was using, but she's not Ginger Stevens," he said. "Ginger Stevens was the name of a New Hampshire child who died more than thirty years ago at the age of four. Not Ginger, actually, but Virginia. Fourteen years ago, someone applied for a social security number in that name." He shook his head, a man used to solving mysteries, who found this one surprisingly hard. "So, other than knowing that she was using a dead person's identity, we have no idea who the woman who called herself Ginger Stevens really was."

They were doing fingerprint searches, but Roland was dubious. If she was in the system at all—or had been—it could have been as a juvenile, given her probable age. Many states were protective about their juvenile records, so the prints might not have been entered. Others had been careless, or the prints hadn't been entered for minor crimes, or the systems didn't communicate well with each other. Modern TV shows have led people to believe information is available at the click of a button. The reality is often far different.

I felt like I'd been sitting on a chair and someone had kicked it out from under me. This morning had been bad enough. Now the mystery about Ginger's death had just gotten a lot more complicated. If she was using a stolen identity, was that because she had some dark secret? And had that dark secret been the reason she was killed?

CHAPTER 7

Soon, the low table held the remnants of our dinner. Crumpled foil and napkins smeared with tomato sauce. The smell of tomato and spice pretty much wiped out anything else. Roland's offhand remark about not having eaten himself, when I knew he was one of those fast metabolism guys who have to eat every few hours to keep going, told me that he felt almost as sick at the thought of meat right now as I did. And he was a tough guy. He might have come late to the party, but that slightly off barbeque smell still filled the house.

Roland looked at the paper splotched with red. "Normally, eggplant wouldn't be my first choice, but…" A long pause. "Some things you never get used to." A hesitation. "It's such a distinctive smell."

I thought about the slipping skin on Ginger's arm. Wondered, briefly, if I would lose my dinner. "I'm just a civilian," I said. "Am I going to have to become vegetarian?"

He shook his head. "Only for a while. As for being *just* a civilian, Thea? If I believe that, you're gonna sell me what? The Penobscot Narrows Bridge?"

"I'd sure like to sell you on the idea that I don't know enough to make this conversation worthwhile."

"And I'm not buying."

He sat across from me on the comfortable mushroom-colored couch, pen poised over his notebook, and started in on his questions.

"This killing wasn't random. It was planned," he said. "You saw what someone did to her."

He gave it a beat as he forced me to remember. A friend, yes, but also a cop with a particularly nasty homicide to investigate. "You're good with people, Thea. You're observant. And they talk to you. At this point, almost anything she might have said would be more than we've got now. Everyone gives us the same line: she was pleasant, she was quiet, she kept to herself. No one knows where she came from. Who her family is. No one is a close enough friend to have been a confidant. Even if she was being guarded about her life, there has to be more than that. No one can be that careful."

"Phone bills?" I suggested, unable to keep from stating the obvious. "They should lead you to people she knew. Her cell phone records? What's on her desk? In her files? Matchbooks, business cards, sales receipts. Things she's scribbled on little pieces of paper. People keep stuff."

He rolled his eyes. "You don't think we're doing that? Of course we'll call those people. But the ones we've contacted so far don't know anything. No one knows if she has parents, siblings, or other relatives, not even people she's worked with for the two years we can document that she's been living in Maine. Her office doesn't even have an application or a resume on file for her. The only person she's ever mentioned other than clients is the boyfriend."

His dark eyes gazed into mine. "Yes, most people keep stuff. But not Ginger. Her apartment is sanitized. As though she wanted to leave no clues to her identity. Unless her killer did that. Frankly, I've rarely seen a place with so few signs of personality. Her clothes are generic. No labels that would give us any clues. Nothing from a boutique, or from a chain that isn't national. There is no paper trail. No names in her books. No stolen library books. No diary, journal, or notebook. No old papers regarding former rentals, places she's owned, bills that aren't recent. No personal letters or photographs. We're going over things again, in case there's something she—or we—missed, but right now, it's like she dropped from the moon about two years ago and brought nothing with her."

"What about her credit history? Car payments?"

"She paid cash for the car. The only credit cards are recent."

I looked at the poised pen and sighed. "That's so odd. She never seemed secretive."

But had she? I tried to think back over our conversations. "I don't know where to begin, Roland. Or how to tap into something I might know. Maybe if you ask me some questions?"

"How long have you known her?"

"I don't know her. She's my realtor."

He gave me a version of Andre's 'get with the program' look. I'd always considered it uniquely my husband's, but maybe it was a cop thing.

I tried to recall our first meeting. "We met at her office. I'd seen a house with her company's sign out front, and when I called, she was the person on the desk…on duty, I guess they call it. She was very pleasant and asked me a bunch of intelligent questions that told me she was really trying to zero in on what I was looking for. At that point I had dealt with a couple other realtors who were real sleazy, or tried to foist their own agendas on me, and Andre and I were getting impatient to find a place. So we made a date, I blocked out some time, and she took me to look at houses."

"When was that?" he said.

"Last fall."

The pen remained static. Of course. I hadn't said anything yet. "She was a smart woman, Roland. Despite what others have told you, I found her very outgoing. Almost chatty. But there was something."

I called up those first impressions. What had there been about her that didn't seem to fit with her affable realtor persona? "She had a way of hesitating before she spoke, like she was weighing her words. Or vetting them. Like she wanted to be careful about what she said. Everything she said. Almost like she had secrets she was afraid might slip out."

I hadn't even known I'd thought that until Roland asked. Or I'd just put it down to caution. Realtors have a lot of requirements about how they represent things. And who they represent.

That he did write down.

I tried to think back to those first times with Ginger, going with her to look at houses. What did I know, or think I knew, about her? We'd spent a fair amount of time in her car, with me as her passenger. I'm rarely in the passenger seat, except when Andre is driving, and since he drives like a cop—too fast, confident, aggressive yet totally in control—I'm often clinging to the edge of my seat and praying that we'll get there alive. Since Ginger drove like a sane person, I'd had a chance to observe her.

"She was sad. I mean, she had an outwardly bubbly personality, the kind of good humor that made her good at her job, but sometimes she'd fall into these silences and get a faraway look, like she'd remembered something sad. They were very brief, and then she'd pull herself back and go on. Most people probably wouldn't have noticed them."

"Can you recall anything particular in your conversations that might have triggered that reaction?"

Could I? I thought about sitting with Ginger in her car. Pulling up in front of a house we were going to look at, smallish but pretty. She'd asked me how many people would be living there. I'd said just the two of us, though we were hoping. And then I'd stopped, because the possibility of a family was a sensitive thing for me. I thought she'd sensed it, and that was the first time I'd seen her do that mental retreat. I described the scene to Roland.

"Family. Children," he said. "Did you notice any kind of a pattern?"

"When I talked about relationships. About me and Andre. How happy we were to be married. She had a boyfriend, but even when I first met her, I got the impression that things weren't working between them. Later, she made those remarks about how he had to go, he was snooping through her things and helping himself to her money. She hinted that maybe he was doing something illegal. She said when she confronted him about it, he said well, she wasn't perfect, either, was she? But I have no idea what he meant. What she meant. She never elaborated. She just seemed very hurt by it. Discouraged about the possibility of having a long-term relationship."

"What else did she say about the boyfriend?"

"His name was Randy. Short for Randolph, not Randall. And he had one of those forgettable last names. Smith or Jones. Or Clark, maybe?"

I thought about driving around with Ginger in her car. The Toyota RAV4 she'd gotten instead of the Prius she wanted. She'd explained it was "because some people are turned off by 'green' cars, and it could create a 'holier than thou' impression." Trying to recall what she'd said about the boyfriend.

Mostly we'd talked about houses. The things people did with them, the awful décor, the neglect, the failure to take advantage of views, or create gardens or lawns. We'd both been appalled at how little some people were willing to do to clean up their houses for a buyer, even when they claimed to be very eager to sell.

One house we'd gone to smelled of dirty diapers and sour milk. Another reeked so badly of cat litter we had to leave. Sometimes, even though they knew we were coming, people hadn't even bothered to make the beds. One had a car up on blocks in the driveway. Ginger had been distressed by that. While I'd looked around, she'd taken the seller aside and had a quiet chat. But these were not things that would interest Roland.

"The boyfriend?" he said impatiently.

I was trying to help. I really was. I forced myself to concentrate, even though I knew memory didn't work like that. Then I changed my strategy. "Ask me more questions," I said. "Prompt my memory. Help me get in the 'remembering' groove."

"The boyfriend. What else did she say about him?"

"Mostly it was about how it wasn't working. I think she felt betrayed. Betrayed and angry. He'd been some kind of a manager. Convenience store, something like that. She said at first it had been all glow and roses. He was unemployed, and discouraged, but she'd been supportive and helped him work on his resume and applications. And he'd seemed so sweet and grateful. So happy to have her help. She said he was fun, at first. Wanting to do things together and making her laugh. Having dinner ready when she got home. A lot of thoughtful things.

"But it wore off pretty quickly. He wouldn't look for work. He was happy to let her work while he sat around and watched TV. He stopped doing things around the house. Despite her encouragement—you know, she even did stuff like tweak his resume and get him set up on LinkedIn—he wasn't trying to find a job."

Had Ginger said anything else about the boyfriend? "She was annoyed that he stopped helping around the house no matter how hard she was working. She'd come home after a long day and he'd be waiting for her to make dinner. Even though he was a good cook. She said he used to work as a cook, before he moved on to managing a store."

I wondered if there was a way the cops could search LinkedIn, and whether knowing only Randolph and Maine would be enough.

"Did their troubles sound like disagreement or did it sound like there might have been violence involved?"

I thought about what I'd seen in that living room. "She never mentioned feeling threatened, and she never seemed to be trying to hide bruises or injuries or moving like she hurt. She was just aggravated. Disappointed. But Roland, the crime, what was done to her—it wasn't some ordinary domestic thing, an angry boyfriend. It felt way too planned. Too ugly and vicious for that. It felt like hatred. Revenge. You're the expert. What do you think?"

He shrugged. Cops. Even the ones I liked could be so infuriating. We're supposed to bare our souls. They get to sit there impassively and refuse to answer our questions.

"Dammit, Roland. Don't play cop games with me."

As soon as the words left my mouth, I regretted them. I knew how this worked. I also knew that I was more deeply affected by this morning's events than I was allowing myself to acknowledge. I was drawing this out, and then I'd go to bed and wait for Andre to come home, listening for every little sound. And in the morning I'd drive to Stafford Academy and immerse myself in work. Handling their problem, working on tasks for other clients. Build a barrier of work between me and this morning.

I was terrified of what would happen if I got into bed, turned out the lights, and closed my eyes. The horror movies would begin. "Sorry, Roland. I'm just. You know. It was horrible."

"Sorry," he said. "Habit."

Our words crossed.

He ducked his head.

I smiled.

He said, "Yes. It looked like it came from something bigger than a domestic spat. But we do see people who get pretty unhinged when they're rejected. All those domestic violence murders where the woman has left some guy and he won't let her go. That deep-seated fear of losing control. She ever suggest that that might be the case with him? That he was controlling? That if she tried to make him leave, he'd lose it?"

I hadn't. "I heard lazy. Leeching. Jerk. Manipulator. I even heard thief, but I didn't know whether that was because he had a record or because he tried to steal money from her. I did get the impression that she thought it would be hard to get him to move out. But not because he'd be violent. My overall impression was more of a weak guy who thought he'd found a sugar mommy than someone likely to go off the rails. More passive-aggressive than aggressive. I never saw signs of him obsessively keeping track of her whereabouts. He didn't call or text her all the time, at least he didn't when I was with her. And she never seemed to be nervous about not responding to calls or texts, which women with controlling husbands or boyfriends are. But we're talking fragments, Roland. Little bits of conversation here and there. We're not talking about hours of girl talk over drinks or pizza. You know what my life is like. I don't have time for girl talk."

If I was looking for sympathy, I wasn't getting it. Perfectly fair. I've made my life the way it is. I don't try hard enough to combat my workaholic genes. I love my work. It's exciting to try and help my clients solve their problems. Andre is no better. The call comes about a crime, and he's out the door in a flash. Buying a house together was supposed to mark the beginning of a new beginning for both of us.

Sometimes I think fate just has it in for me. Us. My partner, Suzanne, recently remarked that she also consults to private schools and she has never come across a body or stared down a dangerous thug. I didn't respond that once I'd beaten my first bad guy, all that kind of stuff came to me. That I had a reputation for being fearless and able to handle difficult situations. Nor did I suggest that I'd be safer if we stopped offering our services in the more serious kinds of campus crises and went back to writing well-researched and detailed reports. Suzanne wouldn't want to hear it.

She was the petite, smiley, wear the chic Chanel suit and make nice with the trustees arm of our operation. She had the Miss Porter's, Wellesley, upper middle class veneer. I was big bad Thea, called in when something hit the fan. I was Oz the Great and Terrible, only without a curtain to hide behind.

Roland cleared his throat, a gentle gesture to draw me back to our conversation. "Did she ever say anything about her background? Family? Where she might have come from? Places she'd lived?"

He was leaning into my space like his physical presence could draw out what his words could not. Telegraphing his sense of urgency. I was doing my best here. I'd carved out a space for him, but I was giving him time I really didn't have. I had prep work to do before my early morning departure. Maybe he was reading that, too. Smart cops are good at reading people and at pursuing their own agendas, regardless of ours. They have to be like that. People don't want to get involved in sordid things like murder. Cooperation often doesn't come easily.

I tried to answer his question. In the back of my mind, there was something triggered by his question about violence that I was trying to recall. But the thought was stuck. I'd just have to wait until it surfaced.

"She said that she'd only lived in Maine a few years, and that she'd been in Florida for a while before that and hadn't liked living there. There was one of her hesitations after that, like she hadn't meant to say it. I figured something had happened in Florida that she didn't want to talk about. I asked where else she'd lived, and she didn't answer. And then I asked her what brought her to Maine and she didn't answer that, either. At the time, I just thought she was distracted. We were looking for a house and it didn't seem to be where the map said it was supposed to be. I thought she was focusing on that. Looking back, I can see she did that several times when I asked her about herself."

"What else did you ask that she didn't answer?"

"I asked if she'd been a realtor in Florida. She said yes. Then she said no, not really. But if she was a realtor down there, there would be a record, right? She'd have to be licensed?"

Roland made a note. "Anything else?"

There was something, but I couldn't call it up. I was having a lot of trouble with recall tonight. Another symptom of notimer's disease. After any day of triage, my brain was fried. Tonight I was double fried.

"Maybe more things will come to me," I said, "but right now, I'm drawing a blank."

"What about friends or relatives? She ever mention any?"

"Not that I remember. I remember making a remark once about my mother being difficult and she said yeah, she knew all about that. But she didn't elaborate."

Roland switched subjects. "Ginger was a realtor," he said. "Lot of people feel about realtors the same way they feel about car salesmen. There can be a whole lot of animosity there. She ever mention disgruntled clients? People she'd had trouble getting along with? Real estate deals that hadn't gone well?"

It was an idea that had never occurred to me. Andre and I had liked Ginger. But I knew sometimes people did feel betrayed by their realtors.

I thought about our conversations. Had she said anything about other clients that might be significant? "Maybe. It's just a snippet, Roland. It was that same day that we were looking for the house we couldn't find. I guess that made her jittery, because she said something kind of defensive, like "none of us are perfect," and "sometimes people expect too much of us," and when I asked her what she meant, because she sounded so down, she said she'd had a really bad day the day before with a seller who thought she was trying to unfairly knock down the price of a house. She said the house was a nightmare. That it needed a ton of work but the seller thought it was a palace and wouldn't listen to any of her advice about how to price it or things he could do to make it more appealing."

I tried to recall if she'd said anything else, anything about the people, or a location. I couldn't remember any other details. "That's all I remember, except that she said curb appeal was really important in her business and why couldn't they understand that? I could probably find the date in my calendar, if that would help. Then maybe you could check her appointments or her clients and see if the people in her office could help you identify who that was."

"That's all?" he said.

I thought it was something, but I bit my lip.

"She never mentioned any other troublesome clients?"

I shook my head.

"But that conflict really seemed to get her down?"

"She was usually pretty upbeat, Roland. I envied her. I couldn't do her job without a whole lot more complaining. I'm good with my clients, but I don't have a lot of patience with whiners."

The truth was that I had to have a lot of patience with whiners and complainers. It was part of doing business. Whiners, complainers, and people who were being deceptive. He'd never believe it, but I sometimes did Roland's job. Leaning on people, pressuring them to do the right thing and tell the truth. It was a supposedly genteel world I worked in, and yet I'd seen every kind of bad behavior. I was grateful when I worked with clients who had manners and self-control. And cared deeply about their students.

I guess we all had versions of the same job. It came with interacting with other humans. Ginger had been mannerly and caring and very forgiving and patient. That seller must have been extremely difficult to get her down like that.

More of the conversation was coming back to me now. "She said the man had called her a cheat and a liar and said she was only out to make a buck and never mind the poor people who were just trying to sell their house."

She'd been really upset. So upset I'd given her a hug and suggested we stop for some cocoa. And she'd taken me up on it. I shared that with Roland.

"Is that the only time she ever mentioned trouble with a customer?"

"The only time I can remember." Ginger had almost been in tears. I told him that. "The thing is that she was pretty unflappable and this really disturbed her. I think it might have been more than just angry words. I think he must have threatened her. She didn't come out and say that. She only said he'd acted 'threatening.' But I read more into it than that."

He sighed and made a note, once again making me feel like I was failing him somehow because I hadn't followed up. But I didn't know what else I could have done. Ginger hadn't wanted to say any more. When people set boundaries, most of us respect them. And I wasn't the prying or gossipy type. I only pried on behalf of my clients.

Then I remembered something else. "There was one other thing. Just the briefest mention, but something that sounded potentially dangerous. Maybe her co-workers can fill you in. We'd gone to see a house, and only the husband was home. His manner was kind of creepy. Too familiar. He followed us through the house, trying to make conversation with her and he kept getting into her space. It made looking at the house impossible. At the time, I thought maybe he was just too eager to sell us on it, but Ginger rushed through it. When we got back to the car, she said something like 'God, some of these guys!' and then she said 'you have to be really careful in this business' and told me about this man who'd called about wanting to see a particular house."

Roland was leaning forward eagerly, like I was finally giving him something useful. "I guess this house was in a pretty remote place. He wanted to meet her there for a showing. She said she didn't like to do that. She liked to meet people at the office first, so she could check them out. I think maybe the office even has some kind of surveillance equipment."

He gave me a funny look and wrote that down, like he'd talked to people at her office and they hadn't mentioned this. Then he gave me a nod. "Go on."

"This guy didn't want to do that. He was pretty insistent about meeting her at the house. Finally, she agreed. She said she needed a sale too much to pass up an eager buyer. Then, at the last minute, some problem came up with the closing on another house and she couldn't go, so she sent someone else. When the other realtor—a guy—got there, the buyer was sitting in his car, waiting. When her colleague got out of the car and the customer saw that it wasn't Ginger, he didn't say anything or walk toward the guy or anything. He just got back in his car and drove away really fast."

Roland was definitely writing that down. I knew what he'd want to know. Was it a car or a truck? Make and model. What had the man looked like? Things he'd have to get from Ginger's co-worker. But it was something.

"If he'd wanted to look at the house, whoever showed up wouldn't matter. So Ginger thought he was trying to get her out there alone. It happens, she said. And you know, she was really cute and her picture was right there on the sign, and on their website, and on her cards. There hasn't been a series of attacks on female realtors, have there?"

I tried to recall when this had happened. Ginger and I had been house hunting for months, when I could find the time or she could find the house. "This might have been back in the fall."

"This customer was driving a car or a truck?" he asked.

"I have no idea."

Roland was tired. He needed coffee. I thought he also needed a nap. That made me think of Andre, who would be just as tired, doing the same thing with other witnesses, or going through Ginger's place and car again, looking for where she might have hidden her secrets.

"Would you like me to make some coffee?"

He unfolded like a stork from the deep sofa. "You mind if I do?"

"Make yourself at home. It's a Keurig. And there are a zillion different k-cups on the counter. Skim milk, half and half, or almond milk in the fridge."

Using the word 'home' stung. I wanted a home, and what I got was this—a too-long day, my husband unavailable, with another police officer asking questions I couldn't answer while I pulled fragments of conversation out of my weary brain. I had too much on my plate, and no clarity about how I kept getting into situations like this. I'd done nothing to bring on this morning's events.

Was it time to change my life? Find something else to do instead? I was good at this. Not at finding bodies—I never wanted to get good at that—but at helping troubled schools. The problem was that my life was beginning to look like one of those TV shows where every place the character goes, someone dies. Except for me, it was closer to the truth to say that people died and then I went there because my clients needed me. Maybe I should trade roles with Suzanne. I could wear the chic suits and the smile and she could face down bad guys. Somehow, I couldn't see it. Smiling isn't my thing. Neither are chic suits.

No one had better die at Stafford. I was tired of people dying. I'd never tell my clients this, but a drug scandal was kind of refreshing.

My life had had more than my share of death in it, but there was no way that Ginger's death had anything to do with me except for the coincidence that I happened to be the client she was meeting. But was it a coincidence? Some of my exploits—Adventures? Disasters?—had been played out pretty graphically in the Maine press. What if someone thought I'd be the perfect addition to their revenge plot against Ginger? But how would anyone even know that I was her client? Was I letting my imagination run in crazy directions?

Goosebumps sprouted on my arms. I pushed myself up and hurried into the kitchen. I needed to test that assumption on Roland.

"Hey," I said, as he deftly poured in the water and stuck in a cup of French roast. "You don't think my being the one to find her was part of someone's plan, do you? I mean—that *I* was meant to find her?"

Roland looked up, surprised. "You mean, do I think that this was somehow directed at you? No. I don't. I think you happened to be the person she was showing that house to on the day when whoever did this found a place and opportunity to act."

"But he called me. He called me, Roland. On her phone. He didn't know when she was having a showing and then set this up. He set this up…moved the showing until later…to…uh…so that I…"

But I didn't know what. To give her time to die? To give her time to almost die? Would my being on time have made any difference? Could Ginger have been saved if I hadn't taken all those phone calls? Driven faster? If I hadn't pulled over to mop up spilled coffee or lingered to admire the dining room?

"Earlier, you said you couldn't remember whether it was a man or a woman who called to change the appointment," Roland said. "Now you think it was a man?"

"It was a man."

I felt one of those sudden chills that happen when knowledge hits home. Whoever did this knew my name, my phone number, and where I worked, while I knew nothing about him.

If I could roll back the clock, meet Ginger at nine instead of 10:30, she might still be alive, and I might have just found my dream house.

Okay. Who doesn't engage in wishful thinking sometimes, especially when reality is so grim and ugly? Instead of Ginger's agonized, terrified face, I'd have living in that lovely house to ponder. Instead, I now had a new worry to come between me and sleep. Along with Ginger's face, I had the disturbing knowledge that a brutal and deliberate killer had my name and number.

"How would the killer get my number? Before I left the office, I mean. Even if he used Ginger's phone, he called me well in advance of when we were supposed to meet, which suggests he knew her schedule and who she was meeting. Or that she was at the house well in advance of our appointment."

"Her office says she had an appointment to show the house to someone else at eight. They didn't have a name or any other information."

I pushed away my irritation at the idea that Ginger had been cheating on me. Showing my dream house to someone else, reminding myself that she was in the business of selling houses. It didn't matter now.

I listened to the sounds of the coffee maker as I stared down at my bandaged hands, sore whenever I flexed them, and pondered. Would the cops find out who did this, and why? Would they find out quickly, so those who were touched by the case could move on? Sleep? Breathe easily? I wondered where Ginger Stevens had come from and what her real name was. What were her secrets, her terrible secrets, that had led to today's events?

CHAPTER 8

After his coffee, Roland left, taking away in his notebook the few bits I'd been able to supply. He and I were both hoping that at some point I'd remember something else. The thought that had lurked in the back of my mind had stayed there. Who knew when it would surface and whether it would be useful?

Maybe, with the information about her having lived in Florida, they could find out more about her. Maybe her colleagues would sleep on it and tomorrow they'd have some helpful information. At least he could ask them about the fleeing customer and the aggrieved seller. That might lead somewhere. And it might prompt their memories in other ways. I wanted this over with. I didn't want Roland coming back with his hopeful gaze and weary shoulders, pressing me to keep remembering.

Before he left, he took me firmly by the shoulders, looked me directly in the eyes, and declared, "This is not about you. Aimed at you. There is no reason for you to be worried about that."

I wished I believed it as fervently as he did. Sometimes it seemed like I lived in a very dark world that was full of bad guys. I still didn't understand how he and Andre kept their balance in that world.

I went back out to my car to grab my coffee stained clothes from this morning so I could throw them in the wash. As I walked through a foggy, dark night that reminded me way too much of another such night on a boarding school campus, I thought about Ginger's last words. "Airy. Bobby. So long. Safe. So sorry." What had she thought she was safe from and what was she so sorry about? Did those regrets have something to do with her killer? With why she was killed?

What if "Bobby" wasn't a name? What if she'd said "baby?" Would a reference to a baby suggest she might be pregnant? Had lost a baby? Or that she was regretting the fact that she'd never get to have a baby? Was she having a premonition of her own death? Did she feel death lingering close by? In a situation as agonizing as that, could a person think about anything but the immediate events?

What about airy? It could be so many things. Like part of the word scary. Or a description of her killer, like she was trying to tell me that he was hairy or scary. It might be a person's name, but there the possibilities were great. It might be Harry, Barry, Larry, Mary, Sherry, Perry, Jerry. Gary. If it even was a name. It certainly didn't narrow the field. And that was only first names. I didn't want to start running the list of last names.

"This is not my problem," I muttered. Right now, my concern was my client's problems.

Who did I think I was fooling?

I cleaned up the coffee table, pouring my undrunk wine down the sink. It seemed there were enough phantoms around tonight. I pretreated the stains and threw the clothes into the washer, then stripped off everything I was wearing and threw that in, too. Even the clothes I'd changed into carried the taint of the morning's awful smoke.

I padded naked into the bedroom, grabbed my nightgown, and then went into the shower. I covered myself with an astringent lavender, salt, and oil scrub, rubbing my skin like I could wash away the singed smell if I worked hard enough, even though I knew it was in my lungs and my sinuses. Andre said it could take days for some smells to go away. I washed my hair, which also smelled of the morning, and bundled it, still damp, into a loose braid.

Lavender is supposed to be soothing, but I didn't feel soothed. I felt like the little kid who knows there is a monster under the bed and another in the closet.

I spent some time making notes about how to approach the Stafford Academy situation, including phone numbers of people I needed to call as soon as it was a civilized hour. That meant from the road, so I wrote them on a yellow sticky that I could put on my dashboard. Hands-free dialing is great, but it's only hands-free if you don't have to look up the number first.

I smiled as I contemplated the first person I'd call. Glen Stryker. Ex-marine. Retired DEA. And big as Godzilla. He was the best person in the world to scare a bunch of high school students straight. And, though the students should never know it, a big pussycat. Glen was one of the good guys. He did what he did to save kids from their own stupidity. Or youthful sense of immortality. His talk would be very effective in giving a wake-up call to the student body while helping Stafford put a good face on their handling of the situation.

I sighed and stretched and wondered if I was a good guy or a weasel. If my white hat was getting gray. No energy tonight to contemplate the question. I needed sleep if I was going to be useful to anyone in the morning. I took a swipe at my teeth, skipped anything resembling a beauty ritual, and crawled into bed. The house was too quiet, the kind of quiet that had me listening carefully for suspicious sounds. Thinking maybe reading would help, I picked up the nice, improving book my mother had given me for Christmas—my mother believes I am badly in need of improving—and started to read. It instantly improved me into a state of lassitude.

I was on the cusp of sleep, and on the cusp of remembering something important that Ginger had said—I do a lot of my best thinking on the way to sleep and in the process of coming awake—when my phone rang.

Expecting the worst—Andre had been shot or the police were raiding the dorms at Stafford, I turned on the light and snatched it up. "Hey," a familiar voice said, "this is your husband. Remember me?"

Andre's call sent sleep, and whatever I was about to remember, skittering away, but I was glad he'd called. He can get so immersed in his cases that it gets too late to call when he's working through the night. It was a stupid question, though. Who can forget a handsome, hunky cop with rock-hard abs, deep brown eyes and testosterone-driven five o'clock shadow on his firm jaw? A guy who may complain about the chances I take, but always has my back? Not me, that's for sure.

"I miss you," I said.

He made a confirming sound, and the barriers I'd erected against my awful day came tumbling down. "That was our dream house," I said, "and now it's tainted. And Lt. Scafaro was so awful. And I don't think I'll ever be able to eat meat again. Never mind going to any barbeques."

Another sound. It was enough. I could have stayed on the phone and listened to him breathe, and it would have been enough. The sound of him breathing in the dark was one of the mainstays of my life.

"I'm afraid to go to sleep without you," I said.

"This sucks," he agreed.

"You making any progress? Roland seemed pretty discouraged."

"This case makes no sense, Thea. Fourteen years ago, she uses a dead child's information to get a social security number. But there's no sign of income, employment, tax returns, credit reports or a driver's license using that number. Nothing. Until six years ago. Then she starts working as a realtor in Florida, and she uses it there.

Roland's going down tomorrow to see what he can learn, but if it's anything like her life here, he's going to draw a great big blank. Then she comes here, works for a couple years, and yet no one knows anything about her. But why did she come here? And where was she for the eight years she was off the grid?"

"Using a different social security number?" I suggested.

He was quiet for a moment, then said, "How was your day?"

"Not too bad. If Suzanne being put on bed rest, a client making us miss a deadline on a big report because they won't furnish essential data, and a potential drug issue at a client school isn't bad. I guess you'd say it's normal for my business."

"Is Suzanne okay?"

"If she doesn't explode with frustration. Or disobey her doctor's orders and bring on a premature delivery."

The sound he made was sympathy for Suzanne and an acknowledgment that we didn't talk about pregnancy at our house.

"I have to go to Connecticut in the morning. Got all the usual stuff to do, and picking up Suzanne's workload, and three other clients yelling at me for things they need. Not to mention Suzanne saying I should stay away from danger and dead bodies. Like I go looking for them."

"I'm sorry," he said. "You didn't need this morning on top of…"

"Nobody needed this morning. It got thrust upon us."

"We could say no."

I was stunned. Our refrain has always been the same. Our lives are crazy, we need a break and more time together, but we love what we do. He didn't mean no to house hunting. Was he suggesting he was falling out of love with detective work? That I should find a safer line of work? Or was he just feeling protective toward me?

"Could you say no?"

He was silent. Then he said, "We can talk about that when we're together. It's too big for a late-night phone call. It's for face-to-face. I'm on my way home, but tonight…uh…this morning, is not the time."

"What have you been doing all day?" I asked.

"Talking to people," he said. "Going through her apartment. Looking for something we might have missed. Figuring out where to go tomorrow. Looking at fingerprints. The ones from the crime scene. From her car. From the house. Whoever did this was careful, though. I'm betting any prints we find on those heaters will belong to someone in a store. And that they were bought over time, in multiple venues. A clerk would remember someone buying eight space heaters and extension cords. Even that many extension cords. Everything about this says planned, right down to the phone call to postpone your appointment."

"Which suggests someone who knew her schedule."

"It does," he agreed. "If we could only find that person."

I tried to remember where the call had come from. I didn't know. Either way it would have said Ginger Stevens or the name of her company. I hadn't looked at the number. "Was the call from Ginger's office?"

"From her cell phone."

"Do you have her cell phone?"

"Yeah. Wiped clean. Of course. Or he wore gloves. We're looking at cell tower pings. Call probably came from the house."

I imagined Ginger tied to that chair for hours. Helpless, maybe struggling to get free at she watched her killer setting up. Would the autopsy show signs of that struggle? "But wouldn't the neighbors have seen someone carrying in those space heaters?"

"No one saw anything. We're thinking he must have done it during the night."

"He?"

"Someone big enough to overpower her."

"And he wasn't noticed on a residential street?"

"Boggles the mind, doesn't it," he said. "A murderer sets up the scene and then kills a woman in broad daylight and no one notices."

"How did he get into the house?"

"Another thing we're looking into. But a million realtors, or former realtors, have keys or combinations for those lockboxes."

I didn't want to play detective. I wanted to leave it in his capable hands. I am so given to wishful thinking. "I've left the light on for you," I said.

"I should be home soon."

I hoped his 'soon' was real and that nothing else called him away. The monsters in the closet and under my bed were usually afraid of Andre. I put down the phone, turned out the light, and tried, once again, for sleep.

In my dream I was being burned alive while a swarm of people dressed like witches circled around me, chanting. They had human bodies and human faces but their eyes were dead and blank and horrible. I kept looking for a truly human face, someone I could make a connection with who might help me, and found not a single one. The smoke was choking me and I was having trouble breathing. I could feel the heat singeing my skin. Feel the agony as it blistered and split. I could hear the little sparks crackle as my clothes and hair caught fire.

Terror seized me. I threw off the covers and sat up, staring into the darkness.

I've woken to a real fire before, a deliberately set "get Thea" fire. I didn't trust that this was just a dream. I got up, turned on the light, and checked the room and the bathroom carefully. Then I checked the rest of the apartment. Everything was clear and still and quiet. I didn't smell any smoke. There was no sign of Andre.

Then I heard a door shut downstairs. I looked out the window and saw his car beside mine in the driveway.

"Take that, monsters," I said. "Daddy's home."

I went to open the door.

"Shower," he said, trying to disengage me, but I was wrapped firmly around him and wouldn't let go.

Finally I relented. I figured that there was room in the shower for two, and a person could never be too clean. That led to the obvious result and cut our time for sleep even shorter, but it was worth it. I had no more bad dreams and slept all the way to morning without interruption.

CHAPTER 9

I yawned as I checked my phone. On the retro analogue clock on the wall, the little hand was almost at five, the big hand at nine. We'd done *The Glass* Menagerie in high school, and the line, "I'll rise but I won't shine," had stuck in my head. I looked across at Andre. Sitting on his side of the bed, already on the phone. We were such a modern couple—Andre on his phone on one side, scribbling notes, me on my phone on the other. Someone should have painted our portraits. Loving Couple. New American Gothic. Looking at him, I wanted to pull the shades, shut off our phones, and get back in bed.

Outside it was very dark, but in the streetlight's glow, I saw that yesterday's fog hadn't dissipated but was thicker. The night's wintery mix had left a few inches of snow. Now, rising temperatures would turn the whole world into a mushy, slushy mess. It was a day to be depressed and think about taking to drink. We both had places to be, but we lingered, a time measured in moments, not really saying anything, just putting off the time when we would spring into action.

But criminals and clients were waiting.

I threw a handful of clean clothes into a shopping bag to replenish the supply in my car, and dragged my raincoat and boots out of the closet. Then I dressed one-handed as I called Reeve Barrows, muttering a litany of ouches as I bent and flexed my burned hands. It was never too early to call an assistant head when a school was in crisis.

He answered, a crisp, slightly frazzled "Reeve Barrows," as I was hopping on one foot, trying to pull on my tights. Tights invariably get caught on my toes when I'm in a hurry.

Reeve was usually a phlegmatic fellow. A worker bee content to trail in the wake of the dynamic younger headmaster, Joel Phelps. Today, though, he barely let me say hello before he was off and running. "It's gotten worse. Much worse. Because of Joel."

I got the tights on and pulled on a warm forest green cashmere dress and an ombre green scarf, juggling the phone from hand to hand as I dressed. There had better not be any fires or other catastrophes today. I was about down to my last good outfit and who knew when I might have time to shop?

"What's up with Joel?"

I could hear him sputtering, so incensed at the predicament Phelps had landed him in that he could barely control himself. "You haven't heard?"

I zipped my boots, and zipped my lip so I wouldn't retort, "How could I have heard?" or mention the psychic hotline.

Across the room, Andre, who'd been grinning at my gyrations while struggling into my clothes, was putting on his coat. I covered the receiver. "You be careful out there," I said.

"Always careful," he said.

"So be more careful. And call me and let me know when you're coming home."

"Likewise," he said, and walked out the door.

I felt a pang every time I watched him leave. The dilemma of the cop's wife. What if he never walked in again?

I brought my attention back to Reeve, who was already off and running. "You know about the new fund-raising campaign to modernize the science buildings, right?" he said. "Well, it's been going great guns. But yesterday, when this whole drug thing was exploding, Joel put the whole thing at risk."

"He put the whole drug thing at risk?"

"Of course not. The fund-raising campaign."

Pretty soon I was going to have to back him up and get an explanation about "the whole drug thing", which was the business that had me up and dressed at this ungodly hour. I was woefully short on information. I figured I'd let him get Joel Phelps off his chest first. I stuck my notes in my briefcase, and the yellow sticky on the outside, ready to be transferred to my dashboard. Grabbed my coat and tried to get downstairs without falling or dropping anything while paying attention to what Reeve was saying.

This was a bad season for anything to go wrong at a private school. Admissions letters were about to go out and anything controversial could jeopardize getting a good incoming class. Some of the premier independent schools still belonged to the age when a person's name appeared in print only when they were born, married, and died, or at least their major donors did. It was no wonder Reeve was in a state.

"Reeve," I said, as I unlocked the Jeep and tossed my spare clothes in the back, "take a breath and then explain to me. What did Joel do?"

I stuck my yellow sticky on the dash, started the engine, flipped on the wipers and backed slowly down the driveway. I'm constantly trying to multitask, but convinced that no one can do it well, including myself. Especially on a foggy morning when the road is covered with slush.

"Oh. Right," he said. "While we were dealing with the crisis involving that student who nearly died, Joel was nowhere to be found."

"But he was eventually found?"

I flipped on the front and rear defrosters to get some visibility. My car fishtailed through a slush ridge, then dove into a puddle that sent a wave of mush onto my windshield.

I turned my wipers on high and tried to listen to Reeve, who was now blasting at me from my dashboard. Another technological wonder that enabled me to do two things at once. I turned up the volume to hear him over the defroster and the wipers.

"Oh, we found him all right. Only after his secretary decided covering for him was no longer in her best interest."

This was like pulling teeth. "Where was he?"

"In bed at a local hotel with our chief fundraiser. With his phone off. Both of them married to other people, of course. While a student nearly died. Once it gets out, his stupidity is going to put the whole campaign at risk."

"Why should it come out?"

In front of me, a car pulled out from a side street without looking. At this time in the morning, they were probably used to being the only car on the road. I blasted my horn as I braked. Through the gloom, I thought I saw the usual polite driver's acknowledgment of wrongdoing, a raised middle finger.

I couldn't do this. "Reeve, the driving is awful. I'll be on the highway in five minutes. I'll call you back then."

"But Thea…"

But Thea was gone. Trying to reach the highway alive.

Once I'd merged onto the turnpike, I called him back and tried to get the details of their drug crisis. We'd helped them write a crisis management plan and he said he was using it, but one of the members of the team he was supposed to assemble was a crisis consultant. That would be me. I was undertaking this journey mostly in response to expressions of desperation and need. Now I needed to gather some facts. I listened to a flood of complaints, questions, and jumbled information, including the fact that Alyce, the VC's daughter who'd actually sold the drug to the girl who'd nearly died, claimed they weren't doing anything illegal because the friend who'd made the pills had used his own formula.

"Believe it or not," he said, "she actually quoted the Synthetic Drug Abuse Prevention Act." Kids today. They might not have heard of the Civil War or read the Constitution, but they were good at keeping current on stuff like this.

When he paused for breath, I jumped in. "I can do a lot more when I get there, but for now, take a deep breath, and write this down."

Ignoring me, he started another litany of complaint and despair. It wasn't getting us anywhere and I needed my attention for driving. Even though there were few cars on the road, the fog, slush ridges, and muck thrown up by everyone's tires meant it was like bumper cars out here, or one of those monster trucks in the mud things. I raised my voice. "Stop," I said. "Take a deep breath. Listen carefully, and write this down."

"I don't know what…"

I was on the verge of yelling 'shut up,' but Suzanne was always on my case about handling clients more gently, so I saved it for later. I was sure I'd need it. "And you won't know what, unless you listen to me. Okay?"

A few blustering words. Finally, he sputtered to a stop and said, "Okay," so I launched into my preliminary advice.

"Now, we have an independent expert who can test those drugs and see if they really are illegal. As I'm sure you know, there's a ton of stuff around that's sold as Molly, or MDMA, that really isn't. And while your student's claim that it isn't illegal because it's a new designer drug is offensive, and she's absolutely broken your rules and put a fellow student at risk, it may be a genuine defense to a criminal charge. So I'll put in a call to our expert. Being able to say you're bringing in an expert will enhance your credibility and help you manage the parents."

I got a sigh, a slightly tremulous "Okay," and then, "Go on."

"I'm going to see if I can get you the drug counselor from hell," I said.

"We've got our own…"

"LISTEN TO ME, Reeve!"

Everyone for a mile around must have heard that, but I was not having an accident out here to avoid bruising his ego. I gave him a moment to shut up as my wipers slapped clods of mush away and a semblance of visibility returned.

"This guy is former DEA, ex-military. He's big and scary and has the demeanor of a drill instructor. He has a power point that will have them cowering under their chairs, which is what you want right now. You want to come on as compassionate, but righteous. You want to send the message that you understand they're kids and they can make mistakes. You also want to drive home both school policy and the risks these kids are taking—legally and physically. His name is Glen Stryker, and he's guaranteed to scare them silly. Or straight."

Reeve asked the stupid, if predictable, question, "Is he expensive?"

"Yup, and worth every penny of it. Look, I know it's daunting, but the faster you get out ahead of this thing and show the right responses, the better you'll look to your current parents and prospective ones. It may feel kind of fake to you, but showing a firm, adult, compassionate response to this can be good PR."

I prayed my way past a semi and asked another question. "What are you going to do about your two students?"

His silence told me they were still contemplating their choices. I knew that tossing the kids could pull them into a fight bigger than they needed, especially with ultra-rich, ultra-protective parents involved. The administration needed to be firm, but they also needed to remember these were kids, and craft punishments that both acknowledged a breach of the rules and were about learning. I couldn't remember, so I asked, "Do your conduct rules allow for on-campus suspension?"

I should know. I'd probably written them. But I'd done it for dozens of schools and not all had adopted this option. Sending students home—the standard punishment for a serious breach—also allowed those students to avoid dealing with their community and isolated them from the approbation and consequences of their acts. It often also allowed them to sink into the arms of defensive and too-forgiving parents whose lives were devoted to protecting their children from responsibility. An on-campus suspension meant the student didn't go home, where they could move about freely, go to the mall and the movies, and generally forget about the wrong they'd done and the harm they'd caused. On campus, they were allowed to attend class, but banned from all extra-curricular activities. They ate their meals in a supervised setting away from other students, had supervised study halls, and did community service tasks in their free time. They also met with counselors to discuss their choices, and, old-fashioned as it sounded, had to write and deliver to the community a paper on whatever risk they'd taken or rule they'd broken.

"They do," he said. "Is that what you'd suggest?"

Before I could respond, he sighed and answered a question I'd been about to ask. "This really shouldn't be my problem, but the chair of our board of trustees doesn't want Joel making any major decisions until they've had time to meet, and as we both know, there are a number of decisions that just can't wait. So…"

I could feel him pondering right through the phone.

"So you would recommend an on-campus suspension?" he finally said.

"I would. And Glen Stryker. Absolutely get Glen."

Another sigh. It's hard to be in the hot seat when you're used to only sitting near the heater. Oops. That was a thought I instantly regretted. And some people have to ponder instead of making quick decisions. Finally, he said, "Okay. That's what we'll do. Can you put me in touch with Mr. Stryker?"

"I'll take care of it. I'll call him, see when he's available, and have him call you. And I'll call the drug analyst. Now I'm going to drive. When I get there, I will help you draft a uniform contact letter to your parents and help you craft your statement to the press and what to say at the school meeting to bring your students up to date. And you might want to remind faculty about the school's media policy."

His only response was a small moan. He didn't have to say it. I knew he was thinking that this shouldn't be his problem. Too bad for him. There's not much room for 'not my problem' in a crisis.

Speaking of problems, I asked, "So what's going on with Joel? Is the Board going to give him a pass on this?"

"Too soon to tell. They're meeting today."

One other thing I'd forgotten to ask. "What year are your two drug dealers?"

"Alyce Crimmons is a senior. Johnny Gordon is a junior. Minority scholarship student."

I figured that meant Alyce was the VC guy's daughter. It was good that she was senior. It gave the school more leverage with the parents. There wasn't time to look for a new school, and plenty of pressure to resolve things so the girl could graduate. "And her parents are coming in with lawyers in tow?"

"They're already here. On the schedule for this morning's meeting."

"And the boy's parents?"

"Parent. Single working mom. She can't take the time off." He sighed. "That's one fewer person to deal with."

And one unprotected kid for the other family to throw the blame on, I thought. "This is awfully hard on you," I said. "Feel free to call me if you need more help. I should be there before nine, road conditions permitting."

There was a pause while I listened to him breathe. Then he said, "I'm feeling better already."

"One more thought. It might garner you some good press if you invite reporters to Stryker's talk. Let them see first-hand what you're doing to inform your students about the risks they're taking."

I left him with that first set of marching orders, finally free to concentrate on my driving. Which was good. It was a nightmare out here. I had one more thing to take care of—something I hoped wouldn't come back to bite me—before I gave myself fully to the insanity of driving. No minority student should have to go up against an arrogant VC daddy and his staff, and I didn't think Reeve would have someone in the kid's corner, so I called my friend Jonetta Williamson, who ran a school for disadvantaged black girls in New York, and described the situation. Jonetta might have some ideas about who could help Johnny Gordon.

CHAPTER 10

Dealing with Reeve's crisis first meant dealing not only with treacherous roads and poor visibility, it meant doing that surrounded by other drivers who seemed oblivious to both. It meant a couple hours in traffic conditions so scary I was clutching the wheel in a death grip and bathed in cold sweat. I can drive. I grew up with New England winters and I've had lessons from the guy who can drive backwards accurately at sixty miles an hour down a dark, curvy road. But the people out here with me hadn't been to Detective Lemieux's driving school. Nor, it seemed, to any other driving school.

It always amazes me how stupid people can be. It's like people believe that turnpikes are magic places where the realities of winter and weather don't apply. Why do they believe that just because they have all-wheel drive, they can stop a huge SUV on a dime? Doesn't it have something to do with basic physics? And fog. Fog is just as treacherous and unpredictable when you have fog lights even if there are three travel lanes. Ice is still ice. Slush is slush, and it can throw a car into another lane just for the damned fun of seeing the driver's panicked face.

Okay. So I was doing—what's it called? anthropomorphizing? Assigning human characteristics to puddles. Anything to get me safely to Connecticut. I took this as a sign that as soon as we got the current batch of crises under control, it might be time for a vacation. Maybe paddle boards and mai tais were in my future. I had a really rocking bikini, a beach cover-up, and a pair of flip flops. I had my arm candy guy who looked so good in a bathing suit women sighed as he walked past. What more could I need?

Time, an evil voice in my head whispered. By the time I'd slain the many-headed hydra, Suzanne would have had this baby and be on maternity leave. I uttered a string of obscenities—hanging around cops is good for enriching my vocabulary, at least—and shifted my thoughts from dreams to reality.

The way the brain makes connections can be so odd. I thought about the slushy puddles pooling into lakes in every depression that was making my driving miserable and somehow the idea of those slush lakes led to swimming pools. From swimming pools, the missing thought about Ginger that I'd been chasing suddenly surfaced. We'd been looking at a house with a postage-stamp sized pool, and she'd said, "I hate pools. I like swimming in ponds. I was a lifeguard one summer at a pond, and I loved it."

I instructed Siri to call Roland as I steered around a puddle and a passing truck threw a wave of opaque mush onto my windshield. As my wipers slapped it away, I got a brusque, "Proffit," with lots of noise in the background. Maybe he was in an airport.

"It's Thea."

"How are you?"

"Muddling along. You?"

"On my way to Florida."

"Nice time of year for it."

"Right. You bet. That's why I packed my board shorts. Got something for me?"

The idea of stork-like Roland in board shorts made me smile. "Just another tidbit. But if I come up with enough of them, they may lead somewhere. At one point, Ginger said that she'd been a lifeguard. At a lake. She said she didn't like pools. I don't know how it helps, but I thought I'd better pass it along."

"Thanks," he said. There was a sigh in his voice, like he'd hoped for more and was grateful for anything. "Keep your thinking cap on."

"I will."

I wanted to throw my thinking cap—my remembering cap—into that black, mushy puddle just beyond the travel lane and go eat donuts. Instead, I left him to the joys of interacting with the TSA and went to deal with my own crisis.

My immediate crisis, that is, which was a humongous black Suburban driving too fast in the slow lane by a driver obviously too young, and too stupid, to have been allowed out in such a vehicle, or out at all on a day like this. She'd gone whipping past me moments earlier, cell phone to her ear, and now, having come upon a driver driving slowly and carefully in the slow and careful lane, had discovered she couldn't shove herself into my lane because it was already occupied by a truck. She'd stomped on her brakes and the resulting chaos was ensuing.

Ah. ABS brakes. The responsive shudder, the car's pulsing attempts to stop. They are good, but not miraculous, and the black babe-mobile fishtailed, swung into the breakdown lane, caught a wheel in a wave of slush, and flew back across the lane, heading straight toward me.

Lucky for me, the lane to my left was open, and I steered carefully over the slush ridge and into it, while she squiggled and swirled, missing me by inches and sending drivers careening desperately in all directions. It all happened with stunning speed and passed just as quickly when the black SUV flew back across two lanes and spun out in the snow beyond the breakdown lane. The rest of us, grateful to be alive and undamaged, were not minded to stop and help.

There was a rest area half a mile ahead, and I pulled in and stopped to let my heart rate slow and to unclench my poor burned hands from the steering wheel. My hands were better today. I'm a fast healer. But they sure hadn't needed this. I thought maybe I'd buy myself a nice café mocha, but getting calm took a while. I noticed a few other cars from the same almost pile-up pulling in to decompress. I was getting out to get my coffee when the black SUV pulled into the parking space beside me and stopped. The stupid young driver got out of the car, still on her phone, laughing as she said to whoever was on the other end, "And I like, spun out and almost ran into like six cars. It was so funny!"

It wasn't funny. She had caused major fear and misery and put a blight on many people's days. I very ostentatiously pulled out my phone and snapped a photo of her—yoga pants, Uggs, elaborate model hair that she must have gotten up at four a.m. to style, and a wholly impractical puffy white jacket—and then of her license plate. To the person on the other end, she said, "Hold on," and then, to me, "Hey, like what do you think you're doing?"

She couldn't, like, tell?

"Taking a picture of your license, and of you. To go with my report to the state police about your reckless driving."

"Oh, right, lady. Sure you will. Like you really think they'll care?"

She said into her bejeweled pink phone, "Hey, Shy, I gotta go. Some old bitch is giving me a hard time about my driving."

Old bitch? I knew this job was aging me, but was it really that bad?

She shoved the pink phone into an oversized red purse. "Look, lady," she said, all chin-jutting, butt-twitching attitude, "what's your problem?"

"My problem? I like people to pay attention when they're driving. You came close to causing a multi-car pile-up. You could have killed someone. You should be ashamed and apologetic, not proud of yourself."

She waggled her yoga-panted butt and tossed her hair. "You're like not really going to tell the police, are you?"

"I absolutely am." I like, really already had.

By this time, two other people had gotten out of their cars and were standing behind me. One of them said, "Honey, you nearly ran me off the road, and I've got a baby in the back." There was a tremble in her voice that said the terror of the experience hadn't left her. "And I did call the police."

Another, an older man, said, "Girlie, don't you get it? You can't drive like that on winter roads."

"Oh, honestly." She drew the word honestly out to about six syllables. "It's no big deal." A flounce of her hips. Another toss of her hair. "The cops aren't going to care anyway."

"Oh, I think they might," I said. "My husband is a state trooper."

But that wasn't why I thought the police might take an interest. Out of the corner of my eye I'd spotted one of those stealth unmarkeds the police were using. A mean-looking gray Camaro. The staties were already here.

I really didn't have time for that coffee. I walked away from her sputtering, got in my car, and headed back to the turnpike, my fog lights painting the tunnel made by my headlights an eerie yellow. Proving what an old fart I was becoming by wondering how we could turn the world over to her generation, a kid who didn't even have the decency to apologize to the woman who'd experienced terrible fear for her baby's life. Before I got to the exit, the ignorant babe sped by me like she was being chased. And behind her, poised for the right moment to stop her, was a state trooper in a mean gray muscle car.

Sometimes the gods are good.

As I continued to navigate the game of almost-bumper-cars that driving entailed, I was suddenly hit by another thought about Ginger. Ginger had been strange about cars. She was obsessive, even though it had been fall and then winter, about making sure the car windows were always slightly open.

She'd been deprecating about it, describing it as just a funny quirk she had, but I'd wondered, once or twice, whether she'd had some kind of an incident involving being trapped in a car. Maybe even a time when she'd driven into the water? I'd noticed that she carried one of those multipurpose tools they advertised that could be used to cut a seatbelt and smash a window. Something else to share with Roland. I couldn't see how it might be useful, but I was just giving him the pieces. Putting the puzzle together was his problem.

Because he was getting on a plane right now, and I might be in a meeting when he called back, I asked Siri to text the new information to his cell phone. I desperately hoped he would learn things in Florida that would let them solve this case. I wanted to stop having these fragments coming at me and wanted the pressure of needing to remember gone. This was like I imagined having malaria might be—the sudden onset of overwhelming symptoms that would come and go, leaving me drained and wretched. Each little memory fragment about Ginger came with images and scents. Ginger in the chair. Ginger on fire. Ginger's terrified eyes begging me to save her.

I spent the rest of the drive on the phone. Catching Bobby up on the report I was handing off, and what was still missing. Like me, he was an early bird seeking that elusive worm. He'd checked his computer, my desktop computer, and the fax. Nothing had come in overnight. That meant another phone call. A stern phone call.

Then I tracked down Glen Stryker. When Glen answered, I said, "I hope it's not too early?"

"Never too early for the most gorgeous girl in the world."

True confession moment here. I love my husband beyond all imagining, but if I didn't know Andre, I would have a totally mad crush on Glen. I must have a thing for manly men or something. I love the fact that his voice alone contains so many qualities—authority, certainty, patience, depth, kindness—that just listening to him makes me feel like the world will be okay if Glen is on the case.

"I've got a problem I need your help with."

"Marital difficulties?" he said. "You finally going to leave that tear ass statie?"

"In your dreams, Glen. We're still newlyweds."

"They're nice dreams though, Thea. So what's the problem?"

I told him my problem. MDMA. Entitled children. The hyperthermic, hypothermic user. Reeve's dilemma. "Sooner is better than later if we're to get out ahead of this thing. So what do your today and tomorrow look like?" Glen was in New York, just a hop, skip, and jump from Connecticut, where it might not even be snowing.

"Gotta go scare a bunch of kids today, but tomorrow is good."

It was a small thing, but with so much going wrong or giving me problems, getting ready agreement sent relief pouring through me. I gave him the details.

"They know they're gonna pay me big bucks for this?"

"They know."

"I should hire you as my publicist," he said.

"A kickback is fine."

"You're gonna get the stuff analyzed, right? You know where to go?" A pause, and he added, "I always feel like a rat when I suggest that."

"You're private sector now, Glen. This is how we pay the bills."

I steered around a terrified man in the middle lane who was going about forty-five. Sometimes slow can be more dangerous than fast, and for some inexplicable reason, slow drivers favor the middle lane. "And yes, we'll get it analyzed. I believe you're the one who taught me about that."

"Compounding my sins. Look, I've gotta run. I'll call you this afternoon and we'll make a solid plan for tomorrow. Anything in particular you'd like me to concentrate on?"

"Cognitive impairment would be good. These kids are fast track and Ivy-bound. And they will have read studies about how this stuff is harmless and the big bad grownups are just trying to scare them. Some graphic evidence to the contrary is always good."

I told him about the girl quoting the synthetic drug law.

"So not just scare 'em straight, but scare 'em straight with facts."

"You've got it. Bye, Glen. Go do good."

"Hey," he said. "Before you go. I saw on the news about that thing with the realtor yesterday. That must be hard."

I didn't have to pretend with Glen. "Yeah. I'm struggling."

"How well did you know her?"

"A lot better than anyone else, it seems. Glen, all we did was look at some houses."

"People talk to you," he said, echoing Roland. "So you probably do know stuff that can help. When it wants to come, don't fight it. Let it come."

"But I *want* to fight it. I want it out of my head."

"Of course you do. But getting past something like this? It's a process. A process that works better if you deal with it. And it takes time. Ask Andre."

I heard keys rattle and a door shut. Like me, he was doing at least two things at once. "Take care, Thea. And don't beat yourself up because you didn't save her. Most likely, the damage was done long before you got there. But what a sicko, setting you up to find her. That's someone who is really twisted."

A car door opened and slammed. Then he said, "I'm sorry. I shouldn't have brought that up. It's not like you needed reminding."

An engine roared to life. Glen drove a big honking double cab truck that sounded like it ate Smart cars for breakfast. "We'll talk later." Then he and the roar of his engine were gone. I went back to focusing on driving.

The traffic conditions improved as I went south. By the time I was west of Boston, it was just drizzle and puddles and the fog was lifting. I wished my mood would lift. Glen had meant to be comforting, but his last remark, that Ginger's killer—the killer who had my name and phone number—must have been sick and twisted, remained stuck in my mind like a splinter.

CHAPTER 11

A little after seven in the morning and I felt like I'd already done a day's work. Choosing the lesser of two evils, remembering details about Ginger being the greater, I asked Siri to check my messages. More calls to return. Problems. Questions. A couple reporters. A possible new project. Among them was an issue that I'd been ducking—a message from my mother. Another unpleasant duty—our relationship is strained at the best of times. Eventually I would have to call her back, though. She wouldn't give up until I did. I get my persistence gene from her.

Like Suzanne has taken to asking: were we having fun yet?

My mother's voice in my head always answered this one by asking, "Whoever told you it was going to be fun?" She was a world-class iconoclast, a woman who could never be pleased, who shared her dissatisfaction with life by making sure she kept the people around her equally unhappy.

With respect to her, I am a very slow learner. I keep trying to please her. This was the third or fourth message from her that I was ignoring, because I knew what it was going to be. Were we coming for Easter dinner? She would guilt me into agreeing to come and agreeing to cook things I didn't have time to cook, even though dinner with my family gives me heartburn before I take the first bite. Not the least because she would go on at length about her desire for grandchildren. She knew about my situation, yet conveniently forgot both my miscarriage and her own several miscarriages. She acted like my failure to get pregnant was willful.

Maybe this year my brother and his toxic wife would announce a pregnancy and I'd finally be off the hook. Their offspring would be the spawn of the devil, a princess or prince-ling born so corrupt and entitled it would steal drugs and command obedience from the staff in the delivery room, but perhaps my mother would be appeased. Temporarily. She could never truly be appeased.

Even in the gloom of late March—spring by the calendar, winter by the weather—the Stafford Academy campus looked manicured. Somehow, their maintenance staff had made the snow orderly. It even looked cleaner than snow anyplace else, like someone came daily and dusted fresh snow over the sandy, sooty mess that prevailed at this season. The paths were swept clean of sand and decaying leaves. The shrubs were carefully wrapped in burlap for protection. There was no litter, no cigarette butts, no casually tossed lottery tickets, cans, coffee cups or bottles. The buildings were warm red brick with immaculate white trim.

The majority of students seemed healthy and lively. Even first thing in the morning, they were striding to class, not shuffling with hoodies up and shoulders hunched. They were talking to each other, not isolated by dangling earbuds. This was a jacket and tie school. Skirts or neat slacks for the girls. There were none of those crotch-between-the-knees pants, swaths of boxers or girls with cleavage, or hoodie-wearers with swaggering attitude.

For a moment, I thought *Stepford students.* A little too easy to segue from Stafford to Stepford. Then I squashed the notion. Spring break in exotic locales could do wonders for the end of winter blues. Their minds might not be any more engaged, but they were rested, well-fed, and had had massive doses of Vitamin D. Jonetta, who runs a school for underprivileged girls in New York City, probably spent as much money to educate her students as these kids spent on grooming products. But I was not here to campaign for economic equality. I was here to help this school deal with a real-world problem. I shelved my politics and went to find Reeve.

Halfway to his office, I had another one of those damned moments of recall. Ginger and I had been in the car, parking outside a house. I was on the phone—when was I not on the phone?—talking to a client school, and when I was done, she'd said, "Is that one of those jacket and tie schools? Where the poor boys have this one ratty jacket that hasn't been to a cleaner in months?"

She'd surprised me with that. I'd said, "Did you go to a private school?" She'd shaken her head and made a face and changed the subject. But later she'd seemed subdued. Was it because she'd accidentally revealed something?

I wished it would stop happening. Remembering was a distraction I couldn't afford right now. I put on a burst of speed, arriving at Reeve's office out of breath. The same order that was evident outside had not found its way in here. There were message slips everywhere. His desk and the conference table in his office were strewn with papers, and he had worried his hair into two strange tufts that stood out like toddler's ponytails on the sides of his head. On toddlers they are adorable. On a middle-aged man, not so much. He rushed at me the moment I'd set down my briefcase, and grabbed my hands in his like a drowning man grips a lifeline. I thought I felt a few small bones snap in response as pain from yesterday's burns flared. I blinked away tears.

"You're here!" he said.

I hadn't remembered him as such a big man. Nor had I realized he was so strong. Maybe his whining and dithering had reduced him in my mind. Today he towered over me like a slightly disheveled bear. An agitated bear. I glanced around for a whip and a chair but all I had to tame him with was experience and reassurance.

I wrestled my hands back and converted my grimace to a reassuring smile. "I'm here." I waved a wounded hand at two comfortable chairs. "Let's sit a minute and you can catch me up."

He perched on the edge of his chair, if it is possible to imagine a bear perching, and clasped his hands like a supplicant. "The trustees are meeting at 9:30."

It was now about quarter to nine. "About Joel?"

"About everything. They'll deal with Joel, of course, but before that they want an update on the situation."

"What is the situation?"

He looked at me like I'd lost my mind and I realized I'd been unclear. "I mean, what has happened since we last talked? What is the situation with the police investigation, if you know? Where do you stand with the two students who were allegedly selling drugs? What is the status of your hospitalized student? What is happening with Alyce's parents?"

I got out my iPad and prepared to take notes. Reeve was chatting at me, but he wasn't saying anything. I put a hand on his arm. "Slow down. Calm down. Let's take this step by step."

Like an engine that didn't want to stop, he sputtered a few times, spewing disconnected information, before he finally fell silent.

"The names of the students suspected of selling Molly?" He'd told me on the phone, but I wanted full names and correct spelling.

"She's Alyce Crimmons. He's Jonathan Wylie Gordon. Known as Flash." He spelled out what I needed spelled.

"What's the relationship between them, if you know?"

"Passionately intertwined since the day he arrived on campus. I think I told you. He's a junior. She's a senior. And she's the wild one. Johnny's pretty conservative. He's a head down, do his work, low profile kid, except when Alyce talks him into doing something crazy. Like this."

"So, as far as you know, she's the one who procured the drugs and brought them to the campus?"

"That's what she says. She says Johnny's not involved. Except that Nina Varshovik—that's the victim, if you can call her that—says she got her pills from Johnny."

"Complicated. And Alyce's parents?"

"Peter and Isabelle Crimmons," he said. "They're here. In town, I mean. With entourage. Their lawyer and his personal assistant. They've demanded a meeting with Joel this morning. He's supposed to call them at their hotel to schedule it."

"What about his mother? Flash Gordon's?" I loved saying that, even though Reeve had called him Johnny. "There's no one representing him?"

"There's no father in the picture. We've left a message for his mother about this morning's meeting but there's been no response." He shrugged. "She works, so she may not have gotten it."

"And Nina's parents?"

"Overseas. So far, just a flurry of angry phone calls." He shrugged. "I think she would have let it slide, but the cops pushed her, and now the parents are squawking about how we've let their little darling down and put her at risk." He shrugged. "In the three years Nina has been here, her parents have shown no interest in anything we've sent them. Never responded to calls and e-mails from her advisors when they were concerned about Nina and her previous antics. And now this."

"Sounds like Nina has been on your radar before?"

He nodded.

"Tell me about that."

He glanced at the clock. "Do we have time?"

"You want me in this meeting, right? Well, I can't go in there and be effective if I don't have a clear picture of what you're…what we're dealing with."

He talked and I typed notes as fast as I could. The teeny keyboard wasn't as easy for me as pen and paper, but I could read what I'd written later, assuming autocorrect hadn't translated it into something truly odd, and the notes would be available on all my devices. Given a choice, I wouldn't have all these electronic pals. But necessity was the bother of invention.

In ten quick minutes, I'd learned that Nina was a party girl for whom studies were far down on her priorities list; a manipulative hedonist who broke rules for the fun of it. Alyce was a neo-hippie who wanted to skip college, go live on a farm in Vermont and grow organic vegetables. She had a taste for drugs, but they had to be "good" drugs. Reeve didn't know if she'd been selling other drugs or if this was just a bit of "letting loose" with graduation on the horizon. Johnny Gordon was an African-American scholarship student, quiet and studious, an unlikely person to be involved, except that he was joined to Alyce at the hip and, being more of a follower than a leader, probably had only delivered the pills to Nina because he usually did what Alyce wanted.

I also knew that Alyce's parents would arrive with a far different vision of their daughter, one that probably blamed this lapse on her unfortunate association with this unsavory minority student who had led their perfect daughter astray. Were the situation not so serious, it would have been amusing to turn Gordon's parents and Crimmons's parents on each other and see how their different scripts would play out. It wouldn't have been fair, though, since Johnny "Flash" Gordon only had one parent, one who wouldn't be there to advocate for her son unless Jonetta found someone to step into that breach, and Alyce's parents had arrived with a whole team.

I'd learned the local police chief was sympathetic to Stafford's situation and would do his best to help the kids avoid legal trouble so long as they got some suitable punishment. Reeve thought Chief Hatchett would be very cooperative and our expert would be welcome to analyze the drugs. Bottom line: his challenge, and ours, would be to manage Alyce's parents. And perhaps Nina's, though that was, as they liked to say on the news, a developing situation.

"What do you know about the source of the pills?"

"According to Alyce, she has a friend at MIT who made them." Reeve shook his head in disbelief. "She won't divulge the friend's name, of course. She says 'sorry but that's just how it is.' That's when she quoted the stuff about synthetic drugs. She's remarkably cool about the whole thing. Except, of course, when I told her that Johnny could get charged with drug dealing and her parents were going to lay the whole thing off on him."

I was thinking that it would be interesting to meet this trio, then realized that there was another question I'd forgotten to ask. "So what's the relationship between Nina and Alyce? Or, for that matter, between Nina and Johnny?"

Reeve made a face. "I believe Nina and Alyce are what's called BFFs. I don't know if Johnny is a BBF, but the three of them are close."

"So none of them wants to get any of the others in trouble?"

"Except that they're already in trouble."

"More trouble?"

Reeve bounced out of his chair. "We're making the trouble. Us. The police. Alyce's parents. And possibly Nina's parents."

I nodded. The mean old grownups were the problem. "How is Nina doing?"

"She's fine," he said. "The young. They recover so fast. First she's nearly dead, and now she wants out of the infirmary because she's missing her friends and falling behind in her classes."

He was pacing the room now, anxious about the upcoming meeting.

"I thought you said she didn't care about classes?"

"Academics are pretty far down her list, but she has to keep her grades up or her mom and dad will jerk her out of here and send her somewhere else. And Nina likes it here.

Easy to take the train down to the city. A couple decent clubs she can sneak out to…"

"Stop!" I said. "You know that she sneaks out and goes to clubs?"

He put his hand over his mouth like a naughty child. "I mean we do now."

Did he really mean now or had the administration's hand on the wheel been shaky for a while now? Had administrative laxity sent students the message that rule-breaking was okay? Not good news for handling upset parents and the local police if that was true. I sighed, made another note, and said, "Let's move on."

"We're going into the conference room in ten minutes," he said. "And we haven't got any kind of a strategy."

We didn't. *I* was developing one, but I needed more information. "About Joel. What's going on with that? Is he confined to quarters? Will he be at the meeting? Have the two of you been talking?"

He held up his hand like a traffic cop. "One question at a time, Thea. Please."

My silenced phone was dancing again. I needed to take a couple minutes before we met with the trustees to be sure there were no new emergencies. I forced myself to be calm. I was supposed to be helping, and I couldn't help Reeve if he imploded before we even got through the door.

"Will he be at the meeting?"

"Yes. Well. First they'll discuss things and then invite him in."

"Have you been consulting with him about this situation—with students and drugs?"

"No." An unconvincing no, if ever I heard one.

"Because?"

"Because Charlotte Ainsley, Chairwoman of the Board of Trustees, told me not to."

His hesitation suggested there was more to the story. Reeve so desperately wanted not to be in charge. A change from many of the people I dealt with—people so eager to be in charge they'd step over their predecessor's dead body if necessary. Some who would step *on* the body. Oh, that was an ugly thought. I hoped it didn't show on my face. Reeve was too busy pacing to be observant anyway. Too full of himself and his own angst.

I was getting a pretty good picture of the situation here, not from what had been said but from what hadn't.

"So is he in the loop at all? Did you fill him in before he was sent to his room?"

Reeve looked so guilty I figured he'd had strict orders to stay away from Joel. "I've tried to keep him informed."

"But while things were happening, while your student was being sent to the hospital, and you were learning who had sold her drugs, he was unavailable?"

He nodded.

I checked the clock. "I'm going to run to the ladies' room," I said.

Reeve wore a 'please don't leave me' look.

"I'll only be a minute." I set a reassuring hand on his shoulder. "Reeve, it's going to be okay."

I left him looking like a man going to his execution and took my dancing phone down the hall to the rest room.

CHAPTER 12

Ordinarily, I don't believe in using phones in the bathroom. It's become a habit for many people, I know, but I find it repulsive and disrespectful. Right now, I didn't have a choice. With Reeve hovering like an aggressive BMW on my bumper, I needed a place to check my phone where he couldn't follow me. At least I wasn't surrounded by flushing toilets.

Despite the angry bee buzzing, there was nothing that couldn't wait a few more hours. Reporters again. Mom again. People who could be called back later. They probably heard my sigh for a hundred miles around—relief, exhaustion, and the effort of pulling myself together to go into the meeting and be effective. I've had the thought more than once that some days it doesn't pay to get up in the morning but by the time we know this, we're already up. I'd been up almost five hours.

My conversation with Reeve had raised some issues that would need to be visited later, about exactly how lax the administration had become, what had caused it—Joel's affair? Reeve's passivity? A cultural failure? A leadership failure?—and how that had contributed to the current situation. But that was for later. Right now, we had to focus on the best way to punish their errant students and on damage control.

I put my phone away, used the facilities, washed my hands, and turned to go. The corridor had been lined with photographs of students. On stage. Playing instruments. Playing sports. That theme had continued on into this little room. On the wall beside the door was a large photograph of a vibrant, smiling young woman, her red hair flying, running across a field. She was wearing shorts and a tank top, arms pumping, a number on her chest, leading a pack of runners. She had a sprinkle of freckles. It was a stunning photo. I could almost feel the runner's pleasure and her strength. What held me there, though, was that except for the red hair, she looked like Ginger, right down to the one slightly crooked tooth.

A total wild card. Still, I whipped the phone back out and took a couple photos. I'd send them to Roland and Andre, who'd probably think I was a nutcase. But they'd told me anything might help. Was it possible Ginger had had a child she'd given up? Could this be a photo of a young Ginger from years ago? A sister or close relative? Mere coincidence? No time for those questions now. The meeting was starting and Reeve would be falling apart. I was here to control damage, not inflict it.

He was literally hovering outside the door, and attached himself to me like a limpet finally finding a rock.

The boardroom was elegant. A long oval table inlaid with exotic woods. Comfortable high backed chairs upholstered in navy and gold—the school's colors. Slate blue walls with what looked like authentic Hudson River School paintings. A credenza with a silver tea and coffee service. A huge oriental rug. Everything spoke of understated class and old money. Charlotte Ainsley, Chanel-suited, straight-backed and adorned with pearls, her perfectly coiffed silver hair flying away from her face in two graceful wings, presided over the room like the distinguished dowager from central casting.

For that matter, the whole board, mostly broad shouldered, graying men in dark suits, looked like the Yankees from central casting. And not the baseball team. Reeve seemed to shrink a few inches when he entered the room, and he took his place at the table like a boy being called on the carpet. Joel wasn't there.

Mrs. Ainsley, who didn't miss much, said, "We've asked Joel to come at ten. And Dr. and Mrs. Crimmons are coming at 10:30." A nod and a hand gesture sent me to the chair beside Reeve. She introduced the people around the table and said, "We really need your help here, Ms. Kozak."

I sat and waited. The Charlotte Ainsleys of the world still had the power to make me feel like an awkward child. The feeling didn't last long. Mrs. Ainsley didn't waste time on small talk. She asked a question, I answered, and we were off and running. I walked them through communications strategies and pulled in aspects of the crisis plan we'd developed that we would need to handle the situation. In particular, I suggested that the faculty be reminded of the school's media policy, so they didn't start talking independently to the media. We agreed that as soon as this meeting was over, I would sit down with the communications director and work out a media strategy, including what would be said to the parents, what would be said to the students, and what would go on the school's website.

On my advice, the school had already sent out a "holding statement" to the press, with the assurance that it would be updated soon. We agreed it was important that any statement lead with the information that the student who'd fallen ill had made a quick and complete recovery.

I told them about Glen Stryker—both his actual value and his PR value—and repeated my suggestion to Reeve that the press be invited to Glen's talk. I explained the complexity of synthetic drugs and my suggestion that we use our own expert to analyze the substance Alyce and Johnny had been selling. I emphasized the separate issue of breaking school rules.

"We've got a pair of very upset parents on our hands," Mrs. Ainsley said. "They're going to fight expulsion, or even a suspension, tooth and nail."

"Tooth, nail, and legal team," one of the other trustees added.

"That's why Reeve and I think an on-campus suspension might be the best solution," I said. "You remember that the rules were amended last year to allow for that."

She raised an eyebrow. "Why would it be better?"

I let Reeve explain. He was supposed to be looking managerial. Headmasterly. If I did all the talking and let him sit there like a chastened child, that wouldn't happen. I was glad we'd gone over all this on the phone.

Thankfully, despite his shambling bear desperation, he'd come prepared. He read the rule, and described how it would work. And the reasons why it was a better plan than sending the errant students away. They kept up with their work. Had to face the approbation of the community. Were forced to acknowledge the problems their behavior caused and admit that they'd broken rules. The value to the community of modeling both firmness and understanding that teenagers made mistakes.

When he finished, there was a murmur of assent around the table.

I took a moment to remind them that even though she had suffered the consequences of her actions, Nina should also be disciplined. She had admitted breaking the school's rules about using drugs. I pointed out that identifying her as a rule-breaker, as well as a victim, also created leverage with her parents.

The minutes flew. It seemed like I'd just sat down when Mrs. Ainsley said, "It's time to meet with Joel, and we haven't discussed that yet. In your experience, Thea, how have other schools handled a situation like this?"

A dozen different ways, I thought. I told her it depended on the egregious nature of the behavior and how much damage had been done to the school. Also on the school's culture. Was it rigid or forgiving? What kind of modeling did they want to do for the students? Did they want to set a stern example? Did they want to send the message that immorality wasn't going to be tolerated in role models?

She listened and nodded. I studied the faces of the men around the table, wondering how many of them had strayed, and whether that would influence their decision here. Whether some of them held the belief some men did that cheating on your wife was not a sign of bad character. That sexual lapses were just part of life and had no impact on a man's ability to do his job. Not a sentiment they were likely to voice in front of Charlotte Ainsley.

"Quite frankly," I said, "it also depends on how much you need Joel to lead you through this crisis. Does he add value or subtract credibility? Because you can be sure that, however circumspect everyone has been about discussing the issue, your students know what has happened. It's something you have to take into account. Can he provide credible leadership in a situation involving rule-breaking and poor decision-making given his own personal failures?"

I gave them a moment to absorb that and added, "And of course you need to think about whether his lapse will damage your fundraising campaign. Whether acknowledging his lapse and offering a sincere apology will be enough. And whether the bigger loss is your erring headmaster or your erring fundraiser."

I wished I felt more optimistic about Reeve stepping into Joel's shoes, even temporarily. But Reeve, while a genuinely likeable human being, was not a leader, and he didn't want to be. I knew it. Everyone around this table knew it. This was an awkward time to be looking for a new headmaster. The school needed leadership now. Strong, decisive leadership in the form of someone willing and able to stand up to Alyce's parents. And Nina's parents, if that evolved into a problem situation.

I wondered if Nina's parents would be content with an offer to refund her tuition for the semester. That was as much as I'd advise the school to do. It was going to take some thought and some finessing even to do that without making them regard it as an invitation for a bigger grab. The fact that she'd suffered the harm while breaking school rules was a good counter.

As the swell of discussion rose around me, I contemplated a new career as a hermit. It was looking very appealing. It wouldn't matter if I spilled coffee on my last good blouse, because no one would see it. I wouldn't have to get up at ungodly hours and drive under horrid conditions. I could throw my cell phone in a pond. There was the small matter of Andre, though. But where it is written that hermits can't have conjugal visits?

Tuning out was a mistake. Not only because I was supposed to be working with them, helping them handle their dual crises, but because the instant my attention wavered from the task at hand, it focused on Ginger instead. That picture, with its striking resemblance to Ginger, surfaced and tried to claim my attention. The smile. The freckles. That slightly crooked tooth that gave her character. I wanted to go back and stare at it. Compare it to my memories of her. Maybe pull up the realtor's website on my phone. If Ginger's picture hadn't been taken down, I could see if I was just imagining all this.

I corralled my mind and dragged it back to the discussion, pushing thoughts of Ginger, and a career change, away. It was well past nine-thirty, and I imagined Joel just outside the door, pacing and practicing his mea culpa speech as the clock ticked toward ten.

It looked like the consensus, pending Joel's interview, was to ask for a formal apology and admission of failure—a teaching moment for the students in which he modeled accepting responsibility—and putting him on some kind of employment probation for a few months to scare some sense into him. I wanted to believe it was the right move, but I didn't know whether this was his first lapse, or if philandering was a habit. Maybe they did.

Finally, Mrs. Ainsley signaled that discussion was over, and asked Reeve if he would bring Joel in. I was curious to observe his demeanor. Joel could be arrogant. I knew that sometimes people met presumed opposition with an attitude. I thought that was not the best approach with this board, but would he?

Joel looked like he'd been spit-shined. Fresh haircut. Fresh shave. Crisp navy suit. Stafford school tie. He was humble. Contrite. Full of apologies for his lapse and for letting everyone down. He was willing to take any punishment they deemed suitable, but hoped they'd give him a chance to help deal with the current pressing situation. I'd forgotten how handsome he was, and how charming he could be. Maybe because he had the kind of charm that he turned on like a faucet, using it where it worked to his advantage and otherwise not bothering. While Joel could be charm itself to those above him, he could be hateful to underlings. Not to Reeve. He needed Reeve. But when I'd consulted with the school before, he hadn't bothered much with me. I was an employee.

Something businesses don't always consider when assessing employees is how they are at 'managing down' as well as 'managing up'. Joel was a model employee with his superiors. He could be a total snot with underlings, and that could have an effect on his ability to manage this crisis, because keeping the faculty on board was critical.

Charlotte Ainsley, despite her shrewd ability to assess character, had a soft spot for Joel. And despite the firmness they'd discussed, the board seemed inclined to forgive their prodigal son and welcome him back to the tiller. Never mind that he'd been absent from the bridge when the ship went aground.

I was getting some insight into how the current situation had come about. Sure, people want to be liked. But they also have to act like grownups. I like charm and good looks as much as the next girl; but as a professional, I put a higher value on substance. While he was probably the best the school had right now, he wasn't the leader the school needed in the long term. Not the easiest thing for an outside consultant to share with Mrs. Ainsley, who had a perpetual air of "not now, young lady." For the present, I would keep my opinions to myself and use my skills to help them through this with whatever they had at hand. When this was over, perhaps I could speak more frankly.

Before too many minutes passed, Joel had been forgiven, Reeve's color was improving, as befitted a man whose death sentence had been reprieved, and it was almost time to call in Dr. and Mrs. Crimmons and their entourage.

Before that happened, Mrs. Ainsley took a moment to update Joel.

"We've discussed Ms. Kozak's suggestion that we give Alyce and Johnny on-campus suspensions, Joel, and the board agrees. It will diffuse many of the family's objections and gives us an opportunity to work on drug issues with the entire community. You'll recall that we added that to the rules last—"

Joel gave me a poisonous look and shook his head. "It's a bad idea, Charlotte. They need to be suspended for the remainder of the term. They need to be sent away."

"Joel," I said. "Let's take a minute and review the advantages of—"

"I'm headmaster," he said. "It's my decision."

Just moments ago, he'd been in danger of being suspended himself. Had he already forgotten?

I looked at Mrs. Ainsley. Would she step in here or simply let Joel have his way? Did she realize that if she didn't set him straight, she was buying the school a boatload of unnecessary trouble?

We didn't get to discuss it. At that moment, the door burst open and a very large, very angry man, trailed by a smaller, officious-looking man carrying a large briefcase, and a slender, overdressed woman, entered.

"You've kept us waiting long enough, Mrs. Ainsley," he bellowed. "It's time to decide what you're going to do about that awful boy who tried to lead our daughter astray."

CHAPTER 13

Dr. Peter Crimmons had one of those famous four hundred dollar haircuts. In his case, not only cut but colored and neatly sprayed into place, and a face that, despite no expense being spared, was as nondescript as a man's face could be. The only outstanding features were the high red color, suggesting imminent heart attack or stroke, and how many gleaming white teeth showed when he bellowed. I could pretty much deduce that he'd never had his tonsils removed and that he'd had both bacon and sausage for breakfast.

Okay. Truth. I'd never met him and I already didn't like him. And since I didn't like Joel, either, the next half hour promised to be a super fun time. Like Suzanne reminds me though, I wasn't here to have fun. I'd just neglected to demand hazardous duty pay for coming into a war zone.

It certainly felt like a war zone. Crimmons stood at the opposite end of the table from Charlotte Ainsley, dominating the table. The room. The conversation. Shooting words in a machine gun ra-ta-tat-tat that allowed no room for response. Mrs. Ainsley seemed to be waiting for a pause in the fire to speak. Joel was just sitting there like he was plugged into some socket that was recharging his charm. Reeve had lost his color again. And—the downside of genteel—all the high-powered men around me were sitting like well-behaved schoolboys.

I guessed none of them had faced down angry militiamen or ax-wielding bad guys or watched someone being cooked alive. Well, I had, and I was not intimidated by this man's bad behavior. Yes. He was concerned about his daughter. But just as I'd felt that Joel ought to show some humility in return for not being terminated on the spot, I thought a man whose daughter was selling drugs that nearly killed a friend on her drug-free school campus ought to take a more conciliatory approach to her school's administration.

Yeah. I'm freaking naïve. I am. Which is why I stood up. In heels, I'm over six feet tall, and while Joel might be able to turn on charm, I can turn on frost.

"Dr. Crimmons," I said. "Perhaps you haven't noticed, but you are interrupting a Stafford Academy board meeting. What's worse, you are behaving inappropriately to the very people who are charged with deciding your daughter's academic fate. Either contain yourself, take a seat, and conduct yourself in a civil manner, or we will call campus security and have you removed from the room."

I keep running across people who seem never to have heard the word 'no' in their lives. Peter Crimmons was one of them. Instead of shutting up and sitting down, both he and his attorney started talking at once.

I did not raise my voice. I didn't look around the table for permission to continue, either. They'd hired me to trouble-shoot and that's what I was doing.

"Dr. Crimmons?" I said.

I turned to Reeve, on my right, and said, "Reeve, would you call Security, please? Tell them we have a situation with a disruptive person in the boardroom."

As Reeve rose and headed for the door, Peter Crimmons stared at me like I was a species he'd never seen before. "Listen, young lady," he began.

"Ms. Kozak," I said.

Something I've learned from hanging around with cops. Some of them have this special quality of authority they call 'command presence'. Today I was channeling Andre Lemieux, trying to pull some of that into this room. Doing what Charlotte Ainsley should have been doing.

"Young…"

"Ms. Kozak." I stood taller and made my voice colder. "Sit down, Mr. Crimmons. Mrs. Crimmons. And if you would please introduce this gentleman?" I gave a perfect Charlotte Ainsley tip of my chin. Across the table, Joel was about to stand, his nose so far out of joint it was practically sideways.

"Hold on, Joel," I said.

I looked at Mrs. Ainsley. She gave him a nod that meant he was to stay in his seat. I had at least a few more minutes to be the grownup here. Perhaps to get myself fired. Ruin my reputation in the business. Put our bottom line in the red and bring Suzanne's wrath down on me. Or do the job I'd been hired to do.

I stood up straighter. "You know Mr. Phelps and Mrs. Ainsley. And these are…" I circled the table, introducing the rest of the board, until I came to the still unnamed attorney. "And sir, you are?"

He was Harold Davenport III, probably 'call me Harry' on friendlier occasions. And like Crimmons, a man used to being the one who dominated the room, or at least to be fighting for dominance. But also one who had the sense to see that this would go better if he could keep his client quiet.

"Thank you. So, as we are all together, this is a good time to discuss the situation concerning your daughter, Alyce, and Jonathan Wylie Gordon."

I turned to Mrs. Ainsley. "Charlotte, is there anyone here from Johnny Gordon's family?"

Talk about theatrical timing. At that moment, Reeve returned, pushing a chair and trailing a majestic African-American woman. She said, "I'm here for Johnny Gordon." She nodded to me and said, "Ms. Kozak."

It took all my newly acquired command presence to keep from rushing up and hugging her. Johnny Gordon's representative was none other than my friend Jonetta. A woman who had more presence than everyone else in here put together. And one of the few people in my circle who makes me feel petite. I guess she hadn't been able to find someone to represent the boy and decided to come herself.

"Jonetta Williamson," she said, crossing directly to Charlotte Ainsley and holding out her hand. They would know each other. The independent school world was a small one.

I did not grin or do a happy dance. I remained standing to ensure that everyone continued to behave themselves until some chairs were shifted and Jonetta was seated. But I was oh-so-happy that Flash Gordon had someone in his camp who could hold her own against Alyce's team.

When Jonetta was seated and Reeve was back in his chair, I said, "Let me lay out the facts as they are known to us." I listed our findings, based on interviews with Alyce, Johnny, and Nina. Across the table, Joel's hands were knotted together so tightly his knuckles were white, and there were thin tendrils of steam coming out his ears.

I'd barely begun to describe what Alyce had said about the source of the drugs and her statement that they were not on the federal list when Davenport said, "Objection," like he was in court.

I'm not just a cop's wife. I'm a lawyer's daughter. I gave him a sweet smile. "Not a court of law, Mr. Davenport. Please let me finish."

He wasn't going to. He wanted—or needed—to impress his client. So he started to explain his objection. I looked at Mrs. Ainsley. She nodded and said, "Mr. Davenport. This is a boardroom, not a courtroom, and we have asked Ms. Kozak to assist us by laying out the facts as they have been told to us by our students. Please allow her to finish."

Perfectly polite. For this round. Davenport might have pit bull qualities, but he wasn't a fool. He held his tongue and I finished. Finished with the facts and then laid out the proposal for the on-campus suspension, and what that entailed. I was afraid, from Joel's dismissive attitude, that he was going to intervene here, destroying our unified front, and giving Alyce's parents leverage. But he held his tongue, and once I'd described it in greater detail than Reeve had, and why it was the best remedy under the circumstances, Mrs. Ainsley was firmly in favor, and the board followed her lead.

Then it was Crimmons's turn. I could see that he wanted to object. To argue for his little girl's innocence. It was obvious that his plan had been to put the blame on Johnny Gordon and claim the boy had led his daughter astray. That wasn't so easy in the face of his daughter's own statements, especially now that Jonetta was here. Instead, he and his lawyer excused themselves and left to room to have a private discussion. I wasn't sure what they would be discussing. The board had already voted.

There was still plenty to negotiate, of course—what would be said to the press and the rest of the parents, what would be shared with the student body. There was the all-important question of what would go into Alyce's and Johnny's school records, whether this could have an impact on college decisions and how that might be averted. Many colleges had a requirement of good character. One they waived all the time with respect to desired athletes, but sometimes applied to other applicants. I assumed that that was what they were discussing. But who knew?

Mrs. Crimmons, in a fussy low-cut animal print blouse and a leather pencil skirt, stayed behind. She was as beautiful for her age as money could buy, with no discernible wrinkles and a forehead that didn't move even when she frowned. She seemed unconcerned about her daughter's fate. Oblivious to the room full of people who were having a meeting, she fiddled with her phone, texting like a teen without social skills and occasionally flipping back an errant curl, her stack of bracelets jingling. She had not said a single word to anyone.

I couldn't resist being a little wicked. "Mrs. Crimmons," I said, "you understand the alternative to our proposal is that Alyce is suspended and sent home, possibly even until the end of the semester. She's admitted to procuring the drugs and bringing them on campus. She'll need structure and supervision from you and Dr. Crimmons, of course."

The mascaraed eyes rose from her phone and stared at me in alarm. She still didn't say anything. She just pushed back her chair and teetered out of the room on her shiny red platform stilettos.

Seriously, now. Who wears red patent stilettos and a plunging blouse to a solemn occasion concerning her daughter's future? A daughter who is a senior in high school with her college admission at stake? A daughter on the verge of being suspended, if not expelled, from school for selling drugs?

Jonetta, who was sitting beside Joel and getting scalded by the steam coming from his ears, smiled across the table at me. Then she took in the whole table with her smile. "Why do I get the impression that Mr. Crimmons and Mr. Davenport think this decision—any of these decisions—belong only to them?" she said. "I don't believe I've heard Jonathan Gordon's name mentioned at all, except in Ms. Kozak's summary."

Another smile. A dazzling smile. "You all do understand that Johnny Gordon's future is at stake as well. Short term and long term? And that the Johnny Gordons of the world have far fewer options than Alyce Crimmons?"

She gestured toward the door. "I'm wondering whether I should be huddled outside with them. Or whether I should hold off raising Johnny's interests until they've returned?"

Mrs. Ainsley's smile was smaller, but no less genuine. "We haven't forgotten about Flash, Jonetta."

I was surprised, and pleased, to hear her use his nickname.

One of the men said, "Flash?"

"Johnny Gordon's nickname."

The clock was running, and we had other things to deal with. What we would tell the parents. The press. The students. A meeting with the police chief later. "While we're waiting, could we use the time to discuss some of our damage control strategies?" I said.

There was a chorus of affirmation. They were busy people, too, with jobs to get back to.

"With respect to the students, Reeve and I have discussed a strategy for…"

"Hold on a minute," Joel interrupted. "I'm the head of school, not Reeve, and I haven't been consulted about any strategies."

I avoided doing a rude eye roll only by bending down and digging in my bag for a tissue. Let Mrs. Ainsley handle this one. I was tired and hungry. I'd left without breakfast. The drive had been long and grueling, and since I'd arrived, no one had offered so much as a cup of coffee. Usually I asked for things like that to be provided when we had a long meeting like this, but I'd been too busy putting Reeve back together. I was grateful when Mrs. Ainsley and a severe looking man who seemed to be her second in command reminded Joel that it was his own fault he'd been out of the loop, and she indicated that Reeve should explain.

He did a decent job of describing why he'd hired Glen Stryker and why he thought the press ought to be invited to that presentation, and the board approved. We moved on to handling the parents and the press and got through most of that as well with no sign of the Crimmonses or their lawyer returning. Once or twice there had been raised voices, mostly hers, but that was all.

Finally, Jonetta said, "I'm sorry, but I have a school to run. So let me speak for Johnny, if I may. First, let me say that he is deeply sorry for the trouble he's caused and for breaking school rules. I hope that you will agree with me, given his record as a good citizen in this community, that this behavior is very much out of character. Second, he is willing to accept any punishment the school deems appropriate, but his preference is for that on-campus suspension the board has chosen, so he can finish his work for the year without losing a semester."

Her eyes circled the table. "I think you all know that Johnny is here on a scholarship. He needs that in order to remain at the school. He has asked me to say that he hopes you will not regard this breach as a reason to take that away from him."

She hesitated. "I believe the words he used, when we spoke, were 'throwing himself on your mercy.' And he needs your mercy. Attending Stafford is a great opportunity for him and he wants you to know he appreciates it. We all know that children—and teenagers are still children—make mistakes. The important thing is that they learn from those mistakes, and that we handle punishments in a way that is rigorous without being unnecessarily cruel. I believe Johnny has learned his lesson. He's contrite and willing to take whatever punishment you choose."

I could see she wanted to say more. Wanted to tell them about Johnny. His background. How he would be the first person in his family to go to college, if this didn't trip him up. How he was trying to be a role model for his younger brothers and sisters, and the impact an expulsion or a loss of his scholarship would have on the entire family. But she held her tongue. She didn't want to guilt the board into making the right decision on preserving Johnny's scholarship. She wanted them to find their own way there.

Oh. Jonetta. She's given her life to educating children with limited opportunities. She could have told them a hundred stories about how education and compassion had made a difference. How forgiveness and firm guidance could change lives. I wondered if Johnny had given her particular instructions. If he hadn't wanted to appear as a charity case in front of Alyce's parents. Compassion, and Jonetta, carried the day for Johnny. The board made some quick decisions about how we would proceed, and delegated the remaining questions—the ones the Crimmonses and their attorney were presumably discussing—to Mrs. Ainsley and Joel to decide.

Then, without ever seeing Dr. and Mrs. Crimmons or Henry Davenport III again, the Board adjourned and went to lunch.

CHAPTER 14

I was so hungry I was actually feeling lightheaded, something Jonetta didn't miss. She's used to my bad habit of forgetting to eat. While Charlotte Ainsley and her board headed off for a congenial lunch, and Joel dragged Reeve away, pointedly ignoring me, Jonetta grabbed me by the arm and dragged me into a corner.

"Lunch," she said. It was not a question.

I tried to argue that I had too much on my plate. But none of it was food. And truth be told, no one functions well without the occasional meal. I'd been working since before five a.m. It was now after noon. Besides, only a fool would pass up a chance to have lunch with Jonetta.

On the other hand, the police chief was coming in half an hour, and while I hadn't been formally invited to the meeting, I was going to be there. I expected that would involve some jockeying with Joel. There was no place I knew of where we could get, and eat, lunch in half an hour. Sadly, I told her that.

"Not a problem," she said, patting her capacious bag. "I know you, remember? And by now, you should know me. They give you an office to work in?"

They hadn't. But we now had the conference room to ourselves, so we settled back into the comfortable chairs, I got us some coffee from the elegant silver urns, and Jonetta produced two huge sandwiches—veggies and cheese—and a stack of napkins from her bag. I may not have a lot of friends, but the ones I have are the best.

Jonetta has a singer's timing. She knows just when to start and what note to start on. She waited quietly while we ate, like she had all the time in the world, and then she surprised me. "Something's happened to you," she said. "Something bad."

Jonetta knows me too well. She's been around for some pretty bad stuff. She knows I'm tough as nails. I can stare down lawyers and bullies and bad guys. But now I threw myself into her arms. "My realtor. Someone killed her. I found the body. Only she was still alive and I tried to save her and I couldn't and it was awful. More awful than anything. It just happened yesterday. It turns out no one knows who she really is and they have no suspects and the cops keep asking me questions I can't answer. And even when they're not, I just can't get it…get her out of my head."

Jonetta's strong arms closed around me and she rocked me like a baby. I felt like a baby. Like there was something wrong with me that I couldn't handle this by myself. And like a baby in that it is amazing how comforting a reassuring hug from strong arms can be.

"Of course you can't get it out of your head," she said. "What kind of person would you be if you could? If you could just brush it off like it didn't matter? Like the victim didn't matter. Were you close?"

"Not really. I liked her. It's…what I'm upset about…it's not about losing a friend, I didn't know her that well, though I liked her. It's about knowing that someone could do something so awful to another person. It's about the horror of it."

I was babbling and couldn't stop. "And the bad guy. He knows my name. He knows where I work. He called me on her phone. He has my number…and even if I could forget or move on, the cops won't let me. They want me to help them. They keep asking me questions like I knew her really well. Because she was so secretive no one knew her really well."

The rocking went on, slow and soothing. "About the bad guys. You've got Andre," she said. "He's not going to let anything happen to you."

"But he's always working, Jonetta."

"And you're not? I thought you two were going to do something about that?"

"We were. Are. It's just…"

"It's just nothing. You want it, you do it. How you ever gonna have yourselves a baby when you never slow down? Babies are smart, Thea. They know there isn't any sense in coming to you. You haven't got time for them."

I could have argued with her. All kinds of people had babies. People who had too many already. People who were too young. Too old. Too sick. People who didn't want them. But somehow, her words felt right. For me. For us. Andre and I weren't making space for the baby we wanted so much. Wasn't it just possible that that was why it hadn't happened?

I never wanted Jonetta to leave. She had command presence, for sure. She also had the most compassionate presence I've ever known. Why would I want to leave here, where I felt safe and comforted, and go tangle with Joel's stupid arrogance? Buck Reeve up again. Handle another ugly crisis. I didn't wanna. Nor did I want to attend to my dancing phone.

"Go away someplace. You and Andre," she said. "Take some time for yourselves and just relax."

Another vote for that elusive vacation. Just as soon as we got some things under control. But that was the trouble. There would always be something else.

As if she was reading my mind, she said, "There's always more work, Thea. You've got to make time to play. And recover. Acknowledge how much experiences like yesterday take out of you and give yourself a chance to heal."

Reluctantly, her arms unwrapped. "I hate to leave you. I don't trust that you're not going to get yourself in even deeper. Because…"

"…that's what I do," I said, finishing her sentence.

She nodded. "Because that's what you do. Solve problems. Right wrongs. Take care of the little people who need someone to stand up for them. What you forget, despite personal evidence to the contrary, is that these situations can be dangerous."

That was me. The big sister. The caretaker. Thea the human tow truck. Always stopping to help those who had broken down on the highway of life.

She might as well have been talking about herself.

We threw our wrappings away and left the quiet of the conference room. Time to move on. Before we parted, she said, "You'll keep an eye on things, right? Make sure they don't backtrack on the on-campus suspension for Johnny once I'm out the door?"

I didn't think they would. The board had decided, but stranger things had happened. "I will."

She hugged me again and swept away. Regal. Powerful. Amazing.

I took another quick break in the ladies' room, trying not to stare at the girl who looked like Ginger and failing miserably. I wanted to talk to her. Ask her who she was. I wanted to never see or think about Ginger again. I was uncharacteristically a mass of emotions. I needed a better lockbox for my mind.

I splashed cold water on my face. There was no improvement. I looked like a tired, overworked woman who wanted to be somewhere else. Someday I'm going to learn to wear makeup. Those who do swear they can change their appearance. I wanted the magic formula in a bottle that made me look rested, eager, authoritative, and youthful. Only a fool believes such a thing exists. What makes someone look rested, eager, and youthful is being rested. Feeling eager instead of always gearing up for battle. And being young. Maybe attitude readjustment would help, though.

I returned seven phone calls, including one from my secretary, Brianna, my third secretary in six months, running down my mail in case there was anything I wanted her to handle. She concluded with, "I put the LL Bean package on your desk." I had an idea what that was. In one of the calls from my mother that I hadn't yet returned, she'd said she was sending me something.

Then it was on to Bobby. I calmed him down about the data that had never arrived. I called the client school, actually found the person who was supposed to have sent the data, and asked him where it was. Got the hesitant, bullcrap response that he was having computer issues. I said I was sending a letter for his signature, extending the deadline on the report. I said it wasn't negotiable. I reminded him they needed the report for their annual meeting and that the delay was on their end. We needed the data to write it. They would have the report two days after that data arrived. He was so surprised by my forcefulness he agreed. I called Bobby back with the good news.

I checked in with Suzanne to see how she was doing. Not well. Neither of us understands the concept of rest. I called the office and sent Magda over to help.

It was four p.m. before I next picked my head up. We'd gotten a lot done. The police chief had been a model of reason and cooperation. I'd only clashed with Joel half a dozen times and only restrained myself from physical violence once.

I'd done what I came to do. Much as I would have liked to stay over and see Glen Stryker in action—I could have watched him count pennies and been entirely happy—I didn't need to. Things were under control. I stuffed my work into my briefcase, said goodbye to Joel, grinning at his barely masked hope that he'd never see me again—and Reeve courteously walked me out.

I couldn't go without asking about the photograph in the bathroom. I wanted to forget Ginger, but that picture haunted me.

"There's a photo on the wall in the ladies' room…a girl running. She has red hair and a big smile and she looks so vibrant and alive. Is she a current student?"

He shook his head. "That's a great picture, isn't it? We just recently put them up, but those pictures were taken years ago, at least fifteen. One of our alums, Jasper Cope, who's a pretty famous photographer now, took those when he was a student here. Recently, he rediscovered them and made us those prints. They've been a big hit."

"Do you know who they're photos of?"

"Not a clue. For most of them, anyway. There are a couple of tennis stars who went on to the professional circuit. I know their names. Otherwise?" He shrugged. "I'm afraid not. Jasper probably does."

"Could you give me his contact information? I'd like to ask him about that girl."

Reeve looked doubtful.

"It's just that she looks so familiar. I'd love to know if it's the same woman I met recently when I was house hunting."

No way was I telling him any more than that.

"I really shouldn't give out his information," he said. "People are always hounding him, he says, and…"

Hounding him? Reeve thought I'd be hounding the man? What my mother calls my 'famous little temper' got away from me. I'd just spent the whole day pulling his ass and everyone else's out of a bunch of fires. And now he treats me like some generic groupie who wanted to bother a famous and important man? I really get tired of people I work hard for treating me like I'm insignificant. Or making assumptions about me when all the evidence is to the contrary.

I turned on him. "Excuse me? You seriously think I'm going to hound the man, Reeve? I just want to ask him a question."

I must not have used dulcet tones because Reeve took a few steps back, looking shocked. “Sorry,” he said. “I’m sorry. I didn’t mean to upset you.”

“Sorry,” I said back. “It’s been a very long day and frankly, from the way he was behaving, I was afraid Joel was going to blow the whole thing. I’m relieved that things turned out so well. Look. About the picture. Just send me Cope’s e-mail address. E-mail is safe. If he doesn’t want to be bothered, he can just ignore it.”

Reeve shook his head. “I’ll send you all his contact info. I know you can be trusted. I don’t know what I was thinking.” He ducked his head apologetically. “I don’t know how we would have done this without you.”

If we were done. The folks at Stafford had better hold firm. No backtracking on what the board had agreed. No underhanded deals with Alyce’s parents that stabbed Johnny Gordon in the back. I was hopeful, but wary. I didn’t want to have to drive back again and set them all straight. Things had a way of unraveling no matter how careful we were, and Joel had been pretty hot-headed about the board’s decision.

“Call me if you need me.”

His soft “I will,” echoed my own uncertainty.

I stumbled out in the chilly darkness, praying it was too warm for black ice, fired up the Jeep, and headed north toward home.

CHAPTER 15

Ah, modern conveniences. It used to be that a car was a car, a home was a home, and an office was an office. Now the car was an office. Home was an office. Everywhere was an office. I liked that my office had a big engine, heated leather seats, and a nice sound system. I liked far less the fact that I couldn't enjoy my sound system, because it was busy helping me communicate via Bluetooth with the many people who still wanted or needed a piece of my time.

The only part of that bluetoothing I enjoyed was the conversation with my husband. He wanted to know if I was coming home, and when I said yes, he said that he was, too, and he going to stop on the way and pick up a piece of swordfish and some potatoes to bake. Did I want him to grab a chocolate cake? Is it any wonder he's the man of my dreams? Yeah. By the time I got there, the potatoes would be in the oven, the grill would be heating up, and there might even be a bottle of good wine breathing quietly on the counter.

Swordfish was a good call. Normally, he would have gotten steak. I didn't know when steak would reappear on my personal menu. Certainly not until long after I got the scent of Ginger's death out of my nose and lungs.

Still, the bright prospects on my horizon made the rest of the drive go better. I fielded questions and shot troubles like a pro, and in a lull between business chats, I tried to reach Jasper Cope at the first number Reeve had texted. No answer. I left a message and made a few more calls. Then I tried Cope's second number. This time, I got an answering machine, and a canned message that said he was away on a trip and would return on the weekend. If I needed assistance before his return, I could contact his assistant. He gave a number, which I couldn't write down. I left my message and said I'd try his assistant in the morning. Then I turned off the phone and pulled up a delicious music mix to carry me home.

My good mood lasted until I pulled into the driveway. It was empty. The apartment was dark and empty. There was no enticing smell of baking potatoes. No heating grill. No wine or chocolate cake. And no Andre. If that wasn't bad enough, when I took off my coat, I found the place was freezing, and when I turned up the thermostat, there was no answering rumble from the furnace. I went downstairs and knocked on the landlady's door. Her car was there, but her apartment was dark, too.

I checked the phone to see if Andre had left a message. He had: Possible sighting of Ginger's ex. I'm following up. Sorry about the cake. I'll call you.

I felt like the kid whose balloon has popped.

I went back upstairs to get a flashlight before investigating the dark, cobwebby basement. Stalling, because spiders are among my least favorite creatures and the place was full of them, I stood in the cold kitchen, smacking the flashlight into my palm and enjoying its heft. This was no ordinary household flashlight. This was a police-approved piece of equipment. It had grooves that gave good grip and a heft that could leave its mark on a bad guy. It had two different controls—UIs or user interfaces in police speak—one on the butt and one on the side, depending on how it needed to be used. It had three different light intensities, or lumens, according my gear-loving spouse. It was good for peering through dark tinted glass during traffic stops, though that wasn't something I usually needed to do here in the house.

I kept stalling, remembering Andre the gear fanatic's lecture on its many features. The low light feature for checking a license or reading paperwork. Sure, hon, I did that all the time. A medium setting for clearing rooms. Not bad. I might actually have to do that, scare the dickens out of those spiders, make that reluctant furnace snap to attention. And then there was the brightest setting for ruining my opponent's night vision. Not to mention the ability to focus a narrow beam or send out a whole wall of light. And the strobe feature. Of course it also had something especially useful for the housewife whose furnace wasn't working—silent switches so the bad guy, or furnace, couldn't hear me coming. Oh, and one-handed operation. I'd never had a chance to use any of them and would be just as glad if tonight wasn't the night that changed.

But things weren't going to be improved by standing here feeling sorry for myself. Wishing would not make it warmer. I headed down the two flights of stairs to the basement to see whether, with my limited home repair knowledge, I could locate the problem. I was armed with my flashlight, a good weapon if one was needed, and my pepper spray. Since my life has led to entanglements with some pretty unsavory characters, I go nowhere without my pepper spray. Those spiders had better stay out of my way.

Usually, the basement was warm. Tonight it was cold, and smelled of damp and must and a hundred years of dust. When I snapped on the light switch, nothing happened. Odd. Our landlady might be indifferent to dust or spiders, but she was a fanatic about light bulbs. The driveway was well lit. The front steps and the staircases, too. She had a deep-seated fear of falling and this was a shared basement.

I clicked on the flashlight and crept carefully down the second flight of stairs. Things didn't feel right. I couldn't remember the last time Mrs. Ames had gone out without taking her car. Her social life, aside from bingo and church, appeared to consist mainly of watching people through her window. The twitch of her curtain as she observed our comings and goings was a regular part of our days. Even in my disappointment at Andre's absence, I'd noticed that no curtain had twitched. Maybe she'd come down here to check on the furnace and fallen?

Stopping halfway down the stairs, I slowly panned the light around the room—medium setting for clearing rooms—the dusty cobwebs bursts of startling white against the dark gray walls. Everywhere the piles of household goods or old coats on hangers made spooky shadows and dark shapes that looked like lurking bad guys. No sign of Mrs. Ames.

I called her name. Called it again. Listening hard, I thought I could hear something. A moan? I held my breath. I was almost sure I could hear someone breathing, but it was hard to hear over the whooshing of my heart.

I wanted to turn around and race back upstairs. I wanted to dive into bed and huddle under the covers until Andre got home. He wasn't afraid of spiders and dark basements and what might be faint moans in the dark. The last time I'd responded to what sounded like someone in distress I'd found Ginger. Just the idea made me break out in a cold sweat. I didn't want to find someone else in distress, injured, or dead. I just wanted some heat.

Down another step, flashing the light around again. The skin on my arms was rising into goose bumps. My chest felt tight. Was I just being foolish, letting myself be spooked by a dark basement? Wait. What was that? I moved the light beam back a few feet. There was a dark, wet-looking patch on the floor between a stack of boxes and some plastic storage bins. It was near the oil tank. Oil leak? Was that why the furnace wasn't working?

I sniffed. I didn't smell fuel oil.

I stepped off the bottom stair onto the cement floor and headed toward the stain. Humans have an inbred sense of impending danger, a primitive instinct left from our cave person days. As I crossed the floor toward the stain, my primitive instincts said run away. Go back upstairs. Do it now. But what if Mrs. Ames was down here and injured?

By the time I was halfway across the room, my sense that something was gravely wrong was overwhelming. The closer I got, the more that pool looked like blood and not an oil leak. Or maybe it was just water looking dark against the dirty floor. Maybe I was deep into wishful thinking. Like wishing I was the type of person who'd never seen a pool of blood.

I stopped. This was stupid. I didn't need to be down here. I could call the oil company and get someone to come and check out the furnace. I could go back upstairs, take a warm bath, crawl into my heaviest flannel nightgown, and get under the covers. Gradually the bed would warm up, and eventually Andre would come home. Then he could handle this.

But what if it was blood and Mrs. Ames was injured and I went back upstairs instead of helping her because I was a scaredy cat? I was already second guessing myself about whether I could have helped Ginger. I didn't need a second person I hadn't helped in time.

I turned in a slow circle, using the flashlight to once again scan the room. I took my time with anything suspicious. A lurking dress form. An ominous hanging raincoat. A laundry basket piled high with clothing. A pair of. Oh God. No. A pair of shoes. A pair of legs. A man. Moving toward me, arms outstretched. A shadowed face under a baseball cap.

He lunged at me.

I swung my flashlight.

His hand grabbed my shoulder as the flashlight connected with the side of his head, knocking the ball cap off. Connected hard. We owned this particular flashlight because it made an excellent weapon.

He dropped his hands, staggering back, one hand going to the side of his head and coming away bloody.

"You've got something that belongs to me, and I want it back," he said. "Just give it to me, and no one gets hurt."

I had no idea what he was talking about. No idea who he was or what he was doing here or even if he was in the right basement threatening the right person. I didn't care, either.

"I don't know what you're talking about," I said, backing away from him as I fumbled in my pocket for my pepper spray.

"Sure you do. Ginger gave the stuff to you. I *know* she did. She said she'd sent it to someone as insurance. And that someone has to be you. You're the only person she knows who's a detective."

What the hell was he talking about? Ginger hadn't sent me anything.

He took a step forward. He had four inches and a hundred pounds on me. If this was the ex-boyfriend, he and Ginger must have been an incongruous couple. Despite the dark and his words, he didn't look so much menacing as thuggish. But I've tangled with thugs before and they can be plenty dangerous.

I backed up. The stupid pepper spray was stuck in my pocket and I couldn't get it out. I played for time. "Ginger?" I said. "I have no idea what you're talking about. She never gave me anything. She was just my realtor. And anyway, I'm not a detective. I'm a consultant to private schools."

I wondered how he'd gotten in here. Mrs. Ames was as careful about locks as she was about light bulbs. There was a bulkhead door leading down here, but it was always locked and it was located within sight of Mrs. Ames's favorite perch—the window from which she watched the driveway and the street.

This wasn't the moment to ask about that. This was the moment to get that damned spray out and put this guy out of commission. The moment when cargo pants, instead of tailored pants with small, tight pockets, would have been a good fashion choice.

"It's not in her apartment. Or at her office. And she said it was her insurance policy."

Insurance policy against what? Against what had happened to her?

I backed up another step and twisted sideways, trying to wiggle the canister out as I evaded his grasp. "Just give it to me, dammit! I'm not playing games here." He lunged for me, treating me to a wave of nervous body odor and the saturated scent of someone who's been drinking so long and hard it was coming out his pores. Drinking because he'd killed Ginger?

I shivered as I swerved aside.

His momentum carried him past me.

The spray came free.

As he whirled and swung his fist, I raised the pepper spray and blasted him in the face. He landed a solid blow to my shoulder and the spray went flying. He screamed, pawing at his face as I flailed at him with the flashlight. I felt the metal connect with something solid, heard an ugly crack, and he buried his face in his hands.

I turned the light out.

As his curses and bellows filled the room, I tried to remember where the stairs were. I thought they were right behind me. Cautiously, I backed up. Three steps and the back of my leg hit something. I bent and touched it. A stair riser.

Turning, I felt for the railing, grabbed it, and rushed up the stairs. I slammed the door, bolted it, and hurried up the next flight to the apartment. I locked that door, too, and called 911. My shoulder was throbbing. The pounding of my heart was so loud I could barely hear the dispatcher on the other end as she went through her litany of questions and I forced out the essential information. I asked for the police and an ambulance, just in case Mrs. Ames was hurt.

If Mrs. Ames was down there with that animal, as I feared, someone with a badge and gun was going to have to find her.

CHAPTER 16

I called Andre. When he answered, I let it all out. No preliminaries. Not even hello. "Ginger's boyfriend is here. In the basement. I'm afraid he's done something to Mrs. Ames. And he hit me, and I hit him and used the pepper spray and I need you to come home right now."

When I paused for breath, he said, "Are you okay?"

A cop question, not a husband question. He should be able to tell I wasn't okay. "Not really. Where are you?"

"Did you call 911?"

"Where are you?"

I wasn't a moron. Just a hysterical woman who'd just found a thug lurking among the spiders.

"Did you call 911?" More insistent now. And immediately began again, in the slow, loud tones you use with someone who's lost focus. "Did…you…call—"

"Yes, of course I called 911," I interrupted. "I asked for police and an ambulance. But I want you. Right here. Right now. Not some local cop who won't even understand what this is about. If that guy, Randy, if he's still down there, you can catch him. What if he's still down there?"

Ginger's ex was a big man, and capable of getting into locked places. I was expecting any moment that the door would be battered in and I'd be doing another fist and flashlight dance. What was the point of being married to a cop if I was the one who had to deal with the bad guys? I was having the irrational wifely thought that I should *not* have to explain this to my husband when I felt a creeping sensation on the back of the hand that wasn't holding the phone.

Looking down, I saw a spider the size of a half dollar crawling up my arm. I screamed as I tried to shake it off. I dropped the phone, dashed it off with my hand, and stomped on it. The spider, not the phone. That I picked up again, hearing Andre's voice, now slightly hysterical himself, saying, "Thea! Thea, what's going on? Are you okay?"

"Spider crawling up my arm. Big spider."

I heard a crash from outside and ran to the window.

"Hold on."

The crash must have been the metal bulkhead door, because someone big and male, so I assumed it was Randy, was running across the lawn toward the road. When he reached the road, he turned right and disappeared behind some trees.

"He's leaving, Andre. He's out on the road. Wait." A dark pickup emerged from the trees and headed off down the road. "He's in a dark truck. Heading toward the highway."

"What color? Make? Double cab?"

I had no idea. What was wrong with truck? Couldn't the police work with that?

Then I took a deep breath, remembering something Roland had said. Sometimes we know more than we think we do. I closed my eyes and tried to focus. To play the game Andre and I liked to play. Trying to be helpful instead of hysterical. "Black or dark green. Double cab. One headlight is dimmer than the other. Right front if you're in the driver's seat. Tape over a broken taillight. Left rear."

"You're a wonder," Andre said. "I'll be there in ten. Keep breathing."

Breathing. If you can breathe you can respond. I breathed in. And out. And in. And told my honey goodbye. "I'm going to go down and check the basement. See if Mrs. Ames is there."

"Be careful," he said.

I said it to him. He said it to me. People always said it to each other. As if the rest of the time we were careless. But I knew what it really meant: be *more* than usually careful.

I would be. Very careful. Of spiders. I didn't think there were more bad guys hiding down there. But then, I hadn't expected the first bad guy.

Armed with my trusty flashlight, I went back down the stairs to the basement. Crazy? Maybe. But what if what I'd seen was a pool of blood? What if Mrs. Ames was lying down there injured and I was cowering up here because I'm such a chicken? What if she died?

What if I lived a different life and none of these things ever happened to me?

Slowly, I went down the two flights of creaky stairs and back into spider land. Back through the air thick with mildew and dust toward that suspicious pool on the floor, scooping up my pepper spray on the way, and shoving it into my pocket. I reached down and touched the pool. Stared at my red-blotched fingers and sniffed. It was definitely blood.

I shifted some boxes and bins and there was Mrs. Ames, lying on the icy floor with a pool of blood under her head. My heart jumped. She looked so still. I knelt and touched her face. Warm. Leaning closer, I could see that she was still breathing. Then her eyes opened.

"Help is on the way," I told her. "You're going to be okay."

I didn't know if it was true, but it was what people said. What the injured needed to hear. I crossed to the heaped-up laundry basket and found an old quilt to cover her. It smelled as musty as the rest of the room, but warmth was the priority here. I tucked it carefully around her, then stepped past her to the silent furnace. Maybe there was something I could do to get some warmth down here. The emergency switch had been turned off, probably by Randy to lure me down here. He'd gotten Mrs. Ames instead. She'd probably heard noises or seen something and come down to investigate. Or gotten very cold. Despite the locks and the lights, she wasn't timid; she was intrepid, a stubborn, self-assured, nosy old biddy. She wouldn't have hesitated to come down here and give an intruder what for.

I flipped the switch to "on" and there was a reassuring roar in response. I was so relieved I wouldn't have to spend the night in a freezing apartment that I almost hugged the ugly beast.

I went back to Mrs. Ames. "I'm going to go outside and see if the police are here yet," I told her. "And the ambulance. I'll be right back."

"Thea. No. That man," she whispered. "That awful man, he might be…"

"Gone. I hit him and zapped him with pepper spray and he ran off."

She patted my hand. "You're a good girl, dear." She moaned and closed her eyes.

I didn't want to leave her, even though Mrs. Ames was what people around here would call a tough old bird. But I didn't know if the police could find us down here in the basement and she needed more than a quilt and some reassuring words. I crossed to the bulkhead door, which was still open, and went up the steps. A police car, lights flashing, was just turning into the driveway and I could see pulsing red in the distance, surging through the trees, that I hoped was the ambulance.

I walked around the house to meet the officer who was getting out of the cruiser. He looked about twelve years old and had a nervous hand on his gun. "Brandon Cooper, ma'am," he said. "Your call said there was a man in the basement?"

Despite the hand on the gun, he was looking at me like I was one of those nervous nellies who are always hearing strange sounds in the basement. In my not-so-humble opinion, if you're going to give a twelve-year-old a gun, you ought to give him some judgment as well. I suppose I could have taken off my shirt and showed him the bruise where Randy's fist had landed. But it was cold out here and anyway I only take off my shirt for one very special cop. And yes, I was tired and cranky and irrational and I didn't want to deal with any more difficult people today. I wanted help, not suspicious looks, and someone competent to take care of Mrs. Ames.

I also wanted a hot bath, a real dinner, a drink, and chocolate cake, followed by twelve hours of deep sleep. I wanted my knight with the shining gold band to ride up in his unmarked and take over this whole mess. Never mind that he was probably just as tired and hungry and cranky and wanted a shower and a drink and baked potatoes and chocolate cake, too. He'd been looking for Randy. I'd found Randy. Or Randy had found me. I didn't know how. Maybe he'd gone through Ginger's files just like he'd gone through her wallet.

From what Ginger had said, I hadn't thought Randy was violent. He'd shown me that he was. And now I wanted to turn the page. It was beginning to look like what Andre and I needed was not a house but a castle, complete with moat and drawbridge. Maybe some knights to defend it as well. I was so sick and tired of bad guys.

"The man I called about is gone," I said. "He attacked me. And my landlady. I fought him off and ran upstairs and called you. Then I heard the bulkhead door crash open and he ran across the lawn and got in a truck." I pointed toward the highway. "He went that way."

Yes. It took all myself control not to say thattaway. Like they used to say on TV. Bad guys always went thattaway.

He looked at the road and then back at me, like he still thought I was a timid sort who'd imagined a strange man in the basement. Bizarre, because I don't think I look timid or helpless. I'm tall and strong and I was wearing serious professional clothes. Those 'ditzy little woman' looks don't go down very well with me.

"I don't know his last name, but his first name is Randy."

The cop was looking over my shoulder, like he was waiting for my parents to show up and take charge. I had to resist the urge to put my finger in front of my nose and say, "Focus. Right here. That's right, look at me and pay attention."

Instead, I raised my voice. "The man who was here, who attacked me and Mrs. Ames? He was the boyfriend of that woman who got killed yesterday. My realtor. Ginger Stevens. The police have been looking for him."

That seemed to register in his boyish little brain. "Ma'am, how long has he been gone?"

I had no idea—time had lost its meaning for me since I'd started down those basement stairs—so I guessed. "Five or six minutes."

He spoke into his radio and took a step toward his cruiser, like he wanted to roar off in pursuit. Then he turned back toward me, remembering his duty to serve and protect. His disappointment at being left here to deal with the ditzy broad and the injured old lady instead of roaring off with lights and sirens blazing in pursuit of a wanted man was all over his face. "Ma'am, are you all right?"

He didn't want my honest answer to this question. "Shaken. Otherwise fine. But my landlady, Gladys Ames, he attacked her. She's in the basement. She's been bleeding. A head wound, I think. She's conscious but in pain. And she's an older woman. I hope there's an ambulance on the way?"

I wasn't wearing a coat, and the icy wind whipped through my clothes. I didn't know whether I was supposed to lead him to the basement where he could take charge of Mrs. Ames or whether we both had to stay there and wait for the ambulance, which seemed to be taking its sweet time driving that last mile. Maybe it had gotten lost? One thinks of public safety vehicles as always being able to find their man or woman, but the roads around here were kind of a tangle. I wrapped my arms around myself, as though that might make me warmer, and stared out toward the road.

The ambulance and Andre's unmarked arrived at the same time, Andre courteously pausing to let the ambulance go first, but he was parked and out of his car before the EMTs were out.

"Thea," he called, "is the bulkhead still open?"

I nodded. Remembered that it was dark, and called, "Yes. She's on the floor behind those boxes near the furnace."

They all headed that way, and I followed, because I was down here without my key and it was my only way back upstairs. Except that when I got to the stairs, young Officer Brandon Cooper blocked my way. "Sorry, ma'am," he said, "but you can't come in here. This is a crime scene."

And I was a crime victim. Also freezing, tired, and totally out of patience. I tried to push past him but he blocked my way. Using pepper spray on him was probably a bad idea, so I said, "Can you ask Detective Lemieux to step over here for a moment?"

Maybe he had some people-reading skills, because he pressed down his officious desire to tell me to go wait in his cruiser, and fetched Andre.

"Detective," I said. "I need to go back upstairs. The door is locked and I don't have my keys because I came down through the basement. Do you suppose you could persuade this officer that it's okay for me to go up the basement stairs to my apartment?"

I could see how badly he wanted to laugh. How much more badly he wanted to shove Brandon aside and sweep me into his arms. Just from the tiniest expressions on his face, and only because I've been reading his face for a long time. Most people wouldn't have seen it.

"Maybe this will help." He dug in his pocket and handed me his keys. Then his radio crackled. They'd stopped a man named Randy Small. He had a broken nose and a head wound and they were taking him to the ER. Did Andre want to meet them there?

Small was a lot like Clark and Jones, wasn't it?

I looked at Cooper. I looked at Andre, who was about to snatch back his keys. "Just let me in first, okay?"

Cooper looked puzzled as Andre stepped past him and the two of us walked away.

"Do you need me to ID him?" I said.

"Maybe later. In a lineup. Just describe him for me."

He unlocked the door, led me through it, and we went up the stairs.

In the kitchen, he pulled out his notebook and I told him what I could about Randy. About 6'2", an easy two fifty, probably heavier. Work boots, jeans, black ski parka with white piping and some kind of logo embroidered on it. Needed a haircut. Needed a shave, missing a canine. A tattoo on his left arm. Big fists. Smelled of sweat and booze. Not bad looking in a thuggish, motorcycle outlaw sort of way.

"Jesus," he said. "And they say eyewitness ID isn't any good."

"I was trained by the best," I said. I stepped closer and he pulled me into his arms. "He was looking for something," I mumbled into his chest. "Something that belonged to him. Some stuff he said Ginger had sent me as insurance. He said she'd chosen me because I was a detective."

He dropped his arms and stepped back. "Did she send you something?"

I shrugged. "I haven't gotten today's mail. Until now there's been nothing. I would have told you. But it doesn't make sense. Why would she send something to me? I wish he'd been clearer about what he was looking for."

But I hadn't been in interview mode, I'd been in survival mode. What had he said? Stuff? Something that belonged to him? I couldn't remember.

"Did he say…?" He broke off. "I'm sorry. We can do all this later. It's just. I don't want…"

He didn't want to go and leave me here alone. I didn't want him to go. But what could I do? I'd married a cop and he was on a case. "Come with me," he said. "I don't want to leave you here. I'll do what I have to do at the hospital and then we can get some dinner."

What girl doesn't swoon at an invitation to the emergency room? Or to bad food in a hospital cafeteria? Which is what it would probably be. Hospitals were notoriously slow and the evening was already crawling on. But I'll do a lot for his company.

"Okay," I said. "Let me get my coat."

"Hey," he said. "Really. Are you okay?"

Hard to hide anything from his cop's eyes. I was moving like the wounded and that was something he was very used to. Before I could answer, he was unbuttoning my blouse and pulling it open so he could inspect the place where Randy's fist had landed. It had been a big fist. Now Andre's warm fingers moved gently on my bruised skin.

Neither of us heard him coming up the stairs until Cooper was in the room. Then what we heard was a strange hissing sound as he sucked in a breath and tried to decide what to do next.

Besides stare at my breasts, that is. Exposed in all their glory. Peeping at my husband like creamy half moons over the top of a black lace bra.

"Officer Cooper," I said, "meet my husband, Detective Andre Lemieux."

CHAPTER 17

Cooper had the grace to lower his eyes. "Detective," he said. "Ma'am."

Being called ma'am always makes me feel ancient.

"He hit you pretty hard," Andre said. "Are you sure…"

"It's a bruise, detective. That's all. Wait 'til you see the other guy." Trying for tough when what I wanted was for Cooper to go away, for duty to go away, and to just stay in Andre's arms until the world felt safe again. Instead, he dropped his hands and I buttoned my blouse and got my coat and purse while Cooper consulted with Andre about whatever he'd come up here to discuss. Then Cooper went back to the basement and we walked out to Andre's car.

Once we were buckled in, he started the engine and was asking questions before we'd gotten onto the road. "Tell me about it. Everything," he said.

"There's not that much to tell. You know what people say. It all happened pretty fast."

I hesitated, reviewing the events before I laid them out. "I was really looking forward to swordfish and chocolate cake, you know."

"No more than I was."

We let the silence of regret and missed opportunities fill the car. I knew he was impatient to hear what had happened and assess it for information and clues and I appreciated his patience. He likes to muscle through things and get them done, has had to school himself in the patience necessary to be a good detective. I'm pretty much the same. We just deal with different populations. Sometimes it takes an effort not to do that with each other. What I wanted to do right now was close my eyes and let the rhythm of the tires lull me to sleep. Now that I wasn't in the midst of crisis, exhaustion had enveloped me like a shroud. I couldn't ever remember feeling this tired.

His hand left the wheel and found mine. Warm and reassuring. "Take your time," he said. We both knew there wasn't much time to take. When we got to the hospital, he'd need to be up and running, already briefed on what had happened.

I knew he wanted to say that I shouldn't have gone down to the cellar, but the truth was I'd just done what any sensible person would have done. Gone down to check the furnace when there wasn't any heat. Regular people don't expect to find bad guys lurking in the basement or bleeding victims behind a pile of boxes. They expected to find the fuel gauge on empty or something inexplicable that would lead to the repairman and the returning burst of warmth. They might expect spiders but they wouldn't expect thugs. Regular people didn't check under their cars or look in the backseat before starting the engine, either. Regular people didn't have industrial strength flashlights or carry pepper spray in their pockets.

Our struggles lately had been toward becoming more like regular people, so this felt profoundly unfair. Not that it mattered. Fair or unfair, the incident had happened, just like the one with Ginger, and would have to be dealt with. I swallowed, summoned up some energy, and told him everything that had happened since I got home.

"Flashlight and pepper spray," he mumbled, when I was done. "I never wanted you to live like this."

"Me neither. I was just trying to buy a house."

I stared out into the dark. Not so foggy tonight, and without precipitation. The headlights cast long bluish shafts of light down the empty gray road. Snowbanks on either side made it feel like we were in a tunnel. It was warm in the car. On another errand, it might have been cozy, alone together and talking in the dark.

"I hope he did it," I said. "I hope when you talk to that piece of crap you find that he's the killer. But I never got that vibe from Ginger."

"Maybe she didn't know him, either," Andre said. "It's rare, but it happens. A guy doesn't show his true colors until the woman tries to leave, and then all that caveman controlling possessiveness comes out. The 'if I can't have her, no one can,' stuff that leads to violence."

"But the attack on Ginger felt so planned. Not like an impulsive burst of violence."

"It didn't," he agreed. "But think about stalkers. They're the ultimate planners. We've had guys who've been convicted and spent years in jail and when they get out, they pick up where they left off. Had a victim once, we finally told her the only thing she could do was get a gun and shoot him, because nothing else would ever stop him. It was hard, telling her that. We're not supposed to give that kind of advice and we're supposed to keep people safe. But we couldn't. No matter where she went, he found her, and we knew, and she knew, that eventually he'd kill her."

That was a story I really didn't want to hear. Bad as Ginger's death was, I didn't want to think of her spending her last days, as well as her last hours, in awful fear. Ridiculous, I knew, wanting to protect her, even though there was nothing anyone could do for her. Except that wasn't entirely true. The one thing we—or least Andre and the other detectives—could do for her now was be sure that her killer was caught.

"I wish we could just drive forever."

"I wish we could go out to dinner, then go home and make whoopee."

Wishing. If only we lived in a Disney world.

"I wonder if Roland learned anything in Florida? It seems like someone, somewhere, had to know who Ginger really is."

"I haven't heard anything."

Tomorrow was another work day. My phone had been buzzing but I didn't want to check it. After a day this long and this complicated, I was, like Pooh, a bear of little brain. I didn't have anything to offer my colleagues or my clients right now. As management experts like to remind us, the world will not end if we aren't there to manage it. I was trying to believe that. And I truly did believe I didn't have to be wedded to my phone every hour of the day.

I might be ignoring my phone, but Andre was working his, getting an update from the hospital, checking that a crime scene team was on their way to our basement, checking on Mrs. Ames, touching base with his boss, Jack Leonard, and with other detectives. As we turned in at the hospital, he disconnected and sighed.

"A vacation is looking really good right now."

"Beach. Warmth. Mai tais." I had the bikini and the cover-up. But I'd have to do some shopping. Without Suzanne's periodic wardrobe replenishments, which she no longer had time for, even my tee shirts were tired.

"You in a bikini," he said. "Oh yes."

That was as far as our planning got. Once he went through the door, he was all business, and I was relegated to a chair in the waiting room. A very dangerous place to be. People around me were bleeding and coughing and moaning. A baby was screaming and its exhausted mother looked like she wanted to throw herself in front of a bus. Across from me, a red-faced toddler in pink overalls was having a meltdown while the woman I assumed was her mother alternately thumbed through a worn magazine and was consoled by the miserable looking man sitting beside her. Neither one of them paid attention to the child.

A sad and skinny old man perched on his chair and rocked, his face a gray mask of pain. Just looking at him made my shoulder ache more. The hateful Randy had landed a serious punch. I hadn't looked at it, but the bruise felt like it was the size of softball. I could hear Suzanne's voice—other people didn't get themselves punched by bad guys—but I couldn't see how this was in any way my fault.

I'd forgotten how much I hated emergency rooms. I've spent far too many hours of my life in places like this, usually when I'm hurting. I've sworn to leave all that behind me. I'd come along because Andre needed to know I was safe, but this swarm of germs and misery didn't make me feel safe at all. It made me feel like a Lilliputian in a petri dish. With Suzanne sidelined, I couldn't afford to get sick.

I also had to fight my "Thea will fix it" impulses. I wanted to rock the baby, pull that weary toddler onto my lap and read to her. Tuck a blanket around the sad gray man and get him a warm cup of tea. Lately, it seemed, I couldn't fix anything. Instead, everywhere I went, chaos ensued.

I tried to take my mind out of here but it was emblematic of my life that there was no place I could go that wasn't almost as bad. Work. The apartment. House hunting. Avoiding my mother. The one bright spot was Jonetta. Seeing her had been a pleasant interlude. Jonetta makes me feel grounded, supported, and safe. Inspired by all that she does. But thinking about Jonetta led to Stafford and that led me to the picture on the bathroom wall. The photograph that looked so much like Ginger and that might be fifteen years old. The timing was right. Fifteen years ago, that could have been Ginger.

In all the commotion, I'd forgotten to send it to Roland and Andre. I'd do that now. Maybe they'd tell me I was crazy. Maybe they'd want to follow up. Even if the photographer decided not to respond to me, he wasn't likely to blow off an official call from the police. It seemed like such a long shot. Why would that be a picture of Ginger? Stafford Academy types didn't generally steal identities and come to live in Maine. But I was generalizing, which was never a good idea, as Andre liked to remind me. Probably Stafford Academy types did all sorts of rulebreaking things. Like selling designer drugs and expecting your parents to bail you out. Or nearly dying from careless drug use.

So much for not checking my phone. Once I took it out to send that picture, I also checked my messages. Anything was better than sitting here aimlessly amidst all this misery. I bent over the screen to see what the end of the day had brought and never got beyond the first message.

Crap. It had brought crap in the form of an urgent message from Jonetta. After she and I left, Alyce Crimmons's parents had started worrying about the effects any suspension, even an on-campus one, might have on their daughter's college choices. Under pressure from them, the administration—that is Joel, since Jonetta thought the board hadn't been consulted—was reconsidering the decisions already made. She'd learned this from a call with Johnny, who'd been talking with Alyce. She had called in to Reeve and Joel, but no one had called her back, and she was worried about everything reverting to some deal using Johnny as the scapegoat. She couldn't take another day off to drive up there and sort them out again. We needed to talk.

My heart sank. I'd had enough conflict today, but this would have to be dealt with. It would take energy and focus when right now I was flattened by the after-effects of adrenaline. When it leaves, it goes like a bad date, leaving weariness and bad feelings behind.

I checked my watch. Jonetta had called me hours ago. Mickey's big hand was edging toward the six and his little hand was halfway between eight and nine. I needed to know if anyone had called her back. I said a prayer to the gods of good sense that they had, that they had stood firm, and that I wouldn't have to make that awful drive again. I kissed my lingering hopes for a decent dinner goodbye. Unless Andre reappeared in the next fifteen minutes or so, our chances of finding an open restaurant were small.

I went outside, where cell phones were permitted, and called Jonetta back.

The first thing she said, when she answered, was, "I'd like to knock their pointy little heads together."

"Does that mean they did you call you back, they called you back with bad news, or they didn't call?"

"Didn't call."

Bad news and very bad form. It meant Reeve was back under Joel's thumb, Joel was using his other thumb to thumb his nose at us, arrogantly demonstrating his lack of good sense, and that what Jonetta feared might happen would happen unless we jointly put some pressure on them. It was also infuriating that neither of them had called me to consult, when we'd spent so much time on the phone and then with the trustees crafting a strategy. Yesterday, Reeve had thought it perfectly okay to call me repeatedly and at any hour when he was desperate for my help. Had they already forgotten that? Did he, or more likely Joel, really believe that smoothing the way for Alyce Crimmons solved all their problems? Could he be that blind and stupid?

I felt like punching something—a very unladylike reaction—but this one had practically been put to bed. I wasn't keen on having it lurch back to life like a Zombie. I kind of liked the notion of Zombie Academy, though. Briefly, because dealing with reality was becoming such a pain, I toyed with the notion of giving up my fun and fabulous consulting career and writing Zombie novels. A fleeting thought. Zombies are pretty much yesterday's news. Most people have already stocked their trunks with anti-zombie essentials in case of the apocalypse and are ready to move on.

"Johnny told you this? He called you?"

"Yes. He's scared. He was fine with the on-campus suspension. Now he's not sure what's going to happen."

"What time was that?"

"Around five."

The wheels were turning. Had Reeve and Joel used me to settle the Crimmons down and get a Board of Trustees decision, then waited for the Trustees to leave and changed the game plan? Was Charlotte Ainsley in the dark? Was this an example of the kind of flouting the chain of command and impulsive decision-making that had led to a lax situation on the campus, or was she a part of this? I couldn't believe she'd okay Joel's unilateral changing of a board decision, however much she liked him. It seemed unlikely, but at EDGE, we've seen things like this happen before—arrogant or careless people under pressure making impulsive decisions without thinking them through.

I was tired of convincing people to act in their own best interest. I was tired of the word tired. I was tired of being so whiny and dull and complaining. Time to stop being such a Debbie Downer and rediscover my inner little Mary Sunshine.

Sometimes a client school went off the rails despite our good advice. When that happened, our concern was the possibility that when things went badly wrong, they'd claim they'd called in the pros to advise them and try to lay off the blame on us. We'd seen it happen before. Schools refusing to take our advice and making their situations worse and then trying to lay the blame on EDGE. I needed to make it very clear that couldn't be the case here.

"Have you talked to Johnny since?"

"Of course. No one has said anything to him. About the suspension or anything else."

Feeling a bit like a backstairs conspirator, I said, "Have him call Alyce and see what he can learn. I'll try Joel and Reeve and if they aren't answering, I'll call Charlotte Ainsley."

"Give 'em hell," she said.

"I'll do my best."

"All I can ask," she said. We disconnected.

It was freezing out here. There's little more depressing than a hospital entrance at night. The few people out here with me were sucking on cigarettes like the things were life savers instead of life takers, or huddled over their cell phones delivering bad news or updates to those who were absent. It felt bleak and dismal.

If I'd had my car, I could have gotten in, turned on the heated seat, and made my calls from there. I didn't have the keys to Andre's car and no idea where he'd gone. I dropped down on a granite bench, knowing it would freeze my ass in no time, and dialed Joel's number.

It went to voice mail.

Then I called Reeve and it went to voice mail again. I left messages on both phones and then scrolled back through my call log to see if I had any other numbers for Reeve. Aha! I did. Because I now suspected he might be ducking me, I went looking for that increasingly elusive device—the pay phone. Sometimes that worked. Despite all the modern features on our phones that allow people to avoid each other on devices designed to allow us to reach each other, there's still a hardwired instinct to answer the phone, especially when the caller's identity is unknown. Especially when those calls come late in the evening. No one calls late in the evening unless it's an emergency.

Bingo. He answered. It took willpower not to yell my "aha!" in his cowardly ear. "Just checking in to make sure everything is still going smoothly and there aren't any glitches in the plans we made before I sign off for the day," I said. My nose grew at least an inch.

"Well…we…uh…we've made, Joel has made…a few alterations to…that is, we're not exactly running with that plan. We're thinking more along the lines of taking another look at Johnny's involvement."

My heart sank even as my temper flared. "There's nothing else to look at, Reeve. We already know everything there is to know about Alyce and Johnny's respective involvements, directly from them."

"Yes," he said, "well, we're not so sure that we've heard the whole story."

"What else do you think you need to know, Reeve? And what alterations are you thinking of making?"

There was a long silence. "Suspending her and expelling him."

I counted to ten. Then to twenty, deleting many excellent expletives.

"Listen to me very carefully," I said. "If you do…if Joel goes ahead with this, with or without board approval…between the bad publicity and Johnny's lawsuit, never mind the likelihood of never attracting another quality minority student to the school…he, and you…are making the biggest mistake of your respective careers." I spoke slowly and precisely, making sure he got the message.

I gave it a beat. "You do know that, right?"

"I just…we just…Joel is concerned that this will—"

"Have a negative impact on Alyce's future? Not if you handle it the way we agreed. Reeve, have you thought this through? She's admitted she was the one who bought the drugs and brought them to campus and arranged the deal. All Johnny did was deliver them at her request."

"Yes, but…"

"There is no *but.*" I desperately wanted to tell him to get his head out of his ass, but it would have been unprofessional.

"What about Johnny's future? Have you thought about that? Or doesn't he matter if he doesn't come with a staff of lawyers and assistants? Of course, after all the publicity and the lawsuit, he'll probably land on his feet, which is more than I can say for Stafford Academy."

There was a long, uncomfortable silence. It was unfair that Reeve had to have this conversation. It should have been Joel. Joel ought to have bent over backward to avoid more trouble and ensure he was forgiven. But he wasn't taking calls. As far as I was concerned, they were still in an emergency situation and he needed to be available to handle it. But I thought it likely that he was only not taking, or returning, calls from me and Jonetta. Which was stupid. Only a fool got on Jonetta's wrong side. Especially in a situation involving a minority student. The kind of bad press they would get if they laid this off onto a minority student and let a privileged princess walk? It would be such a disaster.

"Seriously, Reeve," I said. "You have no response? Have you considered the risks? The fairness? Whether this is even consistent with the school's own written policies? And what about going against a vote of the board?"

"Joel thinks it's what we should do." Like someone who can't or won't think for himself.

"Your school. Your decision. Just understand that EDGE can't work with Stafford if you won't listen to our advice. If you go behind my back and change things after the trustees have agreed without even consulting me, it's not just damaging to the school's reputation, it's damaging to mine."

Damaging to our bottom line, too, but if we didn't have standards, and protect our reputation, our bottom line would suffer in bigger ways. EDGE had to be perceived as giving solid, reliable advice to clients in trouble. We couldn't afford the world we worked in to think we'd advised the disastrous course Stafford was embarking on.

I sucked in some air, trying to keep my voice level and calm, grateful that I wasn't in the same room with him right now. Otherwise I might have a second broken nose on my conscience. Two broken noses in one day? And I knew too well what it felt like to have my nose broken.

"If you proceed in the way you've just described, in a manner that is grossly unfair to the minority student involved and that goes against the known facts in the statements of the students themselves—and targeting the one with the lesser involvement with the greater penalty—EDGE will terminate our connection with Stafford and make it clear why we did. And consider yourself on notice that if you make any representations that these new decisions were advised by or sanctioned by us, our denials will be loud, clear, and very public."

I hung up.

CHAPTER 18

I needed to call Jonetta back. Instead, I huddled on the icy bench. I didn't know what to say. Telling her the school was screwing around and I was pissed wouldn't be helpful. She still had to protect Johnny from their blundering—a real live human being who needed her help—while my job was, or had been, to protect our client's reputation and now was becoming one of protecting our own.

After my endless day, the unpleasant conversation with Reeve left me feeling like someone had drained off most of my blood. I put the phone away and stared out into the parking lot. My shoulder ached. I was so hungry my stomach was singing the blues and a headache was joining my other miseries. It happens when I get overtired and don't eat. Right now, my to-do list was very short: call Jonetta. Find food.

My phone rang as I was reaching for it. Reeve. I let him go to voice mail. If he was coming to his senses, it wouldn't hurt to let him stew a bit. If he'd called back to argue, I wasn't interested.

Behind me, I heard the automatic doors open and the scuffle of feet as two people with lowered voices headed for the parking lot. As they passed me, I saw, just beyond them, a flash of pink. They were oblivious, heads together in some private grief, as the small girl from the waiting room streaked past them toward the parking lot. She was moving fast, bent on escape, too little to pay attention to the ambulance that was flying toward her, sirens on and light flashing.

I jammed the phone into my pocket as I streaked to my feet, dashing past the slow-moving couple and into the street. I grabbed the child with no seconds to spare, swinging her out of the way and landing hard, my hip slamming into the curb, as the ambulance finally came to a stop fifteen feet away. A man's furious face glared at me from the passenger window. Despite obviously being some kind of medical professional, his words were not "Are you okay?" or "Is she okay?" but "You stupid bitch. You nearly got your child killed." He didn't bother to exit the vehicle to find out if we were okay.

I was blinking away tears from the pain as I tried to comfort the terrified child when a familiar voice from behind me exploded, "And if you hadn't been driving too fast, my wife wouldn't have had to rescue the child. Who…is…not…hers!"

My knight in shining armor. As he bent over me, words of concern pouring out, I handed him the little pink bundle. He had many nieces and nephews and far more experience with children. Despite her wails and angry red face, she was a tiny, adorable creature with sweaty blonde curls and deep brown eyes.

"Her parents are in the waiting room."

The image of my handsome husband, who so desperately wanted a child, holding this one brought on the tears I'd been holding back.

"Thea. Are you okay?" He extended his free hand and pulled me to my feet.

"My hip hurts. I think it's just bruised."

It had better be just bruised. I didn't have the time or inclination to submit myself to medical ministrations. The attitude of the guy in the ambulance pretty much summed up my experience with emergency rooms and medical interventions. All sweetness and light and reassurance. All care and comfort and billing a thousand dollars for a bandage. In my short, sweet life I've had more stitches than a baby quilt.

Self-diagnosing, I concluded that I needed a good meal, a soft bed, and at least eight uninterrupted hours of sleep. Maybe a couple of Advil. A shot of strong whiskey. Somewhere on the prescription pad there was also Andre and chocolate cake.

Andre looked like he wanted to drag me into the ER. I wasn't going. "Are we done here?" I asked.

"Almost."

I hoped his 'almost' referred to handing off the little runaway, and not further business with the evil Randy. I knew Andre would want to take a minute to ream the ambulance guy and hoped he wouldn't. Reaming might be in order, but I wanted to be out of here. Right. Now.

To test how long he might be, I said, "I'll wait right here."

"Better come inside where it's warm."

So, a long almost, not a short one. I followed him to the waiting room. The little girl's parents were still in their chairs. She had her head on his shoulder, he had his head on hers, and they were both asleep. I stayed back while Andre put his hand on the man's shoulder and shook him gently.

He came awake and stared at a strange man holding his child. "What the fuck?" he said.

An eloquent response. One I might have used myself, if my mother hadn't worked so hard to make me ladylike.

"Is this your child?" Andre asked, using his best 'I'm a cop so don't fuck with me you asshole' voice.

"Yeah. So?"

"So while you were in here taking a nap, she just ran out into the parking lot and came within inches of getting struck by an ambulance. My wife nearly got killed saving her."

I watched belligerence morph into "Oh my God!" The man shook the woman awake, then rose and held out his arms for the child. He folded her against his chest, murmuring "Sidney, sweetie. Thank God!" and began to cry.

At that moment, a nurse with a clipboard called the woman's name and she rose unsteadily, both hands pressed against her stomach, and followed the nurse and clipboard through a door. The man watched her go, then stammered out an explanation to Andre that involved two back-to-back twelve-hour shifts, a sick wife, a mother with Alzheimer's who kept wandering and other complications. All the while rubbing his child's back and nuzzling her soft curls with his chin.

Yes, they'd been careless. And yes, a child had been at risk and I would have preferred he skipped the foul language. But they weren't the careless parents I'd imagined. So easy to be judgmental and so hard, sometimes, to be parents.

Then Andre was ready to go. At least he was heading for the door. I trailed after him gratefully until I saw that he was actually heading toward a uniformed state trooper who was just coming in. I'd begun an inward string of curses when I saw that the trooper was carrying a pizza box and a paper bag. He gave them to Andre with a crisp, "Here you go, sir. I hope that's everything."

"Thanks for doing this," Andre said.

The trooper headed back to the cruiser parked at the curb and vanished into the night. Andre turned to me. "Veggie pizza, salad, and chocolate cake okay?"

"You are my hero," I said. "Let's go home. I've got a call to make and then you can fill me in."

As the car warmed and we headed off into the black night, the air around us filled with the smells of hot cheese and onions. I was almost too hungry to wait. I filled the time with a call to Jonetta. She was disappointed, not too surprised, and already formulating her battle plan. Reeve had called back two more times. I ignored him. The next eight hours were mine. Mine and Andre's. I was going to have a picnic and chocolate cake, and keep the rest of the world and its problems out somewhere on the periphery. It would all come swooping back soon enough.

"Sounds like your people are as cooperative as my people," he said, when I finished with Jonetta. "You want to hear about Randy?"

I could tell from his tone that Randy had given them nothing, and neither of us was in the mood for another helping of nothing. "Not right now."

"My thoughts exactly. Except you might want to know that you broke his nose."

I should have had regrets at hurting another person, but Randy had done his share of hurting first. I'm working on becoming a tough old bird like Mrs. Ames.

He drove at cop speed, and we were home in record time. We hurried up the stairs, shucked our coats, and spread out our feast on the coffee table. Andre put on a romantic music mix he'd made for Valentine's Day. I opened a bottle of red wine. I took a couple of Advil and told my various aches and pains to go play somewhere else. I had a handsome man across the table and big plans for later that did not involve anyone else's problems. We settled down on cushions on the floor and had ourselves a picnic. Being in the here and now here and now.

Tomorrow, as Scarlett has taught us to say, was another day.

CHAPTER 19

It took willpower not to check my phone again or ask about Ginger's ex boyfriend. Andre was struggling, too, but somehow we avoided talking about our work. We enjoyed our food, though I was so tired I only had a few sips of the wine. We ate impossibly large hunks of chocolate cake. We snuggled and we kissed and we had ourselves a fine old time. We let tomorrow come.

All too soon, it was morning. A morning that began, as so many of them do, with the phone ringing before six. In March, before six, it is almost as black as at three a.m. It was his cell phone, so I pulled the covers over my head and contemplated another hour of sleep. I wasn't going to be a road warrior today. I only had to go to the office. I could take my time.

Ha!

He wasn't too many minutes into his call when the phone rang. Not my cell. I'd turned that to vibrate and left it to silently collect the calls from Reeve. When I stopped counting, Reeve had called seven times. This was the landline.

It was bound to be for Andre, but since he was occupied, I flipped off the covers and grabbed it. "Thea? It's Roland. Where on earth did you get that picture?"

Oh crap. And a cheerful good morning to you, too.

"Roland?" I scrabbled around for clear wits, hoping it might help if I turned on the light. I fumbled for the switch.

"That picture of Ginger," he said impatiently. "Where did you get it?"

"I told you in the email. It was on the bathroom wall at the school I was at yesterday. The Stafford Academy in Connecticut. It's an old photo—maybe fifteen years or so, taken by one of their famous alums. They had a whole display of his work. And I don't know that it's Ginger."

"It's her. It's got to be her," he said. "What does Andre think?"

"I haven't asked him. We were kind of busy last night after I found Ginger's ex-boyfriend Randy hiding in my basement."

"Say what?"

"Where are you?" I said.

"At the airport. Waiting for my flight."

"Back to Maine?" Probably a stupid question. Where else would he be going? Unless he'd found a lead to another part of Ginger's past.

"Yeah. It's been delayed two hours. Well, show it to him, Thea. Right now. See what he thinks. Maybe she's in an alumni directory. In a yearbook. Maybe someone remembers her. Maybe the photographer remembers her."

There was a commotion of airport noise in the background. "Is Andre there?" he said.

I thought he was jumping the gun, getting too excited about something that was probably just a resemblance. I looked over at Andre, still pacing with the phone pressed to his ear. "He's here. On the phone about something."

I waved the phone at him and he held up two fingers. "Two minutes," I told Roland.

I flopped back against the pillows and pulled up the comforter. I wanted Roland to go away and the day to hold off a little longer. My body was one big bruise. My shoulder was stiff and aching from Randy's fist and my hip and thigh felt black and blue from rescuing that toddler.

Suzanne was right. I needed to reform. But I didn't see how I could predict, and thus avoid, thugs in my basement or tiny children bent on escape unless I started consulting psychics. Would Suzanne want me to let the child get run over? I didn't think so.

I shifted and groaned. Maybe the man of my dreams would bring me some Advil when he got off the phone.

"Are you okay?" Roland said.

"Not really."

"What happened?" He sighed, like he shared Suzanne's opinion of my propensity for getting into bad situations. That sigh did nothing to improve my mood.

I gave him the short version. Despite the pleasant time I'd spent with Andre, I was in a foul mood this morning. My phone was like a tiny Pandora's Box. I knew that the moment I opened it a heap of problems would tumble out. Things would only get worse when I got to the office. I thought of Andre's suggestion last night. We should take a vacation. Get away from the cold and ice and snow. Go someplace where furnaces didn't break and we didn't know anyone and wouldn't get drawn in if there was a mugging or a murder.

That brought a mental note to check on Mrs. Ames's condition when I would rather be pawing through storage boxes looking for my bikini. Maybe the rest of our clients would follow Stafford's lead, become impossible, and I could fire them all and become blissfully unemployed. Except then Bobby and Lisa and Magda and Suzanne and Brianna would also be out of work. And we all needed the income. Crap. Note to self: avoid businesses where other people depend on you.

Across the room, Andre kept pacing, phone pressed to his ear. In nothing but blue boxers, he looked like a million dollars. He's one of those men who have naturally great bodies. He also looked like a man getting bad news.

"Andre's still on the phone," I said. "You want to wait for him?" A little mental loop played the too frequent question: would you still like to hold or shall I put you through to his voicemail?

"I want to know what he thinks about that picture." Like I was a bit simple and likely to have forgotten.

I had no idea what Andre would think of the picture. Maybe he hadn't looked at it yet. We'd been busy last night. "Did you learn anything useful in Florida?"

"Pretty much the same as here. No close friends. No paper trail. She appeared from nowhere and disappeared almost without a trace. People liked her. She was pleasant. Good at her job. The reason she gave her boss for leaving was that she'd met a guy and he was moving to Maine. It seemed plausible to him, if a bit sudden."

What would it be like to live an entire life so carefully? To never allow yourself to make connections or have close friends? "You learn anything about the guy?"

"I'm not sure there was one," he said. "No one ever met him. No one ever saw him."

"So maybe it was just an excuse to leave. But people around here hadn't met Randy, either. And he's way too real."

Andre lowered his phone and I held out the one I'd been talking on. "It's Roland."

I gave up on peace and quiet and the possibility of being waited on and headed into the bathroom to get my own painkillers. My body was not with the program. It screamed and creaked all the way across the room. I gobbled some pills, probably destroying my stomach. What helps one thing hurts another. That could be another of my mottoes.

Anticipating the soothing wonders of a hot shower, I limped back into the bedroom to get clean underwear. Mother says one must wear it, and given my track record for ending up in emergency rooms, unlike much of what she had to offer, it was good advice. Before I could secure the necessaries, Andre was pointing at my phone and making "show me" gestures.

Shower postponed, I scrolled through my photos to the ones of the happy, athletic girl in the picture on the bathroom wall. I clicked on the first one and passed my phone to Andre.

He studied the picture, covered the receiver, and said, "Why didn't you show me this last night?"

Dark thoughts involving divorce or domestic violence bubbled to the surface as I turned to my dresser and pulled out a handful of black lacy items. When I turned back, he was still waiting for an answer. A tenacious follow.

"It was such a long shot," I said. "And I did send them. To you and to Roland. When you didn't say anything, I figured you thought the pictures didn't matter. Besides, I didn't want to spoil the little time we had together."

His cop's face said that wasn't satisfactory.

"They're fifteen years old, Andre. I did find out who took them. I called the photographer and left a message. His recording said he was out of the country."

"I'll need his number. This could be important," he said.

Although nothing had been mentioned about Randy and last night, I was getting the impression, from the importance he was putting on these photos, that he didn't think Randy was the killer. I wasn't so sure. While the sense I'd gotten from Ginger was that Randy wasn't dangerous, last night he'd exhibited a serious propensity for violence. I also thought I'd brought Andre and Roland a heck of lot of information, when I wasn't even a detective, and he should stop looking at me like I was a rather dim civilian.

I stumped out to the living room to get my notebook, wrote down the photographer's name and contact information, and gave it to Andre. Then I gathered up my dainties and headed for the shower. Once again postponing the unpleasant task of retrieving my messages. Between voicemail, texts, and e-mail, an increasingly large piece of my day is taken up with electronic communication. The upside? It's fast. The downside? People don't read attentively anymore. Send a message asking three questions and get an instant answer to one of them. Suzanne says just send three separate e-mails. It's a habit I'm slow to learn.

The hot water felt good. I thought about bagging the whole day and spending it here in the shower, where the world was sealed off by a wall of steady, comforting sound and my bruises were soothed. If anyone asked—Andre, that is—I would say I was meditating. He'd be gone soon anyway; duty was obviously calling, and despite my usual regret at his departure, today I'd almost be glad to see him go. It was fine when we were each busy with our own work, but this time I kept getting dragged into his. I wanted a few Ginger-free hours.

I didn't get to enjoy my grouch, or my shower, for long because I wasn't very good at being selfish. Ginger would never have another delicious warm shower. Never find someone to love and trust. Never smile her cute smile. People mattered. Ginger mattered. Finding her killer mattered.

I was about to turn off the water and go face the day when the shower curtain was drawn back and Andre stepped in. "I'm sorry," he said, "for being an ass."

I smiled. "Such a nice ass."

"Better than yours," he said, "which is seven shades of blue and purple."

"Attractive only to another baboon."

"I love you no matter what color you are."

"Don't get all mushy on me, detective." But mushy implies soft and he was anything but.

"I'd like nothing better than to show you how attractive I find you," he said, "but—"

"Duty calls," I said.

"Too right. But keep thinking about that bikini. No matter how much work we've got, when this one is put to bed, we're going away. Even if it's just a long weekend."

"You've got a date," I said.

We stepped out and grabbed our towels. This bathroom was too small. I wondered for a brief second what the bathrooms were like in the house I never got to see. Big, probably. Bright and airy and modern. Maybe even with a bathtub big enough for two.

"Sorry about that photo. For not looking at it. I thought it was—"

"Unrelated?"

"Yeah. And it may still be. But it looks so much like her, and at this point, anything is worth following up."

"What about Randy?"

"I don't think he's the killer. Funny thing about him is that he's no more Randy Small than she was Ginger Stevens. His name is Robert Dorman and he's got a record for theft in Florida."

Had Ginger known or had he lied to her? And what discoveries had she made that led to their breakup? He'd been stealing from her—she'd told me that. Had she discovered he'd been stealing from other people? She couldn't tell us and he wouldn't. What items was he looking for in our house last night that were worth attacking people over? And why didn't this suggest he might have killed her?

As I stepped into my underwear, the phone rang. Andre was shaving, so I went to answer it.

"Thea. Thank goodness. I thought I'd never reach you." A pause. "It's Joel Phelps. At Stafford. We've got a situation."

CHAPTER 20

"Hold on," I said. I was not having this conversation in my underwear. It was cold in the bedroom despite the revived furnace.

"Don't hang up on me," he was saying as I put the phone on the bed. I grabbed a charcoal cashmere tunic and pulled on a pair of black jeans. The mirror said good, if slightly sinister. The look needed a statement necklace or a scarf.

I fumbled through my drawer as I picked up the phone. "Okay?"

"It's Jonetta Williamson," he said. "She says if we expel Johnny Gordon and give Alyce Crimmons a suspension, she'll make sure it gets into every newspaper in the country."

"Sounds about right," I said.

"Thea!" he exploded. "She could destroy us."

"No, Joel. If you give the admittedly guiltier party, a white, well-connected girl, a lesser penalty while expelling a minority boy, you're destroying yourself. Never mind going against the vote of the board and ignoring something everyone agreed on as the best solution. What are you thinking? Do you want to make Stafford Academy look like a retro bastion of white elitist stupidity?"

"Excuse me?" he said.

"Let me reword that: Are you trying to destroy the school's excellent reputation by doing something outrageously stupid and unfair to appease one set of powerful parents?"

"I was hoping you could talk to her."

"Talk to whom?"

"Jonetta."

"And say what? That I agree with her? That you're ignoring all of my advice? That I think you're being arrogant and pigheaded and making a huge mistake that will result in long-term damage for the school?"

I realized that I hadn't called Charlotte Ainsley. "Have you shared your new plan with Mrs. Ainsley? Does she agree?"

"I didn't think I—"

"You can stop at 'I didn't think,' Joel. Now calm down, think this through carefully, and if you are sure you want to proceed with the scenario Reeve outlined to me last night, then you have to share that with her and be certain that she and the trustees are on board."

I gave that a chance to penetrate, and added, "and, as I'm sure Reeve has told you, you may not represent that this change of strategy has EDGE's approval. In fact, you must tell Mrs. Ainsley and the Board that we objected to the change and have made it clear that we will terminate our connection with Stafford Academy if you go forward with your new proposal."

"You're kidding," he said.

It's useless trying to talk with someone who refuses to listen, as his last remark made clear. Yesterday he'd treated me like crap. Today he calls for help and he still won't listen. I was wasting my time. I disconnected. Maybe he'd get the message. Maybe he'd think it was a dropped call. I moved on to the rest of my messages, taking the time to listen through Reeve's increasingly anxious calls in case at any point he'd said anything I needed to be concerned about. Nothing.

By the time I'd made my way through those, Andre was dressed and tying his shoes. There were three discarded shirts on the bed beside him. "I need shirts," he said. "And socks. And new shoes. And pants."

Being a cop can be hard on a guy's wardrobe. And we both hate to shop.

My own wardrobe was pretty shabby as well. It looked like it was time to call up some catalog sites and do some hefty ordering. Not that that worked very well. At 5'11" with a full chest and long legs, clothes never fit me. Ordering clothes for Andre works better. A man can buy something and it fits. Many times I've longed for clothes sized by chest width, inseam, and sleeve length.

"I'll take care of it," I said. I could have told him to do it himself, but then it would never get done. Besides, it didn't take long. If I left it to him, the results might be disastrous. I liked my husband to look good. He might be a brilliant interviewer and able to read crime scenes in a single bound, but he wasn't especially good at knowing what size he was or what looked good on him. And he was impatient, an attribute that had once resulted in him ordering three pink shirts. Tough guy detectives do NOT wear pink shirts.

Ah. Domestic bliss.

Having given domestic bliss its moment, I went back to my phone as Andre clattered away down the stairs. A moment later, his engine roared to life and he crunched away down the drive. I'd never learned what happened last night with evil Randy, never mind where Andre was headed off to now. We needed a vacation if only to have some time to talk. Last night, we'd been too tired for talk. I wasn't complaining, though. We'd found the energy for some nonverbal communication.

I decided I could go to work in jeans, and added a beautiful black, white, and gray ombre scarf to pull the ensemble together. Over coffee and a bowl of the kind of too healthy cereal that takes energy to chew, I went back to my phone and scrolled through the rest of the messages. Nothing but bad news. Lisa needed an hour of my time.

Bobby needed to review our strategy for the school that was still withholding their data. Did we move on to another client? Suzanne needed a sit-down to strategize for the next few weeks. Two client schools needed me to walk them through some problems.

My doctor, dentist, and eye doctor all wanted to remind me that I was overdue for yearly exams.

Jonetta wanted to talk.

My mother wanted to talk. My mother still wanted to talk. My father wanted to know why I wasn't returning my mother's calls, didn't I know I was upsetting her? And prize-winning mixed blessing of the day, my brother Michael's hateful wife Sonia was pregnant. Maybe I would finally be off the reproductive hook. Instead, I would be forced to wonder how to be a good aunt to the little devil spawn. Not the kid's fault. I knew that. There was nature as well as nurture. But my brother's form of nurture? Ghastly. And what if the poor little thing also inherited their natures? I had a brief image of my sister-in-law Sonia pregnant. She's one of those affirmatively skinny women—the kind who starve their poor bodies into submission—and she'd look a lot like a vertical snake that had swallowed a rat.

Yes. I was being unkind. My family, bless their collective souls, brings that out in me. All I can say, in the words of a defiant child, is: they started it.

I quickly moved on to things I could deal with. It was too early to call Suzanne but early enough to be blissfully quiet at the office, my favorite time to get some work done.

I zipped my feet into my warm, lined boots, something else I was tossing on the equinoxial fire along with my tired winter jacket and some sweaters I'd seen way too much of, grabbed briefcase and keys, and headed out into the still dark morning. I didn't know of any bad guys who might be lurking, but life has made me wary. I paused on the step to survey the driveway and yard—the stop, look, and listen carried forward from childhood—and checked the backseat and underneath the car before I got in. Better safe than sorry. I was too well acquainted with sorry.

Enroute, I began to make my list of things to do, struggling to push back images of a warm sand beach, drinks with little umbrellas, and having no to-do lists beyond making the choice between paddle boarding in turquoise water or having a hot stones massage. More like a to-enjoy list. At the top, not of the to-enjoy but the to-do list, as soon as it was a civilized hour to make phone calls, was Charlotte Ainsley. I couldn't really deep six Stafford Academy without doing her the courtesy of making sure she was on board with Joel's program. Farther down, after connecting with Bobby and Lisa and Suzanne, was Andre's wardrobe.

The car still smelled of spilled coffee and the faint remnants of burning that drew me, inevitably, back to Ginger. When I pulled in at my favorite coffee place to grab a coffee and one of their fabulous glorious morning muffins, I pulled up that photograph again and stared at it. Then I dug in my briefcase and pulled out the listing sheet with Ginger's card clipped to it. I held the card next to the phone and looked from one to the other. Even though the photos were small and not high quality, the one from Stafford seemed so much like the one from her business card. I stared at them, wishing she had a mole or a scar or something else indelible. Was I seeing too much in a straight nose, crooked tooth, and freckles?

I figured that by now the photographer had been inundated by messages from Andre and Roland, but I texted him anyway, reminding him of my call and asking if he remembered the girl's name and anything about her. Looking at the young, happy face depressed me so much I had to go back inside for a second muffin.

I turned my phone off for the rest of the drive, treating myself to some silence before the day's craziness began. I didn't even turn on music, just listened to the thump and swish of my tires on the wet pavement.

My desk, as usual, was piled with message slips and things that needed my attention. I worked my way through them, moving from right to left, assessing and assigning.

Gradually, the room filled up around me, people murmuring soft greetings as they headed for their own desks. By the time I'd reached the bottom of the stack, the staff was in and it was a decent hour to make a call to Mrs. Ainsley.

There was just one more thing in that pile. The package from my mother, something she'd mentioned in one of those unreturned calls. A sweater she said was perfect for me. She might be aggravating in most ways, but when she decided to buy me clothing, she was right on the money. Those random packages were her way of admitting something she couldn't come out and say—that she knew she was difficult and we had trouble getting along, but she loved me and wanted me to be happy.

I decided to postpone it until after a visit to the restroom. If my mother had come through as usual, it would be a bright spot in my frazzled day. When I got back to my desk, as if the independent school universe knew I wanted a break from thoughts of Ginger, there was a missed call and a voice mail and Brianna hovering, waiting to tell me that the Blackwell School had a major emergency and they needed me right now. "I'll get back to you, I promise," I told the package, and reached for the phone.

I called the head of school, Patricia Gorham, for the details. Their bad situation involved a longtime, and beloved, faculty member, Dr. Charles Harrington, who had been discovered to have child pornography on his computer. So far, dispersal of the news had been controlled, but once other parents heard about the situation, there would be an uproar. This kind of case topped headlines for weeks, even when there wasn't any news. Fox in the chicken house. Beloved professor is secret predator!

Trish had done the right thing—the man had been immediately fired and he'd been moved out of campus housing within hours of the discovery. But now the trustees wanted a big, tough, trouble-shooter—that would be me—to parachute in and make everything nice again. It was not a situation that could be made nice.

EDGE Consulting specialized in private school issues, and increasingly in public relations emergencies. In a media-obsessed world, damage control couldn't wait. Blackwell's porno-collecting professor was a situation we'd seen before. We'd seen it before because—no surprise—the same people who are attracted to child pornography often situate themselves in jobs that serve children. That didn't make it any less awful for those in charge, but at least it meant I would know what I was doing when I got there.

We were starting off on a good footing. Trish Gorham hadn't dithered about what to do or whether she had to protect her employee's rights, as sometimes happened. She'd correctly chosen to protect her students and acted promptly and decisively to move the man out of campus housing.

The school was an hour and half away. I was hoping I'd be able to get there, get damage control underway, and still drive home tonight. But just in case, I needed to know where there were hotels nearby. I'd leave the logistics to Magda, who loved us all like we were her children and looked after our welfare accordingly. She'd have a list compiled and sent to my phone before I was done here. Brianna was too new, and too timid, to rely on for something like this. And Magda knew what I liked.

I told Trish I would be on my way soon, and started running the list of issues she needed to be aware of. Trish was one of those women who was so competent she scared me. So competent I tried to talk her out of hiring us. She beat me to the punch.

"I know what you're going to say, Thea. That I…that we…don't need you. But we do. I want you to handle the PR issues, shaping what we say to the parents and the press, so I can focus on working with local law enforcement and making sure my kids feel safe."

There was a pause, and then, with deep regret in her voice, "Make sure my kids *are* safe. Were safe. That he hasn't been…"

She took a deep breath. Too often, these discoveries were about someone deeply embedded in the community. Someone people have trusted and had faith in, even loved. It was a tremendous blow when that trust and faith were betrayed, when friends and colleagues were torn between loyalty and what had to be done. It was the kind of betrayal that made people question themselves and their judgment, which made it harder to respond quickly and effectively.

"This is such a shock. I am not naïve. No one could accuse me of it. But I never saw this coming."

"No one does, Trish. People like Dr. Harrington are good at what they do. They present a credible, decent public face. Become members of the community. They're often brilliant manipulators who assess situations and make connections precisely so they can do this without getting caught. What we hope is that he is only a viewer and a collector and not someone who makes and shares his own pornography."

Did it sound like I didn't think viewing and sharing was so bad? What I really thought was that by doing viewing and sharing they victimized the victims over again and created the market for the sick people who produced the stuff.

"Oh, God, Thea. I hope not."

We both hoped not. The situation was already bad; it would be far worse if any of her students were victims. I had to get on the road, but I decided to collect a few more facts before I let her go. "How did you find out?" I asked.

"He called our tech services people because his computer had a virus. Can you believe it? All those disgusting images and he asks someone to look at his computer?"

"Encryption," I said. "They think they're too clever to get caught. They think no one will find the stuff. The longer they get away with it, the more sure they become that they're bulletproof. And they never think that their dirty pictures might bring viruses along. Except…" I hesitated, thinking of one case we'd had. "Except sometimes they feel guilty and want to be caught. To be stopped."

"I don't think that's the case here," she said. "I doubt guilt is in Harrington's vocabulary."

The clock was ticking and there were things I had to tie up here. "I've got to go, Trish. I'll call when I'm on the road."

"Wait," she said. "There's one more thing. One more problem. The tech who went to help him and found the stuff? It was a student. They do that for each other. Students who have computer expertise will acts as techs for the others. We've got…we've got technical people on staff. But none of them were available, so we sent a student. We never thought…It was a student who discovered the images. A sharp, competent boy who spotted those images and said he'd need to take the computer with him to work on it. He got it out of there before Dr. Harrington could object, and brought it straight to me."

CHAPTER 21

A student had found those pornographic images. She was right. That made it much worse. "I'm on my way," I said, grudging the time I'd have to spend on the road, the way I'd get farther behind on everything else. But this was why people called us.

I shoved some papers into my briefcase and grabbed a fresh pad of paper. Stopped at Bobby's desk and then Lisa's and arranged times to call them when I was underway, my rush toward the door impeded by one thing after another. I called Suzanne, explained our emergency, and told her I'd call her back as soon as I could. All the while, Trish's emergency loomed large as I ran the list of things that needed to be done, hoping she stayed on top of things until I could get there.

As I rushed back to grab one more thing, I spotted the thick plastic LL Bean envelope still waiting on my desk. I might as well bring it along. Anything new was better than the stuff in my suitcase. I shoved it in my bag. Once it was on my back seat, covered by my coat, I totally forgot it.

Today the roads were mercifully clear of both ice and traffic. As soon as I was on the highway, I called Charlotte Ainsley. Joel had not been in touch with her.

With a slight sense of the kid tattling to the teacher, I told her about my conversations with Reeve last night and with Joel this morning and the fallout I predicted. "I don't know what actions they have taken, or plan to take. All I know is when I spoke with Joel this morning, he still seemed to be intent on his plan to give them different punishments and ignore the idea of on-campus suspension, despite my warning about the public relations nightmare that will result."

I waited for her response, got none, and continued, "I made it clear that if he goes ahead, against our advice, Stafford Academy cannot represent that EDGE consulting was involved in this decision. I told him, and now I'm telling you, that we will have to terminate our relationship with the school."

Again, I waited for her response. Again there was none. Her silence went on so long I wondered if this was a dropped call and I'd been talking to the air instead of to her, but when I said, "Mrs. Ainsley, are you there?" she made an affirmative noise. But only a noise. I had no idea what I was dealing with. Maybe the Crimmonses and their lawyers had gotten to her, too. Maybe all my work had gone to waste. Maybe they really did think they could outgun Jonetta and ignore a rash of negative press.

Financially, of course, they could. But Jonetta had powerful people in her camp, and knew a thing or two about using the media. I hadn't been engaging in hyperbole when I told Joel he was taking a huge risk.

I steered around a small car poking along in the passing lane, the driver talking on her cell phone, laughing and gesticulating wildly with the hand that wasn't holding the phone. She had no hands on the wheel. I was on the phone, but I was paying attention and had both hands on the wheel. Someday I'm going to have a car with a lightbar that spells out messages, like: DRIVE MUCH? or HANG UP AND DRIVE. It will also have a harpoon mounted on the hood, which Andre has named the

"Carpoon," to spear errant drivers. Someday I'm really going to break loose. Andre might say that I already have.

Still nothing from Mrs. Ainsley. Her silence unnerved me. What was I missing? Was I making some big mistake here? Maybe Suzanne would have some insight. Outside of work, my life was full of murder and death. I really needed work to go smoothly. No guns, no bodies, no violence, just using my expertise to help clients in difficult situations. I was no Pollyanna. I just needed some arena where things went right.

"Mrs. Ainsley?"

Nothing. Maybe she'd put down the phone and gone to get a medicinal sherry. Or someone was holding her at gunpoint. If so, that was not my department. Been there. Done that. Not doing it again.

I gave up. "I have to go," I said. "Please let me know what you and the Stafford Board decide." I disconnected. The second person I'd hung up on today. To ward off the wave of self-doubt that was threatening to drown me, I quickly moved on to other business.

Getting back to Bobby, Lisa, and Suzanne kept me on the phone the rest of the trip. Like I've said, the car has simply become another office. Bobby and Lisa's problems took some time, but they were things we all knew how to deal with, we just needed a strategy. In the midst of my conversation with Lisa, a thought hit me. That was how things were happening lately—I'd be doing my job and suddenly something about Ginger would surface. This time it was what Randy had said when we were circling each other down in the basement. That Ginger had given me something, his "stuff" or whatever he'd called it, and he wanted it back. What if that package wasn't a sea green cashmere sweater at all, but despite the packaging saying LL Bean it was something from Ginger?

I pushed the thought aside. I didn't have time right now. I kept driving and I kept making phone calls. The list of things Suzanne and I need to discuss was long. I saved

Charlotte Ainsley and the Stafford situation for last. When I described my latest interactions with Joel and Mrs. Ainsley, Suzanne fell into a silence that mimicked theirs.

My anxiety cranked up a few more levels.

Finally she said, "I know what you're thinking. That somehow you've blown it. That you're missing something. You aren't." A pause, and then she said, "We keep seeing this. Client schools thinking their actions don't have real world implications. People lulled into complacency by the insular nature of campus life, forgetting that we live in a world of instant communication, media scrutiny, and greater accountability. Ten years ago, a school could be arbitrary. They could sweep things under the carpet, kowtow to important alums and high-powered parents, and that was just the way it was. They still can and still do. But increasingly, it can have bottom-line repercussions. It's not just the parents who have opinions and politics. The students do and social media gives them a forum."

"Yes, but how—"

She sighed. "I know. All we can do is make them aware of the risks. Give them our best advice. After that, it's up to them."

"But Charlotte seemed—" Or didn't seem. Charlotte had been eerily silent.

"She may still do the right thing. Or there may be so much money on the table that she won't. Or she may at least have the good sense to make sure they give Johnny and Alyce the same penalties, which will get Jonetta off her back."

"But not be good for the students or the school."

"Good for the bottom line," she corrected, "bad for character building, student body morale, or, ultimately, the school's reputation. In the end, it's not our problem. As long as we've documented that we gave good advice, and made clear that they can't use our reputation to justify irresponsible actions, we just send a bill and move on."

She was so much better at this. She was tiny. Looked delicate. And was currently bed-ridden and as big around as she was high. But she was better at the business side while I was good at delivering the tough advice in person. One reason we made good partners.

"We can't win them all, Thea. Nobody can."

True, if not much comfort.

I didn't stop for a coffee, or to check my messages, or for anything else. In a remarkably short time, probably because I drove like fiends were chasing me, I was at the rest stop just before my exit. As though a heavy foot on the pedal could exorcise my demons or make my clients rational. I decided to get a coffee and give myself a biobreak. Once I got to Blackwell, there might not be time for either one.

When I grabbed my coat off the back seat, the mystery package sat there like an unspoken reproach. I might as well open it. I assumed it was the sweater from my mother, but what Randy had said last night nagged at me. What if it contained the stuff he was looking for? Things that Ginger had sent me for safekeeping? There could be something Andre needed. A confessional letter. Birth certificate. There could be stolen jewels or Randy's pet rock. If I ignored it, it would become another distraction. I didn't need more distractions. The rebellious crew at Stafford was more than enough.

Tossing down my coat and grabbing the package, I got back in the car and started working the tape loose. First carefully, then, as the tape resisted, I gave up and tore my way in. Inside was a box sealed with tape.

I hesitated. This wasn't how my mother usually wrapped things, nor like merchandise from Bean. What if it wasn't from her? What if there was something dangerous in here? A snake? A poisonous spider? What if it was a bomb, set to go off when I lifted the lid? I couldn't think of anyone who might do that, but I have tangled with some serious bad guys. What if this was an example of the saying: Revenge is a dish best served cold?

Time pressed on me like lead. I was too far away now to call Andre and tell him to come and deal with it. I didn't have time for dithering. I either had to take a chance and open it, or put it down, grab that coffee, and get myself to Blackwell.

I knew of no mechanism for making this decision. I closed my eyes, resorting to purely brilliant decision-making—childhood's eenie meenie miney moe.

I opened the box.

CHAPTER 22

Not a sweater. There were three zippered plastic bags inside, nestled in white tissue paper. The first held only one thing—a small gold locket that looked antique, on a delicate, intricate chain. I found the clasp and opened it. A picture of a young Ginger, about the age of the girl in the Stafford photo, and a picture of a toddler girl with her hair in pigtails with pink bows. Had Ginger had a sister? A child?

With shaky hands, I took out the second bag, heavy when I lifted it. It held jewelry. I'm no expert, I don't care much about jewelry beyond the gold band on my left hand, but it looked like expensive stuff to me. Like real gold and real stones. Some pretty big stones. Was this what Ginger had over her ex that he'd been looking for last night? Randy had been a thief in Florida, though I doubted Ginger had known that then. Was it possible he'd continued doing that here, possibly even been a thief who had used her realtor's card, opened lockboxes, and stolen from her real estate clients? That would certainly explain her sadness and sense of betrayal.

I fished around in the tissue and brought out the third bag. Photographs. Hoping this might be the clue Andre and Roland needed to finally track down Ginger's identity, I pulled them out, holding them carefully by the edges. There were five of them. Three were blurred pictures of a man. Dark haired, tall and thin, looking about Ginger's age. Hard to make out anything distinctive. He was standing beside a vehicle and staring fixedly at something. I couldn't tell anything about the color or make of the vehicle. Maybe the police had some experts who could. He didn't appear aware that his picture was being taken.

The fourth was a woman, again too blurred to tell much about her. Longish dark hair, jeans and a turtleneck and a winter coat. She looked a little like the man in the way that thin, dark, sharp-featured people might look alike from a distance. The fifth was so blurry I couldn't make anything out at first. Gradually, as I stared at it, I realized it was a license plate. Maine. Only the first three numbers and letters visible. 4X7. I checked the backs. Nothing on the plate or the woman's picture. On one of the ones of the man, a name. Very faint and in pencil. I thought it was Jordie. Finally, something useful for Andre. With a name and license plate, he might locate this man and find out who Ginger was, why she had taken these pictures, and why she had sent them to me.

It was something Andre needed to see. He'd want this stuff right away and I'd foolishly brought it with me. Carefully, I slid them back into the box, then the envelope. When had she mailed this? I checked the postmark. It had been mailed the day she died. Maybe it had been in her office and someone had mailed it for her. Or she'd stopped at the post office on her way to our showing. Randy had called me a detective, but that hadn't made any sense. Maybe I was supposed to give these to Andre? She had known he was a detective. Why wasn't there a note? Maybe she'd just sent the stuff to keep it safe, intending to tell me about it when we met. But then, why not just give it to me? Had she had some premonition?

Too damned many whys and the only person who had the answers was dead. So much better if I'd just left the package on my desk and called Andre to come and pick it up. If I hadn't been expecting a sweater. Didn't there have to be a note? I pulled out the white tissue wrappings and shook them. Nothing on the envelope. Then I inspected the box. Scrawled on it, in pencil so faint I'd missed it before: *Here are the things I told you about.*

She must have planned to tell me at the showing and never got the chance.

I needed to call Andre now and tell him what I had. He'd be furious that I'd brought this package with me. When he's nose-down and following a scent, he isn't easily distracted by reasoning. My reasoning. He'd think I somehow should have known. Or that I should have opened the damned package before I left.

The clock was running. Trish was waiting. I put everything back in the envelope and put it on the floor in the backseat, covering it with an umbrella and an old raincoat. I'd decided that my next car would have a trunk, which this Jeep did not. Then I ran inside, used the restroom, skipped the coffee because the line was too long, and hit the road, dialing Andre as soon as I hit the highway.

I got voicemail, as usual, and left a brief message about the package and asked him to call. Five minutes later, he called me back, far from being all sweetness and light. His opening words set the tone. "You did what? You took the package with you? Have you lost your mind?"

The rest of the conversation consisted of a few stammering responses from me, beginning with "I thought it was from my mother," and a shower of abuse and fury from him.

"I've been busy. I wasn't thinking about..." was met with "This is a goddamned murder investigation, Thea. Why weren't you thinking?"

"But there was no return address," met with cold silence.

It was the worst fight we'd ever had. Except it could hardly be called a fight when I never had a chance to share my side. We'd argued before, but it had been face-to-face. He'd walked out. Left me. We'd broken up because he thought I was too pigheaded and he couldn't stand that he couldn't protect me from danger. This was different. I got accused of "interfering with a critical police investigation" and being "too stupid to be allowed out."

Only years of dealing with abusive clients kept me able to drive under such a barrage. In the end, it was so painful I hung up on him. Hanging up was fast becoming my new MO for everything. I ignored the tears streaming down my face—just another thing I'd deal with when I reached my destination.

Eight minutes later, still stinging from Andre's angry words, I was turning into the school gates and contemplating divorce for the second time in twenty-four hours. If I was husbandless as well as childless, I could get so much more done.

I wanted to confront my husband and remind him of our different realities. Instead, I shoved Ginger and my marital dilemma into one of those lockboxes Andre had taught me about and slammed it shut. Even though I wanted to brood and sulk and beat on things with my fists, I needed to be present and effective for my client. I blotted my tears with a tissue, took a few deep breaths, and went to deal with someone else's problems.

There are ways in which all New England boarding schools are alike—there will be the clusters of bikes and sporting gear, a lot of Abercrombie and J. Crew, and this year, when we had endured the winter from hell, along with the shuffling awkwardness of Uggs and a thicket of plaid shirts, there was a renaissance of Bean boots. There will be noisy knots of students and then the outliers and the plugged-in walking alone. And all are distinctly different. Some have a red-brick solidity, like Stafford Academy. Some campuses are more modern, with architectural touches and more stone and wood. Some are a mix. Blackwell leaned heavily toward the Victorian.

I knew that the original buildings had been a private mental facility, a cluster of eight massive white buildings that looked more like overblown houses for enormous

Victorian families than institutional structures. They had been built by a successful businessman with a mentally ill son who had believed that people with mental illnesses—the insane, back in his day—might recover their faculties more readily if they were housed somewhere that looked like home. When the experiment had failed to produce the hoped-for results, and the fashion in mental health treatment had moved on to big state institutions, one of Mr. Blackwell's enterprising and educationally progressive heirs had had the idea of a boarding school, and the buildings had been the beginning of The Blackwell School.

The campus center looked like a small New England town, with houses set in broad lawns and a circular drive that ran around a common. The common had a gazebo at one end, and a walking path dotted with benches than ran around a small lake. In better weather, the lake was blue and hosted ducks and students playing around in tubby wooden rowboats. When winter weather permitted, it was a skating pond. Now, in the shoulder season of March, it was a bowl of unfriendly gray mush.

At the far end of the common, a house that had sprouted two immense wings served as the administration offices and a few larger classrooms. The more modern classroom buildings housing the science labs, the infirmary, the music studios, and a wonderful gym facility were tucked away in the woods behind it. In the parking lot on the building's right, faculty and staff cars shared the space with a handful of police cars.

I wished I'd had some time on the drive to get my thoughts in order, just like I wished Ginger would stay out of my mind so I could forget Andre's anger and my wonderings about what the things in that package meant. She lingered there, though, like that wisp of hair you brush away that creeps back toward the corner of your eye.

I stuffed my phone in my purse—seeing that there were several new messages I didn't have time for—grabbed my briefcase, and hurried inside to find Trish. I'd been stuffing so many things into the briefcase it felt like it was full of lead. It was only when I grabbed my coat off the backseat that I realized I'd come here to help a client deal with a public relations nightmare wearing tight black jeans. Probably there was still something in my suitcase or in the bag I'd brought along to replenish it, though the clothes in the case, like everything else, were getting a little threadbare. I try to have clothes for any eventuality. I didn't have time to change now.

Trish's office had the same serene elegance I'd remembered—a subtle combination of feminine yet academic—but Trish, while outwardly calm, was looking frayed around the edges. She was impeccable in timeless gray Eileen Fisher, with a hand-dyed pleated silk scarf in a glorious muddle of purples and magentas that I would have mugged her for if she weren't a client. Her normally orderly desk was the only outward sign of the chaos she was feeling. Instead of a few isolated items awaiting her serial attention, it was heaped with folders and pink message slips and two half-finished cups of coffee.

We sat on comfortable mossy green loveseats flanking a gas fireplace while she filled me in in more detail. The fire was on, for which I was very grateful. The thermometer said it wasn't that cold for March, but the day had damp undertones.

"The boy who found the pictures…" I began. The flames flickered in my peripheral vision. I fought off the pictures of other flames that crowded my mind and pulled myself firmly into this room.

"Sophomore," she said. "A sweet, geeky boy. Quiet. Funny. Super responsible. Even an adult might have had trouble getting out of there with the computer without spilling the beans, but this boy—Thomas Hoover—carried it off without a hitch. I've already spoken with his parents. Tom doesn't seem the least bit upset, but his mother insists on flying in to make sure. I think he's more upset about that than about the pictures, to tell you the truth."

She ducked her head, a little embarrassed, as she said, "One of our unfortunately too typical families. Nasty divorce, both parents have new families, no real place for Tom. Up to now, my impression is that between second husband and new family, his mother's barely given her boy the time of day. Now she's becoming Momzilla."

Another duck, an acknowledgment she was being particularly frank. "Don't get me wrong. I have no problem with caring parents. Until they become overbearing—and goodness knows we're seeing plenty of that—they make our lives easier. Maybe I'm being paranoid, but I'm getting the feeling that this is more in the way of someone contemplating a lawsuit. The damage we've done to her poor Tommy, exposing him to that horrible smut. Never mind that we've got him working when he's here to study. I doubt that she'll be interested in hearing that being a tech is considered cool. That they're highly valued by the student body and students covet the job."

She smiled. "Another reason we need you."

Another parent contemplating legal action because of the risks to their poor darling, never mind that the poor darlings had affirmatively sought to put themselves in the situations that upset their mothers. I thought we ought to introduce Nina's mother to Tom's. Let them conspire together while we did what was really necessary to make their children's schools safe. What ever happened to talking about things, anyway? These days, everything seemed to go immediately to anger and blame and litigation.

I did not want to think about anger and people who had trouble talking. Instead, I was running scenarios in my mind. Making a list of questions I'd need to ask about their procedures. Wondering if there *were* problems with using students as computer techs or if her positive spin would be enough. Thinking about other parents at other schools and how difficult it could be to get them to listen.

"You want me to beat her up?"

Trish smiled. "In a genteel way. Beat her to the punch, at least. Help us be sure we've dotted our i's and crossed our t's."

"Well, you absolutely did the right thing in getting Dr. Harrington off campus immediately."

"I'm glad you agree."

There were flowers on the coffee table between us. Lilies. Normally, I love the scent of lilies. Right now, I still smelled the residual stench of burning flesh that had permeated my sinuses. Fainter now, but not gone. I'd have to ask Andre how long I'd carry Ginger's last moments with me. If we were ever speaking again. It was also on my coat—another reason I wanted to throw it on the equinoxial pyre.

I dragged my attention back to what Trish was saying.

"I'm sure his lawyer doesn't think so. But it's in the contract that we reserve the right to remove someone from campus housing without notice if there is a violation of our rules." Her eyes went to a portrait on the wall, a Blackwell alum who'd become Chief Justice of the Massachusetts Supreme Judicial Court. "Due process be damned."

"I wouldn't say that in public."

She smiled again, a little wearily this time. "I don't think you have to worry about that."

I'd had headmasters who couldn't keep their mouths shut. Others with a poor sense of self-protection. Never mind the one I dealt with yesterday whose judgment seemed to have departed entirely. I didn't think I'd have worry about that with Trish.

Belatedly, and with an embarrassed shrug of her shoulders, she asked if I'd like some coffee or tea. What I wanted was food, despite having had breakfast and a muffin. Although I miss as many meals as I eat, I am something of a stress eater. Meanwhile, I could put milk and sugar in my coffee. That would have to do.

"Thanks," I said. "I'd love some coffee."

I had had to pass a security guard to get through the gate, which meant Trish had taken my advice, and the students were being protected from having their campus swarming with reporters and news vans. We couldn't block out cell phones or social media, but she affirmed that they had sent a message to all of their students, asking them to voluntarily refrain from comments until the community could come together and be given the details of the situation. That meeting was scheduled for four p.m., when classes would be over.

"Where is the computer now?" I asked.

"The police have it."

"Personal computer or one that belongs to the school?"

"Personal."

That was good, I thought. Good in that it created more distance between the school and the errant employee. Not so good, maybe, in terms of any claims of privacy Dr. Harrington might have. But he had voluntarily given the school's tech access to the computer. In a campus residence. And presumably used the campus internet system to download his porn.

"Of course, the detective I spoke with said we may have to view the…uh…materials. To see if any of our students are involved."

"Any idea when?"

She shook her head. "When they've finished going through them, I guess." Then shook her head again, in a slow, wondering way. "We've been so careful with our hiring. Background checks. Genuine talks with people's last employers, knowing they may tell us things in confidence they wouldn't put it writing. All the things we're supposed to do. And then this! Someone who has been a respected member of the community forever. Someone nobody would ever suspect of something like this."

She had the tails of her scarf gripped firmly in her hands, holding on like they were a lifeline, endangering the fragile silk.

I tried to reassure her. "As I said on the phone, they get away with this because they're good at it. At least he's not someone you hired. And it may well be, repulsive as his behavior is, that he doesn't act on what he sees, he only watches it."

She sighed. "I know. I guess that would be some small relief. I'm worried that it might have gone farther. He's always had such a parade of students in and out of his rooms. Tutoring. Giving advice. Just generally being someone the kids…" She hesitated, "Someone the boys…were comfortable confiding in."

Another sigh. "Their age, you know. Boys gravitate toward male advisors, girls toward female, so it was never so obvious how most of his contact was with the boys. Ask me last week and I would have said he was one of our stars. His students excel. He's generous with references. Alums come back to visit him…"

"Excuse me, Dr. Gorham." It was her assistant, from the doorway. "There's that police detective on the phone."

I listened as she made an appointment to meet with him for a preliminary conversation about what the detectives had found. She looked like the conversation was causing her physical pain. When she was done, she replaced the receiver like it was too hot to handle, and came back to the couch. "Young adolescent boys," she said angrily. "That's what he has on his computer. So of course we have to get some of our longtime faculty to look at the stuff, to see if they recognize anyone. Current or former students. I just hope…"

She tortured the scarf again, then resolutely let it drop. "I could kill that man, Thea, for doing this to all of us. And if there are any of our students in those photographs…I don't know how we'll recover. Other schools…"

She didn't need to finish. We both knew how damaging a scandal could be in the competitive world of boarding schools. Image mattered so much, and parents, however neglectful they might be themselves, needed to feel that they were entrusting their children to a safe place. There had been schools that had swept things like this under the rug. Schools that had covered up for their errant faculty. That had once been the genteel thing to do. But increasingly, there was mandatory reporting and public pressure to prosecute child molesters or those who collected and traded pornography. And this was such a bad season for a scandal.

We spent the next hour working on a damage control plan. What information would be released to the press. What she would say at the all school meeting. How they would stress the fact that the instant inappropriate materials were found, the offending faculty member had been fired and removed from the campus. We debated saying that it appeared no students were involved, and decided it was too soon. Giving false reassurance would only backfire on us if we were wrong. We talked about openly dealing with their bafflement and broken trust. Dr. Harrington had been extremely popular, so the betrayal was that much worse. It was important to acknowledge that.

Together, we drafted the call script that administrators and faculty would use when they contacted the parents. That would start just as soon as the all school meeting ended. She would gather her people, give them the script and call lists, and every parent would receive a personal call.

We reviewed the importance of making sure all her faculty and staff were on message. It wasn't only what the students might say that could be damaging. A careless comment by a faculty or staff member would be jumped on by the press and would be extremely difficult to call back. I'd seen it happen. Luckily, Trish had good control of her world, and a great relationship with her staff. She'd made a habit of getting out of her office and into classes, the gyms, the dining halls, and around the grounds. As a result, she knew everyone. But also as a result, because she'd believed she really had a handle on her school and its culture, this devastating discovery made her question everything she thought she knew.

I talked. Trish made notes. My stomach grumbled. The day wore on as we reviewed the usual details of any boarding school crisis—counselors available and comfort food wherever the students like to congregate. Ensuring that the resident faculty in the dorms kept their doors open and made themselves available. Ensuring that at least one advisor was always in the dorm in case a student needed to talk. I suggested that she issue an open invitation to the students to come and see her if they had any information about Dr. Harrington, or any personal concerns. And no coffee ever appeared.

I suggested she offer the same open door policy to her faculty. Sometimes faculty members had seen or heard something—received a confidence or entertained a suspicion but hadn't come forward. It could be hard to buck the tide, especially for a newcomer or a junior faculty member, when Dr. Harrington had been such a popular teacher. Sometimes an event like this could also cast something seen or heard and discounted in a new light.

One thing that I really needed to know about was what kind of training and guidance they gave the kids who served the community as computer techs. Had they been warned about uncovering illegal things like this and given any strategies for dealing? She said she would have her tech services supervisor in to brief us about that. And she'd get me a copy of the tech's handbook.

It seemed like things were in good shape. Good enough so that it was possible I could go home tonight, though I would probably have to come back tomorrow and do some more handholding. Ideally, I would be going home to Andre, but that would depend on the status of his investigation. And our relationship—we rarely fought and never like this. But he needed that envelope even if we weren't speaking.

Before I moved on, though, I had one more question. Something about the situation wasn't ringing quite true. Trish was being straightforward and open with me, but there was a lingering hesitation. Something in her manner that seemed the teeniest bit off.

It's a risky business to challenge a client. They pay the bills. They call the shots. But one thing I've learned from my years as the girl in the white hat, the one who rides in to save people when they're in trouble—sometimes what they tell me isn't the truth, the whole truth, and nothing but the truth. Even good people hold things back to protect themselves or their institutions or don't share the small niggles and suspicions that can bloom into trouble later.

So instead of gathering up my bag and taking a break to check my messages before the school meeting, I looked into Trish's face and said, "There's something you aren't telling me, isn't there?"

While she struggled with her answer, I supplied it. "Something that should have made you suspicious and you discounted it. Because of who he was. The affection and respect people had for him. Someone tried to clue you in, or something happened to make you wonder, and you brushed it off. Am I right?"

There was a moment while I watched her struggle with whether she would tell me. Then Trish buried her head in her hands. "Oh, God. Thea. You're so right. This is all my fault."

After a few minutes, she dropped her hands and told me the story.

CHAPTER 23

It's one of the hardest things in the world, I've found, to get people to forgive themselves and see that they're only human. Trish's clues had been slight, and her source a notoriously unreliable one—a young female faculty member being sacked for incompetence. During the exit interview, the woman had argued that if she was going to be fired, certain other staff members should be, too. She'd reeled off a list, along with the reasons they should be canned. Harrington had been on that list, the allegation that he was gay.

As a precaution, Trish had looked into some of the allegations against other faculty, and when they didn't pan out, she'd never finished running the list. Being gay wasn't a firing offense, not that there had ever been any indications that Dr. Harrington *was* gay. He'd simply been seen as that staple of the private school world, the perennial bachelor devoted to school and students. There had been no other allegations or suggestions of misconduct. Now, in hindsight, Trish worried that somehow she'd failed to do her job. The rest of the world would never know this had happened unless the aggrieved former employee saw an opportunity for revenge. I told Trish that if that happened, we could get out in front of it pretty easily. As far as she knew, no one on campus had ever observed Dr. Harrington behaving improperly, and there had been nothing in his file from before her tenure to suggest others had had any suspicions.

Trish's tenure was fairly recent, so in the back of both our minds was the fear that others before her had been suspicious but had buried those concerns or not acted on them. That was the elephant in the room—was there something she hadn't been told? It happened too often—the closed community that protected its own rather than protecting the students it served. Private schools can be like small towns where everyone has an interest in protecting the community secrets. Or like the Catholic Church.

There was little we could do about that now. I knew she would sit down with some of her closest allies on the faculty and explore the question, probing into whether there were suspicions that had been ignored or allegations that had been buried. We would both hope that there would be no ugly surprises.

Something still felt unfinished, but I couldn't put my finger on it. Just a niggling worry that there was a question I hadn't asked or Trish hadn't fully answered. I reviewed our conversation and nothing popped out. Maybe it would come to me later. Or maybe I was becoming too cop-like for my own good. So cop-like that I was developing that special sense they called cop's gut. An instinct for what lay beneath. My husband would probably disagree.

Coffee arrived just as I was gathering my things to leave for the meeting, smelling delicious and accompanied by a plate of oatmeal cookies. Trish shrugged, then apologized with a rueful smile. "We're just not ourselves today."

It was an understatement that fit both our situations perfectly. I snagged two cookies and followed her out. My phone had been jumping all the time I was with Trish so I took some time to check my messages, stepping out of the building for some fresh air and privacy. I regretted the move almost immediately as that longed-for fresh air slid its chilly March fingers inside my coat and wrapped me in a damp chill.

The first message was from Charlotte Ainsley. I hesitated a moment before I played her voice mail, reluctant to add any more conflict to my day. I was at the point where I was viewing my phone as an evil messenger tasked with bringing me nothing but bad news. But, cherishing the hope that perhaps she had come to her senses and would put Stafford back on the right track, I listened.

"Thea, it's Charlotte. Charlotte Ainsley. I'm calling to apologize for my behavior earlier. Perhaps you'll understand if I say that I was so shocked by your report about Joel's behavior I was temporarily speechless."

I realized I'd been holding my breath. I resumed normal breathing as she continued.

"I'm sure the Board bears much of the responsibility for not keeping closer tabs on him or being clearer about our relationship and who has the final authority. Evidently, he thought…" She left that unfinished. "In any event, I have spoken with him and reaffirmed the Board's decision. I think we can both rest easy about that."

A hesitation. A throat clearing. I could picture her squaring her shoulders and raising her chin, taking charge of her wayward headmaster and wayward school. Charlotte Ainsley probably didn't have to apologize very often. "And I hope that you, and EDGE, will reconsider and not terminate your relationship with us. I do not believe we've seen the last of this situation and it is very useful to have your input."

I felt fifty pounds lighter as I pressed the buttons to call her back.

There were more calls—this little black rectangle was vying to become the phone that broke the consultant's back, but the meeting would be starting and Trish wanted me there. I put it back on vibrate and went inside. Charlotte Ainsley's call had confirmed that at least something in my life was working. Maybe this was how it was. Sometimes the marriage worked and some days the work worked. Except our marriage always worked. It was only because the lines had gotten so blurred and the personal had become the professional that we were in this mess. Except I didn't exactly know the parameters of this mess.

Andre was angry with me—angry being a mild term for it—for not calling him the instant I saw that package on my desk. He was cutting me no slack for being busy, or distracted, or running out the door, and thought I was a total idiot for not thinking Ginger instead of mom and sweater and help for my weary wardrobe. Maybe I was an idiot—am an idiot—for not calling him immediately and for not leaving that package on my desk, but I'm not supposed to be able to think like a cop. I have my moments. Some of it has definitely rubbed off. But I'm a consultant with clients to serve and the way my mind works is that when I'm wrapped up in my client's business, I'm not so capable of also solving mysteries. More affirmatively—I do not want to be solving mysteries.

As I was putting my phone away, I saw there was a text from Andre. "Roland is on his way to get that package."

Poor Roland. He barely gets off the flight from Florida before he's sent, like a faithful retriever, to pick up something from me.

Hot on the heels of 'poor Roland' was another thought—Andre could have come himself. What a coward.

The day was fading into gloom. Across the road, the campus pond looked like the cauldron of a black-hearted witch. Fog hung about everywhere, slithering among the rain-darkened tree trunks like it was alive. It was such a spooky scene I practically ran back to Trish's office, arriving out of breath, to find she'd already left for the meeting. I got directions from her assistant and hurried after her.

It was the usual thing—anxious students needing help processing the news about Dr. Harrington who needed to be calmed, reassured, and given information about where to go for help. Unusually, the faculty, who were supposed to be calm and supportive, were not much better. I made a quick mental note that the next thing Trish and I needed to deal with was her faculty. They needed a strong heads-up about their role and a reminder not to discuss the situation with anyone outside the school, along with acknowledgment of their own concerns and the reminder that Trish's door was always open. There were also two guys in suit coats hanging around in the back, trying to look innocuous and so obviously cops they might as well have been wearing neon signs announcing their purpose.

Trish and I were supposed to reconvene in her office after the meeting to get on to the stack of issues that still needed attention, but before I could reach the podium from my seat at the back, the two suit coats converged on her, swept her up, and the three of them disappeared. She'd taken a moment to send me a text: Gone with the detectives to look at some pictures.

My heart sank. If there *were* students involved, this would be really bad news. Nothing I could do about that. I might as well go back to her office and get some work done.

As I passed her assistant's desk, he held out an envelope. "It's a copy of our student handbook," he said. "She asked me to give it to you. And this is the training manual for the computer techs. Trish is really sorry not to be here, but says she'll be back soon. And we have coffee and sandwiches on the way."

My heart leapt up at that, but it plummeted when he added, "And Thomas's mother is supposed to be arriving from the airport any minute. Trish asked if you could handle her until the detectives are done."

So the coffee and sandwiches weren't for me. They were to pacify the upset mom.

"What's her name? His mother?"

"Adeline. Adeline Savage."

But Thomas's name wasn't Savage, which prompted another question. "And Thomas's father isn't coming?"

"I believe the parents are divorced and Mrs. Savage has remarried. There's been no mention of a husband. Or father."

Something went click in my head. "Has the father been notified?"

"I believe that he has, Ms. Kozak, but I will check on that." An important thing to check. Situations with divorced parents could get very sticky if one was in the loop and the other was not. Far too often, children became pawns in the game of revenge when a marriage went bad.

I left him shuffling through some papers, and went into Trish's office to fortify myself with coffee and a sandwich, hoping I'd have time to brush the crumbs off my front and check my teeth for green bits before my duties as nursemaid to an angry mother began. Luckily, the sandwiches were tuna. I still wasn't up for eating meat.

In the entertaining Mrs. Savage department there was a reprieve. Because of the fog, her plane was delayed and it was likely she wouldn't arrive until the following morning. I could have some fun with the idea of a savage arriving, especially given some of the parents I'd seen, but I reined in my wicked mind. I was here to help Trish with her crisis and this pause would be a good time to catch up on other business so I could focus on her issues when she returned.

My first other business was to find myself a place to stay. It was clear we weren't going to get everything done tonight, especially not with Trish having to spend time with the police. I checked my mail and found that Magda, on top of things as always, had booked me a room at a nearby inn. I could remember a time when I thought staying at inns and B&Bs was exciting. Now I just hope the bed won't be lumpy, the lamps will have bulbs that are bright enough to read by, and that there will be a desk. I also have a fondness for reliable hot water, which is sometimes hard to come by, and a decent breakfast.

I checked my texts to see if there were any updates from Andre. Something sweet like "please return to bed and board all is forgiven" would have been nice. Or even a simply "sorry." No such luck. Just a terse "Roland delayed 'til morning please snap photos of jewelry and send to me ASAP" followed about five minutes later by "and the photos." Yessiree bob, I lived but to serve. I would grumble, but I would do it, even though I knew photos of blurry photos would be next to useless.

Taking those pictures meant going out to the car. It was dark now, and I have developed a reality-based aversion to dark private school campuses. I hoped the parking lot was well lit.

Grabbing my coat, I went out. The lot was *not* well lit, and even though I had no reason to fear for my safety here, the chill and eerie fog sent little fingers of fear creeping up my neck. I hesitated on the steps and gave myself a pep talk about having nothing to fear, then bustled across the lot to where my car now sat by itself in the dark back row.

I'd left Ginger's envelope in the back. I quickly unlocked the door and reached in to unearth it from the stuff I'd piled on top of it. Behind me, in the quiet night, I heard footsteps. I froze, holding my breath, a perfect target here, bent over and illuminated by the interior lights. As the steps came closer, I stuck my hand in my pocket, feeling for my pepper spray.

"Evening, ma'am," a deep male voice said. "Everything okay here?"

Campus security. My breathing resumed as relief flowed through me. "Yes. Fine. Just grabbing something from my car."

"Have a good evening," floated back as the footsteps moved away.

I grabbed the envelope and hurried inside. What had I been expecting? That Dr. Harrington would suddenly appear out of the night, bent on revenge? But I had been expecting something. It wasn't just my experiential paranoia. It was a thread of lingering doubt about what Trish had told me. A subject we hadn't adequately explored.

When she returned from her meeting with the detectives, probing her concerns about him would be the first thing on our agenda.

CHAPTER 24

Ever the good little doobie, I dumped my coat over a chair, spread out Ginger's materials, and did my best to take useful photographs which I sent along to Andre. Maybe he'd learned something that would make their relevance clearer. He had information that Randy was a thief. Perhaps the jewelry would confirm it. Be a lever to get a confession. Maybe he'd even get some clues to Ginger's identity. I figured he could definitely do something with that partial license plate.

Even though photos might be too small to be useful, I also took pictures of the locket and the pictures of Ginger and the little girl. I thought the locket was an important clue—something that linked Ginger to an earlier time. Tomorrow, it would be in Roland's hands and the police could figure out its significance.

But I am not someone who can leave things alone. I blame it on all the people who've called on me for help, then tried to keep things hidden and unsaid. They've made me into someone who digs in and asks hard questions. I'm not so much nosy as simply doing my job. Tonight, tucked up in my room at the inn, I would take that locket apart and see if there was anything more to learn. It was probably going to destroy evidence or fingerprints or somehow make

Andre even angrier. But this was my problem, too. Ginger had sent me this stuff because she needed my help. I hadn't saved her but maybe I could still help get her justice. Andre might disagree that I had any special talents, especially now, when he was angry, but maybe there was something I would see that he might not.

I put everything back in the envelope, stuffed it in my briefcase, and started through the rest of my messages. An ominous one from Suzanne that simply said, "Call me." Two words, but they carried the weight of doom.

She answered on the first ring.

"It's Thea. What's up?"

"My doctor says bed rest is supposed to mean bed. And rest. Not doing a day's work from a horizontal position. He thinks I'm too stressed." A pause, as bedding rustled. "I am going to lose my mind."

"It's only a few weeks, Suzanne. Watch some television. Read chick lit. Get Paul to paint your toes some luscious color."

"Humbug," she said.

"What's really the matter?"

"I feel like everything is falling apart. Our clients are impossible. Lisa wants to work less. Bobby is feeling stressed and thinks he needs a vacation, though we both know that's Quinn talking, not Bobby. You *do* need a vacation and I'm about to have a baby."

"You won't believe this," I said, "but everything will work out."

"Work out how?" She was almost yelling. "Let the business tank and then we won't have to worry about all this?"

"Stafford is back on track. Bobby finally has the data to finish that report. Things are going well here at Blackwell. We can get another part-timer to take the pressure off Lisa and Bobby. And having a baby is a good thing."

"You sound like a damned Pollyanna."

Right. Because my life was all sweetness and light. I'd been in the middle of gruesome murder scene. I'd been assaulted by a bad guy and nearly hit by an ambulance and was bruised from head to toe. My husband wasn't speaking to me. I suspected my client was holding out on me and we were about to have a heavy 'tell me the whole truth' conversation, and I was having a hard time seeing silver linings myself. But Suzanne was supposed to be staying calm and I needed to help with that.

"Too true. I'm such a ridiculous optimist, as you well know. And my life has been so charmed it's hard for me to imagine that anything could ever go wrong."

There was silence on her end. Finally she said, "Sorry. I'm being an idiot, aren't it?"

"Just temporarily losing your perspective. I can't imagine bed rest."

"Neither can I. Paul threatened to borrow Andre's handcuffs and fasten me here."

It was a laugh out loud image, neat and dainty Suzanne, cuffed to her bed in her feminine pink pajamas. I didn't think she found it funny.

"I know you're doing your best," I said.

She muttered an unconvincing "Yeah."

"Let Magda do more. She'll do anything for you. You know that."

"I do. It's more a matter of control. I'm not so good at delegating."

"Who is? You don't build a business, especially one based on your own talent and credibility, by doing a lot of delegating." I hoped she was listening. "And it's only for a few weeks."

"Like you are a model of patience and self-control," she grumbled.

She had me there. "I should be done here tomorrow. I'll come back. We'll talk. We'll make a plan."

"Okay." She sounded like a sulky child, but I understood. She was sulking about the fact that her body had betrayed her right into bed and she hated it when there wasn't a way to improve a situation. Like me, Suzanne was a fixer. A control freak. The hardest thing in the world for her was a situation she couldn't manage.

"I'll call you tomorrow. Meanwhile, don't do anything to make Paul pull out those handcuffs. Think about your sweet little girl. Nuzzling her yummy downy soft newborn head. Those darling pink outfits. Her precious, perfect fingers and toes." My stomach clenched. I wanted that so badly for myself.

"I'll try."

It was all I could ask.

I moved on down through my messages, making notes as I went of what needed a prompt response and what could wait. Sent a long e-mail to Bobby. Another one to Lisa. I would have preferred conversations, but they deserved some hours of the day when they didn't have to concentrate on business, and tomorrow morning I expected to be very busy here. I sent some advice to a school that had a planning question.

The building grew silent and empty around me and Trish still hadn't reappeared. Strange, empty places at night are kind of creepy, so I immersed myself in work to stave off anxiety. I was Thea the Great and Terrible. Nothing was supposed to scare me. Not wind around the building or mysterious creaks or the fact that I was in a situation I didn't fully understand. I don't like uncertainty.

I worked my way through my email queue, mostly deleting the junk that had accumulated. Ignoring the ads that promised to find me the perfect wardrobe and shoes I needed, and the lover I didn't, as well as the delicious recipes for dinner tonight, a cruel tease for someone who doesn't have time to cook, whose last two dinners had been fast food courtesy of the Maine State Police. Why did this thing designed to help us stay connected have to be such a turnoff?

In the midst of my frenzy of deletion, I almost missed a message from Jasper Cope. It had the terseness of a text, of someone tying things up before disappearing, as his words made clear. *Thanks for yr note. Luv that pic, too. Off in an hour to Kenya. Without e-mail ten days. Girl's name Penelope. Nickname Pen or Penny. I forget her last name. JC*

I forwarded the message to Andre. Maybe he could send Roland down to Stafford to look at old yearbooks. Or go himself to have another opportunity to avoid me.

My chores done, I spent a productive half hour ordering my grouchy husband some new clothes, and wishing I didn't have to try things on. At least one of us would be decently dressed. I did get myself some new boots and a pair of rather sexy, strappy sandals. If we went on vacation, new sandals would be nice.

Just as I'd decided to quit for the night, Trish bustled in, looking like she'd been gnawed on. Spending time with the police will do that to you. Heck, even talking to *some* cops on the phone can do it.

She grabbed a sandwich and dropped into her chair. "I'm exhausted," she said. "Dealing with that detective has just about done me in."

"What did he want?"

"My soul, I think. Something I can't understand—why can't the police treat us like the well-intentioned and decent people that we are instead of likely suspects?"

I knew just how she felt, and that she wanted to vent, but what I needed right now was to be brought up to date. "Seriously."

She sighed and pushed her hair behind her ears. "Seriously? He wanted me to look at an endless succession of horrible pictures to see if I recognized anyone. The Dean of Students, who has been here for decades, a science teacher who was a close friend of the departed Dr. Harrington, and I got to spend the last two plus hours looking at things that make me want to jump in the shower and stay there for the rest of my life. And he wants us to do more of that tomorrow morning."

She took a breath. "I had no idea that people did…that there were…it's just. I mean, I don't think I'm naïve, Thea, but I don't see how anyone could take pleasure in looking at pictures like those. The very thought that Charles Harrington was sitting right here on my campus, surrounded by the students who've been entrusted to our care, and doing that, is sickening. It's…it's beyond sickening."

She'd finished her sandwich and now stared blankly at her empty plate. I gave her another sandwich and she started eating. She seemed so upset I figured I'd better walk her through this, so I asked the critical question. "Did any of you recognize current or former students in the pictures?"

Her silence went on so long I was expecting the worst. Finally she sighed and said, "No."

"But?" Because there was definitely a 'but' there. Someone had recognized something.

"But the science teacher, Ruven Lanport, did recognize one of the boys. It's from a while back. At least ten years ago. A local boy who used to play with one of Ruven's sons." She shook her head. "Never mind the students, I think Ruven is going to need some crisis counseling himself. He's devastated, thinking he unwittingly exposed the boy to this." She stared down at her clenched fists. "And wondering if there are other pictures we haven't seen. Pictures of his own son. He and Harrington were close."

Another hesitation. "There are evidently a lot more pictures that we haven't seen yet."

I was thinking about the boy Lanport had recognized. Maybe Harrington had carefully kept his predation out of his own community. Not an uncommon strategy. Prey on the locals, but not the boys at his own school. It was such a classist kind of manipulation, along with all the other things that were wrong with it. As though children who didn't belong to his exclusive circle were fair game.

"All young boys," she said. "And oh my God, Thea. The pictures."

She didn't just look stunned, she looked ill. Made physically ill by what she'd been forced to watch. She probably needed a tumbler of Scotch and a hot bath. But crises don't go on hold while the people in charge get themselves under control. Life isn't like that.

I moved on to what seemed like the most immediate issue on our agenda. "We'd better brace ourselves for Mrs. Hoover's…I mean, Mrs. Savage's arrival, which looks like it has been delayed until morning. Sometimes fog can be your friend." She almost smiled at that. "So, anticipating that her focus may be on finding a way to blame Blackwell School for trauma to her son, do you have any idea how much of this he saw before he confiscated Dr. Harrington's computer?"

"Very little," she said. "Tommy told me that he'd seen one or two pictures and observed that there were many more. He was concentrating on how he was going to get out of there with the computer, not on exploring further. He said he figured that was a job for the police. Actually…" Despite her distress, this time Trish did smile. "He was pretty proud of himself for his ruse and said he'd enjoyed playing detective."

"That's good news."

"We hope."

"He said this to the police, as well as to you?"

"He did. If this thing has any bright side, it's that Tommy, who's kind of a geeky kid, has achieved a kind of hero status on the campus. Suddenly, despite their distress about Dr. Harrington, they're noticing that having some tech savvy can be a pretty interesting thing. But…"

I sensed she was about to change the subject, but we weren't done with Tommy yet, so I walked her through my questions. Had his father also been notified? Yes. How had he reacted? With indifference. And they weren't expecting him to show up? No. Had Tommy been offered counseling? Yes, but he hadn't thought he needed it. So far, so good.

I had the manuals but hadn't looked at them yet. A job for when I got to the inn. It looked like sleep was nowhere on my horizon.

She stared out the dark window like there was something to see, absently reducing her half-eaten sandwich to a pile of crumbs. "I've tried to be so careful, Thea. I don't know what else I could have done."

More staring and silence. If I was reading her correctly, she was wrestling with something she wanted to tell me, and couldn't figure out how to say it. I gave her some space, hoping she'd reach a decision soon, share the information, the two of us could outline tomorrow's work, and we could get some sleep.

The silence went on for what felt like a very long time.

"Charles Harrington," she said. And stopped. "Dr. Harrington. His public persona is all avuncular charm and good feeling. The beloved professor who loves teaching and loves his boys. And that's not really who he is."

CHAPTER 25

Unable to keep Ginger and her secret identity out of my thoughts, I asked, "What do you mean? You mean that's not really his name?"

"It's not that. I mean the lovable, avuncular professor—that's not really his nature. When I say 'public persona' I mean the face he put on for the world. And, to some extent, for his fellow faculty. But I've had some run-ins where I've seen a very different side of him."

Yesterday she'd told me that she hadn't investigated him despite a suggestion that he needed looking into because he was such a respected and beloved faculty member. Was she now telling me something different? Was she saying she had knowledge that he posed some kind of threat to the community that she had chosen to overlook? Was this what yesterday's hesitation had really been about? Something she'd planned to hide from me, the revelation of which had been prompted by the images she'd seen? I was already wondering how we would spin it if she did know dark secrets about him.

"You're going to have to explain."

Too much time with the police again—I watched her wrestling with whether to lie. She decided, wisely, to tell the truth. "He has a violent streak. Or an anger management problem. I'm not sure how to describe it exactly. It rarely raises its head, but I've encountered it, and it was frightening."

I waited for her to explain.

She fidgeted, reducing the crumbs to finer crumbs. "The first year I was here, he was passed over for a faculty award he believed he should have gotten. He was perfectly nice and gentlemanly in public—the genial, 'it doesn't matter to me, I know I'm loved' facade—but a few days later, he found me alone in my office…late in the evening after the staff had gone home…and he let me know exactly how angry he was."

She trailed off, staring at the mess of fine crumbs on her plate.

This was going to take some prompting. "How did he let you know?"

She pointed at the dark, elegant cabinet that held the school's collection of Cantonware. "He took out one of those lovely pieces and smashed it."

She dumped the crumbs into the wastebasket and pushed the plate aside. "Did you eat something? I was gone so long…I figured you'd understand, though."

"I ate. So, he smashed it how?"

"By aiming it right at me. I ducked and it hit the wall behind me."

"And you didn't fire him on the spot? Or at least put him on leave and require anger management counseling?"

"I was new," she said, bowing her head like a chastised child, aware that her explanation was inadequate, "and he was hurt. And he was immediately profusely apologetic. He said he'd never done anything like that before. That he'd been taking some new medication and it must have had a peculiar effect on him. He seemed shocked himself. So I gave him a pass. As far as I knew, that was the only time he'd behaved like that. And then yesterday…"

Without crumbs to play with, her hands fluttered helplessly through the air.

"What happened yesterday?"

"I heard about another incident. From a rather timid female faculty member. Something that happened earlier this year. I think she was honestly afraid to come forward until he'd been removed from the campus. It was another totally out-of-control outburst of anger. She had parked in what he believed to be 'his' parking space." A pause. "Faculty don't have assigned parking spaces, but he'd somehow got it in his head that this space belonged to him. Anyway, when he confronted her and she quite reasonably declined to move her car, he picked up a rock and smashed her windshield."

The depleted look she'd worn when she returned from talking to the police had morphed into one I recognized—the one people got when someone they knew and trusted turned out to have a dark side. A stunned mixture of betrayal and disbelief. The look of someone who expected more bad news, yet hoped it was all a big mistake and yes, there really were fairies and unicorns and Santa Claus. I'd seen far too many of these looks from my clients. People naturally want to believe that others are good. That the world is a decent and safe place.

I knew it wasn't. Because EDGE parachutes in when there's a crisis, we often see how an act of kindness, like her being understanding about his violent outburst, can come back to haunt you. Even though it's necessary, it feels foreign to most people to keep defensive personnel records and document incidents like this. It's challenging to teach people not to be so trusting—that there's a difference between business and friendship, and that running a school was running a business. But when things blow up, or when a difficult employee needs to be fired, it's important to have that paper trail.

For all we knew, Harrington had had issues with the previous headmaster that he, too, had let pass. It was a question that needed to be asked. The whole issue needed to be explored, and shared with the police.

For right now, though, I thought we had to move on to the work of managing our current crisis. But when I tried to nudge Trish into action, and mentioned our to-do list, and the ticking clock, and how we ought to plan for the morning, she didn't leap into action. And she still wore the look that said there were things she wasn't telling me.

"What is it?" I said. "There's more?"

"I'm afraid so."

Again she made me wait. Waiting was not my strong suit, especially with so much on my plate. When we'd spoken earlier, I'd been confident that however bad Dr. Harrington's behavior had been, Trish had things well under control and working with this school was going to be straightforward. Now I felt a growing anxiety in the pit of my stomach as I waited for another big, bad shoe to drop.

Her fingers danced over her desktop, fiddling with papers and pens. Finally, in a voice so diminished I could barely make out her words, she said, "Yesterday, when I confronted him with what we'd found on his computer, and told him he had to pack his personal belongings and would be escorted off campus immediately, I saw that rage again. He said I had better think twice about my actions, because if I went through with it, he was going to make me, personally, and the Blackwell School, very, very sorry."

"You had security there with you?"

She nodded. "The head of security and two other officers."

That was a lot of officers. "So you were expecting trouble?"

The hesitation before answering that told me she really didn't want to admit this. "I was. But it was also the proper way to proceed. To be cautious. Take witnesses. Have enough personnel available to remove him, and his property, expeditiously. The last thing I wanted was for him to have any reason to return to the campus, like having to come back for the rest of his things. I delivered my message. Told him what had been discovered, that it was in violation of his contract with the school, and that he was forthwith to remove himself and his property and would be barred from entering the campus again. And that his laptop had been turned over to the police."

"Sounds like you were prepped by your lawyer."

She nodded.

"Did you tell the officers with you about your concerns that he might turn violent? At least tell your head of security that it was a potentially risky situation?"

She shook her head, refusing to look at me. So she'd deliberately withheld important information that might have made her staff safer. Luckily, nothing bad had happened. No sense in lecturing her now.

"Did they hear his threat?"

Another nod.

"Did you tell the police when you called them about the computer?"

"Tell them what?"

"That he could be explosively violent."

She shook her head. "I thought it was enough to get him off campus. I was only thinking about getting him gone and then managing the fallout."

"He hasn't been arrested yet, has he?"

"No."

So he wasn't gone. Not in a way that meant others were safe. That meant *she* was safe. God. I thought Trish was tough as nails and here she was acting like some apologetic nice girl who doesn't want to damage someone's ego. Who thinks if she ignores it, the bad stuff will go away. I sucked in a breath, ready to read Trish the riot act, then slowly let it out again.

Suzanne likes to remind me to treat our clients gently. "Kid gloves, Thea," is one of her common refrains. But kid gloves under these circumstances were stupid. It would be totally irresponsible for me to sit here and try to *nudge* Trish toward doing the right thing. The situation was too dangerous. Yet she didn't seem to have put two and two together and seen that danger.

"Then it's not enough," I said. "It's far from enough. You know this yourself. What you've just told me is that Dr.

Harrington is someone who indulges himself in fits of rage when he doesn't get his own way. Who smashes things and threatens people when he feels that his privileges and rights have been disrespected. And that's for a minor frustration like a parking space. He's gotten away with criminal behavior for years, believing he wouldn't get caught and now he's been caught. How do you suppose he's going to react to that?"

I waited for her response. I had enough experience with violent people to understand the danger.

Her fingers were still dancing and she had a faraway look. Either she wasn't really listening to me, or she was formulating defenses.

I raised my voice. "Trish, this situation is very serious. I can't emphasize this strongly enough—Dr. Harrington poses a major threat to you and your community. You have to tell the police about this immediately. You have the lead investigator's number, right?"

When she still didn't respond, I left my chair and leaned over her desk, right into her personal space where she couldn't ignore me. "You need to call him right now and tell him what you just told me."

Trish didn't move.

"Now, Trish. You need to do this right now."

She made shooing motions with her hands, trying to push me away. "It can wait 'til later. In the morning. I…we…have so much to do and I've already spent so much time with the police."

But I don't shoo easily. I stayed right there in her personal space where she couldn't ignore me.

"Trish. Listen to me. There's no sense in moving on to the other things we have to do if we don't deal with this. They're all damage control and image preservation. No amount of damage control regarding your present situation will do any good if he commits some violent act, especially if you knew it was possible and didn't try to prevent it. What if he hurts someone?"

She blinked like she was waking from a trance. "You really think he might?"

"After what you've just told me? I do. And if you're honest with yourself, so do you."

She sighed—deep, troubled sound from down in her chest—and located the lead detective's card. Then, with another sigh, she picked up the phone. She listened, then spoke briefly, leaving a message asking him to call her, and hung up. She looked at me guiltily. "Voicemail," she said.

"What's his number?"

"I already left…"

I grabbed the card, and dialed the number for Det. Leonard Furst on my own phone. When I got voicemail, I said, "Detective Furst, I'm calling for Patricia Gorham. She wasn't sure she'd adequately conveyed her concerns about Charles Harrington's propensity for violence. We're very worried about the possibility of an incident on campus. Please call me back at this number or Trish in her office immediately."

I disconnected and said, "Call your head of security and be sure that they're aware of the possibility of Dr. Harrington returning to the campus. Enforce in the sternest possible terms that he presents a danger to the community and make sure that whoever is controlling entrances and exits should be on the lookout for him."

She looked at me like I'd just done something obscene, when the real obscenity would be if Charles Harrington returned to this campus and carried out his threat. There were a dozen ways he could make her sorry—kill a student, kill a faculty member, kill her, start a fire, run into something or someone with his car—and, coupled with his threat, she'd just described enough incidents to make that a very real possibility. Could she honestly fail to understand the implications of what she'd just told me?

"Thea, I know that you think I don't understand what you're saying, but I'm not sure you appreciate my position. I'm trying to preserve a sense of normalcy on this campus.

To minimize the police presence. Who knows what kind of a response this might bring. Do you really think this is…"

"Necessary? It's way past necessary, Trish."

I had such a bad feeling about this. Maybe because she'd buried it. Because she'd almost 'forgotten' to tell me about it and I'd had to pry it out of her and it had taken multiple conversations to get the whole story. Maybe my unconscious was busy communicating with the psychic hotline. Or this was my version of the cop's gut, developed from being around them so much. I could be overreacting. She'd only described two instances in the three years she'd been here. Three, counting his reaction when she fired him. But all of those had occurred when Harrington's sense of honor and entitlement was offended, which being fired, escorted off campus by security, and interviewed by the police unquestionably did.

"I don't want to alarm them when we don't know…"

Didn't she get it? We wouldn't know until it was too late. People who execute vengeful acts of violence don't normally give warnings first. She'd already had her warning—from his past behavior and his own words.

"You won't alarm them, Trish. Security is their job. What else do you need to know? That's he's currently contemplating violent behavior? That he's done something? What, exactly, might you be waiting for?"

Okay. Okay. Time to rein myself in. My client was looking shell-shocked and yelling at her wouldn't help. And it was a fact that Trish and I had a lot of other stuff to get through.

I counted to twenty and took a couple of calming breaths. "I know this is hard for you. You're feeling betrayed by someone you trusted and those detectives have just put you through the wringer. Believe me, Trish, I'm not trying to make your life worse. I'm trying to make it better. I'm doing what I'm supposed to do, which is protect you and The Blackwell School. I'm anticipating potential damage and trying to head it off."

She nodded and took some calming breaths herself. I watched her resolutely push the shell-shocked look away and become the take-charge woman I admired. "I'll call security and alert them," she said.

From my listener's stance, I got the impression Trish was very surprised by her security chief's reaction. At first I thought it was because she had to talk her way past the common assumption that Harrington was a good guy and this was all a mistake. But when she hung up, she just looked at me and shook her head. "This is looking worse than I imagined. He said he'd already put the word out, anticipating something like this. I couldn't exactly ask why, since he seemed to think I already knew. But something odd is going on here. It's like there's a conspiracy regarding Harrington, some body of knowledge I'm not a party to."

Neither of us had to say it. This was very bad news. Trish's bent head looked penitent, though I didn't know yet what she had to do penance for. It looked like she didn't, either.

With her head bent, the overhead light illuminated the part in her hair. Trish had thick gray hair professionally colored with dramatic dark streaks. Today, too much gray was showing. It was time to visit her colorist.

That random thought conjured up an image of Ginger, bent down to get a house key from a lockbox. The sun shining on her head and showing me that she was indeed a redhead. I remembered thinking how odd it was for someone with lovely red hair to dye it brown, even a warm, pleasing brown. Until this moment, I'd forgotten about that. It explained the major discrepancy between the Ginger I'd known and the girl in the photograph.

My mind went zinging out of this room, where it needed to be, to one of those odd thoughts nice people shouldn't entertain. Would they be able to tell at autopsy that she was a redhead, or did I need to share this information with Roland?

Focus, Kozak. Focus. I massaged my forehead as I dragged my attention back to the here and now.

I was surprised that one of us hadn't gotten a call back from Detective Furst, but for all I knew, he was still deeply immersed in exploring Harrington's porn collection. Or interviewing witnesses. Or conferring with other detectives. Or snoring happily in his warm, comfortable bed. Or reading a story to sleepy little Fursts. It was unreasonable of me to expect him to be sitting by the phone, eager to return my call. He was gathering the necessary information to make an arrest. Perhaps he was even making the arrest. If that was the case, of course he didn't need to instantly respond to an issue regarding Harrington's potential for violence.

I hoped he *was* making that arrest. Saving us from some explosive event that would put Blackwell on the front page for all the wrong reasons. There was nothing more I could do about that. Trish and I had both been diligent about reporting the threat. I only hoped my sense of urgency was the product of too many bad guys in my own life, and not something I was reading from this room.

CHAPTER 26

I tucked my anxiety away, and the two of us went to work. I couldn't quite shake off my sense of impending disaster, though, and suggested to Trish that she contact her predecessor and see if he had had, or knew of, any disturbing encounters with Dr. Harrington.

It was late, so she decided to do that in the morning. Putting anything off seemed wrong to me, but I reminded myself, yet again, that she was the client. Delay didn't do anything for my anxiety levels.

At ten, we gave up, both too tired to work any longer. She headed for her stately home and I to my unknown inn. Crossing the parking lot, I had that uneasy feeling again, but the night was still and quiet. I reached my car without any trouble, checked the backseat and underneath, then got in and quickly locked the doors.

Would anyone, seeing this, really believe I was a consultant?

It was a quick five-minute drive, and by the time I'd tucked retrieved my luggage, and staggered inside, I could see that my fears about lumpy mattresses and forty-watt bulbs were unfounded. Magda had come through for me. The elegance of the front hall told me there would be light, and a wonderful mattress, hot water and a decent breakfast.

It was the first thing that had gone right in days, and I had to hold myself back from doing a happy dance. It would have been a pretty minimalist dance. I ached from head to toe.

A pleasant-faced woman appeared to greet me, signed me in, swiped my card, and led me up the broad stairway. When she opened the door, I almost hugged her. A perfect room right down to the welcoming gas fire and comfortable armchair, appliances for making coffee or tea and a tray of scones in case I wanted a late-night snack. The only thing missing was Andre, and right now, he would not have been a benefit.

"We don't have a minibar," she said, "but if you'd like something—a drink or a glass of wine—I can bring it. And there's wifi. You don't need a password."

I wanted half a bottle of bourbon and oblivion. I opted for tea and scones. That sandwich in Trish's office seemed very long ago. A deep bathtub in a pretty bathroom beckoned but there was something else on my agenda first. Ginger's locket. I settled in by the fire with my tea and pulled it out, delicately using the tip of a nail file to work loose the frames that held the photos. On the back of hers, faintly in pencil, *Penny 98*. And on the back of the little girl, *Babette*. That was all. No hidden key or lock of hair or secret message. I carefully replaced the photos and snapped the frames back into place, then put all of Ginger's materials back in the envelope.

Babette. Did I have enough clues yet? If I did an internet search, would *Penelope and Babette*, or *Penny and Babette*, bring me anything? Did something happen in or around 1998? Was that too long ago to locate news articles? No way to answer that question but to try.

Nothing for *Penelope and Babette*. Nothing for *Penny and Babette*. I thought of the things that Ginger's death or her fears suggested. I tried fires. I tried drownings. I tried accidents.

What had the relationship between Penny and Babette been? Not her child, I thought. Little sister? It had to have been some significant relationship for Ginger—Penny—to have had the child's photo in a locket. Even then, it seemed like an odd thing for a teenage girl to have made for herself, unless she'd been a very sentimental one. Ginger hadn't seemed sentimental, but people changed. Maybe Babette was a sibling's child to whom she had been a doting aunt? Maybe little Babette's mother had given it to her. Whatever the source, it was a strong enough connection for her to have kept it all these years. Kept it when she'd carefully sanitized the rest of her life and assumed someone else's identity.

I closed my tired eyes and tried to think of other search strategies. Without any last names, this was going to be tough. Babette was such a distinctive name. Maybe I should try searching for it by itself. If that didn't pan out, next I'd try *Penny and Stafford Academy. Penelope and Stafford Academy*. Maybe she'd been a track star or some other athletic standout.

Maybe I should give up and go to bed so I'd be fresh for my client in the morning. Let the cops handle this. They were very capable. Perhaps this was just stubborn pride on my part, and a waste of my time.

Good thinking, Kozak, I told myself. I stood and stretched. Got my nightgown and toiletries from my bag and went into the bathroom. The rush of water into the tub was a soothing promise of the delights that lay ahead. I tossed in a handful of lavender bath salts and went back to the bedroom. I took off my boots and clothes and hung up what I'd need for the morning—a creamy cowl neck cashmere sweater and a long cream and black tweed skirt. My last good outfit. The way things seemed to go with me, EDGE ought to build some kind of wardrobe replacement line item into our contracts.

I put on the plush robe from the closet and headed for the bathroom.

Turned off the water and went back and checked my phone. Nothing from Andre. My earlier calls had gone to voicemail—the electronic equivalent of he wasn't speaking to me, so I wasn't going to call him again. But I would text him with the names. Yes. He'd be angry that I'd opened the locket. So let him be angry. Angrier. As Popeye says, I yam what I yam. I had to tell him I wouldn't be home anyway, just in case, being a detective, he hadn't already deduced that.

I sent the text and headed for the bathroom. Turned back to my computer. I wasn't ready to be soothed. My mind was still jumping with possibilities. A few more searches and I'd take that bath. It wasn't just Ginger that was making me restless. Lurking behind those thoughts, like an elusive shadow, was Dr. Harrington. I was troubled that Furst hadn't called me back. That no one had. More deeply troubled, based on my own experiences with angry people, about the potential for something dreadful happening because no one was taking this seriously. It was some comfort that campus security was on top of it. I had no idea, though, how good they were.

Maybe Furst had called Trish and I didn't have anything to worry about. Maybe Harrington had been arrested. Maybe Andre wasn't calling because they were arresting Ginger's killer. Maybe while I was sitting here in a strange room obsessing in an information void, the world was being set right. Maybe pigs can fly and I'm an optimist. I went back to trying to set the world right myself.

An hour later, having found nothing, I quit. I warmed the water up, took my bath, swallowed some Advil and crawled into bed.

It should have been a wonderful night. The sheets were crisp, the mattress was soft, the room was dark and quiet—but my mind was frenzied. I probably slept less than two hours—and even that much sleep was plagued with dark, ugly dreams. So much for being fresh and rested for my client. Maybe the smell of burning was still in my lungs and sinuses, because I kept dreaming I was at a barbeque and waking up thinking the building was on fire.

Morning came much too soon. Another gloomy, foggy day. The inn's delicious breakfast temporarily pushed back the gloom, but I didn't have time to savor it. Doom and gloom flowed back around me when I checked my phone. A text from Andre. Roland would be here at ten, could I let him know where to find me. Nothing more from my loving husband. There were plenty of messages from other people, though, including one from Trish, saying she'd spoken with the last headmaster and we needed to talk. If voices were printed words ***We Need to Talk Right Away*** would be in bold italics.

Feeling more like a one-armed firefighter than my usual one-armed juggler, I threw things into my suitcase, shoved my laptop and Ginger's stuff in my briefcase, and headed back to Blackwell. I parked, took Ginger's package and shoved it under a coat, and hurried inside.

Trish was already behind her desk, in the middle of what looked like a long phone call, beautifully dressed in severe charcoal gray, looking like she was about to attend her own funeral. Before she could fill me in, the assistant head, Caswell Brigham, arrived. Cas was middle aged, middle sized and except for some rather lovely, if slightly too-long graying curls—his only sign of vanity—a man who would disappear in a crowd. He had been supervising the faculty and staff members who were contacting the parents, and wanted to give us an update.

In keeping with the seriousness of the situation, he'd abandoned his everyday corduroy jacket in favor of a severe charcoal suit and the kind of dark striped tie funeral home functionaries wore. His expression was a version of Trish's shell-shocked look. Not surprising. He'd been dealing face-to-face, or at least ear-to-ear, with parents expressing their shock and dismay, or asking their litany of questions about the implications of Harrington's behavior.

When we'd written a script for the faculty and administrators who were making the calls, we'd also given them answers to the questions we'd anticipated. But these were not people working in a call center in India, barely comprehending the language and unable to deviate from their scripts, these were people who shared the parents' concerns about the students' safety. They'd started the calls last night, gotten part way through, and stopped because, Cas said, they wanted to sit with us, get debriefed, and get some advice on how they should be answering the kinds of questions they were getting.

Some of the parents had asked to be called back with answers. Others weren't taking it well. The staff and faculty callers were seeing the whole gamut of contemporary parenting—beyond concern and thoughtful questions, there was plenty of yelling, threats to helicopter in, abuse, and unreasonable demands. The same people who tolerated indifference and imperfection in themselves had no tolerance for it in the people they'd hired to raise their children. He said some of his staff were beginning to feel like they might need to talk with a counselor themselves.

All of that was doable. I suggested we gather in the adjoining conference room as soon as everyone could be assembled and added that he should ask their head of counseling to join us. It sounded like the situation needed more professional help than I was qualified to give.

He left to do that just as Trish got off the phone. I filled her in on how things were going with Cas, shared my suggestion about counselors, and got a distracted nod. I focused on her puzzled expression. Something had happened in the call. I tried to bring myself up to date and to focus her.

"Did you hear back from Furst?"

She shook her head.

"You said you spoke with your predecessor this morning?"

She nodded.

"What did he say about Harrington?"

She rolled her eyes. "I should have had you call him. He was so damned evasive I wanted to crawl through the phone and throttle him. But there's more…"

She'd said we needed to talk right away. Now she was being evasive again. I had to find out why.

Consultants are supposed to present a calm and confident face to the world. I forced myself to be patient, despite my anxious sense of time rushing past while we dealt with everything at a painfully slow pace. I'm a 'take things in stride' type, checking whatever life throws at me off the list. Slay dragon? Check. Leap small building in a single bound? Check. Bring unruly headmaster under control while walking upside down on the ceiling? Check. Defeat bad guys without rumpling my linen? Check. I'd come into this situation in a rattled state. I tried to shove my sense of impending doom into an imaginary locker, but it wouldn't be shoved.

"And?"

"In the end, he admitted he'd had a confrontation with Harrington not too different from mine. Right down to the throwing and breaking of a valuable object. In his case, it was an antique vase."

Trish massaged her forehead like she was trying to rub away bad news.

"But he didn't warn you?"

"I felt like I was talking to my clone. He hadn't wanted to make waves. Harrington had a reasonable explanation. It didn't happen again. The whole thing."

Trish shook her head. "Before I took this job, I asked all the right questions. I specifically asked him if there were any smoldering issues, any situations—or people—I should keep an eye on. I asked straight out about the skeletons in the closet. Every place has some. He never mentioned this."

She kneaded her forehead like she was trying to kill pain or wipe away cobwebs, still talking. "It's worse," she said. "Because, when I pressed him, he admitted he also knew of other instances of Harrington's rage boiling over. He never recorded it for the files or took any other action, because, in his words, Professor Harrington was so popular with the alumni and so good at bringing in contributions, he didn't want to 'look a gift horse in the mouth.'"

She searched for something in a desk drawer. "Just little things, he said. But when I asked what he meant by that, he backpedaled like crazy. And when I reminded him that I'd specifically asked about things like this before I took the job, he said it was all in the package Cas had given me and that he had another call he had to take and hung up on me."

She gave up and slammed the drawer shut. "But I never got any package. I have no idea what he was talking about. Now I'm wondering who else knew about Harrington and why I wasn't informed. Cas? Some of our trustees? Other faculty? I feel like I'm embroiled in a conspiracy I knew nothing about, one that other people covered up until it landed on my plate. Now I've protected a man unworthy of protection and it's going to look like I did it for the same reasons everyone else did—because he helped our bottom line and no one wanted to rock the boat. Something I would never do. Thea, I am so pissed!"

She opened the drawer and slammed it again. Women like Trish—elegant, serene, authoritative—did not slam drawers. Nor did they say 'pissed.'

I fished around in my briefcase, found the Advil, and handed it across the desk. I consider it one of the basic food groups.

She shook out two, grabbed her cut glass tumbler of water, and swallowed them.

I watched as she regained control. Head up. Shoulders squared. She took a moment to put her desk in order and then picked up her phone and asked her assistant to find Cas and send him back in.

Cas had barely landed on his chair before launching into an account of the issues they were having with their calls to the parents. The parents of girls wanted to know if Harrington had targeted girls as well as boys. The parents of boys demanded to know whether there were any photos of their sons on Harrington's computer. Our carefully worded script hadn't gone into that kind of detail. We didn't have those answers yet—except, perhaps, to be able to say with some certainty that Harrington's preference ran to boys.

Trish cut him off. She hadn't called him in for that. That was next on our agenda. First, there was a mysterious package. "Before we get to that, Cas, I have some questions about Dr. Harrington. And what I am supposed to have known."

She took out a tiny recorder, ostentatiously pressed some buttons, and set it on the desk. "I'm going to record this conversation. I think it is in all of our interests to have a record of what is discussed here. I assume you don't have a problem with that?"

Professionals who read body language can tell a lot about a person without hearing a single word. I wasn't even a professional, but Cas's whole body said he knew he was screwed. Even before his first precatory words, "I don't know what you mean," Trish and I both knew that there was plenty he could tell us, and his hesitation following that declaration said he was going through an internal analysis of how much he would disclose and how likely he was to be able to get away with an abbreviated version of the truth.

He also looked from her to the little silver recorder and then to the door, like a prisoner assessing his chances of escape.

"The truth, Cas. The whole truth. Don't waste your time or mine trying to figure out the best way to cover your ass, because if I think you're lying or holding back on me, you are going to be cleaning out your desk and being escorted off this campus even faster than Charles."

Trish gave that half a beat and said, in a calm and pleasant voice, "Are we clear?"

Beads of nervous sweat were appearing on his forehead, and he fumbled out a monogrammed white handkerchief to mop them up. That done, he opted for the offensive. "Look, Trish. I don't like the way you're..."

Her voice cracked like a whip. "You don't like the way I'm doing what, Cas? Trying to save this school and all of our jobs? Trying to do my job because it looks like you and my predecessor and I don't know who else failed to do theirs? A failure that has landed this awful situation on my watch and exposed who knows how many children to harm?"

She lowered her voice until it was almost a growl. "Maybe you don't appreciate how serious this is. We are in a situation that could destroy this school. At the least, do it terrible damage. I'm trying to keep that from happening. So sure, instead of helping with that, why don't we talk about how my approach bothers you?"

"What I meant was..." He squirmed on his chair and made another attempt at belligerence. "We didn't know anything about this...uh...the pictures. And I don't see how rehashing that other..."

"It's not rehashing if I've never heard any of it, Caswell. Is it?"

He mopped again. Swallowed. Studied his hands, his feet, and the floor like they were fascinating objects he'd just discovered. Finally, grudgingly, he gave up a sentence. "We thought we had it under control."

Her body stiffened, and for a moment I thought Trish was going to come right over the desk and strangle him, but she had more class than that. She just poised her pen over a pad of paper and said, very softly and very slowly, enunciating every word, "What is *it*? Did you know Dr. Harrington collected, traded, and probably created child pornography?"

Brigham stared at her, shocked. "Of course not. Of course not! We never would have condoned anything like that. I had no idea. No one had any idea."

He flicked at some invisible lint on his pants like he could brush the awful suggestion away.

"So what is it that you *did* condone?"

Some might think it cruel to reduce a man who prides himself on his dignity to the status of a worm, but if you act like a worm, you may find yourself trying to wriggle off a hook. Trish wasn't doing this to him. He'd brought this on himself by not being honest. A lack of honesty that had contributed to this whole terrible situation. I was curious, though, about how they thought they had Harrington contained. Or even what they thought they had contained. Also who "they" were. I was on the edge of my chair, waiting to see what he would say.

"His temper. Those destructive, irrational outbursts."

"They happened often?"

"No. Well. Often enough."

"How did you think you had him contained? What steps had you taken that made you believe that Dr. Harrington would control himself?"

"We had written reports. Even a couple of videos. He was told that they had been given to you, and if there was one more outburst, he would be fired."

Trish looked at me as she said, with both astonishment and disbelief, "So that was the package I never got. The one that would have gotten him fired and off the campus long before this."

The outburst where he threw the pottery at her had been a test. He'd used a moment of pique to see if she had the goods on him. He'd called her bluff and she hadn't even known it because the responsible parties had failed to clue her in. Then, reassured, he had continued with his self-indulgent ways and his life of predation.

She turned back to Brigham. "This wasn't your call. So who knew about his outbursts? Who compiled these records?"

"Bill Dormont, of course. And Larry Delmonico. And Marianne Hazelton. Bill compiled the records with Larry's help."

The last headmaster. The head of security. And the chair of the Board of Trustees. An across-the-board betrayal. Unless they all thought Cas *had* given her the records and it was her failure to act that had led to this debacle.

"Who has these records that were supposed to be given to me, Caswell?"

His long silence was answer enough.

"But you never gave them to me?"

He shook his head.

"I need a verbal answer, for the recorder," she said, sounding like my dad the trial lawyer.

His "no" was so shaky it barely got past his lips.

"And you didn't give them to me because?"

A silence so long I felt my hair go gray and started to think about retirement homes.

"I knew you'd fire him."

CHAPTER 27

If we're lucky, there are not many moments in our lives that provoke the contemplation of justifiable homicide. Trish was having one of them right now. It's a cliché to talk about looks that can kill, but she was giving Cas one. For a moment, as his hand went to his chest and a panicked look crossed his face, I thought that's what might have been happening.

"You still have those documents?" she said.

He nodded.

"Get them. Right now. And bring them to me."

Before he reached the door, she added, "Thea, go with him and make sure he comes back."

Like an obedient sheepdog, I followed. Cas stopped a few steps down the hall and glared at me. "I'm going to the men's room. Are you going to follow me in there, too?"

"Let's get those materials first," I suggested. "Then I won't have to."

The rest of the way down to hall to his office, he slammed his feet down like a sulky kid. His behavior reinforced a thought I'd been having for a while—that before people are hired for high stress or high visibility jobs, or for jobs that require tact and grace under pressure, regardless of their excellent resumes, references, and presentation, there ought to be a stress test of some sort. In our world, that might mean navigating an obstacle course under fire, while wearing a business suit, and then having to give a coherent speech to a room full of prospective parents. I'd had numerous stress tests over the past few days and passed. Cas was having one right now and flunking.

He pulled a black duffle off the shelf in his office closet, unzipped it, and pulled out a thick padded envelope. He briefly checked the contents, then thrust it at me. "Here."

I wanted to tell him to stop acting like a child, to man up and deal. As my mother was fond of telling me, you make a mess, you clean it up. Instead I put on my friendly consultant's smile. "I think Trish wanted you to deliver this yourself."

He swung around suddenly and kicked his desk chair, barely missing my leg and sending it crashing to the floor.

"Hey! Watch yourself," I said. "That was an assault."

"No way. I never touched you!" Another bit of sulky brat behavior. It had pretty much been a whole week full of men behaving badly.

"An assault is creating the apprehension of bodily harm, Cas. Which fits your behavior perfectly. It's battery that involves the actual touching."

I considered, given the mess we were in partly because of him, doing a bit of battery myself. I did not want to dance this dance, though. I hadn't come here to teach manners or be a babysitter. My job was to deal with the here and now. Handle the mess that now existed. There was real work to be done and other people on my to-do list who were willing to pay for my time.

"Let's get those papers to Trish. Then there are people waiting in the conference room. It would be impolite to keep them waiting any longer."

I sheepdogged the sulky fellow back to Trish's office, where the envelope was offered and received. Well, not received, exactly. Trish told him to put it on the desk, but refused to touch it. I guessed she was thinking defensively.

About fingerprints. About making the case that she really didn't know about this stuff. That she had never touched that envelope. What a world we lived in.

Cas went on to the conference room. I stayed behind for a moment with Trish.

"I've called Marianne," she said. "She was shocked that Cas had never delivered the documents. She's on her way, and is calling other board members. And I have Larry coming over to fill me in on what he knows."

She lifted her phone. "I've sent the audio recording to Marianne, as well. Some small comfort, I suppose, that he admitted what he's done. But there's the matter of protecting myself, and then there's the larger matter of how, being properly informed, I could have protected the school. Firing Harrington might have been sticky, but nothing compared with the mess we're facing now. It makes me seethe to think that this all could have been prevented."

Not all of it, I thought. If Harrington had been caught some other way, the authorities would still have looked at Blackwell. "Can you send me that audio as well?" I said. Better to have copies in many places. I'd known schools that went to great lengths to sweep things under rugs. Of course, the school was really my client. But I prefer my clients to behave honestly.

"All of that is small comfort now," Trish continued. "This situation was preventable, but it wasn't prevented. We have to deal with that reality."

She waved a hand at the door that led to the adjoining conference room. "Now what are we going to do about that?"

"Sit with them. Listen to them. We've brought counseling in to help us craft some helpful replies for students and faculty. We need to remind our callers not to engage and give them some strategies for disengaging. Assure anxious parents that a letter explaining the situation more fully is coming. Overall, the consistent message has to be that you believe their children are safe. That you've taken every precaution to ensure that and are continuing to do so."

"Wish we could tell them with certainty that there are no current or former students involved."

"You can't be that definitive. Not yet. You can say that his files are being examined and there's no sign any current or former students are involved."

She walked to the window, staring out at the gloomy day. "So far. But what if something turns up?"

"Then we deal with it."

She turned toward me. "Have you ever been in a car crash?"

"Yes."

I had. More than one. They were among the things I didn't like to remember.

"Me, too. That's what this feels like. Like those long, awful moments when you're sliding toward inevitable disaster and there isn't a thing you can do about it."

Crash or no, while our car was careening toward the cliff, we had to keep steering, trying to ward off disaster. We scheduled a meeting with the director of communications and his staff for eleven. We needed a uniform message and a strategy for getting that message out to the press and the public. We also needed their help drafting the definitive message to faculty about not speaking to the press or saying anything except our agreed-upon message. Trish had sent an e-mail, but we wanted a formal sheet with bullet points spelling out the whats and whys and the rules they'd agreed to. We also wanted to keep providing updates and reassuring information to the students.

Her assistant interrupted to tell us that Mrs. Savage's plane was still delayed. Bad news for Mrs. Savage but good news for us. Thinking in bad puns, I believed we had a savage enough situation here already.

I was heading for the door when Trish's phone rang and I saw her start. Before I could ask what was wrong, my phone rang. I said, "Thea Kozak," and the gruff male voice on the other end said, "Detective Furst. You called me?"

"Yesterday," I said.

No response, so I continued, "I'm a consultant working with Dr. Gorham on damage control strategies. Yesterday, we uncovered some information about Dr. Harrington that we thought you ought to know. Specifically, about his propensity for violent outbursts when he's criticized or thwarted in some way. When he was fired, he made some threats to the school. We're concerned there may be an incident…"

Still no response.

"Dr. Gorham can explain it in more detail if you…"

"We're on our way," he said. "Be there at eleven." And that was all.

Conversing with cops. As satisfying as talking to my foot. Normally, I made Andre the exception to this statement. Today, he fell under that umbrella as well. Except we weren't conversing unless texts, mostly one-sided, were a conversation. I hoped Furst would be more responsive in person and that he would have some strategies to keep everyone safe. Better yet, I hoped he would tell us Harrington had been arrested and we could all breathe more easily.

Trish was still on the phone, probably talking to someone about the undisclosed information. I had to go to that meeting. I checked my watch. Roland would be arriving in about fifteen minutes. I texted him I would be in a meeting and asked him to let me know when he arrived. Then I wrote: "Furst on his way, here at eleven, move communications meeting?" and slipped the note onto Trish's desk.

Like Reeve Barrows at Stafford, Caswell Brigham was usually an effective assistant headmaster. Also like Reeve, this morning he was playing passive and helpless and waiting for direction. Passive and sulking. What is it with people who bring things down on themselves and then look for someone to blame? I thought the two of them could start a club, the "please don't put me on first 'cuz I'm a wuss" club, unless it was the "this isn't really my job" or the "don't blame me for screw-ups" club. They could meet in their secret clubhouse and whine about how put upon they were and let the rest of us get on about the business of the day. Or they could found a law firm—Barrows and Brigham lent itself to that—and sit around being pompous and important all day when they weren't sweeping things under carpets or singing lusty choruses of "Not my Job."

People who know me understand I don't suffer fools gladly. I try to be patient and kind, but when the situation calls for action, I'm likely to knock the ditherer off the podium and take over. What the assembled faculty and administrators needed was someone to reassure them and give them guidance. What Cas was doing—to the extent that he was doing anything at all—was getting them more upset. So I knocked him off the platform and took over the meeting. I acknowledged their dilemma. Described some strategies for handling difficult conversations, promised them a revised script and a written version of my strategies, and then drew the head of counseling into the meeting.

From the corner of my eye, I watched Cas seethe. Another attribute common to members of the club—not wanting to do the job, but resenting it when someone else did.

Lucky for all of us, the head of counseling was a gem. Though we'd given him little notice, he'd thought this through and was prepared. He was comforting, assured, and informative. He gave a quick outline of the students' dilemmas, then of the parents', and then identified some of the dilemmas the people in the room were experiencing, validating them and assuring them it was normal, expected, and okay. He was relatively new to the school—one of Trish's hires—and I watched them go from being unsure whether they could trust him to being totally in his camp.

Roland's fifteen minutes came and went, then half an hour. It worried me. Roland wasn't usually late. If something had come up, he would have let me know. Now I was worried he'd been in an accident. Or something else bad had happened. I could too easily imagine the possibilities. For a cop's wife, both phone calls and the absence of them can be bad news.

It was almost time for Furst and company to appear in Trish's office. Faculty and administrators needed to get to their classes and offices. We wrapped it up with my confirmation that they'd have revised call packets on their desks by noon. Normally, in a situation like this, I'd have Bobby or Lisa with me to help out, so I could delegate jobs like the call sheet to them. Today, I was on my own and feeling frantic about how I would get things done.

Calm down, I told myself. Take it one step at a time. Things would get done. I went back to Trish's office to check in and ask for a place where I could work.

She shook her head when I appeared. "Larry is delayed. Minor problem he had to deal with. Marianne had a flat and is waiting for roadside assistance. Furst will be here soon. I've got all these things I want to deal with and hand off and I can't get anything off my desk. I've rescheduled communications for eleven-thirty. How's your morning going?"

"About the same. Until they get here, I could use a place to work. I've got to write some things up and print them out for the team that's making phone calls."

She nodded. "There's an empty office upstairs. Andrew will show you."

We both stared at the unopened envelope, a plain brown wrapper that held so much mystery, intrigue, misjudgment, and trouble.

"I'm not touching it," she said.

Before I could reply, a man appeared in the office door.

I'd never met Charles Harrington, but the tweedy jacket and tortoise-rimmed glasses looked distinctly academic, despite his unshaven face and uncombed hair, and the unsteady gun in his hand was as good as a calling card.

CHAPTER 28

He was so focused on Trish I don't think he knew I was in the room. "You've ruined my life," he said.

She stood, gathering her authority around her like a cloak, her severe dark gray cardigan and skirt and buttoned up white blouse seeming almost like a nun's habit. "Charles. You do not want to do this. Shooting me will not make anything better and it will make your situation far worse."

"You're wrong," he said. He was using his professor's voice, large and resonant and meant to fill, and control, a room. "It can't get worse. I've lost my job. I've lost my stature. You've ruined my reputation. For twenty years…more than twenty years…I've been a part of this institution and this community. People call me Mr. Blackwell or Dr. Blackwell because I'm so well known and so closely affiliated with the school."

He gesticulated wildly with the gun, then steadied it so it was aimed at her.

Her eyes followed the gun through every swing but whatever fear she was feeling didn't show on her face.

"And now you. YOU! Some newcomer, some feminist affirmative action hire with no sense of history and connection, no respect for this institution, have the audacity to accuse me of a crime I didn't commit and suddenly I'm thrown out of my home, I'm barred from my classroom and my campus and my students...Correction. *You've* thrown me out of my home and barred me from my classroom. You! With no respect for my service or my dedication."

The more he talked, the louder he got. *Please*, I thought. *Somebody hear him and send for help.*

This was not the moment to remind him that he'd ruined his own life, never mind damaging hundreds of others—the children he'd victimized by creating a market for the vile stuff he collected. Children he'd victimized by taking and sharing their pictures. This was the moment to keep him talking, keep him from pulling the trigger, and hope that Furst and company were close. Or Larry from security. Or the missing Roland. Someone who knew how to handle situations like this.

I was so scared I had to remind myself to breathe, the downside of knowing about this man's propensity for violence. He absolutely felt entitled to harm people. I wanted to run. I was close to the door. I could probably escape before he could turn and shoot me, but I couldn't leave Trish alone with this.

If she was scared, she didn't show it. She remained calm, speaking to him in a steady, quiet voice. Affirming his connections to the school, the many students he'd taught who looked up him. The minds he'd shaped, the legacy of excellent teaching he'd created. All of that, she said, would be forever tainted if he shot someone on the campus. She went on, eerily calm, as she spoke of his love for the Blackwell School, and how he would irrevocably damage the school if he were to carry out his threat and shoot her. She kept it not about her but about the school, something he cared for. A place, as he had said, that he was so deeply linked with.

"This is not about whether you shoot me, Charles. It's about whether you shoot the headmaster of Blackwell School and how that will reverberate through the independent school community. This is about the many parents who will then view this as a dangerous place and withdraw their children. The many students who care for you who will now see you in a different light."

She leaned toward him like she was trying to draw him into the conversation, a slow, stately bending. She understood that abrupt movements might spook him. "Then your legacy won't be that you were an inspiring professor who influenced generations of Blackwell graduates. It will be that you were a selfish, vengeful man who destroyed a wonderful institution. I don't believe that's how you want to be remembered."

I was slightly behind him, standing very still, my briefcase in my hand, hoping his monofocus was so strong he wasn't aware I was there. Or didn't care. He'd come for Trish.

I couldn't get out my phone and call for help. Or turn it off. Any movement would draw his attention and might startle him into firing. I wracked my brain, trying to remember whether I'd left it on vibrate. The last thing we needed was for Roland to call or text me and my ringtone to spook Harrington into shooting us.

I listened, holding my breath, hoping for the sound of approaching footsteps. The building was so quiet it might have been deserted. No ringing phones. No bustle. No doors opened or shut. Could that unnatural silence be a sign that help was on the way? Was it wishful thinking that made me hope this meant cops were in the building and making their stealthy way toward this room?

I beamed the mental message to Trish: Keep him talking. She couldn't look at me or nod, of course, but I saw her take a breath and get ready to go on.

She almost had him. For a moment, that gun waivered, paused, and started toward the floor.

Then it came up again.

"Oh, no," he said. "Oh, no. You're not sucking me in with that legacy bullshit. This isn't about the school. This is personal. This is about you and those pathetic cowards on the Board of Trustees. About how they hired you with specific instructions to get rid of me. That's been your agenda all along. You're Marianne's hit woman. You're the toady the board was looking for when they got rid of Bill. Bill was my friend. He would never have fired me. Couldn't have. I had the goods on Bill and that affair he had. So they canned him and brought you in."

It was all about him. Pretty common with bad guys. Their actions are always okay, always justified, because the world has treated them unfairly. They are only doing what they have to do.

"Oh no," he repeated. "This community knows me. They know who I am and what I've done for them. They'll know this is about you and not about me. That you hounded me until this became inevitable. They'll understand this was a set-up. How you had that student plant incriminating evidence on my computer and then used it as an excuse to fire me."

The words got out before Trish could stop herself. "Charles, there were hundreds of images on that computer, including pictures taken years ago. Pictures that were recognized. Some of them taken when the student who checked out your computer was only six years old. No one…not me, not Marianne…not the board…set you up. You…"

She grabbed a breath to go on. I knew the next thing she said was likely to be the trigger. No matter what it was. Her last statements were a mistake, but despite the wavering gun, what she said probably didn't matter. In the end, words might give him pause, but Harrington wasn't going to be talked out of his revenge. He hadn't come here to have a dialogue. He'd come here to kill. In his mind, he needed to destroy the thing—Trish—that was questioning who he was. That was not respecting him. Trish had taken away all the things he believed he was entitled to.

The silent building stayed silent. No one appeared in the doorway and said, "Police! Drop your weapon."

The cavalry wasn't coming and we were running out of time. I swung up my briefcase, stepped forward, and slammed it into the side of Harriman's head. As he staggered sideways, I dove past him and went right over the desk, grabbing Trish and pulling her onto the floor as an explosion of bullets slammed into the desk, the chair, and the wall above us. I heard glass on a painting shatter, the antique porcelain lamp on the desk explode.

In moments of extreme stress, our minds can behave strangely. Even as I pulled Trish down and heard the bullets thudding into the wall and the desk, and felt something stab into my arm, I was hoping that after he finished with us, he wouldn't turn the gun on the cabinet full of Cantonware. The stuff was so very gorgeous.

I thought about how I might never get a chance to make things right with Andre. How silly our fighting was in the large scheme of things. Two people sulking over a misstep when they might never see each other again.

Another part of my brain—the closet accountant perhaps—was counting bullets. I thought I'd heard about a dozen shots and wondered how many he might have left. I've deliberately failed to be diligent in my firearms education. I learned to shoot because Andre wanted me to, and that turned out to be a useful skill. A lifesaving skill at one point. But I hate guns. I won't carry one. And I resist learning much about them other than the necessary information about how to make them work. I can load a magazine, put it in the gun, pull back the slide, and fire. I can't tell you how many bullets a magazine holds. Still, I counted.

I was grateful that Trish hadn't gone for a delicate, feminine desk, but had retained a massive ark of a thing, heavy wood with sturdy, file-filled drawers that had slowed or stopped the bullets he'd managed to aim at us. At least I thought it had stopped them. A person could be injured and not even notice, and something had struck my arm. This was not the time to unfold ourselves and check.

In the silence after the first barrage, Trish's breathing was so loud in my ear I couldn't hear much else. Her breath and a low keening noise. Then I heard a man's voice. Strained and full of deadly menace. "Dr. Gorham. You have ruined my life. Now I'm going to ruin yours. And I want to see your face when I do it. I want to put a bullet right between your fucking eyes."

His heavy footsteps lumbered toward the desk. Just like I'd counted bullets, I counted steps. I figured it was about twelve or thirteen steps from where he'd been standing to where we were huddled.

His threat had been to her, but I doubted that he'd spare me.

I didn't want to go without a fight.

I had no weapons.

There was nothing to grab or throw or swing.

My pepper spray was in the briefcase I'd flung at him.

I held my breath, counting. Three, four, five, six. What could I do? Just crouch here like an animal and let him shoot us? Attack him in the hope that he'd be too surprised to shoot?

There was a flurry of rushing feet and a commanding voice said, "Police, Dr. Harrington. Drop your weapon."

"I'm afraid I can't oblige you," Harrington said.

"Drop your weapon and put your hands on your head. Drop your weapon! Drop your weapon!" Loud and insistent. Filling the room.

There was an endless silence.

An explosion. A single shot.

Then a flurry of explosions. If Harrington didn't kill us, the cops coming to our rescue probably would.

Then a silence, feeling louder than the gunfire, followed by a commotion of voices.

The air had the singed scent of gunpowder. My ears were ringing. Trish was sobbing softly. I unwrapped from her, not realizing until then that I'd been protecting her with my body, and slowly pushed to my feet, pulling her up with me as I rose on shaky Gumby legs.

A uniformed policeman was crouching by Harrington's body and shaking his head. Another still had his gun out, staring at us like he thought we might be more bad guys. I figured the hard-faced man in the sports coat who filled the doorway was probably Furst.

"Please. Ask him to put that gun away," I said.

Not my voice, but one borrowed from someone smaller and more timid. The voice of a woman who's just been shot at. Who has been anticipating the impact, the pain, the end. I'm no fainter, but I could feel a swirling darkness out at the edges. Two bodies in a single week is more than the average consultant should be expected to deal with. More than I *could* deal with.

Trish just stared at Harrington's sprawled body and didn't say anything, her expression stunned.

I could hear her breathing go shallow, the way someone breathes when they're about to be sick. She was making small moaning sounds. I had to get her out of here. Get her to the bathroom and then get her into a room without a body in it. Get her a sweater and some hot tea and that wonderfully competent head of counseling in to hold her hand.

I've stared down the barrel of a gun pointed at me. It does something to the soul. You can hold yourself together while it's happening, as Trish had done, but it occupies the landscape and imbeds itself in your brain in a way that can't easily be shaken off. It will be with you for a long time. Maybe forever. It becomes the wallpaper that decorates the inside of your head.

In his foolishly dramatic death, Harrington had managed one last violent act. He'd done all the things Trish was warning him about. Confirmed his reputation as a bad person. Hurt the school. Hurt her, badly, even if she hadn't been wounded.

I figured we'd need to leave the room to them to do their crime scene stuff, and that once we left, we probably wouldn't get back in for hours. I would need my laptop and my files. Steering Trish by the arm, I took a step toward my briefcase, which was between us and the door, my belongings spilling out onto the floor. God. Harrington was still warm, blood oozing onto the carpet, and the consultant in me was already thinking about damage control strategies.

The officer with the gun swung toward me, gun still raised. A sudden, terrifying gesture. I let go of the scream that had been building since Harrington appeared in the door.

"Put the damned thing away, Bobby!" Furst barked.

Bobby.

Flipper hits the ball, ball hits the bumper, careens up the table and everything lights up. Ding! Ding! Ding!

Ginger hadn't said Bobby and she hadn't said baby. She'd said Babi. Short for Babette.

Whoever Babette was, she had something to do with Ginger's death.

CHAPTER 29

Then Furst stepped in and shut the pinball machine down. "What happened here?"

I thought it was pretty obvious. Considered my first smartass reply, "You're the detective, figure it out," and rejected it. But I wanted to get Trish out of this room, while he might have a different agenda, so I didn't want to antagonize him.

"Dr. Harrington came with a gun."

What did we used to say as kids when we played Clue? I wish to make my accusation? Dr. Harrington, with a gun, in the headmaster's office. Dear me, why had I ever wanted to be a grownup?

It wasn't easy being a functioning grownup right now. I was feeling lightheaded and holding off an earthquake of tremors that wanted to shake me like a rag doll. Trish was a couple strange shades of green and dead white and clearly about to throw up. I wished Furst would use his detecting skills and notice our condition so I didn't have to explain about our being crime victims and all.

I took a step toward the door, towing Trish with me. "I…we…We need to get out of here…Please…can we go…somewhere else?"

"Hold on," he said. "You're bleeding. Did you get shot?"

When I didn't immediately respond, he repeated his question in the slow, loud way people talk to the shell shocked.

Had I been shot? I dropped my gaze to the arm he was staring at. Not shot. Impaled. A thick sliver of wood had stabbed through the creamy cashmere and buried itself in my arm. Below it, a ribbon of red ran down to my wrist and across the back of my hand. Brilliant, shiny drops of red formed on my fingertips and dripped onto the carpet.

I looked back at him, the tears in my eyes turning him into a blur, then squeezed my eyes shut. Just a splinter, officer. A Godzilla-sized splinter. Adrenaline can keep pain at bay, and I was charged with adrenaline. Now that I'd seen it, though, it started to hurt.

"I really liked this sweater."

From the doorway, I heard Roland's voice, and then his rushing steps as he crossed to me. "Thea! What the hell! Are you okay?"

"Who the hell are you?" Furst demanded.

"Detective Roland Proffit, Maine State Police."

Roland had drawn me, and Trish, because I wasn't letting go of her, into a reassuring embrace. Two big hands patting two trembling backs.

"Maine? This isn't frigging Maine," Furst said. "What the fuck are you doing here? This is a crime scene."

"So don't keep these ladies standing around in it," Roland said. He started steering us toward the door, then paused and turned back. "Thea, is that your briefcase?" Pressed against his chest, I didn't lift my head, I just nodded.

"And the package I'm supposed to pick up?"

"Is in my car."

"Okay," he said. "I'll grab the briefcase and we'll all go some place quiet." He shifted his address to Furst. "It looks like this lady…" He meant Trish. "Needs a restroom. And fast." Over our heads, he asked, "Okay if I take these ladies out of here before one of them loses her breakfast all over your crime scene?"

In my limited experience, cops really don't like it when you're sick. Furst didn't object. Surprisingly, he didn't even object when Roland retrieved my briefcase. I figured Trish and I could get our purses later. It was my work that I needed to save right now.

Roland plunked me down in a chair in the hallway, and, still holding Trish firmly by the arm, said, "Restroom?"

She made a faint gesture toward the end of the hall and he half led, half carried her there. When the door had closed behind her, he came back to me.

"What am I going to tell your husband?"

"Nothing. We're not speaking right now."

"Thea!"

Okay. No sense in being a brat or making this harder than it already was. "The dead guy? Venerated faculty member fired for having a computer full of child porn. I guess he didn't take it very well. He decided to punish Trish for firing him and I happened to be in the room."

"He shot at her?"

"And at me, after I walloped him with my briefcase and dragged her behind her desk."

"Nobody gets into the situations you do, Thea." He shook his head. "Wallop a guy holding a gun with a briefcase? You don't know the meaning of scared."

Guess I had him fooled with my tough girl act. "Oh, I think I do, Roland. I didn't know what else to do. He was going to shoot her."

The shakes got me then. I couldn't hold them off any longer. They grabbed me and shook me like a ragdoll. Roland, who had been my rock before, didn't fail me. He dropped into the chair beside him and put his arms around me. It must have been like holding a flopping fish.

"That's it," he said. "I'm calling an ambulance."

Through trembling lips I said, "No ambulance. No hospital. I hate hospitals, Roland."

"You're bleeding and you're in shock."

What I meant as "It's just a big splinter and the shock will pass" came out as gibberish. He waited, patiently holding me, until I found my voice again. Finally I managed to say, "Tea?" and he went to find someone who could help with that.

I needed a pair of scissors so I could cut my sweater and explore the extent of my injuries. It felt like someone had pounded a stake through my arm. That was something I would deal with in a while when I didn't feel so much like a boiled noodle. I just wanted to pull the darned thing out. That was what heroes did, right? And weren't we all the heroes of our own stories? But I didn't know if that would do more damage and then I couldn't drive home. Probably I could only figure that out by going to a hospital, and hospitals are the enemy.

I huddled on my chair, annoyed with my body for letting me down and knowing I was being totally irrational. Weren't crime victims allowed to be irrational? After a while, when she didn't come back, I figured I'd better go and check on Trish. She'd left the door unlocked and I found her huddled in a corner, arms around her knees, looking forlorn.

"Roland is finding us some tea," I said, holding out my hand. The one that wasn't dripping blood. Reluctantly, she let me pull her to her feet.

"He was going to shoot me," she said. She looked dazed and was still horribly pale. With reason. She'd just been the target of a fusillade of bullets and heard her attacker say he was going to shoot her right between the eyes.

I got out my phone. "Your counseling service. What's the number?"

She told me and I called, awkward with one-handed dialing. Bryan O'Connor said he would be right over. I lowered the phone, surprised to find that simple act had taken so much effort. I hadn't bled much, as far as I could tell, but I felt like I was down a few pints. I wanted to find a dark room with an empty bed, crawl in, and pull the covers over my head. Someone else could be Thea the Great and Terrible for a change. The take charge, expert fix-it person who helped people with their emergencies.

Instead, I moved on to another one-handed dialing job. To the office. To Bobby. I didn't care what had to be put on the back burner, I needed him, or Lisa, here as soon as possible to help handle this mess. Once I'd briefed one of them, made sure things here were on the right track, I was taking myself out of service and back to the shop for repairs.

"I can't believe you did that," Trish said.

"Did what?"

"Hit him with your briefcase."

"As a device to stop him, it didn't work very well."

"Or maybe it saved my life. Our lives."

I didn't have much memory of the situation. Life changing things can happen so fast.

Roland came down the hall, followed by Trish's assistant, Andrew. Andrew stared at me, momentarily speechless. I'd been cradling my damaged arm against my body and now there was blood there, too.

"It looks much worse than it is," I said.

"I've got tea in the conference room," he said, swallowing and trying to look away. "And Larry's in there."

Head of Security. Or in this case, insecurity. But I didn't say anything. None of my flippant thoughts or remarks fit this situation. We were just grateful to be alive. Soon enough, Furst and the gun-happy Bobby would reappear and want to do interviews. We were lucky to be given some time to recover.

Following Andrew's gaze, Trish stared at the blood. She looked like she might be going to be sick again.

"Maybe you've got someone in the infirmary who could take a quick look at it?" I suggested. "Someone who could come here?"

I didn't want to leave Trish alone yet.

She nodded and looked at Andrew. "If you could?" she said. He turned, the perfect assistant, ready to do her bidding. Then he turned back. "Let's get you settled in the conference room and then I'll make that call."

An hour later, fortified by tea and scones, Trish was setting up shop in the conference room. Our purses had been retrieved from the crime scene and Furst had sent a minion to tell us to be ready, he would want to talk to us soon. The splinter from hell had been extracted and I'd been bandaged. Bobby was on his way. The Director of Communications was bringing his staff over so we could start dealing with the fallout.

I walked Roland out to my car so I could give him Ginger's package. Opening that locket and searching the internet last night felt like they had taken place years ago. Back in a time when I was still young and energetic. Now I was old and weary, uncertain how I would even summon the energy to drive myself back to Maine. Assuming I was ever done here.

I had no idea what time of day it was. Just that it was cold and gray and gloomy. I was sick of winter. Right now, I was sick of everything. I crunched across the icy parking lot with Roland at my side, ready, I knew, to grab my arm if I started to slip. The arm that wasn't injured. He's such a gentleman. He's such a hero. I love the old-fashioned guy who stands ready to serve and protect. Today I had badly needed some serving and protecting. In a perfect world, it would have been Andre. That was something to be dealt with later.

I unlocked the car and took out the envelope. "One thing," I said. "I don't know if Andre told you, or what it means, but there's a locket in here with two photos. One is Ginger, except that we now can assume her name is Penelope. The other is a little girl named Babette."

Time to share my under-the-desk epiphany. Talking about it would drag me back there. But I'd be talking about Harrington and the gun with Furst anyway. There was no way I could protect myself from bad stuff today.

"You remember, the morning Ginger was killed, that she said a few words?"

He nodded.

"I thought one of them was *Bobby*. Now, having seen the locket—a thing she kept when she otherwise completely sanitized her life—I think what she said was *Babi*, a nickname for Babette."

He had his notebook out and was writing this down. "Remind me what else she said."

"Babi. Airy. Safe. So sorry." Words that would be burned in my mind forever. As I said them, I could smell burning again. See Ginger's desperate face. What had happened in her life that had made that strong, exuberant young runner named Penelope change her name to Ginger and live so carefully all these years? If *Babi* was a name, I thought *airy* had to be a name, too. There might be something I could track down, if I did more searching. I wanted so badly to have the whole business over and done. I wanted Ginger out of my head.

"I'm heading down to Stafford now, to look at yearbooks," he said. "See if I can get a last name, maybe even something that will lead us to her family. And that, in turn, may help us locate her killer. It has to have something to do with why she changed her name."

But he didn't go. Instead, he bent down, studying me with eyes that read people for a living. "I don't want to leave you like this, Thea."

Like what? Like a consultant with too much work on her plate who just got another big helping? Someone broken and wounded and about to be at the mercy of Detective Furst? Abandoned by her horse's ass of a husband? Was I worse off than I thought? I hadn't looked in a mirror and didn't want to. For once, I kept my mouth shut. Roland had been nothing but good.

"I'll be okay. I'm tough. You need to go catch Ginger's killer."

"There's no sense in telling you this, knowing how stubborn you are, but you don't have to stick around here and keep working. You are allowed to say you can't right now, and go home. Take some time to process this. You do know that, don't you? That you aren't superwoman? That even Andre or me, in a case like this, would take some time. We're human."

I was feeling all too human. "Thanks, Roland. I know. I just need...You know me, I need to get things here under control. We both also know that until he's done his interview, there's no way Detective Furst is letting me leave. But as soon as that's done and I've briefed the guy who's taking over, I am out of here."

He nodded. He couldn't argue with that.

"So you need to get out of that bloody sweater, do whatever needs to be done here, and get yourself back home. Take a day off. Get some rest."

He patted my shoulder, his hand warm and firm, giving me his 'you'd better tell the truth' look as he asked, "Are you going to be okay to drive with that arm?"

"I've driven with worse."

He rolled his eyes.

I did not want him to go and couldn't ask him to stay. I wished Andre had come instead and yet was grateful to Roland for being himself. A true friend. A totally decent man.

"At least, thanks to you, we have something to work with," he said.

"I hope so."

"I know so. You've pretty much given us everything we've got that's useful. Now I'm going to wait while you get something clean out of the suitcase you always keep in there, and then I'm going to walk you back to the building."

"I'm not a baby, Roland."

"Nope. You're a babe, Thea. And I'm walking you back."

I fumbled in my suitcase to find something I could slip on over my damaged arm. Then I slid my good arm through his and let him escort me back to the building. I stood on doorstep, watching him walk away, then turn and wave. I hoped he couldn't see my tears. When his car was out of sight, I turned, too, and went inside.

CHAPTER 30

The rest of the day was a blur. The interview with Detective Furst, which wasn't as awful as I'd feared. Assigning Marianne to watch over Trish and getting her and the erring Cas to take on whatever they could do to help. I sat with the Communications people and drafted a press release and a message to the parents. Because of his popularity and the shocking nature of the events, we drafted a different letter to former students, briefly explaining what had happened. The phones were ringing off the hook with press, parents and people who wanted answers, but it was the best we could do. An extremely stern memo went out to faculty and staff, reiterating their responsibility to defer all comment to the Communications staff. We called another all-school meeting to explain the morning's events to the students, a faculty meeting to do the same.

The upside of being so insanely busy was that I didn't have time to think much about what had happened in Trish's office, never mind wondering what the things in that envelope might help Roland and Andre learn about Ginger. In the dark times, it's important to look for some silver linings, and being busy was definitely that. I wasn't even checking my phone, which vibrated like a forgotten pleasure device in my pocket.

By midafternoon, Bobby had arrived. I was so grateful to have help I almost threw myself into his arms and wept. Bobby would have been okay with that, but I thought it might spook him—Bobby is a tender soul—and I needed him businesslike and steady. He was already under enough pressure from his husband, Quinn, who thought he worked too hard and wasn't appreciated. Quinn refused to accept that Bobby liked to work and was valued as highly as gold at EDGE Consulting.

As I was bringing him up to speed, Trish's assistant, Andrew, appeared. "Excuse me, Ms. Kozak," he said, "but your husband is on the phone." He wore the slightly deflated look of someone who has been yelled at. Cautiously, as though he thought he was bringing me bad news and I might yell at him, too, he said, "He says he'll keep calling until you speak with him."

He pointed at the blinking light on the phone on our borrowed desk. "So would you. Please? It's line 2."

I reached for the phone and Bobby tactfully followed him out into the hall.

"God, Thea, are you okay?" Andre said, and before I could answer, "I'm sorry I've been such a horse's ass." And still not giving me a chance to speak, he said, again, "Are you okay? Roland told me about...about this morning."

"This has not been my best week," I said, trying not to dissolve into tears. I was still in 'hold it together for the clients' mode. And with what tattered remnants of emotion I had left, kind of annoyed with my husband, despite my under-the-desk epiphany.

"You could have called me back last night," I said. He didn't respond. "You could have come instead of Roland. Then you would have been here."

More silence. Then he said, "I know. You're right. We're just not very good at fighting. I hate it. Being a sulky bastard just makes me feel even more like a horse's ass. Roland told me about the locket, and the connection you made. And now he's got a family name for Ginger. For Penelope. We're trying to track them down."

"Unless they moved away. Or changed their names, too."

"A big unless. But it's something."

There were noises in the background. Voices and phones. Wherever he was, there were people around. "Roland's looking for high school friends. People who might know Ginger's story."

"What about the photos? Does that license plate help at all?"

"We're working on it."

What else could he say? Of course they were working on it. And maybe some astute detective would be able to do something with that partial plate. They did it all the time on TV. I didn't know how often it worked in real life.

I didn't want to talk about Ginger. Or Roland. But it was what was happening in his life. I'd moved on to another death. Or added another death. Had I told Andre and Roland everything? I thought I had, but things had been so scattered and some of my memories were so slight. If I ever sailed out of this tempest and into some peaceful waters, I'd take some time to go over everything I thought I knew and share it with Andre. Unless, as I fervently hoped, they'd solved the case by then.

"Roland says you're coming home."

"As soon as I get things squared away here. But there's still a lot of squaring to do."

"Call me when you're on your way."

"Will you be home?"

A stupid question. He'd be home if he could, but if something came up, a break, a lead, he would follow it. It was his job.

"I'll try." He hesitated. "I'll be home."

Whatever that meant. Still feeling a little defensive, or resentful, because it can be hard for me to let things go, I said, "I'm sorry I didn't just give you Ginger's package. But I thought it was a sweater from my mother. And you might not have made that connection between Babette and Babi."

I stopped myself from adding, 'even though you're a great detective,' because we were trying patch things up.

"I know." He stopped himself from saying that this would all have been easier if I were there instead of here and we could just talk face to face. Because we respected each other's work. "Vacation," he said. "As soon as we put these things to bed."

"Beach?"

"Beach. Sun. No winter coats, boots or gloves."

"Okay. Soon. And by the way, you scared Trish's assistant half to death."

"Cops are supposed to be scary. It's how we get things done. Speaking of which, the detectives down there treating you okay?"

"Surprisingly."

A glimmer of suspicion arose, and I had to ask, "You didn't talk to them, did you?"

He laughed. My husband laughing is a lovely sound. "Didn't have to, did I? Roland was there."

Gangly, story-telling Roland Proffit, my guardian angel.

"I hope I'll see you later," I said.

"I hope I'll see you later."

I put down the phone. We'd met when my little sister Carrie was killed. This awkward balancing between awful and normal had always been part of our lives. I pushed domestic issues and other deaths from my mind and went back to bringing order out of Blackwell's chaos.

Hours later, I was ready to hand things off to Bobby and head for home. Trish had shown amazing resilience for someone who'd nearly been killed, and we had decided that she would share the story of what happened with the whole school. She had used it as a call to come together to care for each other in their shock and dismay. It had been very effective. My drive wasn't long, but it wouldn't be an easy one. I felt like a vampire had sucked me dry. Trish and

Bobby both thought I was unfit to drive, but I wanted to be home, sleeping in my own bed, hopefully with my husband.

Bobby tried reasoning with me but quickly gave up. "No one has ever been able to stop you when you've made up your mind about something," he said. "Just promise that you'll stop for coffee. Eat something nice and healthy, like a jelly donut, and text me when you're safely home."

I promised. One of the best things about working at EDGE—we had the greatest people and everyone looked after everyone else. Bobby was staying here overnight, which Quinn would resent, but I could see that Bobby was really settling into his role here and that his calm good nature was having a positive effect on those around him. Some people have a gift for calming the waters.

"You'll be okay?" I said.

"We'll be fine here. Go home. Drive carefully. And let Uncle Bobby know you're safely there."

"Uncle Bobby?"

"Yeah. Sounds a bit venerable, doesn't it?"

"Much as I love you, I can't put you and venerable in the same sentence."

He placed his forearm against his forehead in an PBS Mystery gesture of mock despair. "Will I never get the respect I deserve?"

"Gray hair is usually the answer." Bobby was fair-haired and boyish. Also over six feet tall, broad-shouldered, and strong as an ox. "Or you could shave your head." Which would be sad because Bobby was so right the way he was.

"Quinn wouldn't like it."

True. Not that Quinn liked much. But Bobby loved Quinn, and it was good that he had someone who cared for him. Otherwise, his sweet nature could have made him vulnerable. He was tough enough with clients, though. Trained in toughness by me and diplomacy by Suzanne, he was the perfect fit for Blackwell's situation.

Was this what it was like to watch your child leave home, I wondered. To hand off the reins of adulthood and responsibility to someone you've trained and nurtured. "I'm so glad I can leave Blackwell in your capable hands," I said.

Bobby's smile was huge, and his face wore understanding about the conversation we didn't need to have. "Thanks. Now you drive carefully. And tomorrow, when you've rested, talk to Suzanne about getting us another employee to train. We're stretched pretty thin here."

So right. And so much one of the team. "Will do."

My briefcase and purse seemed almost too heavy to carry as I walked to the car. I cranked up some driving music and hit the road. Following Bobby's instructions, I made one stop for coffee and yes, a jelly donut that was a challenge not to spill on my clothes, and got home in record time to a dark apartment and no Andre.

I was too tired to be depressed about that. He'd get here when he got here. On the other hand, I had encountered so much death and violence this week that I was not lying down or closing my eyes unless Andre was with me. He expected to be home in the next hour.

I texted Bobby that I was home safe, then changed out of my consultant duds and pulled on my softest old sweats. My arm was one big ache. Combined with my earlier injuries, I was pretty much a bundle of misery. Hurting, exhausted, and despite having gotten little sleep last night, not yet ready for sleep. I needed some dull, routine tasks to send me toward sleep. Work. There was always work. I checked my phone for messages, made a list of things to deal with tomorrow, and caught up on my mail. More things to go on the to-do list, including what promised to be a long call with Stafford first thing in the morning.

My work done, I sat and thought about Ginger. Was Andre getting anywhere? I hoped so. What someone had done to her was so horrific the perpetrator had to be punished. Horrific and specific. Killing someone with heat was so unusual the method had to be significant.

I thought about what I knew. That Ginger's real name was Penelope. That she had gone to Stafford Academy where she'd been an athlete. That she'd had some connection with a child named Babette. Something had happened in her life that had made her change her name and hide her identity and forced her live a guarded life forever. From the time I'd spent with her, I'd seen that something about children made her wistful or sad. She had been afraid of being trapped in a car.

Whatever it was, with her full name to aid his search, Andre must have found it by now. Still, I was curious. And possibly a little competitive. Andre might have chastised me for carrying away that envelope, but Ginger had sent it to me because she thought I was some kind of detective. Or because she thought it would help keep her safe. So while I waited for my husband's return, I would pretend I *was* a detective, and see if I could unearth her story.

I started another round of searches. I tried *Babette* and *car accident*. *Babette* and *fire*. *Babette* and *drowning*. Nothing. I added *Penelope* to the mix. Still nothing. What did those heaters mean, if not fire? What if they meant heat?

Heat and cars and Babette?

The phone rang. Andre. "I'm five minutes out," he said. "I'm thinking about bourbon. And you."

Despite my best intentions, the first words out of my mouth were, "Did you find him? Has he been arrested? I tried to find him, but I couldn't figure it out."

"Find who? Has who been arrested?"

"Ginger's killer. Or killers. From the names? The pictures? That license plate?"

"We're working on it," he said, then, "Hey, I thought you'd be asleep by now, or treating yourself to a big medicinal whiskey. Don't tell me you've been playing detective again?"

I didn't think I'd been playing at anything. I didn't think 'play' applied to anything I'd done lately. Play was something I was going to add to my schedule when I had time. Play was what we'd do on our beach vacation. "I'll tell you when you get here."

I'd been feeling pretty good, imagining that the case must be over and Ginger's killers under arrest. Now it looked like that hadn't happened yet. A medicinal whiskey was looking pretty good, too. Even better when I had Andre to share it with. I got out two of the gorgeous Irish crystal glasses we'd gotten as wedding presents, took down the new bottle of Knob Creek, my current favorite, and got out a tray of ice cubes. Yum. I could almost feel the heat.

Now all I needed was him.

CHAPTER 31

I looked at the notes spread out on the table, the written record of the conversation I'd been having with myself. The blind alleys and false starts. Car accidents and fires. Andre was almost home. I could abandon all this and let him fill me in. Let him be the detective while I went back to being a consultant. No. Back to being a wife. I could stop holding up the huge wall I'd built between myself and the horrors of the past week. Finally start really feeling safe.

While I'd worked on my internet search, I'd let obsession take over. Now I felt relief flow through me as I imagined letting go of this and pushing Ginger out of my thoughts.

I hadn't felt like eating since breakfast. The only thing in my stomach to cushion the effects of strong drink was a jelly donut. Not good. I dug in the cupboard for some fancy mixed nuts and poured them into a dish. Found two pieces of cheese that hadn't been eaten by mold, some olives, and a loaf of good bread in the freezer that I stuck in the oven to heat. We even had some hummus and baby carrots—the vegetable course. A veritable feast. And we had leftover chocolate cake.

I'd just finished spreading things out on the coffee table when I heard feet on the stairs. I checked the driveway for his car—there had been enough surprises from bad guys this week—and opened the door.

I could barely see him behind the bouquet he was holding. Incredibly fragrant lilies. My favorite. In the depths of March. He held them out stiffly, like a little boy doing a chore his parents were making him do. "Roland said I had to bring these."

But above the stiff arm, his eyes were shining. In the other hand, he held a box of fancy chocolates. A big box of chocolates. "And I knew I had to bring these. Did you know medical science has determined that chocolate is the best remedy for puncture wounds?"

I took the flowers and laid them carefully on the counter. Did the same with the chocolates, and then walked forward into his arms. "I miss you too much when I'm away."

"Not as much as I miss you. And long distance fighting is impossible."

"Maybe we could have some close-up reconciliation?" I was thinking chocolate cake and make-up sex. After we had our feast.

He raised an eyebrow. "Excuse me, ma'am, but are you aware that I'm a police officer?"

I tried to make my eyes wide and innocent. "Are police officers not allowed to participate in domestic reconciliation?"

"Only with their wives."

I wrapped myself around him and wouldn't let go. He gestured with his chin toward the waiting glasses, because his hands were busy. "Do I detect the signs of an adult beverage?"

"In my experience, detective, it takes both chocolate and an adult beverage to properly treat a wound."

I shelved my questions about their progress in finding Ginger's killer. Instead, I asked, "Did you get dinner?"

He shook his head. Like me, he eats when he can when he's working, but often misses meals.

He unwrapped my clinging arms and poured us each a drink that would have put lesser mortals under the table. I put the flowers in water, took out the hot bread and sliced it, and we took our drinks to the coffee table, where I'd spread out our feast. An unspoken pact that for a few minutes, we would suspend work and just be together. Eat bread and cheese and olives and nuts, breathe in the perfume of flowers, and let our eyes drink in each other's bodies and the promise of things to come. A peaceful interlude before we ventured onto difficult topics like gun-wielding professors and dead realtors. The frustrations of his case and the dangers of my work.

The interlude didn't last long. Being a detective, as soon as he'd grazed the feast and left devastation behind, his gaze shifted to the dining room table, where I had spread out the results of my search. "What's all this?"

Before I could answer, he'd picked up my notes and was scanning them.

I didn't want to go there. Just a few sips of my drink had made me feel tipsy, and we'd exchanged a bourbon-flavored kiss that had me tingling to my toes. I was thinking make-up sex and deep, safe sleep. Regarding work I had only one word: tomorrow.

My husband, though, had clicked into detective mode and now he was like a bloodhound on scent. "What is all this?" he repeated.

"I was trying to figure it out. Ginger's—that is Penelope's or Penny's—connection to the little girl, Babette. What Ginger said when she was dying. Roland told you, didn't he? That it wasn't Bobby but Babi? Babette? The little girl in the locket."

He nodded. "He did. And?"

"You remember how I told you—told you or told Roland—that Ginger had this weird thing about cars? How she always wanted the windows down? Kept that tool in the car in case she went into the water or needed to escape? So I tried water and drowning and accidents. Got nothing, so I tried Penelope or Penny and Babette and fires. More nothing."

I paused to take a little of my medicine and Andre did the same. "Go on."

"I thought using those heaters had to be deliberate. I struck out with *fire* so I wondered, if not fire than what? Heat?"

I waved my hands at the papers. "That's where I was when you called. So far, I've got nothing. But you're close to finding him, right?" I thought about Ginger's pictures. A man and a woman. "Or them? Ginger's killers?"

"Not yet."

My spirits sank. I'd been so sure that with the information from Stafford, plus Ginger's photos and that partial license, he'd find them. Arrest them. Lock them up. And I could sleep peacefully again.

"So what was your next search going to be?" my husband the bloodhound asked.

I gave up on our floor picnic and the promise of that kiss and joined him at the table, taking my glass with me. I let the hot, sweet bourbon roll over my tongue as I looked at my notes. Normally I loved bourbon. Tonight I didn't feel much like drinking. I was too tired.

"Hot cars and Babette. Then hot cars and Babette and Penny."

"Why would you leave Penny out?" he said.

"If she was a juvenile, they wouldn't have printed her name. Would they?" I didn't know what kind of assumptions detectives made when they did searches like this. "Did you find out anything about her from Stafford Academy?"

He shook his head. "Athlete. Good student. Her parents' names and address. She withdrew after her junior year. They moved and we haven't been able to trace them yet." He gestured toward the computer. "Go ahead and try your search."

I shifted my gaze from my notes to his face. Was he serious?

"Why not?" he said. "I don't care how we catch the killer."

"You got mad about the package," I reminded him. "I thought you didn't want me involved."

"I said I was sorry. And you are involved."

He looked sorry. He'd brought me presents. And we both wanted Ginger's killer caught.

I sat down at the computer. Andre pulled a chair up beside me. I tried *hot cars* and *Babette* in a couple different iterations in the archives of Maine newspapers and BINGO! Hours after I started a desultory search, pretending to be a detective to pass the time until Andre came home, and late at night when we both should have been sleeping, I uncovered Ginger's ugly secret.

Andre read over my shoulder as the lurid headlines in the Maine papers declared:

Sitter Leaves Toddler in Hot Car to Tryst with Boyfriend

Hot Car Toddler in Critical Condition

Reckless Sitter Charged with Child Endangerment

Hot Car Toddler May Be Permanently Impaired

Babette Ingram was the hot car toddler. The parents were at their child's bedside and refusing to give interviews. The careless babysitter wasn't identified because she was a juvenile, but one paper had slipped up, perhaps deliberately, and published her first name. Published it in a virulent interview with Babette's older brother, Jordan Ingram, age nineteen. In that interview, he had promised that if his little sister didn't make a full recovery, he would see that Penny suffered just as Babi had suffered. His sister, Mary Ingram, had declined to comment. The papers reported that Mary Ingram and the babysitter had been close friends and attended the same private school in Connecticut.

The babysitter had been caring for little Babi that day because the rest of the family had to attend a funeral. In the middle of the afternoon, she had left Babi in the car because the little girl was asleep, and spent her boyfriend's break time with him outside the local ice cream shop. The temperature that day had been in the nineties. When she got back to the car, the toddler was unconscious. The babysitter had opened the windows, turned on the air-conditioning, and raced to the hospital emergency room. The toddler was revived but was critical and had suffered potential brain and kidney damage. The news stories all reiterated the risks of leaving children in hot cars.

One article stated that despite the babysitter's statements, which were corroborated by her boyfriend and the boyfriend's boss, police did not believe the toddler had been unattended for less than twenty minutes. Penny Martin—always referred to as "the juvenile"—had been arrested, bailed, and was in seclusion. Without the sensation of a trial—the "juvenile" had agreed to a plea deal—the story quickly died away. I could find no follow up articles about what became of little Babi.

I stared at my screen and then down at my notes.

"I thought Ginger said 'airy,'" I told Andre. "She probably said 'Mary.' Oh God. Mary. She was trying to tell me she'd recognized her killers."

I thought of all she'd tried to put into those few painful words. Mary. The connection to Babette. That she'd thought she was safe. That she was still sorry for what had happened. I tried to imagine two people so consumed by hate and a desire for vengeance they'd carried it all these years and planned something so horrible. Done something so horrible.

I'd loved my little sister, Carrie, and wanted her killer caught and punished, but I couldn't imagine myself doing something like this.

"So there were two of them," Andre said. "The two people in those pictures. The man and the woman. Jordan and Mary Ingram," he said. "At some point, she must have spotted them and taken those pictures."

"And wrote *Jordi* on the back. Because even though Ginger had changed her name and colored her hair, and was fifteen years older, she'd made the mistake of coming back to Maine, and continuing to work as a realtor, where her picture would be everywhere. Safe. She thought she was safe. She'd suffered for fifteen years from a momentary mistake. Maybe she was homesick? She did say she'd hated Florida."

Had she been stupid? Or hopeful? Had her boyfriend—ex-boyfriend—played any part in this? Was that what his comment about her not being perfect had been about? If her story in Florida was true, maybe she'd loved him enough to follow him to Maine? Had she also foolishly trusted him enough to confide in him and been betrayed?

My head was spinning from unanswered questions. I was trying not to imagine Ginger's horror, the moments of realization of who her killers were and what they intended—the slow, awful way they arranged for her to die or at least suffer horrible damage. The call they'd made so I'd be delayed. Ginger had sat in that room in slowly increasing agony for more than an hour, hoping for rescue. And I didn't come.

Had they stayed and watched? Waited until she was writhing with pain? Had they watched the horror and desperation in her eyes? Maybe even taken pleasure from it? Ginger—Penelope—had been a kid who made a bad mistake. And I believed it had only been that ten or fifteen minutes. I'd done a little reading on heatstroke. Little children were so vulnerable and the temperature in a car could go up many degrees in only minutes.

The Ingrams had been adults. Methodical, vengeful adults who had done something unspeakably horrible to another human being.

Seeing my face, he said, "You're thinking about Carrie."

"I am. But mostly I was thinking about how tragic it all is. As a teenager, she makes a poor decision and puts a child at risk. She served her time, changed her name, and lived a circumscribed life ever after. But something about Maine—or a romantic miscalculation—drew her back, and coming back got her killed. Despite changing her identity, she made the mistake of working in a profession where her photograph was everywhere. Maybe she thought she was so changed no one would recognize her. But it looks like the Ingrams never got over the incident. Someone, Mary or

Jordan Ingram, or someone they knew, must have seen her picture and made the connection. And they planned their horrible revenge."

Revenge, Shakespeare has written, is a dish best served cold. In this case, more than a decade cold. Clearly, though, the desire for revenge still burned red hot.

CHAPTER 32

"The truck you saw driving away," Andre said. "Did you notice anything about the occupants?"

I thought back to that morning. The dark truck charging at me, well over the line in my lane. Roland had asked if I remembered anything about the truck. I'd been trying to rescue my spilled coffee and dealing with an anxious client. But if I thought really hard, was there anything I could remember? Was this another case where the remembering game we played could be a real world help? What had I told Roland? Dark truck, double cab.

I thought that was all I remembered. Now, I closed my eyes and put myself back in that moment. I pictured it. The glass was heavily tinted, but I thought there had been two people in the truck. A woman driving. A man in the passenger seat. There had been a quick moment, in the midst of my swearing and damage control, when I'd registered surprise at a woman driving a truck so fast and so carelessly.

"The truck I saw that morning? There were two people in it, a man and a woman. Do you think it might have been them?"

I tried to recall Ginger's blurry photo, wondering if it was of a truck, but I couldn't. Minutes ago, I'd been looking forward to a quiet evening with my husband, drinking and eating and tumbling into bed. Now I wanted him to strap on his armor and go do battle with the forces of evil.

"Do you think you can find them?"

"I'll call Roland, tell him what we know—or think we know—and see what he can find out."

"Roland's still at work? He must be exhausted."

"Roland is as tenacious as a pitbull. You know that." A smile. "I'd be there, too, if he hadn't made me come home." He studied my face. "What? You're disappointed I wanted to spend some time with you?"

I wasn't disappointed. I was conflicted. I wanted the killers caught as soon as possible. I also didn't want Andre to leave me. I wanted him strapping on that armor and going forth to do battle, and I wanted him no more than a hair's breadth away.

He kissed me. Another one of those kisses with promise. "Relax. I'm not going to rush out into the night when I've been drinking. I'm going to make a couple phone calls. Get people working on some things."

He touched my cheek, his hand warm and reassuring. "Don't worry. We'll get them. I'm not the only competent detective with the Maine state police. After I make those calls?"

He did his signature eyebrow waggle and leered at me. "I'm going to personally inspect all your injuries. I'm going to kiss all your boo boos, and I'm…"

"Shut up," I interrupted, "and make those calls."

I'd flipped my mental coin and come down on the side of here and now. Keeping him here and now. Tomorrow, when I was back to sorting out errant schools and solving their problems, he could go catch bad guys.

As he made his calls, I basked in pleasure that together Andre and I had done some good detective work, hadn't had a fight, and maybe had taken a big step toward justice for Ginger.

Tonight the monsters would stay in the closet and there would be no bad guys in the basement. I went to take some painkillers for my throbbing arm. I could barely keep my eyes open. It was time for sleep. In my big soft bed. With Andre.

Somehow, the powers that be must have gotten the message that we needed a good night's sleep, because the phone didn't ring and no bad guys came to call. It was such a good night's sleep that I forgot to set my alarm and Andre forgot to set his. The only reason we finally woke, when it was almost nine, was because someone was knocking on our door.

I struggled into my robe and went to answer it, because Andre doesn't have a robe, and while he may be magnificent in—or out—of his skivvies, that's a pleasure I reserve for myself. I found Mrs. Ames on the doorstep holding a plate of muffins so fresh from the oven they were still steaming.

"Raspberry walnut and blueberry lemon," she said, holding out the plate. It hadn't taken much detective work on her part to figure out that we were still home. All she had to do was look out the window. Despite the bandage on her head, she looked good. Like folks said, she was a tough old bird. "A little thank you for rescuing me the other night. I hope you're doing okay?" She peered at me as though she could see damage through the robe.

"I'm fine, thanks. Especially knowing that thug is behind bars."

"Thanks to you. Next time, I'm calling the furnace man," she said. "Let him deal with whatever is down there."

"Me, too," I agreed. "I'm glad to see you looking so well."

"Oh, you know. I'm a tough old bird." She said it with a twinkle in her eye. It was almost as if she enjoyed having been attacked in her basement. It gave her something interesting to talk about. Our comings and goings weren't much fodder for gossip.

"I'll be off now. I'm sure you two have to be getting to work."

Oh, she had that right. We two were already very late for work. I had a call in ten minutes and heaven only knew what awaited Andre. I hoped it would be arrests and interrogations. I set the plate on the counter, wincing at the detritus from last night's feast still covering the coffee table, and went into the bedroom to be sure he was awake. The bed was empty. I could hear the shower running and he was singing something cheerful, loudly and way off the tune. He has many gifts, but singing isn't among them.

My arm was throbbing and my whole body reminded me that I'd recently leapt over a desk and crashed to the floor. I expected I was more black and blue than flesh-colored at this point. I dressed without looking. Whatever life threw at me today, it couldn't be as bad as yesterday.

In record time, my hubby was shaved and clothed and ready to rock and roll. Unless it was lock and load. He gave me a kiss full of promise, snagged a muffin, and headed for the door, already on the phone with Roland.

"Go catch bad guys," I said, "and call me when you've got 'em." A comment as light as a feather. Did he know how much I meant it?

He lowered the phone and said, "I will. And I will." And he was gone, leaving the faint scent of freshly showered man in the air. I missed him before the door had finished closing. The minute he wasn't there to hold it at bay, I felt an unshakable unease, as though last night, while I was doing my search on the bad guys, they were doing their own search on me. They did have my name and number, after all. Probably knew where I lived and worked. I hadn't 'til this moment thought about Ginger's files, where all kinds of client information was kept. Had she had them with her? Had her killers taken them or were they securely in a locked office or with the police?

Suddenly, my position seemed very vulnerable. I was the one who'd heard Ginger's words. The one Ginger had trusted enough to send things to. And I had seen them—if it had been them in the truck—leaving the scene. I was pretty much the only witness. And the story had been all over the papers.

I shivered.

I'd planned to do my call with Stafford from home this morning. Instead, I decided to do it from the office where there would be other people around. I made a quick call to Charlotte Ainsley, saying there had been a complication and I'd call her again in fifteen minutes. Then I did a hasty toilette—I didn't much care how I looked, especially if I wasn't meeting with clients today. Black jeans and a sweater were fine for the office. I grabbed my briefcase and purse and headed for my car. Have briefcase, will travel. Maybe I needed a steel-lined briefcase, one that would make a better shield. Did they even make such a thing?

I'd toyed with the notion before—what about chic designer wear for people in semi-dangerous professions? Silk, cashmere, and metallic thread flack vests? Statement necklaces that kept bad guys from compressing the neck? Steel-toed stilettos? Perfume atomizers containing pepper spray? That last one probably already existed.

I sighed. I didn't want to be someone who needed weapons to do her job, never mind needing a bodyguard in order to buy a house. I shifted my thoughts to my upcoming conversation with Charlotte Ainsley. Damage control of a type I understood.

I was just out the door when Mrs. Ames appeared, still shoving her arms into her coat sleeves. There was an eagerness on her face I'd rarely seen. "I forgot to ask," she said, "when I delivered them muffins. You know someone who drives a big green Ford truck? There was one hanging around here yesterday. Drove past a couple times and then turned into the driveway one time. No one got out or anything, and I couldn't make out much about the driver. It just seemed kind of odd, you know?"

More than odd. "You didn't happen to get a license, did you?"

"They was too fast for me," she said. "I only got a partial." She said partial like she'd watched a lot of TV cop shows. "Hold on a minute, I'll get it for you, maybe your husband can figure out who it was. After the other night, I'm not keen on people snooping around here, if you know what I mean."

I knew exactly what she meant. I wasn't partial, either. Or keen.

She came back with a scrap of paper torn from a yellow pad. "There was two people in it, but that's all I can say. I don't know of anybody who'd be interested in doing me no harm, but you never can tell. I've got Lester's guns here, still, and people are always looking to steal guns. So just to be on the safe side, I've got one of 'em loaded and right here by the door."

She grabbed my arm—luckily the uninjured one—and practically hauled me into her entry. "See!"

Leaning against the wall was a shotgun. For a moment, I wanted one, too. But I'd had enough encounters with guns and their aftermath. I didn't want to make them a routine part of my life.

"Bet they wouldn't come back if they knew about this," I said.

"Oh. They do know. I waved it at 'em when I saw 'em turning in yesterday, after all them times they drove past. This is why I only got that partial, you see, because my hands were kind of busy."

"You didn't happen to call the police, did you?"

She shook her head. "Wouldn't know what to tell 'em. That some guy kept driving past in a truck? They'd just take me for a crazy old lady. I get enough of that already, being solitary and opinionated and all. I just mentioned it to your husband when he come home last night. Forgot to give him that license plate, though. He was pretty hot to get upstairs with them flowers."

I thought it was a good thing Mrs. Ames had a gun, but I didn't know whether she was adept with firearms or was likely to blow her foot off or put a hole through the ceiling.

I fluttered the piece of paper. "Thanks for partial. I'll let Andre know about this." I pulled out one of my business cards and circled my office number. "If you see that truck again, call me at this number. Please."

She looked disappointed. "I thought it might be kinda fun to take a shot at 'em."

"But if they aren't up to something bad, you'd only get yourself in trouble."

"That's right," she agreed. "Well, I'll be careful then. And you be careful, too. If they're in any way connected to what happened the other day, these are very bad people." She looked down at the shotgun, then back at me. "You know how to use a gun?"

"I've done it a few times."

"Well, I've got more inside. Why don't you take this one with you? Just in case."

I could have used it yesterday, that was for sure. But I'm not easy around guns. If I brought her shotgun along, I'd probably be so distracted I'd drive off the road. "Thanks," I said, "but I'd better not. As likely to shoot myself as some bad guy."

Her eyes narrowed as she squinted toward the road. "Well, okay," she said dubiously. "But if you see a big green truck in your rearview, you skedaddle to someplace where there are a lot of people around."

It was good advice, except that there were thousands of green pickups in Maine. I'd be skedaddling all the way to work. And Mrs. Ainsley was waiting for my call. I tossed my purse and briefcase in the Jeep and headed for the office.

Half a mile down the road, as I passed the dirt road that led to the closed town dump, a green truck pulled out behind me.

CHAPTER 33

My heart jumped. I reminded myself that there were green trucks everywhere. But there was no reason for anyone to be coming out of that road. It was a dirt track to nowhere. I was still a couple miles from the highway, and there was only one place with a lot of people that I could skedaddle into—a gas station with a Dunkin' Donuts. I didn't have time to stop. Because of my conversation with Mrs. Ames, I was already late for my scheduled call, which I couldn't do from the car because I needed my notes.

Grimly, I drove on past and so did the truck. It stayed a steady distance behind me, never getting any closer or falling back, and it followed me onto the highway. Because my car offered the magic of Bluetooth, I instructed my dashboard to call Andre. When he didn't pick up, I left a message about Mrs. Ames and the green truck and the partial plate numbers. I even added that I was feeling nervous about the truck that was following me. Make a record, Andre says.

Make a record? Dammit! All I wanted to do was buy a house and now I seemed to be looking over my shoulder all the time. Everything was conspiring to make me feel insecure this morning. When was I going to get back to normal?

Did my crazy life even have a normal? Or *was* this normal?

I try to stay on an even keel because I need to be steady for clients who are freaking out themselves. But this morning, I couldn't even find my keel, never mind steadying it. I wanted that green truck gone so I could shift my attention to something that really mattered.

I moved over a lane and slowed down, then into the slow lane where I poked along like a granny, feeling the clock ticking and visualizing work piling up on my desk, a heap of papers topped, like strawberries on an ice cream sundae, with pink message slips.

The green truck stuck to me like a baby duck following mama. Never close enough so I could see the occupants, never far enough back so I could hope its presence was just a coincidence.

Finally, we reached my turnoff. When I left the highway to drive the short distance to my office building, the green truck came right along with me, following through the twists and turns that led to my building.

By now, I was wishing that I had accepted Mrs. Ames's offer of one of her spare guns.

I parked as close to the door as I could, noting that the green truck had parked farther along in another row. I watched it. No one got out.

Just as I was about to grab my bags and sprint for the door, I noticed that there was another green truck, bigger, fancier and with a lot more chrome, backed into the row behind me. The windshield had a dark tint, so I couldn't see much, but it looked like there were two people inside. I settled back in my seat, the pressure of work warring with my instinct for self-preservation. The insane part of my brain, the part that tries for humor in situations like this, said there had been an invasion of menacing green trucks. Right now, that wasn't funny.

I tried Andre again and went to voice mail. Then I tried Roland, with the same result. Where are the cops when you really need help? Like where had Furst been yesterday?

I'd parked as close to the building as I could, but I was late this morning and it wasn't close. The door was at least sixty feet away. If someone was waiting for me, I'd be exposed for too long. I debated. Like Mrs. Ames, I couldn't imagine calling the police. What would I say? That I'd suddenly become leery of green trucks? That I was sure someone was following me in a green truck? But no, officer, I hadn't seen them, didn't know who they were, and they'd done nothing menacing. Yet.

I had to get upstairs to my desk and make that phone call. I'd just break the rules and park right by the door. From there, I could jump out and run into the building. What was the worst thing that could happen? My car got towed? It was better than a run-in with the pair who'd killed Ginger. I started the engine and began backing out.

The engine on the shiny green truck roared to life.

I stopped. If I backed up any farther, the truck could accelerate right into my driver's side. I pulled back into my space, shoved the car into park, and watched helplessly as the truck pulled forward until it was almost on my bumper, pinning me there. A man and a woman got out. Even from Ginger's grainy photos, I recognized him. Tall, thin and dark. The woman wasn't the one in the photos. She was pudgy and moonfaced and hung back by the truck. His movements were purposeful, his face set. He was carrying what looked like a splitting maul.

I snatched up my phone and was dialing 911 when the glass on the window beside my head exploded. I tried to squeeze down under the steering wheel. It was like trying to put a Great Dane in a mini poodle carrier.

In my hand, a distant voice said, "911, Dispatcher Belcastro, this call is being recorded, what is your emergency?"

"I'm in the parking lot at 3373 West Main, the office building, and there's a man with a splitting maul smashing my car windows."

I grabbed some air and forced the words out. "I'm inside the car."

"We're sending some officers. Ma'am, may I have your name please?"

I fumbled it out as Ingram moved forward and my windshield exploded, showering me with glass. "Please. Hurry. He's smashing everything!"

"Officers are en route, ma'am. Please stay on the line."

His face set in a fanatical grimace, the man I assumed was Jordan Ingram started raising his weapon again. As I waited for the blow that would come right through the missing window and smash into me, I heard a man's voice say, "Police. Drop your weapon, drop your weapon. Step away from that car, and put your hands on your head."

Then, more slowly, and louder, "Police. Drop your weapon and step away from the car." I knew that voice. Roland Proffit. I had no idea what he was doing here, but I couldn't be more grateful.

My husband's voice, "Give it up, Ingram. You've lost."

Jordan Ingram hesitated, but he wasn't complying. I peeked from under my arm and saw the maul still poised to strike. My car was at an angle and he was in front of me and beside the hood, in the narrow slot between me and the car beside me.

I wasn't waiting to see if he'd listen to Roland, or for the blow that might kill me. I'd had it with bad guys.

I reached up and shifted into drive, pressing down on the accelerator while swinging the car sharply in his direction. I might miss him completely and just smash some poor innocent's car, but it was better than getting smashed myself. The car lurched forward. Man and maul disappeared from sight.

In the distance, I could hear sirens.

Closer, the crunch of metal and a man's screams. I took my foot off the gas.

The screams went on.

It made no sense, but Andre and Roland must have been in the green truck that followed me. Acting, I guess, on Mrs. Ames's information.

After that there was a commotion of voices and grunts, in the midst of which my beloved stuck his head in the window and said, "It's okay. It's okay. Put it into park, Thea. Stay right there. I'll get you out in a minute." I could barely hear him over the pounding of my heart. I'd come too close to getting mauled.

I guess he'd never pushed himself off a console and curled his own 6'1", glass-encrusted self into a ball in a space that was several sizes too small. Or deliberately tried to run down another human being.

Or maybe he had?

I needed to get out of this car. Now. Not in a while when the police were done with whatever they were doing. A zillion things were sticking into me. I was wearing what looked like a fancy glass dress.

Beside my door, Roland and Andre were dealing with Ingram. I couldn't get out. With the grace of an elephant going through the eye of a needle, I levered myself over the console and climbed out the passenger side. I stood there in the March cold as little chunks of glass rolled off and bounced on the pavement at my feet. Somewhere out at the periphery, my suspicious little nature wondered if Andre and Roland had used me as bait.

One thing I was now sure of—my call to Charlotte Ainsley was indefinitely postponed.

Ten feet away from me, the woman who had been with Ingram stood in her baggy pink sweats, staring at us without comprehension. She had a doll clutched to her chest. Babi. Little Babette. This was what Jordan Ingram had been avenging.

When Andre and Roland had the snarling, spitting Ingram subdued and cuffed, and turned over to waiting troopers, they came over to me. Andre's shrewd cop's eyes assessed me for damage.

"Did you know about this?" I said, which was a stupid question, because otherwise, why would they have been following me? I knew Mrs. Ames had told him about the suspicious green truck.

I decided to save my remarks about their timing for a day when I had more self-control. Jordan Ingram might not have landed that last blow but the experience had taken years off my life.

Failing to get an answer, I tried to brush off some of the glass, and decided that was not a smart move. But what were my choices? Disrobe in the parking lot? There have been times, in my romantic past, when my beloved has plucked glass shards from my hair. This was a larger task, and I could see that once he'd established I still had all my limbs and wasn't bleeding badly, he was hot to get Ingram into an interview room, go at the man with all his skill and tenacity, and close this case.

I, on the other hand, was on the cusp of collapsing onto the cold pavement and weeping. I gestured toward Babi, still standing patiently, waiting for someone to take charge and tell her what to do. "What are you going to do about her? About Babi?"

He looked over and I saw comprehension on his face. "So that's what this was about."

"I'll get him booked and into an interview room," Roland said. "And take care of his sister. We've got people here for that. You take care of Thea."

Roland gave me one of his reassuring smiles. "That was quick thinking, just now. You probably saved your life."

Andre looked at me, surprised. My hands and face were bleeding and I was glittering with bits of broken glass. I'd just been attacked by a murderer. Andre's initial assessment had been the cop's assessment of an accident victim—conscious, coherent, not seriously bleeding. Thinking he'd catch the bad guy and then deal with the victim. Maybe I've played the part of Thea the Great and Terrible too well. So well even my husband actually believed I was a tough guy when I felt just like my car windows. Shattered.

Now he saw the error of his ways. Glass and all, he carefully gathered me into his arms. Over my head, he was already consulting with Roland about locating Mary Ingram and arresting her and getting warrants for the truck and their residences as more bits of glass, sparkling like jewels in the March sun, landed with icy crashes at my feet.

CHAPTER 34

From my lounge chair, the white sand beach, swaying palm trees, and rolling blue waves seemed almost too good to be true—like a picture in a travel brochure, though the sun's heat on my winter weary skin and fading bruises said it was real. Also looking too good to be true was Andre, snoozing beside me in the red Speedo that he owned like few men could.

Sun and rest and yummy snacks delivered right to my beach chair were working their magic. It had taken a few weeks before we could get away and we'd arrived exhausted wrecks. Andre had gotten confessions from the Ingrams. I'd put out all the client fires I could, set the process in motion to hire more staff, and resolutely kept other issues out of my mind. I only found myself crying a few times a day now. Sudden, spontaneous tears that seemed to come from nowhere, triggered by the silliest things. A small child offering me a shell. The waiter's kind smile as he set down my nachos. A man putting a possessive hand around his wife's waist as they walked past. A smiling dad romping with his small girls in the surf.

Kindness. Warmth. Tender, loving gestures. People behaving decently. How had I come to live a life where these were the surprises, the gifts, instead of the norm?

Where it was all work and no play and I was losing sight of who I was and what I wanted? This vacation was helping me get rebalanced. Also making me smile, and tear up, was picturing Suzanne, back home, snuggling her new baby daughter.

"Want to try paddle boards this afternoon?" Andre said, sliding his warm hand across my back.

There it was again. I started to cry.

"It will get better," he said.

"It's already better," I said. "I think I've figured out why I'm such an emotional wreck."

"Trying to save a murder victim, then being attacked by a gun-wielding professor, and again by a man obsessed with revenge would make anyone an emotional wreck," he said. "Never mind all your crazy clients."

"True. But that's not it."

I rolled over onto my back, then took his warm hand and placed it on my stomach. "It's hormones," I said. "I'm afraid little Claudine or Mason or Oliver is taking a toll on mama." Claudine. Mason. Oliver. The names we'd picked for the baby we lost.

He made a sound, something deep and visceral and primitive, as his big hand spread out protectively. Then the handsomest man on the beach, the hunky guy in the red bathing suit that stopped conversation and made women sigh, joined his tears to mine. Happy tears. This time, fingers crossed, our lives would be safe and normal, and along about Halloween, our own little pumpkin would appear.

The End

THE THEA KOZAK MYSTERY SERIES

Chosen for Death
Death in a Funhouse Mirror
Death at the Wheel
An Educated Death
Death in Paradise
Liberty or Death
Stalking Death
Death Warmed Over
Schooled in Death

Turn the page for an excerpt from

SCHOOLED IN DEATH

A Thea Kozak Mystery

Book Eight

Kate Flora

It was Monday. Always the worst day of the week in the working world. So when my phone rang before I'd showered, brushed my teeth, or even opened my eyes, I knew I was about to be the recipient of bad news and a summons to someone else's troubles.

I was not wrong.

"Is that Thea, then?" a man's voice asked. Reluctantly, I agreed that it was.

He didn't need to give his name. His gentle Welsh lilt announced my caller was Gareth Williams, headmaster of Simmons Prep. Gareth was the most optimistic person I knew. Usually, just hearing his voice instantly improved my mood. Today, his tones were shot with pain at the situation he found himself in, a situation he rapidly described. One of their young boarding students, a girl no one knew was pregnant, had given birth in her dorm bathroom during the night and left her baby in the trash. It was only because another student had heard the faint sounds of crying that the tiny infant had been saved. Now the baby was fighting for life in a neonatal ICU and the young, terrified mother, only a child herself, was facing potential criminal charges.

Gareth needed my help—or the help of my business, EDGE Consulting—to manage the situation on his campus and in the wider world. Immediately if not sooner. That was the problem with being a private school trouble-shooter—when people called me, usually their emergencies were already underway and they were rarely something I could handle over the phone. Today was no exception. Gareth needed me on campus now. He was two hours away in the crawl of morning traffic and my calendar was already full.

"It's complicated, Thea," Gareth said, "The girl insists that she has never had sex, never mind been pregnant, and the baby can't possibly be hers, even though she has obviously just given birth. And she seems, as much as one can judge under these circumstances, to be utterly sincere." In the background, I could hear a Palestrina mass.

A million questions immediately presented themselves about the girl and her situation. Questions of drugs and date rape and mental illness, among others. But those would wait until Gareth and I were face to face.

On the other side of the bed, my husband Andre gave up trying to sleep and grimaced at a clock that said 5:45. He tossed off the covers and stood. Naked. Gorgeous. The outline of his little red Speedo the only untanned part of his body. A wonderful sight to start the day. It's not just me, though I readily admit to being prejudiced in his favor. Perfect strangers of the female persuasion sigh softly when he passes. He mouthed, "Shower. Join me?"

I nodded as he headed for the bathroom, throwing off my own covers so I could cross to the desk and make some notes on what Gareth was saying. Damage control was my specialty. He needed me there as soon as possible. I would have to do some rearranging if I was going to be able to help.

"She's not been arrested, which is something," Gareth said. "They took her to hospital and now she's in our infirmary. But the investigation's on-going, and the police are considering charges."

"What's our girl's name?"

"Heidi," he said. "Heidi Basham."

That name, Heidi, conjured up images of blond pigtails and the Swiss Alps and Grandfather and some goats.

"What year is she?"

"Sophomore. But this is her first year at the school."

So yes, I thought, *the girl is awfully young.* "You've called her parents?"

"Of course. And they're on their way. Her mother and stepfather, at least. Flying in from the West Coast," he said. "It's a divorce situation. The mother said she'd let the father know."

I wasn't comfortable with his decision to let the mother control the news, but that could wait until I was showered, dressed, and on the road. I preferred to handle details when my eyes were open and my brain was fully operating.

As if he'd read my mind, he said, "We've tried to reach the father. This time and others. He's…uh…difficult to reach. I gather he travels a lot."

The traveling parent. Another reason kids got sent to private school. No one at home had time for them. I felt a spike of sympathy for this girl, wondering if this pregnancy might have been a grab for attention that went horribly wrong.

Anticipating my next question, he said, "And yes, I was on the phone to our lawyer as soon as ever it happened. Once he'd established that she hadn't been arrested, I got a quick paragraph of instructions and a 'call me back in the morning,' which I took to mean at a more civilized hour. We'll for sure get him in later this morning, but I'm expecting he'll be telling me that the poor girl will need her own lawyer. I'll get some suggestions from him so we'll be prepared when mother arrives. Obviously, Heidi being a minor, we'll need mother's consent for that."

The clock was ticking. I had calls to make to free up my day if I was going to drive to Simmons, so I said, "I'll be there as soon as I can, Gareth. I'll call you from the road and we can continue this."

"I'm beyond relieved to know you're coming," he said. "I'm afraid I'm a bit thrown by all this."

"All this" had happened in the night, but the facts would soon spread across the campus. Boarding schools were like small towns. Everyone—students and faculty alike—lived in each other's pockets and news and gossip traveled at the speed of light. Gareth was already reeling from the implications of the event for his school and anticipating the sorrow and confusion his students would feel over such shocking behavior by one of their own. Any headmaster would be struggling with this. Heidi's unusual situation, and assessing her denial of the facts and getting at the truth, was a significant complication.

The other complications were the kind that occurred whenever there was a crisis involving a student on a boarding school campus: managing the disclosure of information to the student body, their parents, the media, and the involved student's parents in a manner least damaging to the school. Divorced parents made things even more difficult, since often the divorces were so bitter they couldn't even be in the same room at the same time, despite the fact that the matter concerned their child. Far too often, when EDGE came into these situations, part of our job ended up being to babysit, or verbally control, a set of warring parents. Also complicating things, of course, would be dealing with the police.

EDGE Consulting works with independent, meaning private, schools. Often, we work with schools on their image, on "branding" their special niche in this small corner of the education world and helping them to promote and protect those brands. Simmons's brand was particularly vulnerable in this situation. Simmons Prep was a small, elite, non-denominational private school north of Boston, with a reputation for educational excellence. Their special niche was nurturing a responsible, caring, community-oriented student body with particular attention to environmental science, social justice, and global awareness. This was part of their core values, as was service to the community.

The Simmons campus was so green and vegan it was practically a sin to wear leather shoes there. Everybody worked in the greenhouses and campus gardens. The students helped run a day-care center for low-income children. They valued diversity of culture and opinion. It was a self-selected community of budding activists, humanistic citizens, and locovores. The last place on earth, in short, to have a pregnant student fly under the radar, never mind surreptitiously deliver a baby and abandon her newborn to almost certain death. The situation would have been bad anywhere, but the value the school placed on personal responsibility made it a particularly bad place for someone to deny responsibility for endangering a vulnerable life.

The independent school world was a small one, and schools vied each year for the cream of students whose parents could afford the stiff tuitions. Schools worked very hard to protect their images. Mostly, EDGE worked on promoting positive images. In cases like this, though, and why Gareth had called me at such an uncivilized hour, was the importance of *protecting* an image. The school needed immediate help with public relations and damage control. My job was shaping the message to the community, parents, and public in a way least damaging to the school. And callus though it might sound, the timing of this couldn't have been worse. Acceptance letters had recently gone out and prospective students were choosing their schools.

In most school populations, information control was difficult. Even five years ago, fewer students had cell phones and social media wasn't so omnipresent in students' lives. These days it was harder to control the message. They were so connected to the world that keeping the story under wraps was impossible. Still, Simmons was a better place for shaping the message than most. It was a community, with shared community values, and a sense of responsibility to that community and the wider world. Students chose to go there because of that.

In this case, the school's unusual character would be a double-edged sword. Gareth would have better control of his students, and what they communicated, because they believed in discussion and consensus within the community, and a more difficult job explaining to his students how one of their own had veered so far from the school's core values.

I urged Gareth to email his students, explain the dilemma they faced with respect to the wider world's understanding and judgment, and ask them to hold off discussing it with those outside the community until the administration could explore the details of what had happened. His message should be that the situation was complicated, called for open minds and compassion, and that when he had the facts, he would bring them together as a student body to explore the implications. That was how they worked at Simmons. Community. Open communication. Respect for a diversity of opinions.

It was a wonderful place. I'd worked with them before and loved it. Simmons students gave me hope for the future. These young people would understand citizenship. Know how to disagree, listen to opposing opinions, and reach decisions based on mutual respect.

As I stumbled across the cold floor to grab some clothes, I ached for the pain they would be feeling. For a student body who felt their values had been betrayed, and for the student whose situation—about which we knew so little—had caused her to betray them.

I knew how the world would judge them. I feared for how the parents would react, even though they'd chosen this special community for their children. But I hoped, a hope Gareth echoed, that within their community they could come to understand what had happened, offer forgiveness and support, and move on stronger.

We both knew he had other things to worry about. He had to consider the impact on applicants for next year's class, and on skittish parents who might consider pulling their children out. He would be worried about damage to the school's reputation as a close and caring community if something like this could happen under their noses. Schools acting in loco parentis were always vulnerable to the charge that they had failed.

I was about to disconnect, but as I pulled out underwear and tights, I had another thought. "You said the girl denies that she was pregnant?"

"She does."

"And her denial seems genuine?"

"She wasn't in the best of shape to answer questions, in the circumstances, but I'd say yes. She seemed credible."

These were critical issues—the age of the young mother, the events leading to the pregnancy, the mother's mental state, the reaction of her family. It was all part of building the story, of translating Heidi from a heartless monster to someone deserving of compassion. From someone indifferent to the welfare of an innocent baby to a desperate child herself, possibly even unaware of her pregnancy, with few options and impaired judgment. Quite possibly a victim herself. I was not being a weasel. The truth mattered. But there were often many versions of the truth, depending on whose point of view you told the story from. There is a Rashomon element to most stories that involve more than one person.

"So have you…or will you…get a good psychiatrist involved?"

"We will. I agree that it's essential. We're collecting names, but you know, it's not a good time of day to try and reach anyone." There was an embarrassed silence, as we both shared the thought that he hadn't hesitated to reach me. Then he went on. "We have some good prospects in hand and as soon as the hour's more civilized, we'll be making those calls." He hesitated again. "I'll ring off now, Thea, and let you get ready. But do, please, call me when you're under way."

He didn't say, "And hurry!" but that was what he meant.

I would. Of course. But first, despite the urgency of my client's situation, I needed a shower, and the world's best inducement awaited me.

I carried my clothes into the bathroom, pulled off my nightgown, and stepped into the shower.

Kate Flora's fifteen books include the star-reviewed Joe Burgess police series. *Redemption* and *And Grant You Peace* won the 2013 and 2015 Maine Literary Awards for Crime Fiction. Her nonfiction includes the Agatha and Anthony nominated true crime *Death Dealer,* winner of the 2015 PSWA award for nonfiction. *Finding Amy*, co-written with Portland, Maine deputy chief Joseph Loughlin, was an Edgar nominee. With retired Maine game warden Roger Guay, she has co-written the memoir, *A Good Man with a Dog*. Her next Thea Kozak mystery, *Death Warmed Over,* will be published in 2017.

A former Maine assistant attorney general in the areas of battered children and employment discrimination, Flora's a founder of the New England Crime Bake, the Maine Crime Wave, and Level Best Books. She was international president of Sisters in Crime. She divides her time between Maine and Massachusetts, where she struggles to keep deer, woodchucks, and rabbits from devouring her gardens. She has two sons, a film editor and a scientist, two lovely daughters-in-law, a perfect grandson and six granddogs.

CPSIA information can be obtained
at www.ICGtesting.com
Printed in the USA
LVHW011542040521
686466LV00002B/275